VAN ▌▌▌ ▌▌▌▌▌▌▌▌▌ ▌▌▌ ARY
DE   W9-BYY-327   5

DISCARDED

HOMELAND

THE LEGEND OF DRIZZT BOOK I

R A
SALVATORE

Sal

THE LEGEND OF DRIZZT
BOOK I
HOMELAND

©2004 Wizards of the Coast, Inc.

All characters in this book are fictitious. Any resemblance to actual persons, living or dead, is purely coincidental.

This book is protected under the copyright laws of the United States of America. Any reproduction or unauthorized use of the material or artwork contained herein is prohibited without the express written permission of Wizards of the Coast, Inc.

Distributed in the United States by Holtzbrinck Publishing. Distributed in Canada by Fenn Ltd.

Distributed to the hobby, toy, and comic trade in the United States and Canada by regional distributors.

Distributed worldwide by Wizards of the Coast, Inc. and regional distributors.

Forgotten Realms, Wizards of the Coast, and their respective logos are trademarks of Wizards of the Coast, Inc., in the U.S.A. and other countries.

All Wizards of the Coast characters, character names, and the distinctive likenesses thereof are trademarks of Wizards of the Coast, Inc.

Printed in the U.S.A.

Cover art by Todd Lockwood
Designed by Matt Adelsperger
First Hardcover Printing: March 2004
Originally published as Book One of the Dark Elf Trilogy in August 1990.

Library of Congress Catalog Card Number: 2003111908

9 8 7 6 5 4 3 2 1

US ISBN: 0-7869-3123-X
UK ISBN: 0-7869-3124-8
620-88851-001-EN

U.S., CANADA,   EUROPEAN HEADQUARTERS
ASIA, PACIFIC, & LATIN AMERICA   Wizards of the Coast, Belgium
Wizards of the Coast, Inc.   T Hofveld 6d
P.O. Box 70   1702 Groot-Bijgaarden
Renton, WA 98057-0707   Belgium
+1-800-324-6496   +322 467 3360

Visit our web site at www.wizards.com

3/04
BdT

THE LEGEND OF DRIZZT

Homeland

Exile

Sojourn

The Crystal Shard

Streams of Silver

The Halfling's Gem

The Legacy

Starless Night

Siege of Darkness

Passage to Dawn

The Silent Blade

The Spine of the World

Sea of Swords

THE HUNTER'S BLADES TRILOGY

The Thousand Orcs

The Lone Drow

The Two Swords
October 2004

Once upon a time, across dusty tundra, a dark elf who'd walked all through the night and was now grimly continuing his trek despite the sunlit day around him, came trudging into our lives.

And the FORGOTTEN REALMS® came a little bit more alive.

I created the Realms over thirty-five (gulp!) years

INTRODUCTION

ago, and for the first twenty of those, it was more or less just my world to play in. I say "more or less" because a band of very talented, brilliant, and demanding players questioned me and pushed me almost constantly to provide more detail, more explanations, and give them more people to meet, treasures to gloat over, and intrigues and mysteries to play with.

It wasn't easy, throwing the gates of the Realms open for everybody—and on some occasions since I've felt very much like the ringmaster of a circus full of performers who were so inspired once they got into the spotlights that they often improvised this, ran off on a tangent doing that, and generally made the ringmaster tear at his hair (and in my case, beard). I understand many Realms editors have felt the same way from time to time.

One of the reasons I shared the Realms was because there was one thing my world couldn't do for me as long as it was just mine: surprise me. I wanted to be surprised and delighted, I wanted to discover corners of the Realms rather than always having to sneak ahead of the story or the role-playing and paint in all the details myself. I wanted the Realms to come alive for *me*.

My chance to do that was to let other creative people step into the Realms and tell their stories. Three early efforts particularly pleased me. Elaine Cunningham's *Elfshadow*, because she *nailed* Waterdeep, from Elaith on up. Jeff Grubb and Kate Novak's *Azure Bonds*, because its characters were zany enough to be welcome in *my* Realms. And Bob Salvatore's Drizzt Do'Urden.

You were wondering when I was going to get to Drizzt, weren't you?

Actually, it wasn't Drizzt alone that grabbed me. It was Bob's entire cast of characters, from Bruenor and Wulfgar and Regis and Cattie-brie to Artemis Entreri and later (in what I still consider the finest FORGOTTEN REALMS® novel yet written, *Homeland*), Drizzt's father Zaknafein. Bob breathed life into the drow of the original ADVANCED DUNGEONS & DRAGONS® game (themselves adapted from real-world legend), and gave us a cruel, Byzantine, and alluring Underdark society of warring drow cities and noble families. He also gave us fictional delights far beyond kill-the-dragon battle scenes, exploring love and revenge and maturing and loyalty and family ties.

And the books sold, and sold, and Drizzt became very well-known to the wider world of fantasy readers beyond gamers. And why? Because this R. A. Salvatore guy can really tell stories.

Stories that stand up to reading again and again, the mark of *good* writing. Don't let professors and critics and snobs tell you any different: in the end, if a tale keeps you enthralled when the storyteller's voice comes at you over the campfire, it's a good story. If you want it never to stop or want to hear it over and over again, it's one of your treasures . . . and we can never have too many treasures in life.

This book just might turn out to be one of yours.

Oh, yes, there was another reason I handed the keys of the Realms to diverse writers and gamers: because one of my delights in gaming and writing is making friends.

I'm honored that Bob Salvatore is one of mine. What a guy.

Ed Greenwood
Realmskeep
August, 2003

Alton DeVir
A young drow mage, a student at Sorcere.

Belwar Dissengulp
A deep gnome burrow-warden who leads a mining expedition close to Menzoberranzan.

Berg'inyon Baenre
Son of Matron Baenre, trains at Melee-Magthere with Drizzt Do'Urden.

Dramatis Personae

Briza Do'Urden
Eldest daughter of Matron Malice, and a high priestess of Lolth.

Dinin Do'Urden
Secondboy of House Do'Urden, son of Matron Malice, and a Master of Melee-Magthere.

Drizzt Do'Urden
Son of Matron Malice, Drizzt is a young drow warrior with purple eyes, unusual among drow. He becomes secondboy of House Do'Urden after serving as a page prince, and is a student at Melee-Magthere.

Gromph Baenre
Son of Matron Baenre, Archmage of Menzoberranzan.

Guenhwyvar
Magical black panther, summoned from the Astral Plane via an onyx figurine.

Hatch'net
Lore-master at Melee-Magthere.

Kelnozz
A common drow who is training at Melee-Magthere.

Masoj Hun'ett
A wizard's apprentice. Trains Drizzt (at Sorcere) in his last year at the Academy.

Matron Baenre
Matron Mother of the First House, the nominal ruler of
Menzoberranzan.

Matron Ginafae
Matron Mother of House Devir and a high priestess, but
out-of-favor with Lolth.

Matron Malice
Matron Mother of House Do'Urden. Skilled in making
salves and potions.

Matron SiNafay
Matron Mother of House Hun'ett and a high priestess of
Lolth.

Maya Do'Urden
Daughter of Matron Malice.

Methil
An illithid that lives in the House Baenre stronghold.

Nalfein
Eldest boy of House Do'Urden, son of Matron Malice, and a
wizard.

Rizzen
A drow warrior, and the current Patron of House Do'Urden.

Shar Nadal
A drow from House Maevret.

The Faceless One
A wizard and Master of the Academy who melted all his
facial features away during an experiment. His real name is
Gelroos Hun'ett.

Vierna Do'Urden
Daughter of Matron Malice, charged with raising Drizzt and
teaching him the drow ways of life.

Zaknafein
The finest weapons master in Menzoberranzan and former
Patron of House Do'Urden.

To my best friend,
my brother,
Gary.

PRELUDE

Never does a star grace this land with a poet's light of twinkling mysteries, nor does the sun send to here its rays of warmth and life. This is the Underdark, the secret world beneath the bustling surface of the Forgotten Realms, whose sky is a ceiling of heartless stone and whose walls show the gray blandness of death in the torchlight of the foolish surface-dwellers that stumble here. This is not their world, not the world of light. Most who come here uninvited do not return.

Those who do escape to the safety of their surface homes return changed. Their eyes have seen the shadows and the gloom, the inevitable doom of the Underdark.

Dark corridors meander throughout the dark realm in winding courses, connecting caverns great and small, with ceilings high and low. Mounds of stone as pointed as the teeth of a sleeping dragon leer down in silent threat or rise up to block the way of intruders.

There is a silence here, profound and foreboding, the crouched hush of a predator at work. Too often the only sound, the only reminder to travelers in the Underdark that they have not lost their sense of hearing altogether, is a distant and echoing drip of water, beating like the heart of a beast, slipping through the silent stones to the deep Underdark pools of chilled water. What lies beneath the still onyx surface of these pools one can only guess. What secrets await the brave, what horrors await the foolish, only the imagination can reveal—until the stillness is disturbed.

This is the Underdark.

✕ ✕ ✕ ✕ ✕

There are pockets of life here, cities as great as many of those on the surface. Around any of the countless bends and turns in the gray stone a traveler might stumble suddenly into the perimeter of such a city, a stark contrast to the emptiness of the corridors. These places are not havens, though; only the foolish traveler would assume so. They are the homes of the most evil races in all the Realms, most notably the duergar, the kuo-toa, and the drow.

In one such cavern, two miles wide and a thousand feet high, looms Menzoberranzan, a monument to the other worldly and—ultimately—deadly grace that marks the race of drow elves. Menzoberranzan is not a large city by drow standards; only twenty thousand dark elves reside there. Where, in ages past, there had been an empty cavern of roughly shaped stalactites and stalagmites now stands artistry, row after row of carved castles thrumming in a quiet glow of magic. The city is perfection of form, where not a stone has been left to its natural shape. This sense of order and control, however, is but a cruel facade, a deception hiding the chaos and vileness that rule the dark elves' hearts. Like their cities, they are a beautiful, slender, and delicate people, with features sharp and haunting.

Yet the drow are the rulers of this unruled world, the deadliest of the deadly, and all other races take cautious note of their passing. Beauty itself pales at the end of a dark elf's sword. The drow are the survivors, and this is the Underdark, the valley of death—the land of nameless nightmares.

PART ONE

S tation: In all the world of the drow, there
is no more important word. It is the calling of their—of our—religion, the incessant
pulling of hungering heart-
strings. Ambition overrides STATION
good sense and compassion
is thrown away in its face, all in the name of
Lolth, the Spider Queen.

Ascension to power in drow society is a simple process of assassination. The Spider Queen
is a deity of chaos, and she and her high priestesses, the true rulers of the drow world, do not
look with ill favor upon ambitious individuals
wielding poisoned daggers.

Of course, there are rules of behavior; every
society must boast of these. To openly commit murder or wage war invites the pretense
of justice, and penalties exacted in the name
of drow justice are merciless. To stick a dagger in the back of a rival during the chaos of a
larger battle or in the quiet shadows of an alley,

however, is quite acceptable—even applauded. Investigation is not the forte of drow justice. No one cares enough to bother.

Station is the way of Lolth, the ambition she bestows to further the chaos, to keep her drow "children" along their appointed course of self-imprisonment. Children? Pawns, more likely, dancing dolls for the Spider Queen, puppets on the imperceptible but impervious strands of her web. All climb the Spider Queen's ladders; all hunt for her pleasure; and all fall to the hunters of her pleasure.

Station is the paradox of the world of my people, the limitation of our power within the hunger for power. It is gained through treachery and invites treachery against those who gain it. Those most powerful in Menzoberranzan spend their days watching over their shoulders, defending against the daggers that would find their backs. Their deaths usually come from the front.

—Drizzt Do'Urden

MENZOBERRANZAN

To a surface dweller, he might have passed undetected only a foot away. The padded footfalls of his lizard mount were too light to be heard, and the pliable and perfectly crafted mesh armor that both rider and mount wore bent and creased with their movements as well as if the suits had grown over their skin.

Dinin's lizard trotted along in an easy but swift gait, floating over the broken floor, up the walls, and even across the long tunnel's ceiling. Subterranean lizards, with their sticky and soft three-toed feet, were preferred mounts for just this ability to scale stone as easily as a spider. Crossing hard ground left no damning tracks in the lighted surface world, but nearly all of the creatures of the Underdark possessed infravision, the ability to see in the infrared spectrum. Footfalls left heat residue that could easily be tracked if they followed a predictable course along a corridor's floor.

Dinin clamped tight to his saddle as the lizard plodded along a stretch of the ceiling, then sprang out in a twisting descent to a point farther along the wall. Dinin did not want to be tracked.

He had no light to guide him, but he needed none. He was a dark elf, a drow, an ebon-skinned cousin of those sylvan folk who danced under the stars on the world's surface. To Dinin's superior eyes, which translated subtle variations of heat into vivid and colorful images, the Underdark was far from a lightless place. Colors all across the spectrum swirled before him in the stone of the walls and the floor, heated by some distant fissure or hot stream. The heat of living things was the most distinctive, letting the dark elf view his enemies in details as intricate as any surface-dweller would find in brilliant daylight.

Normally Dinin would not have left the city alone; the world of the Underdark was too dangerous for solo treks, even for a drow elf. This day was different, though. Dinin had to be certain that no unfriendly drow eyes marked his passage.

A soft blue magical glow beyond a sculpted archway told the drow that he neared the city's entrance, and he slowed the lizard's pace accordingly. Few used this narrow tunnel, which opened into Tier Breche, the northern section of Menzoberranzan devoted to the Academy, and none but the mistresses and masters, the instructors of the Academy, could pass through here without attracting suspicion.

Dinin was always nervous when he came to this point. Of the hundred tunnels that opened off the main cavern of Menzoberranzan, this one was the best guarded. Beyond the archway, twin statues of gigantic spiders sat in quiet defense. If an enemy crossed through, the spiders would animate and attack, and alarms would be sounded throughout the Academy.

Dinin dismounted, leaving his lizard clinging comfortably to a wall at his chest level. He reached under the collar of his *piwafwi*, his magical, shielding cloak, and took out his neck-purse. From this Dinin produced the insignia of House Do'Urden, a spider wielding various weapons in each of its eight legs and emblazoned with the letters "DN," for Daermon N'a'shezbaernon, the ancient and formal name of House Do'Urden.

"You will await my return," Dinin whispered to the lizard as he waved the insignia before it. As with all the drow houses, the insignia of House Do'Urden held several magical dweomers, one of which gave family members absolute control over the house pets. The lizard would obey unfailingly, holding its position as though it were rooted to the stone, even if a scurry rat, its favorite morsel, napped a few feet from its maw.

Dinin took a deep breath and gingerly stepped to the archway. He could see the spiders leering down at him from their fifteen-foot height. He was a drow of the city, not an enemy, and could pass through any other tunnel unconcerned, but the Academy was an unpredictable place; Dinin had heard that the spiders often refused entry—viciously—even to uninvited drow.

He could not be delayed by fears and possibilities, Dinin reminded himself. His business was of the utmost importance to his family's battle plans. Looking straight ahead, away from the towering spiders, he strode between them and onto the floor of Tier Breche.

He moved to the side and paused, first to be certain that no one lurked nearby, and to admire the sweeping view of Menzoberranzan. No one, drow or otherwise, had ever looked out from this spot without a sense of wonder at the drow city. Tier Breche was the highest point on the floor of the two-mile cavern, affording a panoramic view to the rest of Menzoberranzan. The cubby of the Academy was narrow, holding only the three structures that comprised the drow school: Arach-Tinilith, the spider-shaped school of Lolth; Sorcere, the gracefully curving, many-spired tower of wizardry; and Melee-Magthere, the somewhat plain pyramidal structure where male fighters learned their trade.

Beyond Tier Breche, through the ornate stalagmite columns that marked the entrance to the Academy, the cavern dropped away quickly and spread wide, going far beyond Dinin's line of vision to either side and farther back than his keen eyes could possibly see. The colors of Menzoberranzan were threefold to the sensitive eyes of the drow. Heat patterns from various fissures and hot springs swirled about the entire cavern. Purple and red, bright yellow and subtle blue, crossed and merged, climbed the walls and stalagmite mounds, or ran off singularly in cutting lines against the backdrop of dim gray stone. More confined than these generalized and natural gradations of color in the infrared spectrum were the regions of intense magic, like the spiders Dinin had walked between, virtually glowing with energy. Finally there were the actual lights of the city, faerie fire and highlighted sculptures on the houses. The drow were proud of the beauty of their designs, and especially ornate columns or perfectly crafted gargoyles were almost always limned in permanent magical lights.

Even from this distance Dinin could make out House Baenre, First House of Menzoberranzan. It encompassed twenty stalagmite pillars and half again that number of gigantic stalactites. House Baenre had existed for five thousand years, since the founding of Menzoberranzan, and in that time the work to perfect the house's art had never ceased. Practically every inch of the immense structure glowed in faerie fire, blue at the outlying towers and brilliant purple at the huge central dome.

The sharp light of candles, foreign to the Underdark, glared through some of the windows of the distant houses. Only clerics or wizards would light the fires, Dinin knew, as necessary pains in their world of scrolls and parchments.

This was Menzoberranzan, the city of drow. Twenty thousand dark elves lived there, twenty thousand soldiers in the army of evil.

A wicked smile spread across Dinin's thin lips when he thought of some of those soldiers who would fall this night.

Dinin studied Narbondel, the huge central pillar that served as the timeclock of Menzoberranzan. Narbondel was the only way the drow had to mark the passage of time in a world that otherwise knew no days and no seasons. At the end of each day, the city's appointed Archmage cast his magical fires into the base of the stone pillar. There the spell lingered throughout the cycle—a full day on the surface—and gradually spread its warmth up the structure of Narbondel until the whole of it glowed red in the infrared spectrum. The pillar was fully dark now, cooled since the dweomer's fires had expired. The wizard was even now at the base, Dinin reasoned, ready to begin the cycle anew.

It was midnight, the appointed hour.

Dinin moved away from the spiders and the tunnel exit and crept along the side of Tier Breche, seeking the "shadows" of heat patterns in the wall, which would effectively hide the distinct outline of his own body temperature. He came at last to Sorcere, the school of wizardry, and slipped into the narrow alley between the tower's curving base and Tier Breche's outer wall.

"Student or master?" came the expected whisper.

"Only a master may walk out-of-house in Tier Breche in the black death of Narbondel," Dinin responded.

A heavily robed figure moved around the arc of the structure to stand before Dinin. The stranger remained in the customary posture of a master of the drow Academy, his arms out before him and bent at the elbows, his hands tight together, one on top of the other in front of his chest.

That pose was the only thing about this one that seemed normal to Dinin. "Greetings, Faceless One," he signaled in the silent hand code of the drow, a language as detailed as the spoken word. The quiver of Dinin's hands belied his calm face, though, for the sight of this wizard put him as far on the edge of his nerves as he had ever been.

"Secondboy Do'Urden," the wizard replied in the gestured code. "Have you my payment?"

"You will be compensated," Dinin signaled pointedly, regaining his composure in the first swelling bubbles of his temper. "Do you dare to doubt the promise of Malice Do'Urden, Matron Mother of Daermon N'a'shezbaernon, Tenth House of Menzoberranzan?"

The Faceless One slumped back, knowing he had erred. "My apologies, Secondboy of House Do'Urden," he answered, dropping to one knee in a gesture of surrender. Since he had entered this conspiracy, the wizard had feared that his impatience might cost him his life. He had been caught in the violent throes of one of his own magical experiments, the tragedy melting away all of his facial features and leaving behind a blank hot spot of white and green goo. Matron Malice Do'Urden, reputedly as skilled as anyone in all the vast city in mixing potions and salves, had offered him a sliver of hope that he could not pass by.

No pity found its way into Dinin's callous heart, but House Do'Urden needed the wizard. "You will get your salve," Dinin promised calmly, "when Alton DeVir is dead."

"Of course," the wizard agreed. "This night?"

Dinin crossed his arms and considered the question. Matron Malice had instructed him that Alton DeVir should die even as their families' battle commenced. That scenario now seemed too clean, too easy, to Dinin. The Faceless One did not miss the sparkle that suddenly brightened the scarlet glow in the young Do'Urden's heat-sensing eyes.

"Wait for Narbondel's light to approach its zenith," Dinin replied, his hands working through the signals excitedly and his grimace seeming more of a twisted grin.

"Should the doomed boy know of his house's fate before he dies?" the wizard asked, guessing the wicked intentions behind Dinin's instructions.

"As the killing blow falls," answered Dinin. "Let Alton DeVir die without hope."

✕ ✕ ✕ ✕ ✕

Dinin retrieved his mount and sped off down the empty corridors, finding an intersecting route that would take him in through a different entrance to the city proper. He came in along the eastern end of the great cavern, Menzoberranzan's produce section, where no drow families would see that he had been outside the city limits and where only a few unremarkable stalagmite pillars rose up from the flat stone. Dinin spurred his mount along the banks of Donigarten, the city's small pond with its moss-covered island that housed a fair-sized herd of cattle-like creatures called rothe. A hundred goblins and orcs looked up from their herding and fishing duties to mark the drow soldier's swift passage. Knowing their restrictions as slaves, they took care not to look Dinin in the eye.

Dinin would have paid them no heed anyway. He was too consumed by the urgency of the moment. He kicked his lizard to even greater speeds when he again was on the flat and curving avenues between the glowing drow castles. He moved toward the south-central region of the city, toward the grove of giant mushrooms that marked the section of the finest houses in Menzoberranzan.

As he came around one blind turn, he nearly ran over a group of four wandering bugbears. The giant hairy goblin things paused a moment to consider the drow, then moved slowly but purposefully out of his way.

The bugbears recognized him as a member of House Do'Urden, Dinin knew. He was a noble, a son of a high priestess, and his surname, Do'Urden, was the name of his house. Of the twenty thousand dark elves in Menzoberranzan, only a thousand or so were nobles, actually the children of the sixty-seven recognized families of the city. The rest were common soldiers.

Bugbears were not stupid creatures. They knew a noble from a commoner, and though drow elves did not carry their family insignia in plain view, the pointed and tailed cut of Dinin's stark white hair and the distinctive pattern of purple and red lines in his black *piwafwi* told them well enough who he was.

The mission's urgency pressed upon Dinin, but he could not ignore the bugbears' slight. How fast would they have scampered away if he had been a member of House Baenre or one of the other seven ruling houses? he wondered.

"You will learn respect of House Do'Urden soon enough!" the dark elf whispered under his breath, as he turned and charged his lizard at the group. The bugbears broke into a run, turning down an alley strewn with stones and debris.

Dinin found his satisfaction by calling on the innate powers of his race. He summoned a globe of darkness—impervious to both infravision and normal sight—in the fleeing creatures' path. He supposed that it was unwise to call such attention to himself, but a moment later, when he heard crashing and sputtered curses as the bugbears stumbled blindly over the stones, he felt it was worth the risk.

His anger sated, he moved off again, picking a more careful route through the heat shadows. As a member of the tenth house of the city, Dinin could go as he pleased within the giant cavern without question, but Matron Malice had made it clear that no one connected to House Do'Urden was to be caught anywhere near the mushroom grove.

Matron Malice, Dinin's mother, was not to be crossed, but it was only a rule, after all. In Menzoberranzan, one rule took precedence over all of the petty others: Don't get caught.

At the mushroom grove's southern end, the impetuous drow found what he was looking for: a cluster of five huge floor-to-ceiling pillars that were hollowed into a network of chambers and connected with metal and stone parapets and bridges. Red-glowing gargoyles, the standard of the house, glared down from a hundred perches like silent sentries. This was House DeVir, Fourth House of Menzoberranzan.

A stockade of tall mushrooms ringed the place, every fifth one a shrieker, a sentient fungus named (and favored as guardians) for the shrill cries of alarm it emitted whenever a living being passed it by. Dinin kept a cautious distance, not wanting to set off one of the shriekers and knowing also that other, more deadly wards protected the fortress. Matron Malice would see to those.

An expectant hush permeated the air of this city section. It was general knowledge throughout Menzoberranzan that Matron Ginafae of House DeVir had fallen out of favor with Lolth, the Spider Queen deity to all drow and the true source of every house's strength. Such circumstances were never openly discussed among the drow, but everyone who knew fully expected that some family lower in the city hierarchy soon would strike out against the crippled House DeVir.

Matron Ginafae and her family had been the last to learn of the Spider Queen's displeasure—ever was that Lolth's devious way—and Dinin could tell just by scanning the outside of House DeVir that the doomed family had not found sufficient time to erect proper defenses. DeVir sported nearly four hundred soldiers, many female, but those that Dinin could now see at their posts along the parapets seemed nervous and unsure.

Dinin's smile spread even wider when he thought of his own house, which grew in power daily under the cunning guidance of Matron Malice. With all three of his sisters rapidly approaching the status of high priestess, his brother an accomplished wizard, and his uncle Zaknafein, the finest weapons master in all of Menzoberranzan, busily training the three hundred soldiers, House Do'Urden was a complete force. And, Matron Malice, unlike Ginafae, was in the Spider Queen's full favor.

"Daermon N'a'shezbaernon," Dinin muttered under his breath, using the formal and ancestral reference to House Do'Urden. "Ninth House of Menzoberranzan!" He liked the sound of it.

⚔ ⚔ ⚔ ⚔ ⚔

Halfway across the city, beyond the silver-glowing balcony and the arched doorway twenty feet up the cavern's west wall, sat the principals of House Do'Urden, gathered to outline the final plans of the night's work. On the raised dais at the back of the small audience chamber sat venerable Matron Malice, her belly swollen in the final hours of pregnancy. Flanking her in their places of honor were her three daughters, Maya, Vierna, and the eldest, Briza, a newly ordained high priestess of Lolth. Maya and Vierna appeared as younger versions of their mother, slender and deceptively small, though possessing great strength. Briza, though, hardly carried the family resemblance. She was big—huge by drow standards—and rounded in the shoulders and hips. Those who knew Briza well figured that her size was merely a circumstance of her temperament; a smaller body could not have contained the anger and brutal streak of House Do'Urden's newest high priestess.

"Dinin should return soon," remarked Rizzen, the present patron of the family, "to let us know if the time is right for the assault."

"We go before Narbondel finds its morning glow!" Briza snapped at him in her thick but razor-sharp voice. She turned a crooked smile to her mother, seeking approval for putting the male in his place.

"The child comes this night," Matron Malice explained to her anxious husband. "We go no matter what news Dinin bears."

"It will be a boy child," groaned Briza, making no effort to hide her disappointment, "third living son of House Do'Urden."

"To be sacrificed to Lolth," put in Zaknafein, a former patron of the house who now held the important position of weapons master. The skilled drow fighter seemed quite pleased at the thought of sacrifice, as did Nalfein, the family's eldest son, who stood at Zak's side. Nalfein was the elderboy, and he needed no more competition beyond Dinin within the ranks of House Do'Urden.

"In accord with custom," Briza glowered and the red of her eyes brightened. "To aid in our victory!"

Rizzen shifted uncomfortably. "Matron Malice," he dared to speak, "you know well the difficulties of birthing. Might the pain distract you—"

"You dare to question the matron mother?" Briza started sharply, reaching for the snake-headed whip so comfortably strapped—and writhing—on her belt. Matron Malice stopped her with an outstretched hand.

"Attend to the fighting," the matron said to Rizzen. "Let the females of the house see to the important matters of this battle."

Rizzen shifted again and dropped his gaze.

⚔ ⚔ ⚔ ⚔ ⚔

Dinin came to the magically wrought fence that connected the keep within the city's west wall with the two small stalagmite towers of House Do'Urden, and which formed the courtyard to the compound. The fence was adamantine, the hardest metal in all the world, and adorning it were a hundred weapon-wielding spider carvings, each ensorcelled with deadly glyphs and wards. The mighty gate of House Do'Urden was the envy of many a drow house, but so soon after viewing the spectacular houses in the mushroom grove, Dinin could only find disappointment when looking upon his own abode. The compound was plain and somewhat bare, as was the section of wall, with the notable exception of the mithral-and-adamantine balcony running along the second level, by the arched doorway reserved for the nobility of the family. Each baluster of that balcony sported a thousand carvings, all of which blended into a single piece of art.

House Do'Urden, unlike the great majority of the houses in Menzoberranzan, did not stand free within groves of stalactites and stalagmites. The bulk of the structure was within a cave, and while this setup was indisputably defensible, Dinin found himself wishing that his family could show a bit more grandeur.

An excited soldier rushed to open the gate for the returning secondboy. Dinin swept past him without so much as a word of greeting and moved across the courtyard, conscious of the hundred and more curious glances that fell upon him. The soldiers and slaves knew that Dinin's mission this night had something to do with the anticipated battle.

No stairway led to the silvery balcony of House Do'Urden's second level. This, too, was a precautionary measure designed to segregate the leaders of the house from the rabble and the slaves. Drow nobles needed no stairs; another manifestation of their innate magical abilities allowed them the power of levitation. With hardly a conscious thought to the act, Dinin drifted easily through the air and dropped onto the balcony.

He rushed through the archway and down the house's main central corridor, which was dimly lit in the soft hues of faerie fire, allowing for sight in the normal light spectrum but not bright enough to defeat the use of infravision. The ornate brass door at the corridor's end marked the secondboy's destination, and he paused before it to allow his eyes to shift back to the infrared spectrum. Unlike the corridor, the room beyond the door had no light source. It was the audience hall of the high priestesses, the anteroom to House Do'Urden's grand chapel. The drow clerical rooms, in accord with the dark rites of the Spider Queen, were not places of light.

When he felt he was prepared, Dinin pushed straight through the door, shoving past the two shocked female guards without hesitation and moving boldly to stand before his mother. All three of the family daughters narrowed their eyes at their brash and pretentious brother. To enter without permission! he knew they were thinking. Would that it was he who was to be sacrificed this night!

As much as he enjoyed testing the limitations of his inferior station as a male, Dinin could not ignore the threatening dances of Vierna, Maya, and Briza. Being female, they were bigger and stronger than Dinin and had trained all their lives in the use of wicked drow clerical powers and weapons. Dinin watched as enchanted extensions of the clerics, the dreaded snake-headed whips on his sisters' belts, began writhing in anticipation of the punishment they would exact. The handles were adamantine and ordinary enough, but the whips' lengths and multiple heads were living serpents. Briza's whip, in particular, a wicked six-headed device, danced and squirmed, tying itself into knots around the belt that held it. Briza was always the quickest to punish.

Matron Malice, however, seemed pleased by Dinin's swagger. The secondboy knew his place well enough by her measure and he followed her commands fearlessly and without question.

Dinin took comfort in the calmness of his mother's face, quite the opposite of the shining white-hot faces of his three sisters. "All is ready," he said to her. "House DeVir huddles within its fence—except for Alton, of course, foolishly attending his studies in Sorcere."

"You have met with the Faceless One?" Matron Malice asked.

"The Academy was quiet this night," Dinin replied. "Our meeting went off perfectly."

"He has agreed to our contract?"

"Alton DeVir will be dealt with accordingly," Dinin chuckled. He then remembered the slight alteration he had made in Matron Malice's plans, delaying Alton's execution for the sake of his own lust for added cruelty. Dinin's thought evoked another recollection as well: high priestesses of Lolth had an unnerving talent for reading thoughts.

"Alton will die this night," Dinin quickly completed the answer, assuring the others before they could probe him for more definite details.

"Excellent," Briza growled. Dinin breathed a little easier.

"To the meld," Matron Malice ordered.

The four drow males moved to kneel before the matron and her daughters: Rizzen to Malice, Zaknafein to Briza, Nalfein to Maya, and Dinin to Vierna. The clerics chanted in unison, placing one hand delicately upon the forehead of their respective soldier, tuning in to his passions.

"You know your places," Matron Malice said when the ceremony was completed. She grimaced through the pain of another contraction. "Let our work begin."

⚔ ⚔ ⚔ ⚔

Less than an hour later, Zaknafein and Briza stood together on the balcony outside the upper entrance to House Do'Urden. Below them, on the cavern floor, the second and third brigades of the family army, Rizzen's and Nalfein's, bustled about, fitting on heated leather straps and metal patches—camouflage against a distinctive elven form to heat-seeing drow eyes. Dinin's group, the initial strike force that included a hundred goblin slaves, had long since departed.

"We will be known after this night," Briza said. "None would have suspected that a tenth house would dare to move against one as powerful as DeVir. When the whispers ripple out after this night's bloody work, even Baenre will take note of Daermon N'a'shezbaernon!" She leaned out over the balcony to watch as the two brigades formed into lines and started out, silently, along separate paths that would bring them through the winding city to the mushroom grove and the five-pillared structure of House DeVir.

Zaknafein eyed the back of Matron Malice's eldest daughter, wanting nothing more than to put a dagger into her spine. As always, though, good judgment kept Zak's practiced hand in its place.

"Have you the articles?" Briza inquired, showing Zak considerably more respect than she had when Matron Malice sat protectively at her side. Zak was only a male, a commoner allowed to don the family name as his own because he sometimes served Matron Malice in a husbandly manner and had once been the patron of the house. Still, Briza feared to anger him. Zak was the weapons master of House Do'Urden, a tall and muscular male, stronger than most females, and those who had witnessed his fighting wrath considered him among the finest warriors of either sex in all of Menzoberranzan. Besides Briza and her mother, both high priestesses of the Spider Queen, Zaknafein, with his unrivaled swordsmanship, was House Do'Urden's trump.

Zak held up the black hood and opened the small pouch on his belt, revealing several tiny ceramic spheres.

Briza smiled evilly and rubbed her slender hands together. "Matron Ginafae will not be pleased," she whispered.

Zak returned the smile and turned to view the departing soldiers. Nothing gave the weapons master more pleasure than killing drow elves, particularly clerics of Lolth.

"Prepare yourself," Briza said after a few minutes.

Zak shook his thick hair back from his face and stood rigid, eyes tightly closed. Briza drew her wand slowly, beginning the chant that would activate the device. She tapped Zak on one shoulder, then the other, then held the wand motionless over his head.

Zak felt the frosty sprinkles falling down on him, permeating his clothes and armor, even his flesh, until he and all of his possessions had cooled to a uniform temperature and hue. Zak hated the magical chill—it felt as he imagined death would feel—but he knew that under the influence of the wand's sprinkles he was, to the heat-sensing eyes of the creatures of the Underdark, as gray as common stone, unremarkable and undetectable.

Zak opened his eyes and shuddered, flexing his fingers to be sure they could still perform the fine edge of his craft. He looked back to Briza, already in the midst of the second spell, the summoning. This one would take a while, so Zak leaned back against the wall and considered again the pleasant, though dangerous, task before him. How thoughtful of Matron Malice to leave all of House DeVir's clerics to him!

"It is done," Briza announced after a few minutes. She led Zak's gaze upward, to the darkness beneath the unseen ceiling of the immense cavern.

Zak spotted Briza's handiwork first, an approaching current of air, yellow-tinted and warmer than the normal air of the cavern. A living current of air.

The creature, a conjuration from an elemental plane, swirled to hover just beyond the lip of the balcony, obediently awaiting its summoner's commands.

Zak didn't hesitate. He leaped out into the thing's midst, letting it hold him suspended above the floor.

Briza offered him a final salute and motioned her servant away. "Good fighting," she called to Zak, though he was already invisible in the air above her.

Zak chuckled at the irony of her words as the twisting city of Menzoberranzan rolled out below him. She wanted the clerics of House DeVir dead as surely as Zak did, but for very different reasons. All complications aside, Zak would have been just as happy killing clerics of House Do'Urden.

The weapons master took up one of his adamantine swords, a drow weapon magically crafted and unbelievably sharp with the edge of killing dweomers. "Good fighting indeed," he whispered. If only Briza knew how good.

2

THE FALL OF HOUSE DEVIR

Dinin noted with satisfaction that any of the meandering bugbears, or any other of the multitude of races that composed Menzoberranzan, drow included, now made great haste to scurry out of his way. This time the secondboy of House Do'Urden was not alone. Nearly sixty soldiers of the house walked in tight lines behind him. Behind these, in similar order though with far less enthusiasm for the adventure, came a hundred armed slaves of lesser races—goblins, orcs, and bugbears.

There could be no doubt for onlookers—a drow house was on a march to war. This was not an everyday event in Menzoberranzan but neither was it unexpected. At least once every decade a house decided that its position within the city hierarchy could be improved by another house's elimination. It was a risky proposition, for all of the nobles of the "victim" house had to be disposed of quickly and quietly. If even one survived to lay an accusation upon the perpetrator, the attacking house would be eradicated by Menzoberranzan's merciless system of "justice."

If the raid was executed to devious perfection, though, no recourse would be forthcoming. All of the city, even the ruling council of the top eight matron mothers, would secretly applaud the attackers for their courage and intelligence and no more would ever be said of the incident.

Dinin took a roundabout route, not wanting to lay a direct trail between House Do'Urden and House DeVir. A half-hour later, for the second time that night, he crept to the mushroom grove's southern end, to the cluster of stalagmites that held House DeVir. His soldiers streamed out behind him eagerly, readying weapons and taking full measure of the structure before them.

The slaves were slower in their movements. Many of them looked about for some escape, for they knew in their hearts that they were doomed in this battle. They feared the wrath of the dark elves more than death itself, though, and would not attempt to flee. With every exit out of Menzoberranzan protected by devious drow magic, where could they possibly go? Every one of them had witnessed the brutal punishments the drow elves exacted on recaptured slaves. At Dinin's command, they jumped into their positions around the mushroom fence.

Dinin reached into his large pouch and pulled out a heated sheet of metal. He flashed the object, brightened in the infrared spectrum, three times behind him to signal the approaching brigades of Nalfein and Rizzen. Then, with his usual cockiness, Dinin spun it quickly into the air, caught it, and replaced it in the secrecy of his heat-shielding pouch. On cue with the twirling signal, Dinin's drow brigade fitted enchanted darts to their tiny hand-held crossbows and took aim on the appointed targets.

Every fifth mushroom was a shrieker, and every dart held a magical dweomer that could silence the roar of a dragon.

". . . two . . . three," Dinin counted, his hand signaling the tempo since no words could be heard within the sphere of magical silence cast about his troops. He imagined the "click" as the drawn string on his little weapon released, loosing the dart into the nearest shrieker. So it went all around the cluster of House DeVir, the first line of alarm systematically silenced by three-dozen enchanted darts.

⚔ ⚔ ⚔ ⚔ ⚔

Halfway across Menzoberranzan, Matron Malice, her daughters, and four of the house's common clerics were gathered in Lolth's unholy circle of eight. They ringed an idol of their wicked deity, a gemstone carving of a drow-faced spider, and called to Lolth for aid in their struggles.

Malice sat at the head, propped in a chair angled for birthing. Briza and Vierna flanked her, Briza clutching her hand.

The select group chanted in unison, combining their energies into a single offensive spell. A moment later, when Vierna, mentally linked to Dinin, understood that the first attack group was in position, the Do'Urden circle of eight sent the first insinuating waves of mental energy into the rival house.

⚔ ⚔ ⚔ ⚔ ⚔

Matron Ginafae, her two daughters, and the five principal clerics of the common troops of House DeVir huddled together in the darkened anteroom of the five-stalagmite house's main chapel. They had gathered there in solemn prayer every night since Matron Ginafae had learned that she had fallen into Lolth's disfavor. Ginafae understood how vulnerable her house remained until she could find a way to appease the Spider Queen. There were sixty-six other houses in Menzoberranzan, fully twenty of which might dare to attack House DeVir at such an obvious disadvantage. The eight clerics were anxious now, somehow suspecting that this night would be eventful.

Ginafae felt it first, a chilling blast of confusing perceptions that caused her to stutter over her prayer of forgiveness. The other clerics of House DeVir glanced nervously at the matron's uncharacteristic slip of words, looking for confirmation.

"We are under attack," Ginafae breathed to them, her head already pounding with a dull ache under the growing assault of the formidable clerics of House Do'Urden.

⚔ ⚔ ⚔ ⚔ ⚔

A second signal from Dinin put the slave troops into motion. Still using stealth as their ally, they quietly rushed to the mushroom fence and cut through with wide-bladed swords. The secondboy of House Do'Urden watched and enjoyed as the courtyard of House DeVir was easily penetrated.

"Not such a prepared guard," he whispered in silent sarcasm to the red-glowing gargoyles on the high walls. The statues had seemed such an ominous guard earlier that night. Now they just watched helplessly.

Dinin recognized the measured but growing anticipation in the soldiers around him; their drow battle-lust was barely contained. Every now and came a killing flash as one of the slaves stumbled over a warding glyph, but the secondboy and the other drow only laughed at the spectacle. The lesser races were the expendable "fodder" of House Do'Urden's army. The only purpose in bringing the goblinoids to House DeVir was to trigger the deadly traps and defenses along the perimeter, to lead the way for the drow elves, the true soldiers.

The fence was now opened and secrecy was thrown away. House DeVir's soldiers met the invading slaves head-on within the compound. Dinin barely had his hand up to begin the attack command when his sixty anxious drow warriors jumped up and charged, their faces twisted in wicked glee and their weapons waving menacingly.

They halted their approach on cue, though, remembering one final task set out to them. Every drow, noble or commoner, possessed certain magical abilities. Bringing forth a globe of darkness, as Dinin had done to the bugbears in the street earlier that night, came easily to even the lowliest of the dark elves. So it went now, with sixty Do'Urden soldiers blotting out the perimeter of House DeVir above the mushroom fence in ball after ball of blackness.

For all of their stealth and precautions, House Do'Urden knew that many eyes were watching the raid. Witnesses were not too much of a problem; they could not, or would not, care enough to identify the attacking house. But custom and rules demanded that certain attempts at secrecy be enacted, the etiquette of drow warfare. In the blink of a red-glowing drow eye, House DeVir became, to the rest of the city, a dark blot on Menzoberranzan's landscape.

Rizzen came up behind his youngest son. "Well done," he signaled in the intricate finger language of the drow. "Nalfein is in through the back."

"An easy victory," the cocky Dinin signaled back, "if Matron Ginafae and her clerics are held at bay."

"Trust in Matron Malice," was Rizzen's response. He clapped his son's shoulder and followed his troops in through the breached mushroom fence.

⚔ ⚔ ⚔ ⚔ ⚔

High above the cluster of House DeVir, Zaknafein rested comfortably in the current-arms of Briza's aerial servant, watching the drama unfold. From this vantage, Zak could see within the ring of darkness and could hear within the ring of magical silence. Dinin's troops, the first drow soldiers in, had met resistance at every door and were being beaten badly.

Nalfein and his brigade, the troops of House Do'Urden most practiced in the ways of wizardry, came through the fence at the rear of the complex. Lightning strikes and magical balls of acid thundered into the courtyard at the base of the DeVir structures, cutting down Do'Urden fodder and DeVir defenses alike.

In the front courtyard, Rizzen and Dinin commanded the finest fighters of House Do'Urden. The blessings of Lolth were with his house, Zak could see when the battle was fully joined, for the strikes of the soldiers of House Do'Urden came faster than those of their enemies, and their aim proved more deadly. In minutes, the battle had been taken fully inside the five pillars.

Zak stretched the incessant chill out of his arms and willed the aerial servant to action. Down he plummeted on his windy bed, and he fell free the last few feet to the terrace along the top chambers of the central pillar. At once, two guards, one a female, rushed out to greet him.

They hesitated in confusion, though, trying to sort out the true form of this unremarkable gray blur—too long.

They had never heard of Zaknafein Do'Urden. They didn't know that death was upon them.

Zak's whip flashed out, catching and gashing the female's throat, while his other hand walked his sword through a series of masterful thrusts and parries that put the male off balance. Zak finished both in a single, blurring movement, snapping the whip-entwined female from the terrace with a twist of his wrist and spinning a kick into the male's face that likewise dropped him to the cavern floor.

Zak was then inside, where another guard rose up to meet him . . . but fell at his feet.

Zak slipped along the curving wall of the stalactite tower, his cooled body blending perfectly with the stone. Soldiers of House DeVir rushed all about him, trying to formulate some defense against the host of intruders who had already won out the lowest level of every structure and had taken two of the pillars completely.

Zak was not concerned with them. He blocked out the clanging ring of adamantine weapons, the cries of command, and the screams of death, concentrating instead on a singular sound that would lead him to his destination: a unified, frantic chant.

He found an empty corridor covered with spider carvings and running into the center of the pillar. As in House Do'Urden, this corridor ended in a large set of ornate double doors, their decorations dominated by arachnid forms. "This must be the place." Zak muttered under his breath, fitting his hood to the top of his head.

A giant spider rushed out of its concealment to his side.

Zak dived to his belly and kicked out under the thing, spinning into a roll that plunged his sword deep into the monster's bulbous body. Sticky fluids gushed out over the weapons master, and the spider shuddered to a quick death.

"Yes," Zak whispered, wiping the spider juices from his face, "this must be the place." He pulled the dead monster back into its hidden cubby and slipped in beside the thing, hoping that no one had noticed the brief struggle.

By the sounds of ringing weapons, Zak could tell that the fighting had almost reached this floor. House DeVir now seemed to have its defenses in place, though, and was finally holding its ground.

"Now, Malice," Zak whispered, hoping that Briza, attuned to him in the meld, would sense his anxiety. "Let us not be late!"

⚔ ⚔ ⚔ ⚔ ⚔

Back in the clerical anteroom of House Do'Urden, Malice and her subordinates continued their brutal mental assault on the clerics of House DeVir. Lolth heard their prayers louder than those of their counterparts, giving the clerics of House Do'Urden the stronger spells in their mental combat. Already they had easily put their enemies into a defensive posture. One of the lesser priestesses in DeVir's circle of eight had been crushed by Briza's mental insinuations and now lay dead on the floor barely inches from Matron Ginafae's feet.

But the momentum had slowed suddenly and the battle seemed to be swinging back to an even level. Matron Malice, struggling with the impending birth, could not hold her concentration, and without her voice, the spells of her unholy circle weakened.

At her mother's side, powerful Briza clutched her mother's hand so tightly that all the blood was squeezed from it, leaving it cool—the only cool spot on the laboring female—to the eyes of the others. Briza studied the contractions and the crowning cap of the coming child's white hair, and calculated the time to the moment of birth. This technique of translating the pain of birth into an offensive spell attack had never been tried before, except in legend, and Briza knew that timing would be the critical factor.

She whispered into her mother's ear, coaxing out the words of a deadly incantation.

Matron Malice echoed back the beginnings of the spell, sublimating her gasps, and transforming her rage of agony into offensive power.

"Dinnen douward ma brechen tol," Briza implored.

"Dinnen douward. . . maaa . . . brechen tol!" Malice growled, so determined to focus through the pain that she bit through one of her thin lips.

The baby's head appeared, more fully this time, and this time to stay.

Briza trembled and could barely remember the incantation herself. She whispered the final rune into the matron's ear, almost fearing the consequences.

Malice gathered her breath and her courage. She could feel the tingling of the spell as clearly as the pain of the birth. To her daughters standing around the idol, staring at her in disbelief, she appeared as a red blur of heated fury, streaking sweat lines that shone as brightly as the heat of boiling water.

"*Abec*," the matron began, feeling the pressure building to a crescendo. "*Abec*." She felt the hot tear of her skin, the sudden slippery release as the baby's head pushed through, the sudden ecstacy of birthing. "*Abec di'n'a'BREG DOUWARD!*" Malice screamed, pushing away all of the agony in a final explosion of magical power that knocked even the clerics of her own house from their feet.

⚔ ⚔ ⚔ ⚔ ⚔

Carried on the thrust of Matron Malice's exultation, the dweomer thundered into the chapel of House DeVir, shattered the gemstone idol of Lolth, sundered the double doors into heaps of twisted metal, and threw Matron Ginafae and her overmatched subordinates to the floor.

Zak shook his head in disbelief as the chapel doors flew past him. "Quite a kick, Malice." He chuckled and spun around the entryway, into the chapel. Using his infravision, he took a quick survey and head count of the lightless room's seven living occupants, all struggling back to their feet, their robes tattered. Again shaking his head at the bared power of Matron Malice, Zak pulled his hood down over his face.

A snap of his whip was the only explanation he offered as he smashed a tiny ceramic globe at his feet. The sphere shattered, dropping out a pellet that Briza had enchanted for just such occasions, a pellet glowing with the brightness of daylight.

For eyes accustomed to blackness, tuned in to heat emanations, the intrusion of such radiance came in a blinding flash of agony. The clerics' cries of pain only aided Zak in his systematic trek around the room, and he smiled widely under his hood every time he felt his sword bite into drow flesh.

He heard the beginnings of a spell across the way and knew that one of the DeVirs had recovered enough from the assault to be dangerous. The weapons master did not need his eyes to aim, however, and the crack of his whip took Matron Ginafae's tongue right out of her mouth.

⚔ ⚔ ⚔ ⚔ ⚔

Briza placed the newborn on the back of the spider idol and lifted the ceremonial dagger, pausing to admire its cruel workmanship. Its hilt was a spider's body sporting eight legs, barbed so as to appear furred, but angled down to serve as blades. Briza lifted the instrument above the baby's chest. "Name the child," she implored her mother. "The Spider Queen will not accept the sacrifice until the child is named!"

Matron Malice lolled her head, trying to fathom her daughter's meaning. The matron mother had thrown everything into the moment of the spell and the birth, and she was now barely coherent.

"Name the child!" Briza commanded, anxious to feed her hungry goddess.

⚔ ⚔ ⚔ ⚔ ⚔

"It nears its end," Dinin said to his brother when they met in a lower hall of one of the lesser pillars of House DeVir. "Rizzen is winning through to the top, and it is believed that Zaknafein's dark work has been completed."

"Two score of House DeVir's soldiers have already turned allegiance to us," Nalfein replied.

"They see the end," laughed Dinin. "One house serves them as well as another, and in the eyes of commoners no house is worth dying for. Our task will be finished soon."

"Too quickly for anyone to take note," Nalfein said. "Now Do'Urden, Daermon N'a'shezbaernon, is the Ninth House of Menzoberranzan and DeVir be damned!"

"Alert!" Dinin cried suddenly, eyes widening in feigned horror as he looked over his brother's shoulder.

Nalfein reacted immediately, spinning to face the danger at his back, only to put the true danger at his back. For even as Nalfein realized the deception, Dinin's sword slipped into his spine. Dinin put his head to his brother's shoulder and pressed his cheek to Nalfein's, watching the red sparkle of heat leave his brother's eyes.

"Too quickly for anyone to take note," Dinin teased, echoing his brother's earlier words.

He dropped the lifeless form to his feet. "Now Dinin is elderboy of House Do'Urden, and Nalfein be damned."

✕ ✕ ✕ ✕ ✕

"Drizzt," breathed Matron Malice. "The child's name is Drizzt!"

Briza tightened her grip on the knife and began the ritual. "Queen of Spiders, take this babe," she began. She raised the dagger to strike. "Drizzt Do'Urden we give to you in payment for our glorious vic—"

"Wait!" called Maya from the side of the room. Her melding with her brother Nalfein had abruptly ceased. It could only mean one thing. "Nalfein is dead," she announced. "The baby is no longer the third living son."

Vierna glanced curiously at her sister. At the same instant that Maya had sensed Nalfein's death, Vierna, melded with Dinin, had felt a strong emotive surge. Elation? Vierna brought a slender finger up to her pursed lips, wondering if Dinin had successfully pulled off the assassination.

Briza still held the spider-shaped knife over the babe's chest, wanting to give this one to Lolth.

"We promised the Spider Queen the third living son," Maya warned. "And that has been given."

"But not in sacrifice," argued Briza.

Vierna shrugged, at a loss. "If Lolth accepted Nalfein, then he has been given. To give another might evoke the Spider Queen's anger."

"But to not give what we have promised would be worse still!" Briza insisted.

"Then finish the deed," said Maya.

Briza clenched down tight on the dagger and began the ritual again.

"Stay your hand," Matron Malice commanded, propping herself up in the chair. "Lolth is content; our victory is won. Welcome, then, your brother, the newest member of House Do'Urden."

"Just a male," Briza commented in obvious disgust, walking away from the idol and the child.

"Next time we shall do better," Matron Malice chuckled, though she wondered if there would be a next time. She approached the end of her fifth century of life, and drow elves, even young ones, were not a particularly fruitful lot. Briza had been born to Malice at the youthful age of one hundred, but in the almost four centuries since, Malice had produced only five other children. Even this baby, Drizzt, had come as a surprise, and Malice hardly expected that she would ever conceive again.

"Enough of such contemplations," Malice whispered to herself, exhausted. "There will be ample time . . ." She sank back into her chair and fell into fitful, though wickedly pleasant, dreams of heightening power.

⚔ ⚔ ⚔ ⚔ ⚔

Zaknafein walked through the central pillar of the DeVir complex, his hood in his hand and his whip and sword comfortably replaced on his belt. Every now and a ring of battle sounded, only to be quickly ended. House Do'Urden had rolled through to victory, the tenth house had taken the fourth, and now all that remained was to remove evidence and witnesses. One group of lesser female clerics marched through, tending to the wounded Do'Urdens and animating the corpses of those beyond their ability, so that the bodies could walk away from the crime scene. Back at the Do'Urden compound, those corpses not beyond repair would be resurrected and put back to work.

Zak turned away with a visible shudder as the clerics moved from room to room, the marching line of Do'Urden zombies growing ever longer at their backs.

As distasteful as Zaknafein found this troupe, the one that followed was even worse. Two Do'Urden clerics led a contingent of soldiers through the structure, using detection spells to determine hiding places of surviving DeVirs. One stopped in the hallway just a few steps from Zak, her eyes turned inward as she felt the emanations of her spell. She held her fingers out in front of her, tracing a slow line, like some macabre divining rod, toward drow flesh.

"In there!" she declared, pointing to a panel at the base of the wall. The soldiers jumped to it like a pack of ravenous wolves and tore through the secret door. Inside a hidden cubby huddled the children of House DeVir. These were nobles, not commoners, and could not be taken alive.

Zak quickened his pace to get beyond the scene, but he heard vividly the children's helpless screams as the hungry Do'Urden soldiers finished their job. Zak found himself in a run now. He rushed around a bend in the hallway, nearly bowling over Dinin and Rizzen.

"Nalfein is dead," Rizzen declared impassively.

Zak immediately turned a suspicious eye on the younger Do'Urden son.

"I killed the DeVir soldier who committed the deed," Dinin assured him, not even hiding his cocky smile.

Zak had been around for nearly four centuries, and he was certainly not ignorant of the ways of his ambitious race. The brother princes had come in defensively at the back of the lines, with a host of Do'Urden soldiers between them and the enemy. By the time they even encountered a drow that was not of their own house, the majority of the DeVirs' surviving soldiers had already switched allegiance to House Do'Urden. Zak doubted that either of the Do'Urden brothers had even seen action against a DeVir.

"The description of the carnage in the prayer room has been spread throughout the ranks," Rizzen said to the weapons master. "You performed with your usual excellence—as we have come to expect."

Zak shot the patron a glare of contempt and kept on his way, down though the structure's main doors and out beyond the magical darkness and silence into Menzoberranzan's dark dawn. Rizzen was Matron Malice's present partner in a long line of partners, and no more. When Malice was finished with him, she would either relegate him back to the ranks of the common soldiery, stripping him of the name Do'Urden and all the rights that accompanied it, or she would dispose of him. Zak owed him no respect.

Zak moved out beyond the mushroom fence to the highest vantage point he could find, then fell to the ground. He watched, amazed, a few moments later, when the procession of the Do'Urden army, patron and son, soldiers and clerics, and the slow-moving line of two dozen drow zombies, made its way back home. They had lost, and left behind, nearly all of their slave fodder in the attack, but the line leaving the wreckage of House DeVir was longer than the line that had come in earlier that night. The slaves had been replaced twofold by captured DeVir slaves, and fifty or more of the DeVir common troops, showing typical drow loyalty, had willingly joined the attackers. These traitorous drow would be interrogated—magically interrogated—by the Do'Urden clerics to ensure their sincerity.

They would pass the test to a one, Zak knew. Drow elves were creatures of survival, not of principle. The soldiers would be given new identities and would be kept within the privacy of the Do'Urden compound for a few months, until the fall of House DeVir became an old and forgotten tale.

Zak did not follow immediately. Rather, he cut through the rows of mushroom trees and found a secluded dell, where he plopped down on a patch of mossy carpet and raised his gaze to the eternal darkness of the cavern's ceiling—and the eternal darkness of his existence.

It would have been prudent for him to remain silent at that time; he was an invader to the most powerful section of the vast city. He thought of the possible witnesses to his words, the same dark elves who had watched the fall of House DeVir, who had wholeheartedly enjoyed the spectacle. In the face of such behavior and such carnage as this night had seen, Zak could not contain his emotions. His lament came out as a plea to some god beyond his experience.

"What place is this that is my world; what dark coil has my spirit embodied?" he whispered the angry disclaimer that had always been a part of him. "In light, I see my skin as black; in darkness, it glows white in the heat of this rage I cannot dismiss.

"Would that I had the courage to depart, this place or this life, or to stand openly against the wrongness that is the world of these, my kin. To seek an existence that does not run afoul to that which I believe, and to that which I hold dear faith is truth.

"Zaknafein Do'Urden, I am called, yet a drow I am not, by choice or by deed. Let them discover this being that I am, then. Let them rain their wrath on these old shoulders already burdened by the hopelessness of Menzoberranzan."

Ignoring the consequences, the weapons master rose to his feet and yelled, "Menzoberranzan, what hell are you?"

A moment later, when no answer echoed back out of the quiet city, Zak flexed the remaining chill of Briza's wand from his weary muscles. He found some comfort as he patted the whip on his belt—the instrument that had taken the tongue from the mouth of a matron mother.

THE EYES OF A CHILD

M asoj, the young apprentice—which at this point in his magic-using career meant that he was no more than a cleaning attendant—leaned on his broom and watched as Alton DeVir moved through the door into the highest chamber of the spire. Masoj almost felt sympathy for the student, who had to go in and face the Faceless One.

Masoj felt excitement as well, though, knowing that the ensuing fireworks between Alton and the faceless master would be well worth the watching. He went back to his sweeping, using the broom as an excuse to get farther around the curve of the room's floor, closer to the door.

⚔ ⚔ ⚔ ⚔ ⚔

"You requested my presence, Master Faceless One," Alton DeVir said again, keeping one hand in front of his face and squinting to fight the brilliant glare of the room's three lighted candles. Alton shifted uncomfortably from one foot to the other just inside the shadowy room's door.

Hunched across the way, the Faceless One kept his back to the young DeVir. Better to be done with this cleanly, the master reminded himself. He knew, though, that the spell he was now preparing would kill Alton before the student could learn his family's fate, before the Faceless One could fully complete Dinin Do'Urden's final instructions. Too much was at stake. Better to be done with this cleanly.

"You . . ." Alton began again, but he prudently held his words and tried to sort out the situation before him. How unusual to be summoned to the private chambers of a master of the Academy before the day's lessons had even begun.

When he had first received the summons, Alton feared that he had somehow failed one of his lessons. That could be a fatal mistake in Sorcere. Alton was close to graduation, but the disdain of a single master could put an end to that.

He had done quite well in his lessons with the Faceless One, had even believed that this mysterious master favored him. Could this call be simply a courtesy of congratulations on his impending graduation? Unlikely, Alton realized against his hopes. Masters of the drow Academy did not often congratulate students.

Alton then heard quiet chanting and noticed that the master was in the midst of spellcasting. Something cried out as very wrong to him now; something about this whole situation did not fit the strict ways of the Academy. Alton set his feet firmly and tensed his muscles, following the advice of the motto that had been drilled into the thoughts of every student at the Academy, the precept that kept drow elves alive in a society so devoted to chaos: Be prepared.

⚔ ⚔ ⚔ ⚔ ⚔

The doors exploded before him, showering the room with stone splinters and throwing Masoj back against the wall. He felt the show well worth both the inconvenience and the new bruise on his shoulder when Alton DeVir scrambled out of the room. The student's back and left arm trailed wisps of smoke, and the most exquisite expression of terror and pain that Masoj had ever seen was etched on the DeVir noble's face.

Alton stumbled to the floor and kicked into a roll, desperate to put some ground between himself and the murderous master. He made it down and around the descending arc of the room's floor and through the door that led into the next lower chamber just as the Faceless One made his appearance at the sundered door.

The master stopped to spit a curse at his misfire, and to consider the best way to replace his door. "Clean it up!" he snapped at Masoj, who was again leaning casually with his hands atop his broomstick and his chin atop his hands.

Masoj obediently dropped his head and started sweeping the stone splinters. He looked up as the Faceless One stalked past, however, and cautiously started after the master.

Alton couldn't possibly escape, and this show would be too good to miss.

⚔ ⚔ ⚔ ⚔ ⚔

The third room, the Faceless One's private library, was the brightest of the four in the spire, with dozens of candles burning on each wall.

"Damn this light!" Alton spat, stumbling his way down through the dizzying blur to the door that led to the Faceless One's entry hall, the lowest room of the master's quarters. If he could get down from this spire and outside of the tower to the courtyard of the Academy, he might be able to turn the momentum against the master.

Alton's world remained the darkness of Menzoberranzan, but the Faceless One, who had spent so many decades in the candlelight of Sorcere, had grown accustomed to using his eyes to see shades of light, not heat.

The entry hall was cluttered with chairs and chests, but only one candle burned there, and Alton could see clearly enough to dodge or leap any obstacles. He rushed to the door and grabbed the heavy latch. It turned easily enough, but when Alton tried to shoulder through, the door did not budge and a burst of sparkling blue energy threw him back to the floor.

"Curse this place," Alton spat. The portal was magically held. He knew a spell to open such enchanted doors but doubted whether his magic would be strong enough to dispel the castings of a master. In his haste and fear, the words of the dweomer floated through Alton's thoughts in an indecipherable jumble.

"Do not run, DeVir," came the Faceless One's call from the previous chamber. "You only lengthen your torment!"

"A curse upon you, too," Alton replied under his breath. Alton forgot about the stupid spell; it would never come to him in time. He glanced around the room for an option.

His eyes found something unusual halfway up the side wall, in an opening between two large cabinets. Alton scrambled back a few steps to get a better angle but found himself caught within the range of the candlelight, within the deceptive field where his eyes registered both heat and light.

He could only discern that this section of the wall showed a uniform glow in the heat spectrum and that its hue was subtly different from the stone of the walls. Another doorway? Alton could only hope his guess to be right. He rushed back to the center of the room, stood directly across from the object, and forced his eyes away from the infrared spectrum, fully back into the world of light.

As his eyes adjusted, what came into view both startled and confused the young DeVir. He saw no doorway, nor any opening with another chamber behind it. What he looked upon was a reflection of himself, and a portion of the room he now stood in. Alton had never, in his fifty-five years of life, witnessed such a spectacle, but he had heard the masters of Sorcere speak of these devices. It was a mirror.

A movement in the upper doorway of the chamber reminded Alton that the Faceless One was almost upon him. He couldn't hesitate to ponder his options. He put his head down and charged the mirror.

Perhaps it was a teleportation door to another section of the city, perhaps a simple door to a room beyond. Or perhaps, Alton dared to imagine in those few desperate seconds, this was some interplanar gate that would bring him into a strange and unknown plane of existence!

He felt the tingling excitement of adventure pulling him on as he neared the wondrous thing—then he felt only the impact, the shattering glass, and the unyielding stone wall behind it.

Perhaps it was just a mirror.

✕ ✕ ✕ ✕ ✕

"Look at his eyes," Vierna whispered to Maya as they examined the newest member of House Do'Urden.

Truly the babe's eyes were remarkable. Though the child had been out of the womb for less than an hour, the pupils of his orbs darted back and forth inquisitively. While they showed the expected radiating glow of eyes seeing into the infrared spectrum, the familiar redness was tinted by a shade of blue, giving them a violet hue.

"Blind?" wondered Maya. "Perhaps this one will be given to the Spider Queen still."

Briza looked back to them anxiously. Dark elves did not allow children showing any physical deficiency to live.

"Not blind," replied Vierna, passing her hand over the child and casting an angry glare at both of her eager sisters. "He follows my fingers."

Maya saw that Vierna spoke the truth. She leaned closer to the babe, studying his face and strange eyes. "What do you see, Drizzt Do'Urden?" she asked softly, not in an act of gentleness toward the babe, but so that she would not disturb her mother, resting in the chair at the head of the spider idol.

"What do you see that the rest of us cannot?"

✕ ✕ ✕ ✕ ✕

Glass crunched under Alton, digging deeper wounds as he shifted his weight in an effort to rise to his feet. What would it matter? he thought. "My mirror!" he heard the Faceless One groan, and he looked up to see the outraged master towering over him.

How huge he seemed to Alton! How great and powerful, fully blocking the candlelight from this little alcove between the cabinets, his form enhanced tenfold to the eyes of the helpless victim by the mere implications of his presence.

Alton then felt a gooey substance floating down around him, detached webbing finding a sticky hold on the cabinets, on the wall, and on Alton. The young DeVir tried to leap up and roll away, but the Faceless One's spell already held him fast, trapped him as a dirgit fly would be trapped in the strands of a spider's home.

"First my door," the Faceless One growled at him, "and now this, my mirror! Do you know the pains I suffered to acquire such a rare device?"

Alton turned his head from side to side, not in answer, but to free at least his face from the binding substance.

"Why did you not just stand still and let the deed be finished cleanly?" the Faceless One roared, thoroughly disgusted.

"Why?" Alton lisped, spitting some of the webbing from his thin lips. "Why would you want to kill me?"

"Because you broke my mirror!" the Faceless One shot back.

It didn't make any sense, of course—the mirror had only been shattered after the initial attack—but to the master, Alton supposed, it didn't have to make sense. Alton knew his cause to be hopeless, but he continued on in his efforts to dissuade his opponent.

"You know of my house, of House DeVir," he said, indignant, "fourth in the city. Matron Ginafae will not be pleased. A high priestess has ways to learn the truth of such situations!"

"House DeVir?" The Faceless One laughed. Perhaps the torments that Dinin Do'Urden had requested would be in line after all. Alton had broken his mirror!

"Fourth house!" Alton spat.

"Foolish youth," the Faceless One cackled. "House DeVir is no more— not fourth, not fifty-fourth, nothing."

Alton slumped, though the webbing did its best to hold his body erect. What could the master be babbling about?

"They all are dead," the Faceless One taunted. "Matron Ginafae sees Lolth more clearly this day." Alton's expression of horror pleased the disfigured master. "All dead," he snarled one more time. "Except for poor Alton, who lives on to hear of his family's misfortune. That oversight shall be remedied now!" The Faceless One raised his hands to cast a spell.

"Who?" Alton cried.

The Faceless One paused and seemed not to understand.

"What house did this?" the doomed student clarified. "Or what conspiracy of houses brought down DeVir?"

"Ah, you should be told," replied the Faceless One, obviously enjoying the situation. "I suppose it is your right to know before you join your kin in the realm of death." A smile widened across the opening where his lips once had been.

"But you broke my mirror!" the master growled. "Die stupid, stupid boy! Find your own answers!"

The Faceless One's chest jerked out suddenly, and he shuddered in convulsions, babbling curses in a tongue far beyond the terrified student's comprehension. What vile spell did this disfigured master have prepared for him, so wretched that its chant sounded in an arcane language foreign to learned Alton's ears, so unspeakably evil that its semantics jerked on the very edge of its caster's control? The Faceless One then fell forward to the floor and expired.

Stunned, Alton followed the line of the master's hood down to his back—to the tail of a protruding dart. Alton watched the poisoned thing as it continued to shudder from the body's impact, then he turned his scan upward to the center of the room, where the young cleaning attendant stood calmly.

"Nice weapon, Faceless One!" Masoj beamed, rolling a two-handed, crafted crossbow over in his hands. He threw a wicked smile at Alton and fitted another dart.

⚔ ⚔ ⚔ ⚔ ⚔

Matron Malice hoisted herself out of her chair and willed herself to her feet. "Out of the way!" she snapped at her daughters.

Maya and Vierna scooted away from the spider idol and the baby. "See his eyes, Matron Mother," Vierna dared to remark. "They are so unusual."

Matron Malice studied the child. Everything seemed in place, and a good thing, too, for Nalfein, elderboy of House Do'Urden, was dead, and this boy, Drizzt, would have a difficult job replacing the valuable son.

"His eyes," Vierna said again.

The matron shot her a venomous look but bent low to see what the fuss was about.

"Purple?" Malice said, startled. Never had she heard of such a thing.

"He is not blind," Maya was quick to put in, seeing the disdain spreading across her mother's face.

"Fetch the candle," Matron Malice ordered. "Let us see how these eyes appear in the world of light."

Maya and Vierna reflexively headed for the sacred cabinet, but Briza cut them off. "Only a high priestess may touch the holy items," she reminded them in a tone that carried the weight of a threat. She spun around haughtily, reached into the cabinet, and produced a single half-used red candle. The clerics hid their eyes and Matron Malice put a prudent hand over the baby's face as Briza lit the sacred candle. It produced only a tiny flame, but to drow eyes it came as a brilliant intrusion.

"Bring it," said Matron Malice after several moments of adjusting. Briza moved the candle near Drizzt, and Malice gradually slid her hand away.

"He does not cry," Briza remarked, amazed that the babe could quietly accept such a stinging light.

"Purple again," whispered the matron, paying no heed to her daughter's rambling. "In both worlds, the child's eyes show as purple."

Vierna gasped audibly when she looked again upon her tiny brother and his striking lavender orbs.

"He is your brother," Matron Malice reminded her, viewing Vierna's gasp as a hint of what might come. "When he grows older and those eyes pierce you so, remember, on your life, that he is your brother."

Vierna turned away, almost blurting a reply she would have regretted making. Matron Malice's exploits with nearly every male soldier of the Do'Urden house—and many others that the seductive matron managed to sneak away from other houses—were almost legendary in Menzoberranzan. Who was she to be spouting reminders of prudent and proper behavior? Vierna bit her lip and hoped that neither Briza nor Malice had been reading her thoughts at that moment.

In Menzoberranzan, thinking such gossip about a high priestess, whether or not it was true, got you painfully executed.

Her mother's eyes narrowed, and Vierna thought she had been discovered. "He is yours to prepare," Matron Malice said to her.

"Maya is younger," Vierna dared to protest. "I could attain the level of high priestess in but a few years if I may keep to my studies."

"Or never," the matron sternly reminded her. "Take the child to the chapel proper. Wean him to words and teach him all that he will need to know to properly serve as a page prince of House Do'Urden."

"I will see to him," Briza offered, one hand subconsciously slipping to her snake-headed whip. "I do so enjoy teaching males their place in our world."

Malice glared at her. "You are a high priestess. You have other duties more important than word-weaning a male child." Then to Vierna, she said, "The babe is yours; do not disappoint me in this! The lessons you teach Drizzt will reinforce your own understanding of our ways. This exercise at 'mothering' will aid you in your quest to become a high priestess." She let Vierna take a moment to view the task in a more positive light, then her tone became unmistakably threatening once again. "It may aid you, but it surely can destroy you!"

Vierna sighed but kept her thoughts silent. The chore that Matron Malice had dropped on her shoulders would consume the bulk of her time for at least ten years. Vierna didn't like the prospects, she and this purple-eyed child together for ten long years. The alternative, however, the wrath of Matron Malice Do'Urden, seemed a worse thing by far.

⚔ ⚔ ⚔ ⚔ ⚔

Alton blew another web from his mouth. "You are just a boy, an apprentice," he stammered. "Why would you—?"

"Kill him?" Masoj finished the thought. "Not to save you, if that is your hope." He spat down at the Faceless One's body. "Look at me, a prince of the sixth house, a cleaning steward for that wretched—"

"Hun'ett," Alton cut in. "House Hun'ett is the sixth house."

The younger drow put a finger to pursed lips. "Wait," he remarked with a widening smile, an evil smile of sarcasm. "We are the fifth house now, I suppose, with DeVir wiped out."

"Not yet!" Alton growled.

"Momentarily," Masoj assured him, fingering the crossbow quarrel.

Alton slumped even farther back in the web. To be killed by a master was bad enough, but the indignity of being shot down by a boy. . . .

"I suppose I should thank you," Masoj said. "I had planned to kill that one for many tendays."

"Why?" Alton pressed his new assailant. "You would dare to kill a master of Sorcere simply because your family put you in servitude to him?"

"Because he would snub me!" Masoj yelled. "Four years I have slaved for him, that back end of a carrion crawler. Cleaned his boots. Prepared salve for his disgusting face! Was it ever enough? Not for that one." He spat at the corpse again and continued, talking more to himself than to the trapped student. "Nobles aspiring to wizardry have the advantage of being trained as apprentices before they reach the proper age for entry into Sorcere."

"Of course," Alton said. "I myself trained under—"

"He meant to keep me out of Sorcere!" Masoj rambled, ignoring Alton altogether. "He would have forced me into Melee-Magthere, the fighters' school, instead. The fighters' school! My twenty-fifth birthday is only two tendays away." Masoj looked up, as though he suddenly remembered that he was not alone in the room.

"I knew I must kill him," he continued, now speaking directly to Alton. "Then you come along and make it all so convenient. A student and master killing each other in a fight? It has happened before. Who would question it? I suppose, then, that I should thank you, Alton DeVir of No House Worth Mentioning," Masoj chided with a low, sweeping bow. "Before I kill you, I mean."

"Wait!" cried Alton. "Kill me to what gain?"

"Alibi."

"But you have your alibi, and we can make it better!"

"Explain," said Masoj, who, admittedly, was in no particular hurry. The

Faceless One was a high-level wizard; the webs weren't going anywhere anytime soon.

"Free me," Alton said earnestly.

"Can you be as stupid as the Faceless One proclaimed you?"

Alton took the insult stoically—the kid had the crossbow. "Free me so that I may assume the Faceless One's identity," he explained. "The death of a master arouses suspicion, but if no master is believed dead . . ."

"And what of this?" Masoj asked, kicking the corpse.

"Burn it," said Alton, his desperate plan coming fully into focus. "Let it be Alton DeVir. House DeVir is no more, so there will be no retaliation, no questions."

Masoj seemed skeptical.

"The Faceless One was practically a hermit," Alton reasoned. "And I am near to graduation; certainly I can handle the simple chores of basic teaching after thirty years of study."

"And what is my gain?"

Alton gawked, nearly burying himself in webbing, as if the answer were obvious. "A master in Sorcere to call mentor. One who can ease your way through your years of study."

"And one who can dispose of a witness at his earliest convenience," Masoj added slyly.

"And what then would be my gain?" Alton shot back. "To anger House Hun'ett, fifth in all the city, and I with no family at my back? No, young Masoj, I am not as stupid as the Faceless One named me."

Masoj ticked a long and pointed fingernail against his teeth and considered the possibilities. An ally among the masters of Sorcere? This held possibilities.

Another thought popped into Masoj's mind, and he pulled open the cabinet to Alton's side and began rummaging through the contents. Alton flinched when he heard some ceramic and glass containers crashing together, thinking of the components, possibly even completed potions, that might be lost by the apprentice's carelessness. Perhaps Melee-Magthere would be a better choice for this one, he thought.

A moment later, though, the younger drow reappeared, and Alton remembered that he was in no position to make such judgments.

"This is mine," Masoj demanded, showing Alton a small black object: a remarkably detailed onyx figurine of a hunting panther. "A gift from a denizen of the lower planes for some help I gave to him."

"You aided such a creature?" Alton had to ask, finding it difficult to believe that a mere apprentice had the resources necessary to even survive an encounter with such an unpredictable and mighty foe.

"The Faceless One—" Masoj kicked the corpse again—"took the credit and the statue, but they are mine! Everything else in here will go to you, of course. I know the magical dweomers of most and will show you what is what."

Brightening at the hope that he would indeed survive this dreadful day, Alton cared little about the figurine at that moment. All he wanted was to be freed of the webs so that he could find out the truth of his house's fate. Then Masoj, ever a confusing young drow, turned suddenly and started away.

"Where are you going?" Alton asked.

"To get the acid."

"Acid?" Alton hid his panic well, though he had a terrible feeling that he understood what Masoj meant to do.

"You want the disguise to appear authentic," Masoj explained matter-of-factly. "Otherwise, it would not be much of a disguise. We should take advantage of the web while it lasts. It will hold you still."

"No," Alton started to protest, but Masoj wheeled on him, the evil grin wide on his face.

"It does seem a bit of pain, and a lot of trouble to go through," Masoj admitted. "You have no family and will find no allies in Sorcere, since the Faceless One was so despised by the other masters." He brought the cross-bow up level with Alton's eyes and fitted another poisoned dart. "Perhaps you would prefer death."

"Get the acid!" Alton cried.

"To what end?" Masoj teased, waving the crossbow. "What have you to live for, Alton DeVir of No House Worth Mentioning?"

"Revenge," Alton sneered, the sheer wrath of his tone setting the confident Masoj on his heels. "You have not learned this yet—though you will, my young student—but nothing in life gives more purpose than the hunger for revenge!"

Masoj lowered the bow and eyed the trapped drow with respect, almost fear. Still, the apprentice Hun'ett could not appreciate the gravity of Alton's proclamation until Alton reiterated, this time with an eager smile on his face, "Get the acid."

4

THE FIRST HOUSE

Four cycles of Narbondel—four days—later, a glowing blue disk floated up the mushroom-lined stone path to the spider-covered gate of House Do'Urden. The sentries watched it from the windows of the two outer towers and from the compound as it hovered patiently three feet off the ground. Word came to the ruling family only seconds later.

"What can it be?" Briza asked Zaknafein when she, the weapons master, Dinin, and Maya assembled on the balcony of the upper level.

"A summons?" Zak asked as much as answered. "We will not know until we investigate." He stepped up on the railing and out into the empty air, then levitated down to the compound floor. Briza motioned to Maya, and the youngest Do'Urden daughter followed Zak.

"It bears the standard of House Baenre," Zak called up after he had moved closer. He and Maya opened the large gates, and the disk slipped in, showing no hostile movements.

"Baenre," Briza repeated over her shoulder, down the house's corridor to where Matron Malice and Rizzen waited.

"It seems that you are requested in audience, Matron Mother," Dinin put in nervously.

Malice moved out to the balcony, and her husband obediently followed.

"Do they know of our attack?" Briza asked in the silent code, and every member of House Do'Urden, noble and commoner alike, shared that unpleasant thought. House DeVir had been eliminated only a few days before, and a calling card from the First Matron Mother of Menzoberranzan could hardly be viewed as a coincidence.

"Every house knows," Malice replied aloud, not believing the silence to be a necessary precaution within the boundaries of her own complex. "Is the evidence against us so overwhelming that the ruling council will be forced to action?" She stared hard at Briza, her dark eyes alternating between the red glow of infravision and the deep green they showed in the aura of normal light. "That is the question we must ask." Malice stepped up onto the balcony, but Briza grabbed the back of her heavy black robe to stay her.

"You do not mean to go with the thing?" Briza asked.

Malice's answering look showed even more startlement. "Of course," she replied. "Matron Baenre would not openly call upon me if she meant me harm. Even her power is not so great that she can ignore the tenets of the city."

"You are certain that you will be safe?" Rizzen asked, truly concerned. If Malice was killed, Briza would take over the house, and Rizzen doubted that the eldest daughter would want any male by her side. Even if the vicious female did desire a patron, Rizzen would not want to be the one in that position. He was not Briza's father, was not even as old as Briza. Clearly, the present patron of the house had a lot at stake in Matron Malice's continued good health.

"Your concern touches me," Malice replied, knowing her husband's true fears. She pulled out of Briza's grasp and stepped off the railing, straightening her robes as she slowly descended. Briza shook her head disdainfully and motioned Rizzen to follow her back inside the house, not thinking it wise that the bulk of the family be so exposed to unfriendly eyes.

"Do you want an escort?" Zak asked as Malice sat on the disk.

"I am certain that I will find one as soon as I am beyond the perimeter of our compound," Malice replied. "Matron Baenre would not risk exposing me to any danger while I am in the care of her house."

"Agreed," said Zak, "but do you want an escort from House Do'Urden?"

"If one was wanted, two disks would have floated in," Malice said in a tone of finality. The matron was beginning to find the concerns of those around her stifling. She was the matron mother, after all, the strongest, the oldest, and the wisest, and did not appreciate others second-guessing her. To the disk, Malice said, "Execute your appointed task, and let us be done with it!"

Zak nearly snickered at Malice's choice of words.

"Matron Malice Do'Urden," came a magical voice from the disk, "Matron Baenre offers her greetings. Too long has it been since last you two have sat in audience."

"Never," Malice signaled to Zak. "Then take me to House Baenre!" Malice demanded. "I do not wish to waste my time conversing with a magical mouth!"

Apparently, Matron Baenre had anticipated Malice's impatience, for without another word, the disk floated back out of the Do'Urden compound.

Zak shut the gate as it left, then quickly signaled his soldiers into motion. Malice did not want any open company, but the Do'Urden spy network would covertly track every movement of the Baenre sled, to the very gates of the ruling house's grand compound.

✗ ✗ ✗ ✗ ✗

Malice's guess about an escort was correct. As soon as the disk swept down from the pathway to the Do'Urden compound, twenty soldiers of House Baenre, all female, moved out from concealment along the sides of the boulevard. They formed a defensive diamond around the guest matron mother. The guard at each point of the formation wore black robes emblazoned on the back with a large purple-and-red spider design—the robes of a high priestess.

"Baenre's own daughters," Malice mused, for only the daughters of a noble could attain such a rank. How careful the First Matron Mother had been to ensure Malice's safety on the trip!

Slaves and drow commoners tripped over themselves in a frantic effort to get far out of the way of the approaching entourage as the group made its way through the curving streets toward the mushroom grove. The soldiers of House Baenre alone wore their house insignia in open view, and no one wanted to invoke the anger of Matron Baenre in any way.

Malice just rolled her eyes in disbelief and hoped that she might know such power before she died.

She rolled her eyes again a few minutes later, when the group approached the ruling house. House Baenre encompassed twenty tall and majestic stalagmites, all interconnected with gracefully sweeping and arching bridges and parapets. Magic and faerie fire glowed from a thousand separate sculptures and a hundred regally adorned guardsmen paced about in perfect formations.

Even more striking were the inverse structures, the thirty smaller stalactites of House Baenre. They hung down from the ceiling of the cavern, their roots lost in the high darkness. Some of them connected tip-to-tip with the stalagmite mounds, while others hung freely like poised spears. Ringing balconies, curving up like the edging of a screw, had been built along the length of all of these, glowing with an overabundance of magic and highlighted design.

Magic, too, was the fence that connected the bases of the outer stalagmites, encircling the whole of the compound. It was a giant web, silver against the general blue of the rest of the outer compound. Some said it had been a gift from Lolth herself, with iron-strong strands as thick as a drow elf's arm. Anything touching Baenre's fence, even the sharpest of drow weapons, would simply stick fast until the matron mother willed the fence to let it free.

Malice and her escorts moved straight toward a symmetrical and circular section of this fence, between the tallest of the outer towers. As they neared, the gate spiraled and wound out, leaving a gap large enough for the caravan to step through.

Malice sat through it all, trying to appear unimpressed.

Hundreds of curious soldiers watched the procession as it made its way to the central structure of House Baenre, the great purple-glowing chapel dome. The common soldiers left the entourage, leaving only the four high priestesses to escort Matron Malice inside.

The sights beyond the great doors to the chapel did not disappoint her. A central altar dominated the place with a row of benches spiraling out in several dozen circuits to the perimeter of the great hall. Two thousand drow could sit there with room to stretch. Statues and idols too numerous to count stood all about the place, glowing in a quiet black light. In the air high above the altar loomed a gigantic glowing image, a red-and-black illusion that slowly and continually shifted between the forms of a spider and a beautiful drow female.

"A work of Gromph, my principal wizard," Matron Baenre explained from her perch on the altar, guessing that Malice, like everyone else who ever came to Chapel Baenre, was awestruck by the sight. "Even wizards have their place."

"As long as they remember their place," Malice replied, slipping down from the now stationary disk.

"Agreed," said Matron Baenre. "Males can get so presumptuous at times, especially wizards! Still, I wish that I had Gromph at my side more often these days. He has been appointed Archmage of Menzoberranzan, you know, and seems always at work on Narbondel or some other such tasks."

Malice just nodded and held her tongue. Of course, she knew that Baenre's son was the city's chief wizard. Everybody knew. Everybody knew, too, that Baenre's daughter Triel was the Matron Mistress of the Academy, a position of honor in Menzoberranzan second only to the title of matron mother of an individual family. Malice had little doubt that Matron Baenre would somehow work that fact into the conversation before too long.

Before Malice took a step toward the stairs to the altar, her newest escort stepped out from the shadows. Malice scowled openly when she saw the thing, a creature known as an illithid, a mind flayer. It stood about six feet tall, fully a foot taller than Malice, most of the difference being the result of the creature's enormous head. Glistening with slime, the head resembled an octopus with pupil-less, milky white eyes.

Malice composed herself quickly. Mind flayers were not unknown in Menzoberranzan, and rumors said that one had befriended Matron Baenre. These creatures, though, more intelligent and more evil than even the drow, almost always inspired shudders of revulsion.

"You may call him Methil," Matron Baenre explained. "His true name is beyond my pronunciation. He is a friend."

Before Malice could reply, Baenre added, "Of course, Methil gives me the advantage in our discussion, and you are not accustomed to illithids." Then, as Malice's mouth drooped open in disbelief, Matron Baenre dismissed the illithid.

"You read my thought," Malice protested. Few could insinuate themselves through the mental barriers of a high priestess well enough to read her thoughts, and the practice was a crime of the highest order in drow society.

"No!" Matron Baenre explained, immediately on the defensive. "Your pardon, Matron Malice. Methil reads thoughts, even the thoughts of a high priestess, as easily as you or I hear words. He communicates telepathically. On my word, I did not even realize that you had not yet spoken your thoughts."

Malice waited to watch the creature depart the great hall, then walked up the steps to the altar. In spite of her efforts against the action, she could not help peeking up at the transforming spider-and-drow image every now and.

"How fares House Do'Urden?" Matron Baenre asked, feigning politeness.

"Well enough," replied Malice, more interested at that moment in studying her counterpart than in conversing. They were alone atop the altar, though no doubt a dozen or so clerics wandered through the shadows of the great hall, keeping a watchful eye on the situation.

Malice had all that she could handle in hiding her contempt for Matron Baenre. Malice was old, nearly five hundred, but Matron Baenre was ancient. Her eyes had seen the rise and fall of a millennium, by some accounts, though drow rarely lived past their seventh—and certainly not their eighth—century. While drow normally did not show their age—Malice was as beautiful and vibrant now as she had been on her one-hundredth birthday—Matron Baenre was withered and worn. The wrinkles surrounding her mouth resembled a spider's web, and she could hardly keep the heavy lids of her eyes from dropping altogether. Matron Baenre should be dead, Malice noted, but still she lives.

Matron Baenre, seeming so beyond her time of life, was pregnant, and due in only a few tendays.

In this aspect, too, Matron Baenre defied the norm of the dark elves. She had given birth twenty times, twice as often as any others in Menzoberranzan, and fifteen of those she bore were female, every one a high priestess! Ten of Baenre's children were older than Malice!

"How many soldiers do you now command?" Matron Baenre asked, leaning closer to show her interest.

"Three hundred," Malice replied.

"Oh," mused the withered old drow, pursing a finger to her lips. "I had heard the count at three-hundred fifty."

Malice grimaced in spite of herself. Baenre was teasing her, referring to the soldiers House Do'Urden had added in its raid on House DeVir.

"Three hundred," Malice said again.

"Of course," replied Baenre, resting back.

"And House Baenre holds a thousand?" Malice asked for no better reason than to keep herself on even terms in the discussion.

"That has been our number for many years."

Malice wondered again why this old decrepit thing was still alive. Surely more than one of Baenre's daughters aspired to the position of matron mother. Why hadn't they conspired and finished Matron Baenre off? Or why hadn't any of them, some in the later stages of life, struck out on their own to form separate houses, as was the norm for noble daughters when they passed their fifth century? While they lived under Matron Baenre's rule, their children would not even be considered nobles but would be relegated to the ranks of the commoners.

"You have heard of the fate of House DeVir?" Matron Baenre asked directly, growing as tired of the hesitant small talk as her counterpart.

"Of what house?" Malice asked pointedly. At this time, there was no such thing as House DeVir in Menzoberranzan. To drow reckoning, the house no longer existed; the house never existed.

Matron Baenre cackled. "Of course," she replied. "You are matron mother of the ninth house now. That is quite an honor."

Malice nodded. "But not as great an honor as matron mother of the eighth house."

"Yes," agreed Baenre, "but ninth is only one position away from a seat on the ruling council."

"That would be an honor indeed," Malice replied. She was beginning to understand that Baenre was not simply teasing her, but was congratulating her as well, and prodding her on to greater glories. Malice brightened at the thought. Baenre was in the highest favor of the Spider Queen. If she was pleased with House Do'Urden's ascension, then so was Lolth.

"Not as much of an honor as you would believe," said Baenre. "We are a group of meddling old females, gathering every so often to find new ways to put our hands into places they do not belong."

"The city recognizes your rule."

"Does it have a choice?" Baenre laughed. "Still, drow business is better left to the matron mothers of the individual houses. Lolth would not stand for a presiding council exacting anything that even remotely resembled total rule. Do you not believe that House Baenre would have conquered all of Menzoberranzan long ago if that was the Spider Queen's will?"

Malice shifted proudly in her chair, appalled by such arrogant words.

"Not now, of course," Matron Baenre explained. "The city is too large for such an action in this age. But long ago, before you were even born, House Baenre would not have found such a conquest difficult. But that is not our way. Lolth encourages diversity. She is pleased that houses stand to balance each other, ready to fight beside each other in times of common need." She paused a moment and let a smile appear on her wrinkled lips. "And ready to pounce upon any that fall out of her favor."

Another direct reference to House DeVir, Malice noted, this time directly connected to the Spider Queen's pleasure. Malice eased out of her angry posture and found the rest of her discussion—fully two hours long—with Matron Baenre quite enjoyable.

Still, when she was back on the disk and floating out through the compound, past the grandest and strongest house in all of Menzoberranzan, Malice was not smiling. In the face of such an open display of power, she could not forget that Matron Baenre's purpose in summoning her had been twofold: to privately and cryptically congratulate her on her perfect coup, and to vividly remind her not to get too ambitious.

WEANING

For five long years Vierna devoted almost every waking moment to the care of baby Drizzt. In drow society, this was not so much a nurturing time as an indoctrinating time. The child had to learn basic motor and language skills, as did children of all the intelligent races, but a drow elf also had to be grilled on the precepts that bound the chaotic society together.

In the case of a male child such as Drizzt, Vierna spent hour after endless hour reminding him that he was inferior to the drow females. Since almost all of this portion of Drizzt's life was spent in the family chapel, he encountered no males except during times of communal worship. Even when all in the house gathered for the unholy ceremonies, Drizzt remained silent at Vierna's side, with his gaze obediently on the floor.

When Drizzt was old enough to follow commands, Vierna's workload lessened. Still, she spent many hours teaching her younger brother—presently they were working on the intricate facial, hand, and body movements of the silent code. Often, though, she just set Drizzt about the endless task of cleaning the domed chapel. The room was barely a fifth the size of the great hall in House Baenre, but it could hold all the dark elves of House Do'Urden with a hundred seats to spare.

Being a weanmother was not so bad now, Vierna thought, but still she wished that she could devote more of her time to her studies. If Matron Malice had appointed Maya to the task of rearing the child, Vierna might already have been ordained as a high priestess. Vierna still had another five years in her duties with Drizzt; Maya might attain high priestesshood before her!

Vierna dismissed that possibility. She could not afford to worry about such problems. She would finish her tenure as weanmother in just a few short years. On or around his tenth birthday, Drizzt would be appointed page prince of the family and would serve all the household equally. If her work with Drizzt did not disappoint Matron Malice, Vierna knew that she would get her due.

"Go up the wall," Vierna instructed. "Tend to that statue." She pointed to a sculpture of a naked drow female about twenty feet from the floor. Young Drizzt looked up at it, confused. He couldn't possibly climb up to the sculpture and wipe it clean while holding any secure perch. Drizzt knew the high price of disobedience, though—even of hesitation—and he reached up, searching for his first handhold.

"Not like that!" Vierna scolded.

"How?" Drizzt dared to ask, for he had no idea of what his sister was hinting at.

"Will yourself up to the gargoyle," Vierna explained.

Drizzt's small face crinkled in confusion.

"You are a noble of House Do'Urden!" Vierna shouted at him. "Or at least you will one day earn that distinction. In your neck-purse you possess the emblem of the house, an item of considerable magic." Vierna still wasn't certain if Drizzt was ready for such a task; levitation was a high manifestation of innate drow magic, certainly more difficult that limning objects in faerie fire or summoning globes of darkness. The Do'Urden emblem heightened these innate powers of drow elves, magic that usually emerged as a drow matured. Whereas most drow nobles could summon the magical energy to levitate once every day or so, the nobles of House Do'Urden, with their insignia tool, could do so repeatedly.

Normally, Vierna would never have tried this on a male child younger than ten, but Drizzt had shown her so much potential in the last couple of years that she saw no harm in the attempt. "Just put yourself in line with the statue," she explained, "and will yourself to rise."

Drizzt looked up at the female carving, then lined his feet just out in front of the thing's angled and delicate face. He put a hand to his collar, trying to attune himself to the emblem. He had sensed before that the magic coin possessed some type of power, but it was only a raw sensation, a child's intuition. Now that Drizzt had some focus and confirmation to his suspicions, he clearly felt the vibrations of magical energy.

A series of deep breaths cleared distracting thoughts from the young drow's mind. He blocked out the other sights of the room; all he saw was the statue, the destination. He felt himself grow lighter, his heels went up, and he was on one toe, though he felt no weight upon it. Drizzt looked over at Vierna, his smile wide in amazement . . . then he tumbled to a heap.

"Foolish male!" Vierna scolded. "Try again! Try a thousand times if you must!" She reached for the snake-headed whip on her belt. "If you fail . . ."

Drizzt looked away from her, cursing himself. His own elation had caused the spell to falter. He knew that he could do it now, though, and he was not afraid of being beaten. He concentrated again on the sculpture and let the magical energy gather within his body.

Vierna, too, knew that Drizzt would eventually succeed. His mind was keen, as sharp as any Vierna had ever known, including those of the other females of House Do'Urden. The child was stubborn, too; Drizzt would not let the magic defeat him. She knew he would stand under the sculpture until he fainted from hunger if need be.

Vierna watched him go through a series of small successes and failures, the last one dropping Drizzt from a height of nearly ten feet. Vierna flinched, wondering if he was seriously hurt. Drizzt, whatever his wounds, did not even cry out but moved back into position and started concentrating all over again.

"He is young for that," came a comment from behind Vierna. She turned in her seat to see Briza standing over her, a customary scowl on the older sister's face.

"Perhaps," Vierna replied, "but I'll not know until I let him try."

"Whip him when he fails," Briza suggested, pulling her cruel six-headed instrument from her belt. She gave the whip a loving look—as if it were some sort of pet—and let a snake's head writhe about her neck and face. "Inspiration."

"Put it away," Vierna retorted. "Drizzt is mine to rear, and I need no help from you!"

"You should watch **how you** speak to a high priestess," Briza warned, and all of the snake heads, **extensions** of her thoughts, turned menacingly toward Vierna.

"As Matron Malice will watch how you interfere with my tasks," Vierna was quick to reply.

Briza put her whip away at the mention of Matron Malice. "Your tasks," she echoed scornfully. "You are too yielding for such a chore. Male children must be disciplined; they must be taught their place." Realizing that Vierna's threat held dire consequences, the older sister turned and left.

Vierna let Briza have the last word. The weanmother looked back to Drizzt, still trying to get up to the statue. "Enough!" she ordered, recognizing that the child was tiring; he could barely get his feet off the ground.

"I will do it!" Drizzt snapped back at her.

Vierna liked his determination, but not the tone of his reply. Perhaps there was some truth to Briza's words. Vierna snapped the snake-headed whip from her belt. A little inspiration might go a long way.

⚔ ⚔ ⚔ ⚔ ⚔

Vierna sat in the chapel the next day, watching Drizzt hard at work polishing the statue of the naked female. He had levitated the full twenty feet in his first attempt this day.

Vierna could not help but be disappointed when Drizzt did not look back to her and smile at the success. She saw him now, hovering up in the air, his hands a blur as they worked the brushes. Most vividly of all, though, Vierna saw the scars on her brother's naked back, the legacy of their "inspirational" discussion. In the infrared spectrum, the whip lines showed clearly, trails of warmth where the insulating layers of skin had been stripped away.

Vierna understood the gain in beating a child, particularly a male child.

Few drow males ever raised a weapon against a female, unless under the order of some other female. "How much do we lose?" Vierna wondered aloud. "What more could one such as Drizzt become?"

When she heard the words spoken aloud, Vierna quickly brushed the blasphemous thoughts from her mind. She aspired to become a high priestess of the Spider Queen, Lolth the Merciless. Such thoughts were not in accord with the rules of her station. She cast an angry glare on her little brother, transferring her guilt, and again took out her instrument of punishment.

She would have to whip Drizzt again this day, for the sacrilegious thoughts he had inspired within her.

⚔ ⚔ ⚔ ⚔ ⚔

So the relationship continued for another five years, with Drizzt learning the basic lessons of life in drow society while endlessly cleaning the chapel of House Do'Urden. Beyond the supremacy of female drow (a lesson always accentuated by the wicked snake-headed whip), the most compelling lessons were those concerning the surface elves, the faeries. Evil empires often bound themselves in webs of hate toward fabricated enemies, and none in the history of the world were better at it than the drow. From the first day they were able to understand the spoken word, drow children were taught that whatever was wrong in their lives could be blamed on the surface elves.

Whenever the fangs of Vierna's whip sliced into Drizzt's back, he cried out for the death of a faerie. Conditioned hatred was rarely a rational emotion.

PART TWO

E mpty hours, empty days.
        I find that I have few memories of that
first period of my life, those first sixteen years
when I labored as
a servant. Minutes   THE WEAPONS
blended into hours,
hours into days, and so on, until the   MASTER
whole of it seemed one long and barren
moment. Several times I managed to sneak out
onto the balcony of House Do'Urden and look
out over the magical lights of Menzoberranzan.
On all of those secret journeys, I found myself
entranced by the growing, and dissipating,
heatlight of Narbondel, the timeclock pillar.
Looking back on that now, on those long
hours watching the glow of the wizard's fire
slowly walk its way up and down the pillar I
am amazed at the emptiness of my early days.
    I clearly remember my excitement, tingling ex-
citement, each time I got out of the house and set
myself into position to observe the pillar. Such

a simple thing it was, yet so fulfilling compared to the rest of my existence.

Whenever I hear the crack of a whip, another memory—more a sensation than a memory actually—sends a shiver through my spine. The shocking jolt and the ensuing numbness from those snake-headed weapons is not something that any person would soon forget. They bite under your skin, sending waves of magical energy through your body, waves that make your muscles snap and pull beyond their limits.

Yet I was luckier than most. My sister Vierna was near to becoming a high priestess when she was assigned the task of rearing me and was at a period of her life where she possessed far more energy than such a job required. Perhaps, then, there was more to those first ten years under her care than I now recall. Vierna never showed the intense wickedness of our mother—or, more particularly, of our oldest sister, Briza. Perhaps there were good times in the solitude of the house chapel; it is possible that Vierna allowed a more gentle side of herself to show through to her baby brother.

Maybe not. Even though I count Vierna as the kindest of my sisters, her words drip in the venom of Lolth as surely as those of any cleric in Menzoberranzan. It seems unlikely that she would risk her aspirations toward high priest-esshood for the sake of a mere child, a mere male child.

Whether there were indeed joys in those years, obscured in the unrelenting assault of

Menzoberranzan's wickedness, or whether that earliest period of my life was even more painful than the years that followed—so painful that my mind hides the memories—I cannot be certain. For all my efforts, I cannot remember them.

I have more insight into the next six years, but the most prominent recollection of the days I spent serving the court of Matron Malice—aside from the secret trips outside the house—is the image of my own feet.

A page prince is never allowed to raise his gaze.

—Drizzt Do'Urden

"Two-Hands"

Drizzt promptly answered the call to his matron mother's side, not needing the whip Briza used to hurry him along. How often he had felt the sting of that dreaded weapon! Drizzt held no thoughts of revenge against his vicious oldest sister. With all of the conditioning he had received, he feared the consequences of striking her—or any female—far too much to entertain such notions.

"Do you know what this day marks?" Malice asked him as he arrived at the side of her great throne in the chapel's darkened anteroom.

"No, Matron Mother," Drizzt answered, unconsciously keeping his gaze on his toes. A resigned sigh rose in his throat as he noticed the unending view of his own feet. There had to be more to life than blank stone and ten wiggling toes, he thought.

He slipped one foot out of his low boot and began doodling on the stone floor. Body heat left discernible tracings in the infrared spectrum, and Drizzt was quick and agile enough to complete simple drawings before the initial lines had cooled.

"Sixteen years," Matron Malice said to him. "You have breathed the air of Menzoberranzan for sixteen years. An important period of your life has passed."

Drizzt did not react, did not see any importance or significance to the declaration. His life was an unending and unchanging routine. One day, sixteen years, what difference did it make? If his mother considered important the things he had been put through since his earliest recollections, Drizzt shuddered to think of what the next decades might hold.

He had nearly completed his picture of a round-shouldered drow—Briza—being bitten on the behind by an enormous viper.

"Look at me," Matron Malice commanded.

Drizzt felt at a loss. His natural tendency once had been to look upon a person with whom he was talking, but Briza had wasted no time in beating that instinct out of him. The place of a page prince was servitude, and the only eyes a page prince's were worthy of meeting were those of the creatures that scurried across the stone floor—except the eyes of a spider, of course; Drizzt had to avert his gaze whenever one of the eight-legged things crawled into his vision. Spiders were too good for the likes of a page prince.

"Look at me," Malice said again, her tone hinting at volatile impatience. Drizzt had witnessed the explosions before, a wrath so incredibly vile that it swept aside anything and everything in its path. Even Briza, so pompous and cruel, ran for hiding when the matron mother grew angry.

Drizzt forced his gaze up tentatively, scanning his mother's black robes, using the familiar spider pattern along the garment's back and sides to judge the angle of his gaze. He fully expected, as every inch passed, a smack on his head, or a lashing on his back—Briza was behind him, always with her snake-headed whip near her anxious hand.

Then he saw her, the mighty Matron Malice Do'Urden, her heat-sensing eyes flashing red and her face cool, not flushed with angry heat. Drizzt kept tense, still expecting a punishing blow.

"Your tenure as page prince is ended," Malice explained. "You are secondboy of House Do'Urden now and are accorded all the . . ."

Drizzt's gaze unconsciously slipped back to the floor.

"Look at me!" his mother screamed in sudden rage.

Terrified, Drizzt snapped his gaze back to her face, which now was glowing a hot red. On the edge of his vision he saw the wavering heat of Malice's swinging hand, though he was not foolish enough to try to dodge the blow. He was on the floor then, the side of his face bruised.

Even in the fall, though, Drizzt was alert and wise enough to keep his gaze locked on to that of Matron Malice.

"No more a servant!" the matron mother roared. "To continue acting like one would bring disgrace to our family." She grabbed Drizzt by the throat and dragged him roughly to his feet.

"If you dishonor House Do'Urden," she promised, her face an inch from his, "I will put needles into your purple eyes."

Drizzt didn't blink. In the six years since Vierna had relinquished care of him, putting him into general servitude to all the family, he had come to know Matron Malice well enough to understand all of the subtle connotations of her threats. She was his mother—for whatever that was worth—but Drizzt did not doubt that she would enjoy sticking needles in his eyes.

⚔ ⚔ ⚔ ⚔ ⚔

"This one is different," Vierna said, "in more than the shade of his eyes."

"In what way, then?" Zaknafein asked, trying to keep his curiosity at a professional level. Zak had always liked Vierna better than the others, but she recently had been ordained a high priestess, and had since become too eager for her own good.

Vierna slowed the pace of her gait—the door to the chapel's ante-chamber was in sight now. "It is hard to say," she admitted. "Drizzt is as intelligent as any male child I have ever known; he could levitate by the age of five. Yet, after he became the page prince, it took tendays of punishment to teach him the duty of keeping his gaze to the floor, as if such a simple act ran unnaturally counter to his constitution."

Zaknafein paused and let Vierna move ahead of him. "Unnatural?" he whispered under his breath, considering the implications of Vierna's observations. Unusual, perhaps, for a drow, but exactly what Zaknafein would expect—and hope for—from a child of his loins.

He moved behind Vierna into the lightless anteroom. Malice, as always, sat in her throne at the head of the spider idol, but all the other chairs in the room had been moved to the walls, even though the entire family was present. This was to be a formal meeting, Zak realized, for only the matron mother was accorded the comfort of a seat.

"Matron Malice," Vierna began in her most reverent voice, "I present to you Zaknafein, as you requested."

Zak moved up beside Vierna and exchanged nods with Malice, but he was more intent on the youngest Do'Urden, standing naked to the waist at the matron mother's side.

Malice held up one hand to silence the others, then motioned for Briza, holding a house *piwafwi*, to continue.

An expression of elation brightened Drizzt's childish face as Briza, chanting through the appropriate incantations, placed the magical cloak, black and shot with streaks of purple and red, over his shoulders.

"Greetings, Zaknafein Do'Urden," Drizzt said heartily, drawing stunned looks from all in the room. Matron Malice had not granted him privilege to speak; he hadn't even asked her permission!

"I am Drizzt, secondboy of House Do'Urden, no more the page prince. I can look at you now—I mean at your eyes and not your boots. Mother told me so." Drizzt's smile disappeared when he looked up at the burning scowl of Matron Malice.

Vierna stood as if turned to stone, her jaw hanging open and her eyes wide in disbelief.

Zak, too, was amazed, but in a different manner. He brought a hand up to pinch his lips together, to prevent them from spreading into a smile that would have inevitably erupted into belly-shaking laughter. Zak couldn't remember the last time he had seen the matron mother's face so very bright!

Briza, in her customary position behind Malice, fumbled with her whip, too confounded by her young brother's actions to even know what in the Nine Hells she should do.

That was a first, Zak knew, for Malice's eldest daughter rarely hesitated when punishment was in order.

At the matron's side, but now prudently a step farther away, Drizzt quieted and stood perfectly still, biting down on his bottom lip. Zak could see, though, that the smile remained in the young drow's eyes. Drizzt's informality and disrespect of station had been more than an unconscious slip of the tongue and more than the innocence of inexperience.

The weapons master took a long step forward to deflect the matron mother's attention from Drizzt. "Secondboy?" he asked, sounding impressed, both for the sake of Drizzt's swelling pride and to placate and distract Malice. "Then it is time for you to train."

Malice let her anger slip away, a rare event. "Only the basics at your hand, Zaknafein. If Drizzt is to replace Nalfein, his place at the Academy will be in Sorcere. Thus the bulk of his preparation will fall upon Rizzen and his knowledge, limited though it may be, of the magical arts."

"Are you so certain that wizardry is his lot, Matron?" Zak was quick to ask.

"He appears intelligent," Malice replied. She shot an angry glare at Drizzt. "At least, some of the time. Vierna reported great progress with his command of the innate powers. Our house needs a new wizard." Malice snarled reflexively, reminded of Matron Baenre's pride in her wizard son, the Archmage of the city. It had been sixteen years since Malice's meeting with the First Matron Mother of Menzoberranzan, but she had never forgotten even the tiniest detail of that encounter. "Sorcere seems the natural course."

Zak took a flat coin from his neck-purse, flipped it into a spin, and snatched it out of the air. "Might we see?" he asked.

"As you will," Malice agreed, not surprised at Zak's desire to prove her wrong. Zak placed little value in wizardry, preferring the hilt of a blade to the crystal rod component of a lightning bolt.

Zak moved to stand before Drizzt and handed him the coin. "Flip it."

Drizzt shrugged, wondering what this vague conversation between his mother and the weapons master was all about. Until now, he had heard nothing of any future profession being planned for him, or of this place called Sorcere. With a consenting shrug of his shoulders, he slid the coin onto his curled index finger and snapped it into the air with his thumb, easily catching it. He then held it back out to Zak and gave the weapons master a confused look, as if to ask what was so important about such an easy task.

Instead of taking the coin, the weapons master pulled another from his neck-purse. "Try both hands," he said to Drizzt, handing it to him.

Drizzt shrugged again, and in one easy motion, put the coins up and caught them.

Zak turned an eye on Matron Malice. Any drow could have performed that feat, but the ease with which this one executed the catch was a pleasure to observe. Keeping a sly eye on the matron, Zak produced two more coins. "Stack two on each hand and send all four up together," he instructed Drizzt.

Four coins went up. Four coins were caught. The only parts of Drizzt's body that had even flinched were his arms.

"Two-hands," Zak said to Malice. "This one is a fighter. He belongs in Melee-Magthere."

"I have seen wizards perform such feats," Malice retorted, not pleased by the look of satisfaction on the troublesome weapons master's face. Zak once had been Malice's proclaimed husband, and quite often since that distant time she took him as her lover. His skills and agility were not confined to the use of weapons. But along with the pleasures that Zaknafein gave to Malice, sensual skills that had prompted Malice to spare Zak's life on more than a dozen occasions, came a multitude of headaches. He was the finest weapons master in Menzoberranzan, another fact that Malice could not ignore, but his disdain, even contempt, for the Spider Queen had often landed House Do'Urden into trouble.

Zak handed two more coins to Drizzt. Now enjoying the game, Drizzt put them into motion. Six went up. Six came down, the correct three landing in each hand.

"Two-hands," Zak said more emphatically. Matron Malice motioned for him to continue, unable to deny the grace of her youngest son's display.

"Could you do it again?" Zak asked Drizzt.

With each hand working independently, Drizzt soon had the coins stacked atop his index fingers, ready to flip. Zak stopped him there and pulled out four more coins, building each of the piles five high. Zak paused a moment to study the concentration of the young drow (and also to keep his hands over the coins and ensure that they were brightened enough by the warmth of his body heat for Drizzt to properly see them in their flight).

"Catch them all, Secondboy," he said in all seriousness. "Catch them all, or you will land in Sorcere, the school of magic. That is not where you belong!"

Drizzt still had only a vague idea of what Zak was talking about, but he could tell from the weapons master's intensity that it must be important. He took a deep breath to steady himself, then snapped the coins up. He sorted their glow quickly, discerning each individual item. The first two fell easily into his hands, but Drizzt saw that the scattering pattern of the rest would not drop them so readily in line.

Drizzt exploded into action, spinning a complete circle, his hands an indecipherable blur of motion. Then he straightened suddenly and stood before Zak. His hands were in fists at his sides and a grim look lay on his face.

Zak and Matron Malice exchanged glances, neither quite sure of what had happened.

Drizzt held his fists out to Zak and slowly opened them, a confident smile widening across his childish face.

Five coins in each hand.

Zak blew a silent whistle. It had taken him, the weapons master of the house, a dozen tries to complete that maneuver with ten coins. He walked over to Matron Malice.

"Two-hands," he said a third time. "He is a fighter, and I am out of coins."

"How many could he do?" Malice breathed, obviously impressed in spite of herself.

"How many could we stack?" Zaknafein shot back with a triumphant smile.

Matron Malice chuckled out loud and shook her head. She had wanted Drizzt to replace Nalfein as the house wizard, but her stubborn weapons master had, as always, deflected her course. "Very well, Zaknafein," she said, admitting her defeat. "The secondboy is a fighter."

Zak nodded and started back to Drizzt.

"Perhaps one day soon to be the weapons master of House Do'Urden," Matron Malice added to Zak's back. Her sarcasm stopped Zak short, and he eyed her over his shoulder.

"With this one," Matron Malice continued wryly, wrenching back the upper hand with her usual lack of shame, "could we expect anything less?"

Rizzen, the present patron of the family shifted uncomfortably. He knew, and so did everyone—even the slaves of House Do'Urden—that Drizzt was not his child.

⚔ ⚔ ⚔ ⚔ ⚔

"Three rooms?" Drizzt asked when he and Zak entered the large training hall at the southernmost end of the Do'Urden complex. Balls of multicolored magical light had been spaced along the length of the high-ceilinged stone room, basking the entirety in a comfortably dim glow. The hall had only three doors: one to the east, which led to an outer chamber that opened onto the balcony of the house; one directly across from Drizzt, on the south wall, leading into the last room in the house; and the one from the main hallway that they had just passed through. Drizzt knew from the many locks Zak was now fastening behind them that he wouldn't often be going back that way.

"One room," Zak corrected.

"But two more doors," Drizzt reasoned, looking out across the room. "With no locks."

"Ah," Zak corrected, "their locks are made of common sense." Drizzt was beginning to get the picture. "That door," Zak continued, pointing to the south, "opens into my private chambers. You do not ever want me to find you in there. The other one leads to the tactics room, reserved for times of war. When—if—you ever prove yourself to my satisfaction, I might invite you to join me there. That day is years away, so consider this single magnificent hall—" he swept his arm out in a wide arc—"your home."

Drizzt looked around, not overly thrilled. He had dared to hope that he had left this kind of treatment behind him with his page prince days. This setup, though, brought him back even to before his six years of servitude in the house, back to that decade when he had been locked away in the family chapel with Vierna. This room wasn't even as large as the chapel, and was too tight for the likings of the spirited young drow. His next question came out as a growl.

"Where do I sleep?"

"Your home," Zak answered matter-of-factly.

"Where do I take meals?"

"Your home."

Drizzt's eyes narrowed to slits and his face flushed in glowing heat. "Where do I . . ." he began stubbornly, determined to foil the weapons master's logic.

"Your home," Zak replied in the same measured and weighted timbre before Drizzt could finish the thought.

Drizzt planted his feet firmly and crossed his arms over his chest. "It sounds messy," he growled.

"It had better not be," Zak growled back.

"Then what is the purpose?" Drizzt began. "You pull me away from my mother—"

"You will address her as Matron Malice," Zak warned. "You will always address her as Matron Malice."

"From my mother—"

Zak's next interruption came not with words but with the swing of a curled fist.

Drizzt awoke about twenty minutes later.

"First lesson," Zak explained, casually leaning against the wall a few feet away. "For your own good. You will always address her as Matron Malice."

Drizzt rolled to his side and tried to prop himself up on his elbow but found his head reeling as soon as it left the black-rugged floor. Zak grabbed him and hoisted him up.

"Not as easy as catching coins," the weapons master remarked.

"What?"

"Parrying a blow."

"What blow?"

"Just agree, you stubborn child."

"Secondboy!" Drizzt corrected, his voice again a growl, and his arms defiantly back over his chest.

Zak's fist curled at his side, a not-too-subtle point that Drizzt did not miss. "Do you need another nap?" the weapons master asked calmly.

"Secondboys can be children," Drizzt wisely conceded.

Zak shook his head in disbelief. This was going to be interesting. "You may find your time here enjoyable," he said, leading Drizzt over to a long, thick, and colorfully (though most of the colors were somber) decorated curtain. "But only if you can learn some control over that wagging tongue of yours." A sharp tug sent the curtain floating down, revealing the most magnificent weapons rack the young drow (and many older drow as well) had ever seen. Polearms of many sorts, swords, axes, hammers, and every other kind of weapon Drizzt could imagine—and a whole bunch he'd never imagine—sat in an elaborate array.

"Examine them," Zak told him. "Take your time and your pleasure. Learn which ones sit best in your hands, follow most obediently the commands of your will. By the time we have finished, you will know every one of them as a trusted companion."

Wide-eyed, Drizzt wandered along the rack, viewing the whole place and the potential of the whole experience in a completely different light. For his entire young life, sixteen years, his greatest enemy had been boredom. Now, it appeared, Drizzt had found weapons to fight that enemy.

Zak headed for the door to his private chamber, thinking it better that Drizzt be alone in those first awkward moments of handling new weapons.

The weapons master stopped, though, when he reached his door and looked back to the young Do'Urden. Drizzt swung a long and heavy halberd, a polearm more than twice his height, in a slow arc. For all of Drizzt's attempts to keep the weapon under control, its momentum spun his tiny frame right to the ground.

Zak heard himself chuckle, but his laughter only reminded him of the grim reality of his duty. He would train Drizzt, as he had trained a thousand young dark elves before him, to be a warrior, preparing him for the trials of the Academy and life in dangerous Menzoberranzan. He would train Drizzt to be a killer.

How against this one's nature that mantle seemed! thought Zak. Smiles came too easily to Drizzt; the thought of him running a sword through the heart of another living being revolted Zaknafein. That was the way of the drow, though, a way that Zak had been unable to resist for all of his four centuries of life. Pulling his stare from the spectacle of Drizzt at play, Zak moved into his chamber and shut the door.

"Are they all like that?" he asked into his nearly empty room. "Do all drow children possess such innocence, such simple, untainted smiles that cannot survive the ugliness of our world?" Zak started for the small desk to the side of the room, meaning to lift the darkening shade off the continually glowing ceramic globe that served as the chamber's light source. He changed his mind as that image of Drizzt's delight with the weapons refused to diminish, and he headed instead for the large bed across from the door.

"Or are you unique, Drizzt Do'Urden?" he continued as he fell onto the cushioned bed. "And if you are so different, what, then, is the cause? The blood, my blood, that courses through your veins? Or the years you spent with your weanmother?"

Zak threw an arm across his eyes and considered the many questions. Drizzt was different from the norm, he decided at length, but he didn't know whether he should thank Vierna—or himself.

After a while, sleep took him. But it brought the weapons master little comfort. A familiar dream visited him, a vivid memory that would never fade.

Zaknafein heard again the screams of the children of House DeVir as the Do'Urden soldiers—soldiers he himself had trained—slashed at them.

"This one is different!" Zak cried, leaping up from his bed. He wiped the cold sweat from his face.

"This one is different." He had to believe that.

7
Ðark Secrets

"Ð o you truly mean to try?" Masoj asked, his voice condescending and filled with disbelief.

Alton turned his hideous glare on the student.

"Direct your anger elsewhere, Faceless One," Masoj said, averting his gaze from his mentor's scarred visage. "I am not the cause of your frustration. The question was valid."

"For more than a decade, you have been a student of the magical arts," Alton replied. "Still you fear to explore the nether world at the side of a master of Sorcere."

"I would have no fear beside a true master," Masoj dared to whisper.

Alton ignored the comment, as he had with so many others he had accepted from the apprenticing Hun'ett over the last sixteen years. Masoj was Alton's only tie to the outside world, and while Masoj had a powerful family, Alton had only Masoj.

They moved through the door into the uppermost chamber of Alton's four-room complex. A single candle burned there, its light diminished by an abundance of dark-colored tapestries and the black hue of the room's stone and rugs. Alton slid onto his stool at the back of the small, circular table, and placed a heavy book down before him.

"It is a spell better left for clerics," Masoj protested, sitting down across from the faceless master. "Wizards command the lower planes;

the dead are for the clerics alone."

Alton looked around curiously, then turned a frown up at Masoj, the master's grotesque features enhanced by the dancing candlelight. "It seems that I have no cleric at my call," the Faceless One explained sarcastically. "Would you rather I try for another denizen of the Nine Hells?"

Masoj rocked back in his chair and shook his head helplessly and emphatically. Alton had a point. A year before, the Faceless One had sought answers to his questions by enlisting the aid of an ice devil. The volatile thing froze the room until it shone black in the infrared spectrum and smashed a matron mother's treasure horde worth of alchemical equipment. If Masoj hadn't summoned his magical cat to distract the ice devil, neither he nor Alton would have gotten out of the room alive.

"Very well, then," Masoj said unconvincingly, crossing his arms in front of him on the table. "Conjure your spirit and find your answers."

Alton did not miss the involuntary shudder belied by the ripple in Masoj's robes. He glared at the student for a moment, then went back to his preparations.

As Alton neared the time of casting, Masoj's hand instinctively went into his pocket, to the onyx figurine of the hunting cat he had acquired on the day Alton had assumed the Faceless One's identity. The little statue was enchanted with a powerful dweomer that enabled its possessor to summon a mighty panther to his side. Masoj had used the cat sparingly, not yet fully understanding the dweomer's limitations and potential dangers. "Only in times of need," Masoj reminded himself quietly when he felt the item in his hand. Why was it that those times kept occurring when he was with Alton? the apprentice wondered.

Despite his bravado, this time Alton privately shared Masoj's trepidation. Spirits of the dead were not as destructive as denizens of the lower planes, but they could be equally cruel and subtler in their torments.

Alton needed his answer, though. For more than a decade and a half he had sought his information through conventional channels, enquiring of masters and students—in a roundabout manner, of course—of the details concerning the fall of House DeVir. Many knew the rumors of that eventful night; some even detailed the battle methods used by the victorious house.

None, though, would name that perpetrating house. In Menzoberranzan, one did not utter anything resembling an accusation, even if the belief was commonly shared, without enough undeniable proof to spur the ruling council into a unified action against the accused. If a house botched a raid and was discovered, the wrath of all Menzoberranzan would descend upon it until the family name had been extinguished. But in the case of a successfully executed attack, such as the one that felled House DeVir, an accuser was the one most likely to wind up at the wrong end of a snake-headed whip.

Public embarrassment, perhaps more than any guidelines of honor, turned the wheels of justice in the city of drow.

Alton now sought other means for the solution to his quest. First he had tried the lower planes, the ice devil, to disastrous effect. Now Alton had in his possession an item that could end his frustrations: a tome penned by a wizard of the surface world. In the drow hierarchy, only the clerics of Lolth dealt with the realm of the dead, but in other societies, wizards also dabbled into the spirit world. Alton had found the book in the library of Sorcere and had managed to translate enough of it, he believed, to make a spiritual contact.

He wrung his hands together, gingerly opened the book to the marked page, and scanned the incantation one final time. "Are you ready?" he asked Masoj.

"No."

Alton ignored the student's unending sarcasm and placed his hands flat on the table. He slowly sunk into his deepest meditative trance.

"*Fey innad . .*," He paused and cleared his throat at the slip. Masoj, though he hadn't closely examined the spell, recognized the mistake.

"*Fey innunad de-min . .*". Another pause.

"Lolth be with us," Masoj groaned under his breath.

Alton's eyes popped wide, and he glared at the student. "A translation," he growled. "From the strange language of a human wizard!"

"Gibberish," Masoj retorted.

"I have in front of me the private spellbook of a wizard from the surface world," Alton said evenly. "An archmage, according to the scribbling of the orcan thief who stole it and sold it to our agents." He composed himself again and shook his hairless head, trying to return to the depths of his trance.

"A simple, stupid orc managed to steal a spellbook from an archmage," Masoj whispered rhetorically, letting the absurdity of the statement speak for itself.

"The wizard was dead!" Alton roared. "The book is authentic!"

"Who translated it?" Masoj replied calmly.

Alton refused to listen to any more arguments. Ignoring the smug look on Masoj's face, he began again.

"Fey innunad de-min de-sul de-keî."

Masoj faded out and tried to rehearse a lesson from one of his classes, hoping that his sobs of laughter wouldn't disturb Alton. He didn't believe for a moment that Alton's attempt would prove successful, but he didn't want to screw up the fool's line of babbling again and have to suffer through the ridiculous incantation all the way from the beginning still another time.

A short time later, when Masoj heard Alton's excited whisper, "Matron Ginafae?" he quickly focused his attention back on the events at hand.

Sure enough, an unusual ball of green-hued smoke appeared over the candle's flame and gradually took a more definite shape.

"Matron Ginafae!" Alton gasped again when the summons was complete. Hovering before him was the unmistakable image of his dead mother's face.

The spirit scanned the room, confused. "Who are you?" it asked at length.

"I am Alton. Alton DeVir, your son."

"Son?" the spirit asked.

"Your child."

"I remember no child so very ugly."

"A disguise," Alton replied quickly, looking back at Masoj and expecting a snicker. If Masoj had chided and doubted Alton before, he now showed only sincere respect.

Smiling, Alton continued, "Just a disguise, that I might move about in the city and exact revenge upon our enemies!"

"What city?"

"Menzoberranzan, of course."

Still the spirit seemed not to understand.

"You are Ginafae?" Alton pressed. "Matron Ginafae DeVir?"

The spirit's features contorted into a twisted scowl as it considered the question. "I was . . . I think."

"Matron Mother of House DeVir, Fourth House of Menzoberranzan," Alton prompted, growing more excited. "High priestess of Lolth."

The mention of the Spider Queen sent a spark through the spirit. "Oh, no!" it balked. Ginafae remembered now. "You should not have done this, my ugly son!"

"It is just a disguise," Alton interrupted.

"I must leave you," Ginafae's spirit continued, glancing around nervously. "You must release me!"

"But I need some information from you, Matron Ginafae."

"Do not call me that!" the spirit shrieked. "You do not understand! I am not in Lolth's favor . . ."

"Trouble," whispered Masoj offhandedly, hardly surprised.

"Just one answer!" Alton demanded, refusing to let another opportunity to learn his enemies' identities slip past him.

"Quickly!" the spirit shrieked.

"Name the house that destroyed DeVir."

"The house?" Ginafae pondered. "Yes, I remember that evil night. It was House—"

The ball of smoke puffed and bent out of shape, twisting Ginafae's image and sending her next words out as an indecipherable blurb.

Alton leaped to his feet. "No!" he screamed. "You must tell me! Who are my enemies?"

"Would you count me as one?" the spirit image said in a voice very different from the one it had used earlier, a tone of sheer power that stole the blood from Alton's face. The image twisted and transformed, became something ugly, uglier than Alton. Hideous beyond all experience on the Material Plane.

Alton was not a cleric, of course, and he had never studied the drow religion beyond the basic tenets taught to males of the race. He knew the creature now hovering in the air before him, though, for it appeared as an oozing, slimy stick of melted wax: a yochlol, a handmaiden of Lolth.

"You dare to disturb the torment of Ginafae?" the yochlol snarled.

"Damn!" whispered Masoj, sliding slowly down under the black tablecloth. Even he, with all of his doubts of Alton, had not expected his disfigured mentor to land them in trouble this serious.

"But . . ." Alton stuttered.

"Never again disturb this plane, feeble wizard!" the yochlol roared.

"I did not try for the Abyss," Alton protested meekly. "I only meant to speak with—"

"With Ginafae!" the yochlol snarled. "Fallen priestess of Lolth. Where would you expect to find her spirit, foolish male? Frolicking in Olympus, with the false gods of the surface elves?"

"I did not think . . ."

"Do you ever?" the yochlol growled.

"Nope," Masoj answered silently, careful to keep himself as far out of the way as possible.

"Never again disturb this plane," the yochlol warned a final time. "The Spider Queen is not merciful and has no tolerance for meddling males!" The creature's oozing face puffed and swelled, expanding beyond the limits of the smoky ball. Alton heard gurgling, gagging noises, and he stumbled back over his stool, putting his back flat against the wall and bringing his arms up defensively in front of his face.

The yochlol's mouth opened impossibly wide and spewed forth a hail of small objects. They ricocheted off Alton and tapped against the wall all around him. Stones? the faceless wizard wondered in confusion. One of the objects then answered his unspoken question. It caught hold of Alton's layered black robes and began crawling up toward his exposed neck. Spiders.

A wave of the eight-legged beasts rushed under the little table, sending Masoj tumbling out the other side in a desperate roll. He scrambled to his feet and turned back, to see Alton slapping and stomping wildly, trying to get out of the main host of the crawling things.

"Do not kill them!" Masoj screamed. "To kill spiders is forbidden by the—"

"To the Nine Hells with the clerics and their laws!" Alton shrieked back.

Masoj shrugged in helpless agreement, reached around under the folds of his own robes, and produced the same two-handed crossbow he had used to kill the Faceless One those years ago. He considered the powerful weapon and the tiny spiders scrambling around the room.

"Overkill?" he asked aloud. Hearing no answer, he shrugged again and fired.

The heavy bolt knifed across Alton's shoulder, cutting a deep line. The wizard stared in disbelief, then turned an ugly grimace on Masoj.

"You had one on your shoulder," the student explained.

Alton's scowl did not relent.

"Ungrateful?" Masoj snarled. "Foolish Alton, all of the spiders are on your side of the room. Remember?" Masoj turned to leave and called, "Good hunting," over his shoulder. He reached for the handle to the door, but as his long fingers closed around it, the portal's surface transformed into the image of Matron Ginafae. She smiled widely, too widely, and an impossibly long and wet tongue reached out and licked Masoj across the face.

"Alton!" he cried, spinning back against the wall out of the slimy member's reach. He noticed the wizard in the midst of spellcasting, Alton fighting to hold his concentration as a host of spiders continued their hungry ascent up his flowing robes.

"You are a dead one," Masoj commented matter-of-factly, shaking his head.

Alton fought through the exacting ritual of the spell, ignored his own revulsion of the crawling things, and forced the evocation to completion. In all of his years of study, Alton never would have believed he could do such a thing; he would have laughed at the mere mention of it. Now, however, it seemed a far preferable fate to the yochlol's creeping doom.

He dropped a fireball at his own feet.

✕ ✕ ✕ ✕ ✕

Naked and hairless, Masoj stumbled through the door and out of the inferno. The flaming faceless master came next, diving into a roll and stripping his tattered and burning robe from his back as he went.

As he watched Alton patting out the last of the flames, a pleasant memory flashed in Masoj's mind, and he uttered the single lament that dominated his every thought at this disastrous moment.

"I should have killed him when I had him in the web."

✕ ✕ ✕ ✕ ✕

A short time later, after Masoj had gone back to his room and his studies, Alton slipped on the ornamental metallic bracers that identified him as a master of the Academy and slipped outside the structure of Sorcere. He moved to the wide and sweeping stairway leading down from Tier Breche and sat down to take in the sights of Menzoberranzan.

Even with this view, though, the city did little to distract Alton from thoughts of his latest failure. For sixteen years he had forsaken all other dreams and ambitions in his desperate search to find the guilty house. For sixteen years he had failed.

He wondered how long he could keep up the charade, and his spirits. Masoj, his only friend—if Masoj could be called a friend—was more than halfway through his studies at Sorcere. What would Alton do when Masoj graduated and returned to House Hun'ett?

"Perhaps I shall carry on my toils for centuries to come," he said aloud, "only to be murdered by a desperate student, as I—as Masoj—murdered the Faceless One. Might that student disfigure himself and take my place?" Alton couldn't stop the ironic chuckle that passed his lipless mouth at the notion of a perpetual "faceless master" of Sorcere. At what point would the Matron Mistress of the Academy get suspicious? A thousand years? Ten thousand? Or might the Faceless One outlive Menzoberranzan itself? Life as a master was not such a bad lot, Alton supposed. Many drow would sacrifice much to be given such an honor.

Alton dropped his face into the crook of his elbow and forced away such ridiculous thoughts. He was not a real master, nor did the stolen position bring him any measure of satisfaction. Perhaps Masoj should have shot him that day, sixteen years ago, when Alton was trapped in the Faceless One's web.

Alton's despair only deepened when he considered the actual time frame involved. He had just passed his seventieth birthday and was still young by drow standards. The notion that only a tenth of his life was behind him was not a comforting one to Alton DeVir this night.

"How long will I survive?" he asked himself. "How long until this madness that is my existence consumes me?" Alton looked back out over the city. "Better that the Faceless One had killed me," he whispered. "For now I am Alton of No House Worth Mentioning."

Masoj had dubbed him that on the first morning after House DeVir's fall, but way back then, with his life teetering on the edge of a crossbow, Alton had not understood the title's implications. Menzoberranzan was nothing more than a collection of individual houses. A rogue commoner might latch on to one of them to call his own, but a rogue noble wouldn't likely be accepted by any house in the city. He was left with Sorcere and nothing more . . . until his true identity was discovered at last. What punishments would he then face for the crime of killing a master? Masoj may have committed the crime, but Masoj had a house to defend him. Alton was only a rogue noble.

He sat back on his elbows and watched the rising heat-light of Narbondel. As the minutes became hours, Alton's despair and self-pity went through inevitable change. He turned his attention to the individual drow houses now, not to the conglomeration that bound them as a city, and he wondered what dark secrets each harbored. One of them, Alton reminded himself, held the secret he most dearly wanted to know. One of them had wiped out House DeVir.

Forgotten was the night's failure with Matron Ginafae and the yochlol, forgotten was the lament for an early death. Sixteen years was not so long a time, Alton decided. He had perhaps seven centuries of life left within his slender frame. If he had to, Alton was prepared to spend every minute of those long years searching for the perpetrating house.

"Vengeance," he growled aloud, needing, feeding off, that audible reminder of his only reason for continuing to draw breath.

8

KINÐREÐ

Zak pressed in with a series of low thrusts. Drizzt tried to back away quickly and return to even footing, but the relentless assault followed his every step, and he was forced to keep his movements solely on the defensive. More often than not, Drizzt found the hilts of his weapons closer to Zak than the blades.

Zak then dropped into a low crouch and came up under Drizzt's defense.

Drizzt twirled his scimitars in a masterful cross, but he had to straighten stiffly to dodge the weapons master's equally deft assault. Drizzt knew that he had been set up, and he fully expected the next attack as Zak shifted his weight to his back leg and dived in, both sword tips aimed for Drizzt's loins.

Drizzt spat a silent curse and spun his scimitars into a downward cross, meaning to use the "V" of his blades to catch his teacher's swords. On a sudden impulse, Drizzt hesitated as he intercepted Zak's weapons, and he jumped away instead, taking a painful slap on the inside of one thigh. Disgusted, he threw both of his scimitars to the floor.

Zak, too, leaped back. He held his swords out to his sides, a look of sincere confusion on his face. "You should not have missed that move," he said bluntly.

"The parry is wrong," Drizzt replied.

Awaiting further explanation, Zak lowered one sword tip to the floor and leaned on the weapon. In past years, Zak had wounded, even killed, students for such blatant defiance.

"The cross-down defeats the attack, but to what gain?" Drizzt continued. "When the move is completed, my sword tips remain down too low for any effective attack routine, and you are able to slip back and free."

"But you have defeated my attack."

"Only to face another," Drizzt argued. "The best position I can hope to obtain from the cross-down is an even stance."

"Yes . . . " Zak prompted, not understanding his student's problem with that scenario.

"Remember your own lesson!" Drizzt shouted. "'Every move should bring an advantage you preach to me, but I see no advantage in using the cross-down."

"You recite only one part of that lesson for your own purpose," Zak scolded, now growing equally angry. "Complete the phrase, or use it not at all! 'Every move should bring an advantage or take away a disadvantage.' The cross-down defeats the double thrust low, and your opponent obviously has gained the advantage if he even attempts such a daring offensive maneuver! Returning to an even stance is far preferable at that moment."

"The parry is wrong." Drizzt said stubbornly.

"Pick up your blades," Zak growled at him, taking a threatening step forward. Drizzt hesitated and Zak charged, his swords leading.

Drizzt dropped to a crouch, snatched up the scimitars, and rose to meet the assault while wondering if it was another lesson or a true attack.

The weapons master pressed furiously, snapping off cut after cut and backing Drizzt around in circles. Drizzt defended well enough and began to notice an all-too-familiar pattern as Zak's attacks came consistently lower, again forcing the hilts of Drizzt's weapons up and out over the scimitars' blades.

Drizzt understood that Zak meant to prove his point with actions, not words. Seeing the fury on Zak's face, though, Drizzt wasn't certain how far the weapons master would carry his point. If Zak proved correct in his observations, would he strike again to Drizzt's thigh? Or to his heart? Zak came up and under and Drizzt stiffened and straightened. "Double thrust low!" the weapons master growled, and his swords dived in.

Drizzt was ready for him. He executed the cross-down, smiling smugly at the ring of metal as his scimitars crossed over the thrusting swords. Drizzt then followed through with only one of his blades, thinking he could deflect both of Zak's swords well enough in that manner. Now with one blade free of the parry, Drizzt spun it over in a devious counter.

As soon as Drizzt reversed the one hand, Zak saw the ploy—a ruse he had suspected Drizzt would try. Zak dropped one of his own sword tips—the one nearest to the hilt of Drizzt's single parrying blade—to the ground, and Drizzt, trying to maintain an even resistance and balance along the length of the blocking scimitar, lost his balance. Drizzt was quick enough to catch himself before he had stumbled too far, though his knuckles pinched into the stone of the floor. He still believed that he had Zak caught in his trap, and that he could finish his brilliant counter. He took a short step forward to regain his full balance.

The weapons master dropped straight down to the floor, under the arc of Drizzt's swinging scimitar, and spun a single circuit, driving his booted heel into the back of Drizzt's exposed knee. Before Drizzt had even realized the attack, he found himself lying flat on his back.

Zak abruptly broke his own momentum and threw his feet back under him. Before Drizzt could begin to understand the dizzying counter-counter, he found the weapons master standing over him with the tip of Zak's sword painfully and pointedly drawing a tiny drop of blood from his throat.

"Have you anything more to say?" Zak growled.

"The parry is wrong," Drizzt answered.

Zak's laughter erupted from his belly. He threw his sword to the ground, reached down, and pulled the stubborn young student to his feet. He calmed quickly, his gaze finding that of Drizzt's lavender orbs as he pushed the student out to arm's length. Zak marveled at the ease of Drizzt's stance, the way he held the twin scimitars almost as if they were a natural extension of his arms. Drizzt had been in training only a few months, but already he had mastered the use of nearly every weapon in the vast armory of House Do'Urden.

Those scimitars! Drizzt's chosen weapons, with curving blades that enhanced the dizzying flow of the young fighter's sweeping battle style. With those scimitars in hand, this young drow, barely more than a child, could outfight half the members of the Academy, and a shiver tingled through Zak's spine when he pondered just how magnificent Drizzt would become after years of training.

It was not just the physical abilities and potential of Drizzt Do'Urden that made Zaknafein pause and take note, however. Zak had come to realize that Drizzt's temperament was indeed different from that of the average drow; Drizzt possessed a spirit of innocence and lacked any maliciousness. Zak couldn't help but feel proud when he looked upon Drizzt. In all manners, the young drow held to the same principles—morals so unusual in Menzoberranzan—as Zak.

Drizzt had recognized the connection as well, though he had no idea of how unique his and Zak's shared perceptions were in the evil drow world. He realized that "Uncle Zak" was different from any of the other dark elves he had come to know, though that included only his own family and a few dozen of the house soldiers. Certainly Zak was much different from Briza, Drizzt's oldest sister, with her zealous, almost blind, ambitions in the mysterious religion of Lolth. Certainly Zak was different from Matron Malice, Drizzt's mother, who seemed never to say anything at all to Drizzt unless it was a command for service.

Zak was able to smile at situations that didn't necessarily bring pain to anyone. He was the first drow Drizzt had met who was apparently content with his station in life. Zak was the first drow Drizzt had ever heard laugh.

"A good try," the weapons master conceded of Drizzt's failed counter.

"In a real battle, I would have been dead," Drizzt replied.

"Surely," said Zak, "but that is why we train. Your plan was masterful, your timing perfect. Only the situation was wrong. Still, I will say it was a good try."

"You expected it," said the student.

Zak smiled and nodded. "That is, perhaps, because I had seen the maneuver attempted by another student."

"Against you?" Drizzt asked, feeling a little less special now that he knew his battle insights were not so unique.

"Hardly," Zak replied with a wink. "I watched the counter fail from the same angle as you, to the same result."

Drizzt's face brightened again. "We think alike," he commented.

"We do," said Zak, "but my knowledge has been increased by four centuries of experience, while you have not even lived through a score of years. Trust me, my eager student. The cross-down is the correct parry."

"Perhaps," Drizzt replied.

Zak hid a smile. "When you find a better counter, we shall try it. But until then, trust my word. I have trained more soldiers than I can count, all the army of House Do'Urden and ten times that number when I served as a master in Melee-Magthere. I taught Rizzen, all of your sisters, and both of your brothers."

"Both?"

"I . . ." Zak paused and shot a curious glance at Drizzt. "I see," he said after a moment. "They never bothered to tell you." Zak wondered if it was his place to tell Drizzt the truth. He doubted that Matron Malice would care either way; she probably hadn't told Drizzt simply because she hadn't considered the story of Nalfein's death worth telling.

"Yes, both." Zak decided to explain. "You had two brothers when you were born: Dinin, whom you know, and an older one, Nalfein, a wizard of considerable power. Nalfein was killed in battle on the very night you drew your first breath."

"Against dwarves or vicious gnomes?" Drizzt squeaked, as wide-eyed as a child begging for a frightening bedtime story. "Was he defending the city from evil conquerors or rogue monsters?"

Zak had a hard time reconciling the warped perceptions of Drizzt's innocent beliefs. "Bury the young in lies," he lamented under his breath, but to Drizzt he answered, "No."

"Then against some opponent more foul?" Drizzt pressed. "Wicked elves from the surface?"

"He died at the hands of a drow!" Zak snapped in frustration, stealing the eagerness from Drizzt's shining eyes.

Drizzt slumped back to consider the possibilities, and Zak could hardly bear to watch the confusion that twisted his young face.

"War with another city?" Drizzt asked somberly. "I did not know . . ."

Zak let it go at that. He turned and moved silently toward his private chamber. Let Malice or one of her lackeys destroy Drizzt's innocent logic. Behind him, Drizzt held his next line of questions in check, understanding that the conversation, and the lesson, was at an end. Understanding, too, that something important had just transpired.

⚔ ⚔ ⚔ ⚔ ⚔

The weapons master battled Drizzt through long hours as the days blended into tendays, and the tendays into months. Time became unimportant; they fought until exhaustion overwhelmed them, and went back to the training floor again as soon as they were able.

By the third year, at the age of nineteen, Drizzt was able to hold out for hours against the weapons master, even taking the offensive in many of their contests.

Zak enjoyed these days. For the first time in many years, he had met one with the potential to become his fighting equal. For the first time that Zak could ever remember, laughter often accompanied the clash of adamantine weapons in the training room.

He watched Drizzt grow tall and straight, attentive, eager, and intelligent. The masters of the Academy would be hard put just to hold a stalemate against Drizzt, even in his first year!

That thought thrilled the weapons master only as long as it took him to remember the principles of the Academy, the precepts of drow life, and what they would do to his wonderful student. How they would steal that smile from Drizzt's lavender eyes.

A pointed reminder of that drow world outside the practice room visited them one day in the person of Matron Malice.

"Address her with proper respect," Zak warned Drizzt when Maya announced the matron mother's entrance. The weapons master prudently moved out a few steps to greet the head of House Do'Urden privately.

"My greetings, Matron," he said with a low bow. "To what do I owe the honor of your presence?"

Matron Malice laughed at him, seeing through his facade.

"So much time do you and my son spend in here," she said. "I came to witness the benefit to the boy."

"He is a fine fighter," Zak assured her.

"He will have to be," Malice muttered. "He goes to the Academy in only a year."

Zak narrowed his eyes at her doubting words and growled, "The Academy has never seen a finer swordsman."

The matron walked away from him to stand before Drizzt. "I doubt not your prowess with the blade," she said to Drizzt, though she shot a sly gaze back at Zak as she spoke the words. "You have the proper blood. There are other qualities that make up a drow warrior—qualities of the heart. The attitude of a warrior!"

Drizzt didn't know how to respond to her. He had seen her only a few times in all of the last three years, and they had exchanged no words.

Zak saw the confusion on Drizzt's face and feared that the boy would slip up—precisely what Matron Malice wanted. Then Malice would have an excuse to pull Drizzt out of Zak's tutelage—dishonoring Zak in the process—and give him over to Dinin or some other passionless killer. Zak may have been the finest instructor with the blade, but now that Drizzt had learned the use of weapons, Malice wanted him emotionally hardened.

Zak couldn't risk it; he valued his time with young Drizzt too much. He pulled his swords from their jeweled scabbards and charged right by Matron Malice, yelling, "Show her, young warrior!"

Drizzt's eyes became burning flames at the approach of his wild instructor. His scimitars came into his hands as quickly as if he had willed them to appear.

It was a good thing they had! Zak came in on Drizzt with a fury that the young drow had never before seen, more so even than the time Zak had shown Drizzt the value of the cross-down parry. Sparks flew as sword rang against scimitar, and Drizzt found himself driven back, both of his arms already aching from the thudding force of the heavy blows.

"What are you . . ." Drizzt tried to ask.

"Show her," Zak growled, slamming in again and again.

Drizzt barely dodged one cut that surely would have killed him. Still, confusion kept his moves purely defensive.

Zak slapped one of Drizzt's scimitars, then the other, out wide, and used an unexpected weapon, bringing his foot straight up in front of him and slamming his heel into Drizzt's nose.

Drizzt heard the crackle of cartilage and felt the warmth of his own blood running freely down his face. He dived back into a roll, trying to keep a safe distance from his crazed opponent until he could realign his senses.

From his knees he saw Zak, a short distance away and approaching. "Show her!" Zak growled angrily with every determined step.

The purple flames of faerie fire limned Drizzt's skin, making him an easier target. He responded the only way he could; he dropped a globe of darkness over himself and Zak. Sensing the weapons master's next move, Drizzt dropped to his belly and scrambled out, keeping his head low—a wise choice.

At his first realization of the darkness, Zak had quickly levitated up about ten feet and rolled right over, sweeping his blades down to Drizzt's face level.

When Drizzt came clear of the other side of the darkened globe, he looked back and saw only the lower half of Zak's legs. He didn't need to watch anything more to understand the weapons master's deadly blind attacks. Zak would have cut him apart if he had not dropped low in the blackness.

Anger replaced confusion. When Zak dropped from his magical perch and came rushing back out the front of the globe, Drizzt let his rage lead him back into the fight. He spun a pirouette just before he reached Zak, his lead scimitar cutting a gracefully arcing line and his other following in a deceptively sharp stab straight over that line.

Zak dodged the thrusting point and put a backhand block on the other.

Drizzt wasn't finished. He set his thrusting blade into a series of short, wicked pokes that kept Zak on the retreat for a dozen steps and more, back into the conjured darkness. They now had to rely on their incredibly keen sense of hearing and their instincts. Zak finally managed to regain a foothold, but Drizzt immediately set his own feet into action, kicking away whenever the balance of his swinging blades allowed for it. One foot even slipped through Zak's defenses, blasting the breath from the weapons master's lungs.

They came back out the side of the globe, and Zak, too, glowed in the outline of faerie fire. The weapons master felt sickened by the hatred etched on his young student's face, but he realized that this time, neither he nor Drizzt had been given a choice in the matter. This fight had to be ugly, had to be real. Gradually, Zak settled into an easy rhythm, solely defensive, and let Drizzt, in his explosive fury, wear himself down.

Drizzt played on and on, relentless and tireless. Zak coaxed him by letting him see openings where there were none, and Drizzt was always quick to oblige, launching a thrust, cut, or kick.

Matron Malice watched the spectacle silently. She couldn't deny the measure of training Zak had given her son; Drizzt was—physically—more than ready for battle.

Zak knew that, to Matron Malice, sheer skill with weapons might not be enough. Zak had to keep Malice from conversing with Drizzt for any length of time. She would not approve of her son's attitudes.

Drizzt was tiring now, Zak could see, though he recognized the weariness in his student's arms to be partly deception.

"Go with it," he muttered silently, and he suddenly "twisted" his ankle, his right arm flailing out wide and low as he struggled for balance, opening a hole in his defenses that Drizzt could not resist.

The expected thrust came in a flash, and Zak's left arm streaked in a short crosscut that slapped the scimitar right out of Drizzt's hand.

"Ha!" Drizzt cried, having expected the move and launching his second ruse. His remaining scimitar knifed over Zak's left shoulder, inevitably dipping in the follow-through of the parry.

But by the time Drizzt even launched the second blow, Zak was already down to his knees. As Drizzt's blade cut harmlessly high, Zak sprang to his feet and launched a right cross, hilt first, that caught Drizzt squarely in the face. A stunned Drizzt leaped back a long step and stood perfectly still for a long moment. His remaining scimitar dropped to the ground, and his glossed eyes did not blink.

"A feint within a feint within a feint!" Zak calmly explained.

Drizzt slumped to the floor, unconscious.

Matron Malice nodded her approval as Zak walked back over to her. "He is ready for the Academy," she remarked.

Zak's face turned sour and he did not answer.

"Vierna is there already," Malice continued, "to teach as a mistress in Arach-Tinilith, the School of Lolth. It is a high honor."

A laurel for House Do'Urden, Zak knew, but he was smart enough to keep his thoughts silent.

"Dinin will leave soon," said the matron.

Zak was surprised. Two children serving as masters in the Academy at the same time? "You must have worked hard to get such accommodations," he dared to remark.

Matron Malice smiled. "Favors owed, favors called in."

"To what end?" asked Zak. "Protection for Drizzt?"

Malice laughed aloud. "From what I have just witnessed, Drizzt would more likely protect the other two!"

Zak bit his lip at the comment. Dinin was still twice the fighter and ten times the heartless killer as Drizzt. Zak knew that Malice had other motives.

"Three of the first eight houses will be represented by no fewer than four children in the Academy over the next two decades," Matron Malice admitted. "Matron Baenre's own son will begin in the same class as Drizzt."

"So you have aspirations," Zak said. "How high, then, will House Do'Urden climb under the guidance of Matron Malice?"

"Sarcasm will cost you your tongue," the matron mother warned. "We would be fools to let slip by such an opportunity to learn more of our rivals!"

"The first eight houses," Zak mused. "Be cautious, Matron Malice. Do not forget to watch for rivals among the lesser houses. There once was a house named DeVir that made such a mistake."

"No attack will come from behind," Malice sneered. "We are the ninth house but boast more power than but a handful of others. None will strike at our backs; there are easier targets higher up the line."

"And all to our gain," Zak put in.

"That is the point of it all, is it not?" Malice asked, her evil smile wide on her face.

Zak didn't need to respond; the matron knew his true feelings. That precisely was not the point.

⚔ ⚔ ⚔ ⚔ ⚔

"Speak less and your jaw will heal faster," Zak said later, when he again was alone with Drizzt.

Drizzt cast him a vile glance.

The weapons master shook his head. "We have become great friends," he said.

"So I had thought," mumbled Drizzt.

"Then think clearly," Zak scolded. "Do you believe that Matron Malice would approve of such a bonding between her weapons master and her youngest—her prized youngest—son? You are a drow, Drizzt Do'Urden, and of noble birth. You may have no friends!"

Drizzt straightened as if he had been slapped in the face.

"None openly, at least," Zak conceded, laying a comforting hand on the youngster's shoulder. "Friends equate to vulnerability, inexcusable vulnerability. Matron Malice would never accept . . ." He paused, realizing that he was browbeating his student. "Well," he admitted in quiet conclusion, "at least we two know who we are."

Somehow, to Drizzt, that just didn't seem enough.

9

FAMILIES

Come quickly," Zak instructed Drizzt one evening after they had finished their sparring. By the urgency of the weapons master's tone, and
by the fact that Zak didn't even pause to wait for Drizzt, Drizzt knew that
something important was happening.

He finally caught up to Zak on the balcony of House Do'Urden, where
Maya and Briza already stood.

"What is it?" Drizzt asked.

Zak pulled him close and pointed out across the great cavern, to the
northeastern reaches of the city. Lights flashed and faded in sudden bursts,
a pillar of fire rose into the air, then disappeared.

"A raid," Briza said of offhandedly. "Minor houses, and of no concern
to us."

Zak saw that Drizzt did not understand.

"One house has attacked another," he explained. "Revenge, perhaps, but
most likely an attempt to climb to a higher rank in the city."

"The battle has been long," Briza remarked, "and still the lights flash."

Zak continued to clarify the event for the confused secondboy of the
house. "The attackers should have blocked the battle within rings of darkness. Their inability to do so might indicate that the defending house was
ready for the raid."

"All cannot be going well for the attackers," Maya agreed.

Drizzt could hardly believe what he was hearing. Even more alarming than the news itself was the way his family talked about the event. They were so calm in their descriptions, as if this was an expected occurrence.

"The attackers must leave no witnesses," Zak explained to Drizzt, "else they will face the wrath of the ruling council."

"But we are witnesses," Drizzt reasoned.

"No," Zak replied. "We are onlookers; this battle is none of our affair. Only the nobles of the defending house are awarded the right to place accusations against their attackers."

"If any nobles are left alive," Briza added, obviously enjoying the drama.

At that moment, Drizzt wasn't sure if he liked this new revelation. However he might have felt, he found that he could not tear his gaze from the continuing spectacle of drow battle. All the Do'Urden compound was astir now, soldiers and slaves running about in search of a better vantage point and shouting out descriptions of the action and rumors of the perpetrators.

This was drow society in all its macabre play, and while it seemed ultimately wrong in the heart of the youngest member of House Do'Urden, Drizzt could not deny the excitement of the night. Nor could Drizzt deny the expressions of obvious pleasure stamped upon the faces of the three who shared the balcony with him.

✕ ✕ ✕ ✕ ✕

Alton made his way through his private chambers one final time, to make certain that any artifacts or tomes that might seem even the least bit sacrilegious were safely hidden. He was expecting a visit from a matron mother, a rare occasion for a master of the Academy not connected with Arach-Tinilith, the School of Lolth. Alton was more than a little anxious about the motives of this particular visitor, Matron SiNafay Hun'ett, head of the city's fifth house and mother of Masoj, Alton's partner in conspiracy.

A bang on the stone door of the outermost chamber in his complex told Alton that his guest had arrived. He straightened his robes and took yet another glance around the room. The door swung open before Alton could get there, and Matron SiNafay swept into the room. How easily she made the transformation—walking from the absolute dark of the outside corridor into the candlelight of Alton's chamber—without so much as a flinch.

SiNafay was smaller than Alton had imagined, diminutive even by the standards of the drow. She stood barely more than four feet high and weighed, by Alton's estimation, no more than fifty pounds. She was a matron mother, though, and Alton reminded himself that she could strike him dead with a single spell.

Alton averted his gaze obediently and tried to convince himself that there was nothing unusual about this visit. He grew less at ease, however, when Masoj trotted in and to his mother's side, a smug smile on his face.

"Greetings from House Hun'ett, Gelroos," Matron SiNafay said. "Twenty-five years and more it has been since we last talked."

"Gelroos?" Alton mumbled under his breath. He cleared his throat to cover his surprise. "My greetings to you, Matron SiNafay," he managed to stammer. "Has it been so very long?"

"You should come to the house," the matron said. "Your chambers remain empty."

My chambers? Alton began to feel very sick.

SiNafay did not miss the look. A scowl crossed her face and her eyes narrowed evilly.

Alton suspected that his secret was out. If the Faceless One had been a member of the Hun'ett family, how could Alton hope to fool the matron mother of the house? He scanned for the best escape route, or for some way he could at least kill the traitorous Masoj before SiNafay struck him down.

When he looked back toward Matron SiNafay, she had already begun a quiet spell. Her eyes popped wide at its completion, her suspicions confirmed.

"Who are you?" she asked, her voice sounding more curious than concerned.

There was no escape, no way to get at Masoj, standing prudently close to his powerful mother's side.

"Who are you?" SiNafay asked again, taking a three-headed instrument from her belt, the dreaded snake-headed whip that injected the most painful and incapacitating poison known to drow.

"Alton," he stuttered, having no choice but to answer. He knew that since she now was on her guard, SiNafay would use simple magic to detect any lies he might concoct. "I am Alton DeVir."

"DeVir?" Matron SiNafay appeared at least intrigued. "Of the House DeVir that died some years ago?"

"I am the only survivor," Alton admitted.

"And you killed Gelroos—Gelroos Hun'ett—and took his place as master in Sorcere," the matron reasoned, her voice a snarl. Doom closed in all around Alton.

"I did not . . . I could not know his name . . . He would have killed me!" Alton stuttered.

"I killed Gelroos," came a voice from the side.

SiNafay and Alton turned to Masoj, who once again held his favorite two-handed crossbow.

"With this," the young Hun'ett explained. "On the night House DeVir fell. I found my excuse in Gelroos's battle with that one." He pointed to Alton.

"Gelroos was your brother," Matron SiNafay reminded Masoj.

"Damn his bones!" Masoj spat. "For four miserable years I served him—served him as if he were a matron mother! He would have kept me from Sorcere, would have forced me into the Melee-Magthere instead."

The matron looked from Masoj to Alton and back to her son. "And you let this one live," she reasoned, a smile again on her lips. "You killed your enemy and forged an alliance with a new master in a single move."

"As I was taught," Masoj said through clenched teeth, not knowing whether punishment or praise would follow.

"You were just a child," SiNafay remarked, suddenly realizing the time-table involved.

Masoj accepted the compliment silently.

Alton watched it all anxiously. "Then what of me?" he cried. "Is my life forfeit?"

SiNafay turned a glare on him. "Your life as Alton DeVir ended, so it would seem, on the night House DeVir fell. Thus you remain the Faceless One, Gelroos Hun'ett. I can use your eyes in the Academy—to watch over my son and my enemies."

Alton could hardly breathe. To so suddenly find himself allied with one of the most powerful houses in Menzoberranzan. A jumble of possibilities and questions flooded his mind, one in particular, which had haunted him for nearly two decades.

His adopted matron mother recognized his excitement. "Speak your thoughts," she commanded.

"You are a high priestess of Lolth," Alton said boldly, that one notion overpowering all caution. "It is within your power to grant me my fondest desire."

"You dare to ask a favor?" Matron SiNafay balked, though she saw the torment on Alton's face and was intrigued by the apparent importance of this mystery. "Very well"

"What house destroyed my family?" Alton growled. "Ask the nether world, I beg, Matron SiNafay."

SiNafay considered the question carefully, and the possibilities of Alton's apparent thirst for vengeance. Another benefit of allowing this one into the family? SiNafay wondered.

"This is known to me already," she replied. "Perhaps when you have proven your value, I will tell—"

"No!" Alton cried. He stopped short, realizing that he had interrupted a matron mother, a crime that could invoke a punishment of death.

SiNafay held back her angry urges. "This question must be very important for you to act so foolishly," she said.

"Please," Alton begged. "I must know. Kill me if you will, but tell me first who it was."

SiNafay liked his courage, and his obsession could only prove of value to her. "House Do'Urden," she said.

"Do'Urden?" Alton echoed, hardly believing that a house so far back in the city hierarchy could have defeated House DeVir.

"You will take no actions against them," Matron SiNafay warned. "And I will forgive your insolence—this time. You are a son of House Hun'ett now; remember always your place!" She let it stay at that, knowing that one who had been clever enough to carry out such a deception for the better part of two decades would not be foolish enough to disobey the matron mother of his house.

"Come Masoj," SiNafay said to her son, "let us leave this one alone so that he may consider his new identity."

⚔ ⚔ ⚔ ⚔ ⚔

"I must tell you, Matron SiNafay," Masoj dared to say as he and his mother made their way out of Sorcere, "Alton DeVir is a buffoon. He might bring harm to House Hun'ett."

"He survived the fall of his own house," SiNafay replied, "and has played through the ruse as the Faceless One for nineteen years. A buffoon? Perhaps, but a resourceful buffoon at the least."

Masoj unconsciously rubbed the area of his eyebrow that had never grown back. "I have suffered the antics of Alton DeVir for all these years," he said. "He does have a fair share of luck, I admit, and can get himself out of trouble—though he is usually the one who puts himself into it!"

"Do not fear," SiNafay laughed. "Alton brings value to our house."

"What can we hope to gain?"

"He is a master of the Academy," SiNafay replied. "He gives me eyes where I now need them." She stopped her son and turned him to face her so that he might understand the implications of her every word. "Alton DeVir's claim against House Do'Urden may work in our favor. He was a noble of the house, with rights of accusation."

"You mean to use Alton DeVir's charge to rally the great houses into punishing House Do'Urden?" Masoj asked.

"The great houses would hardly be willing to strike out for an incident that occurred almost twenty years ago," SiNafay replied. "House Do'Urden executed House DeVir's destruction nearly to perfection—a clean kill. To so much as speak an open charge against the Do'Urdens now would be to invite the wrath of the great houses on ourselves."

"What good then is Alton DeVir?" Masoj asked. "His claim is useless to us."

The matron replied, "You are only a male and cannot understand the complexities of the ruling hierarchy. With Alton DeVir's charge whispered into the proper ears, the ruling council might look the other way if a single house took revenge on Alton's behalf."

"To what end?" Masoj remarked, not understanding the importance. "You would risk the losses of such a battle for the destruction of a lesser house?"

"So thought House DeVir of House Do'Urden," explained SiNafay. "In our world, we must be as concerned with the lower houses as with the higher ones. All of the great houses would be wise now to watch closely the moves of Daermon N'a'shezbaernon, the ninth house that is known as Do'Urden. It now has both a master and a mistress serving in the Academy and three high priestesses, with a fourth nearing the goal."

"Four high priestesses?" Masoj pondered. "In a single house." Only three of the top eight houses could claim more than that. Normally, sisters aspiring to such heights inspired rivalries that inevitably thinned the ranks.

"And the legions of House Do'Urden number more than three hundred fifty," SiNafay continued, "all of them trained by perhaps the finest weapons master in all the city."

"Zaknafein Do'Urden, of course!" Masoj recalled.

"You have heard of him?"

"His name is often spoken at the Academy, even in Sorcere."

"Good," SiNafay purred. "Then you will understand the full weight of the mission I have chosen for you."

An eager light came into Masoj's eyes.

"Another Do'Urden is soon to begin there," SiNafay explained. "Not a master, but a student. By the words of those few who have seen this boy, Drizzt, at training, he will be as fine a fighter as Zaknafein. We should not allow this."

"You want me to kill the boy?" Masoj asked eagerly.

"No," SiNafay replied, "not yet. I want you to learn of him, to understand the motivations of his every move. If the time to strike does come, you must be ready."

Masoj liked the devious assignment, but one thing still bothered him more than a little. "We still have Alton to consider," he said. "He is impatient and daring. What are the consequences to House Hun'ett if he strikes House Do'Urden before the proper time? Might we invoke open war in the city, with House Hun'ett viewed as the perpetrator?"

"Do not worry, my son," Matron SiNafay replied. "If Alton DeVir makes a grievous error while in the guise of Gelroos Hun'ett, we expose him as a murderous imposter and no member of our family. He will be an unhoused rogue with an executioner facing him from every direction."

Her casual explanation put Masoj at ease, but Matron SiNafay, so knowledgeable in the ways of drow society, had understood the risk she was taking from the moment she had accepted Alton DeVir into her house. Her plan seemed foolproof, and the possible gain—the elimination of this growing House Do'Urden—was a tempting piece of bait.

But the dangers, too, were very real. While it was perfectly acceptable for one house to covertly destroy another, the consequences of failure could not be ignored. Earlier that very night, a lesser house had struck out against a rival and, if the rumors held true, had failed. The illuminations of the next day would probably force the ruling council to enact a pretense of justice, to make an example of the unsuccessful attackers. In her long life, Matron SiNafay had witnessed this "justice" several times.

Not a single member of any of the aggressor houses—she was not even allowed to remember their names—had ever survived.

⚔ ⚔ ⚔ ⚔ ⚔

Zak awakened Drizzt early the next morning. "Come," he said. "We are bid to go out of the house this day."

All thoughts of sleep washed away from Drizzt at the news. "Outside the house?" he echoed. In all of his nineteen years, Drizzt had never once walked beyond the adamantine fence of the Do'Urden complex. He had only watched that outside world of Menzoberranzan from the balcony.

While Zak waited, Drizzt quickly collected his soft boots and his *pi-wafwi*. "Will there be no lesson this day?" Drizzt asked.

"We shall see," was all that Zak replied, but in his thoughts, the weapons master figured that Drizzt might be in for one of the most startling revelations of his life. A house had failed in a raid, and the ruling council had requested the presence of all the nobles of the city, to bear witness to the weight of justice.

Briza appeared in the corridor outside the practice room's door. "Hurry," she scolded. "Matron Malice does not wish our house to be among the last groups joining the gathering!"

The matron mother herself, floating atop a blue-glowing disk—for matron mothers rarely walked through the city—led the procession out of House Do'Urden's grand gate. Briza walked at her mother's side, with Maya and Rizzen in the second rank and Drizzt and Zak taking up the rear. Vierna and Dinin, attending to the duties of their positions in the Academy, had gone to the ruling council's summons with a different group.

All the city was astir this morning, rumbling in the rumors of the failed raid. Drizzt walked through the bustle wide-eyed, staring in wonderment at the close-up view of the decorated drow houses. Slaves of every inferior race—goblins, orcs, even giants—scrambled out of the way, recognizing Malice, riding her enchanted carriage, as a matron mother. Drow commoners halted conversations and remained respectfully silent as the noble family passed.

As they made their way toward the northwestern section, the location of the guilty house, they came into a lane blocked by a squabbling caravan of duergar, gray dwarves. A dozen carts had been overturned or locked together—apparently, two groups of duergar had come into the narrow lane together, neither relinquishing the right-of-way.

Briza pulled the snake-headed whip from her belt and chased off a few of the creatures, clearing the way for Malice to float up to the apparent leaders of the two groups.

The dwarves turned on her angrily—until they realized her station.

"Beggin' yer pardon, Madam," one of them stammered. "Unfortunate accident is all."

Malice eyed the contents of one of the nearest carts, crates of giant crab legs and other delicacies.

"You have slowed my journey," Malice said calmly.

"We have come to your city in hopes of trade," the other duergar explained. He cast an angry glare at his counterpart, and Malice understood that the two were rivals, probably bartering the same goods to the same drow house.

"I will forgive your insolence . . ." she offered graciously, still eyeing the crates.

The two duergar suspected what was forthcoming. So did Zak. "We eat well tonight," he whispered to Drizzt with a sly wink. "Matron Malice would not let such an opportunity slip by without gain."

". . . if you can see your way to deliver half of these carts to the gate of House Do'Urden this night," Malice finished.

The duergar started to protest but quickly dismissed the foolish notion. How they hated dealing with drow elves!

"You will be compensated appropriately," Malice continued. "House Do'Urden is not a poor house. Between both of your caravans, you will still have enough goods to satisfy the house you came to see."

Neither of the duergar could refute the simple logic, but under these trading circumstances, where they had offended a matron mother, they knew the compensation for their valuable foods would hardly be appropriate. Still, the gray dwarves could only accept it all as a risk of doing business in Menzoberranzan. They bowed politely and set their troops to clearing the way for the drow procession.

✕ ✕ ✕ ✕ ✕

House Teken'duis, the unsuccessful raiders of the previous night, had barricaded themselves within their two-stalagmite structure, fully expecting what was to come. Outside their gates, all of the nobles of Menzoberranzan, more than a thousand drow, had gathered, with Matron

Baenre and the other seven matron mothers of the ruling council at their head. More disastrous for the guilty house, the entirety of the three schools of the Academy, students and instructors, had surrounded the Teken'duis compound.

Matron Malice led her group to the front line behind the ruling matrons. As she was matron of the ninth house, only one step from the council, other drow nobles readily stepped out of her way.

"House Teken'duis has angered the Spider Queen!" Matron Baenre proclaimed in a voice amplified by magical spells.

"Only because they failed," Zak whispered to Drizzt.

Briza cast both males an angry glare.

Matron Baenre bade three young drow, two females and a male, to her side. "These are all that remain of House Freth," she explained. "Can you tell us, orphans of House Freth," she asked of them, "who it was that attacked your home?"

"House Teken'duis!" they shouted together.

"Rehearsed," Zak commented.

Briza turned around again. "Silence!" she whispered harshly.

Zak slapped Drizzt on the back of the head. "Yes," he agreed. "Do be quiet!"

Drizzt started to protest, but Briza had already turned away and Zak's smile was too wide to argue against.

"Then it is the will of the ruling council," Matron Baenre was saying, "that House Teken'duis suffer the consequences of their actions!"

"What of the orphans of House Freth?" came a call from the crowd.

Matron Baenre stroked the head of the oldest female, a cleric recently finished in her studies at the Academy. "Nobles they were born, and nobles they remain," Baenre said. "House Baenre accepts them into its protection; they bear the name of Baenre now."

Disgruntled whispers filtered through the gathering. Three young nobles, two of them female, was quite a prize. Any house in the city gladly would have taken them in.

"Baenre," Briza whispered to Malice. "Just what the first house needs more clerics!"

"Sixteen high priestesses is not enough, it seems," Malice answered.

"And no doubt, Baenre will take any surviving soldiers of House Freth," Briza reasoned.

Malice was not so certain. Matron Baenre was walking a thin line by taking even the surviving nobles. If House Baenre got too powerful, Lolth surely would take exception. In situations such as this, where a house had been almost eradicated, surviving common soldiers were normally pooled out to bidding houses. Malice would have to watch for such an auction. Soldiers did not come cheaply, but at this time, Malice would welcome the opportunity to add to her forces, particularly if there were any magic-users to be had.

Matron Baenre addressed the guilty house. "House Teken'duis!" she called. "You have broken our laws and have been rightfully caught. Fight if you will, but know that you have brought this doom upon yourself!" With a wave of her hand, she set the Academy, the dispatcher of justice, into motion.

Great braziers had been placed in eight positions around House Teken'duis, attended by mistresses of Arach-Tinilith and the highest-ranking clerical students. Flames roared to life and shot into the air as the high priestesses opened gates to the lower planes. Drizzt watched closely, mesmerized and hoping to catch a glimpse of either Dinin or Vierna.

Denizens of the lower planes, huge, many-armed monsters, slime covered and spitting fire, stepped through the flames. Even the nearest high priestesses backed away from the grotesque horde. The creatures gladly accepted such servitude. When the signal from Matron Baenre came, they eagerly descended upon House Teken'duis.

Glyphs and wards exploded at every corner of the house's feeble gate, but these were mere inconveniences to the summoned creatures.

The wizards and students of Sorcere then went into action, slamming at the top of House Teken'duis with conjured lightning bolts, balls of acid, and fireballs.

Students and masters of Melee-Magthere, the school of fighters, rushed about with heavy crossbows, firing into windows where the doomed family might try to escape.

The horde of monsters bashed through the doors. Lightning flashed and thunder boomed.

Zak looked at Drizzt, and a frown replaced the master's smile. Caught up in the excitement—and it certainly was exciting—Drizzt bore an expression of awe.

The first screams of the doomed family rolled out from the house, screams so terrible and agonized that they stole any macabre pleasure that Drizzt might have been experiencing. He grabbed Zak's shoulder, spinning the weapons master to him, begging for an explanation.

One of the sons of House Teken'duis, fleeing a ten-armed giant monster, stepped out onto the balcony of a high window. A dozen crossbow quarrels struck him simultaneously, and before he even fell dead, three separate lightning bolts alternately lifted him from the balcony, then dropped him back onto it.

Scorched and mutilated, the drow corpse started to tumble from its high perch, but the grotesque monster reached out a huge, clawed hand from the window and pulled it back in to devour it.

"Drow justice," Zak said coldly. He didn't offer Drizzt any consolation; he wanted the brutality of this moment to stick in the young drow's mind for the rest of his life.

The siege went on for more than an hour, and when it was finished, when the denizens of the lower planes were dismissed through the braziers' gates and the students and instructors of the Academy started their march back to Tier Breche, House Teken'duis was no more than a glowing lump of lifeless, molten stone.

Drizzt watched it all, horrified, but too afraid of the consequences to run away. He did not notice the artistry of Menzoberranzan on the return trip to House Do'Urden.

10

STAIN OF BLOOD

Zaknafein is out of the house?" Malice asked.

"I sent him and Rizzen to the Academy to deliver a message to Vierna," Briza explained. "He shan't return for many hours, not before the light of Narbondel begins its descent."

"That is good," said Malice. "You both understand your duties in this farce?"

Briza and Maya nodded. "I have never heard of such a deception," Maya remarked. "Is it necessary?"

"It was planned for another of the house," Briza answered, looking to Matron Malice for confirmation. "Nearly four centuries ago."

"Yes," agreed Malice. "The same was to be done to Zaknafein, but the unexpected death of Matron Vartha, my mother, disrupted the plans."

"That was when you became the matron mother," Maya said.

"Yes," replied Malice, "though I had not passed my first century of life and was still training in Arach-Tinilith. It was not a pleasant time in the history of House Do'Urden."

"But we survived," said Briza. "With the death of Matron Vartha, Nalfein and I became nobles of the house."

"The test on Zaknafein was never attempted," Maya reasoned.

"Too many other duties preceded it," Malice answered.

"We will try it on Drizzt, though," said Maya.

"The punishment of House Teken'duis convinced me that this action had to be taken," said Malice.

"Yes," Briza agreed. "Did you notice Drizzt's expression throughout the execution?"

"I did," answered Maya. "He was revolted."

"Unfitting for a drow warrior," said Malice, "and so this duty is upon us. Drizzt will leave for the Academy in a short time; we must stain his hands with drow blood and steal his innocence."

"It seems a lot of trouble for a male child," Briza grumbled. "If Drizzt cannot adhere to our ways, then why do we not simply give him to Lolth?"

"I will bear no more children!" Malice growled in response. "Every member of this family is important if we are to gain prominence in the city!" Secretly Malice hoped for another gain in converting Drizzt to the evil ways of the drow. She hated Zaknafein as much as she desired him, and turning Drizzt into a drow warrior, a true heartless drow warrior, would distress the weapons master greatly.

"On with it, then," Malice proclaimed. She clapped her hands, and a large chest walked in, supported by eight animated spider legs. Behind it came a nervous goblin slave.

"Come, Byuchyuch," Malice said in a comforting tone. Anxious to please, the slave bounded up before Malice's throne and held perfectly still as the matron mother went through the incantation of a long and complicated spell.

Briza and Maya watched in admiration at their mother's skills; the little goblin's features bulged and twisted, and its skin darkened. A few minutes later, the slave had assumed the appearance of a male drow. Byuchyuch looked at its features happily, not understanding that the transformation was merely a prelude to death.

"You are a drow soldier now," Maya said to it, "and my champion. You must kill only a single, inferior fighter to take your place as a free commoner of House Do'Urden!"

After ten years as an indentured servant to the wicked dark elves, the goblin was more than eager.

Malice rose and started out of the anteroom. "Come," she ordered, and her two daughters, the goblin, and the animated chest fell in line behind her.

They came upon Drizzt in the practice room, polishing the razor edge of his scimitars. He leaped straight up to silent attention at the sight of the unexpected visitors.

"Greetings, my son," Malice said in a tone more motherly than Drizzt had ever heard. " We have a test for you this day, a simple task necessary for your acceptance into Melec-Magthere."

Maya moved before her brother. "I am the youngest, beside yourself," she declared. "Thus, I am granted the rights of challenge, which I now execute."

Drizzt stood confused. He had never heard of such a thing. Maya called the chest to her side and reverently opened the cover.

"You have your weapons and your *piwafwi*," she explained. "Now it is time for you to don the complete outfit of a noble of House Do'Urden." From the chest she pulled out a pair of high black boots and handed them to Drizzt.

Drizzt eagerly slipped out of his normal boots and put on the new ones. They were incredibly soft, and they magically shifted and adjusted to a perfect fit on his feet. Drizzt knew the magic within them: they would allow him to move in absolute silence. Before he had even finished admiring them, though, Maya gave him the next gift, even more magnificent.

Drizzt dropped his *piwafwi* to the floor as he took a set of silvery chain mail. In all the Realms, there was no armor as supple and finely crafted as drow chain mail. It weighed no more than a heavy shirt and would bend as easily as silken cloth, yet could deflect the tip of a spear as surely as dwarven-crafted plate mail.

"You fight with two weapons," Maya said, "and therefore need no shield. But put your scimitars in this; it is more fitting to a drow noble." She handed Drizzt a black leather belt, its clasp a huge emerald and its two scabbards richly decorated in jewels and gemstones.

"Prepare yourself," Malice said to Drizzt. "The gifts must be earned." As Drizzt started to don the outfit, Malice moved beside the altered goblin, which stood nervously in the growing realization that its fight would be no simple task.

"When you kill him, the items will be yours," Malice promised. The goblin's smile returned tenfold; it could not comprehend that it had no chance against Drizzt.

When Drizzt again fastened his *piwafwi* around his neck, Maya introduced the phony drow soldier. "This is Byuchyuch," she said, "my champion. You must defeat him to earn the gifts . . . and your proper place in the family."

Never doubting his abilities, and thinking the contest to be a simple sparring match, Drizzt readily agreed. "Let it begin, then," he said, drawing his scimitars from their lavish sheaths.

Malice gave Byuchyuch a comforting nod, and the goblin took up the sword and shield that Maya had provided and moved right in at Drizzt.

Drizzt began slowly, trying to take a measure of his opponent before attempting any daring offensive strikes. In only a moment, though, Drizzt realized how badly Byuchyuch handled the sword and shield. Not knowing the truth of the creature's identity, Drizzt could hardly believe that a drow would show such ineptitude with weapons. He wondered if Byuchyuch was baiting him, and with that thought, continued his cautious approach.

After a few more moments of Byuchyuch's wild and off balance swings, however, Drizzt felt compelled to take the initiative. He slapped one scimitar against Byuchyuch's shield. The goblin-drow responded with a lumbering thrust, and Drizzt slapped its sword from its hand with his free blade and executed a simple twist that brought the scimitar's tip to a halt against the hollow of Byuchyuch's chest.

"Too easy," Drizzt muttered under his breath.

But the true test had only begun.

On cue, Briza cast a mind-numbing spell on the goblin, freezing it in its helpless position. Still aware of its predicament, Byuchyuch tried to dive away, but Briza's spell held it still.

"Finish the strike," Malice said to Drizzt. Drizzt looked at his scimitar, then to Malice, unable to believe what he was hearing.

"Maya's champion must be killed," Briza snarled.

"I cannot—" Drizzt began.

"Kill!" Malice roared, and this time the word carried the weight of a magical command.

"Thrust!" Briza likewise commanded.

Drizzt felt their words compelling his hand to action. Thoroughly disgusted with the thought of murdering a helpless foe, he concentrated with all of his mental strength to resist. While he managed to deny the commands for a few seconds, Drizzt found that he could not pull the weapon away.

"Kill!" Malice screamed.

"Strike!" yelled Briza.

It went on for several more agonizing seconds. Sweat beaded on Drizzt's brow. Then the young drow's willpower broke. His scimitar slipped quickly between Byuchyuch's ribs and found the unfortunate creature's heart. Briza released Byuchyuch from her holding spell then, to let Drizzt see the agony on the phony drow's face and hear the gurgles as the dying Byuchyuch slipped to the floor.

Drizzt could not find his breath as he stared at his bloodstained weapon.

It was Maya's turn to act. She clipped Drizzt on the shoulder with her mace, knocking him to the floor.

"You killed my champion!" she growled. "Now you must fight me!"

Drizzt rolled back to his feet, away from the enraged female. He had no intention of fighting, but before he could even drop his weapons, Malice read his thoughts and warned, "If you do not fight, Maya will kill you!"

"This is not the way," Drizzt protested, but his words were lost in the ring of adamantine as he parried a heavy blow with one scimitar.

He was now into it, whether he liked it or not. Maya was a skilled fighter—all females spent many hours training with weapons—and she was stronger than Drizzt. But Drizzt was Zak's son, the prime student, and when he admitted to himself that he had no way out of this predicament, he came in at Maya's mace and shield with every cunning maneuver he had been taught.

Scimitars weaved and dipped in a dance that awed Briza and Maya.

Malice hardly noticed, caught in the midst of yet another mighty spell. Malice never doubted that Drizzt could defeat his sister, and she had incorporated her expectations into the plan.

Drizzt's moves were all defensive as he continued to hope for some semblance of sanity to come over his mother, and that this whole thing would be stopped. He wanted to back Maya up, cause her to stumble, and end the fight by putting her in a helpless position. Drizzt had to believe that Briza and Malice would not compel him to kill Maya as he had killed Byuchyuch.

Finally, Maya did slip. She threw her shield out to deflect an arcing scimitar but became overbalanced in the block, and her arm went wide. Drizzt's other blade knifed in, only to nick at Maya's breast and force her back.

Malice's spell caught the weapon in mid-thrust.

The bloodstained adamantine blade writhed to life and Drizzt found himself holding the tail of a serpent, a fanged viper that turned back against him!

The enchanted snake spat its venom in Drizzt's eyes, blinding him, then he felt the pain of Briza's whip. All six snake heads of the awful weapon bit into Drizzt's back, tearing through his new armor and jolting him in excruciating pain. He crumbled down into a curled position, helpless as Briza snapped the whip in, again and again.

"Never strike at a drow female!" she screamed as she beat Drizzt into unconsciousness.

An hour later, Drizzt opened his eyes. He was in his bed, Matron Malice standing over him. The high priestess had tended to his wounds, but the sting remained, a vivid reminder of the lesson. But it was not nearly as vivid as the blood that still stained Drizzt's scimitar.

"The armor will be replaced," Malice said to him. "You are a drow warrior now. You have earned it." She turned and walked out of the room, leaving Drizzt to his pain and his fallen innocence.

⚔ ⚔ ⚔ ⚔ ⚔

"Do not send him," Zak argued as emphatically as he dared. He stared up at Matron Malice, the smug queen on her high throne of stone and black velvet. As always, Briza and Maya stood obediently by her sides.

"He is a drow fighter," Malice replied, her tone still controlled. "He must go to the Academy. It is our way."

Zak looked around helplessly. He hated this place, the chapel anteroom, with its sculptures of the Spider Queen leering down at him from every angle, and with Malice sitting—towering—above him from her seat of power.

Zak shook the images away and regained his courage, reminding himself that this time he had something worth arguing about.

"Do not send him!" he growled. "They will ruin him!"

Matron Malice's hands clenched down on the rock arms of her great chair.

"Already Drizzt is more skilled than half of those in the Academy," Zak continued quickly, before the matron's anger burst forth. "Allow me two more years, and I will make him the finest swordsman in all of Menzoberranzan!"

Malice eased back on her seat. From what she had seen of her son's progress, she could not deny the possibilities of Zak's claim. "He goes," she said calmly. "There is more to the making of a drow warrior than skill with weapons. Drizzt has other lessons he must learn."

"Lessons of treachery?" Zak spat, too angry to care about the consequences. Drizzt had told him what Malice and her evil daughters had done that day, and Zak was wise enough to understand their actions. Their "lesson" had nearly broken the boy, and had, perhaps, forever stolen from Drizzt the ideals he held so dear. Drizzt would find his morals and principles harder to cling to now that the pedestal of purity had been knocked out from under him.

"Watch your tongue, Zaknafein," Matron Malice warned.

"I fight with passion!" the weapons master snapped. "That is why I win. Your son, too, fights with passion—do not let the conforming ways of the Academy take that from him!"

"Leave us," Malice instructed her daughters. Maya bowed and rushed out through the door. Briza followed more slowly, pausing to cast a suspicious eye upon Zak.

Zak didn't return the glare, but he entertained a fantasy concerning his sword and Briza's smug smile.

"Zaknafein," Malice began, again coming forward in her chair. "I have tolerated your blasphemous beliefs through these many years because of your skill with weapons. You have taught my soldiers well, and your love of killing drow, particularly clerics of the Spider Queen, has aided the ascent of House Do'Urden. I am not, and have not been, ungrateful.

"But I warn you now, one final time, that Drizzt is my son, not his sire's! He will go to the Academy and learn what he must to take his place as a prince of House Do'Urden. If you interfere with what must be, Zaknafein, I will no longer turn my eyes from your actions! Your heart will be given to Lolth."

Zak stamped his heels on the floor and snapped a short bow of his head, then spun about and departed, trying to find some option in this dark and hopeless picture.

As he made his way through the main corridor, he again heard in his mind the screams of the dying children of House DeVir, children who never got the chance to witness the evils of the drow Academy. Perhaps they were better off dead.

GRIM PREFERENCE

Z ak slid one of his swords from its scabbard and admired the weapon's
wondrous detail. This sword, as with most of the drow weapons,
had been forged by the gray dwarves, then traded to Menzoberranzan.
The duergar workmanship was exquisite, but it was the work done on the
weapon after the dark elves had acquired it that made it so very special.
None of the races of the surface or Underdark could outdo the dark elves
in the art of enchanting weapons. Imbued with the strange emanations
of the Underdark, the magical power unique to the lightless world, and
blessed by the unholy clerics of Lolth, no blade ever sat in a wielder's hand
more ready to kill.

Other races, mostly dwarves and surface elves, also took pride in their
crafted weapons. Fine swords and mighty hammers hung over mantles as
showpieces, always with a bard nearby to spout the accompanying legend
that most often began, "In the days of yore . . ."

Drow weapons were different, never showpieces. They were locked in
the necessities of the present, never in reminiscences, and their purpose
remained unchanged for as long as they held an edge fine enough for
battle—fine enough to kill.

Zak brought the blade up before his eyes. In his hands, the sword had
become more than an instrument of battle. It was an extension of his rage,
his answer to an existence he could not accept.

It was his answer, too, perhaps, to another problem that seemed to have no resolution.

He walked into the training hall, where Drizzt was hard at work spinning attack routines against a practice dummy. Zak paused to watch the young drow at practice, wondering if Drizzt would ever again consider the dance of weapons a form of play. How the scimitars flowed in Drizzt's hands! Interweaving with uncanny precision, each blade seemed to anticipate the other's moves and whirred about in perfect complement.

This young drow might soon be an unrivaled fighter, a master beyond Zaknafein himself.

"Can you survive?" Zak whispered. "Have you the heart of a drow warrior?" Zak hoped that the answer would be an emphatic "no," but either way, Drizzt was surely doomed.

Zak looked down at his sword again and knew what he must do. He slid its sister blade from its sheath and started a determined walk toward Drizzt.

Drizzt saw him coming and turned at the ready. "A final fight before I leave for the Academy?" He laughed.

Zak paused to take note of Drizzt's smile. A facade? Or had the young drow really forgiven himself for his actions against Maya's champion. It did not matter, Zak reminded himself. Even if Drizzt had recovered from his mother's torments, the Academy would destroy him. The weapons master said nothing; he just came on in a flurry of cuts and stabs that put Drizzt immediately on the defensive. Drizzt took it in stride, not yet realizing that this final encounter with his mentor was much more than their customary sparring.

"I will remember everything you taught me," Drizzt promised, dodging a cut and launching a fierce counter of his own. "I will carve my name in the halls of Melee-Magthere and make you proud."

The scowl on Zak's face surprised Drizzt, and the young drow grew even more confused when the weapons master's next attack sent a sword knifing straight at his heart. Drizzt leaped aside, slapping at the blade in sheer desperation, and narrowly avoided impalement.

"Are you so very sure of yourself?" Zak growled, stubbornly pursuing Drizzt.

Drizzt set himself as their blades met in ringing fury. "I am a fighter," he declared. "A drow warrior!"

"You are a dancer!" Zak shot back in a derisive tone. He slammed his sword onto Drizzt's blocking scimitar so savagely that the young drow's arm tingled.

"An imposter!" Zak cried. "A pretender to a title you cannot begin to understand!"

Drizzt went on the offensive. Fires burned in his lavender eyes and new strength guided his scimitars' sure cuts.

But Zak was relentless. He fended the attacks and continued his lesson. "Do you know the emotions of murder?" he spat. "Have you reconciled yourself to the act you committed?"

Drizzt's only answers were a frustrated growl and a renewed attack.

"Ah, the pleasure of plunging your sword into the bosom of a high priestess," Zak taunted. "To see the light of warmth leave her body while her lips utter silent curses in your face! Or have you ever heard the screams of dying children?"

Drizzt let up his attack, but Zak would not allow a break. The weapons master came back on the offensive, each thrust aimed for a vital area.

"How loud, those screams," Zak continued. "They echo over the centuries in your mind; they chase you down the paths of your entire life."

Zak halted the action so that Drizzt might weigh his every word. "You have never heard them, have you, dancer?" The weapons master stretched his arms out wide, an invitation. "Come, then, and claim your second kill," he said, tapping his stomach. "In the belly, where the pain is greatest, so that my screams may echo in your mind. Prove to me that you are the drow warrior you claim to be."

The tips of Drizzt's scimitars slowly made their way to the stone floor. He wore no smile now.

"You hesitate," Zak laughed at him. "This is your chance to make your name. A single thrust, and you will send a reputation into the Academy before you. Other students, even masters, will whisper your name as you pass. 'Drizzt Do'Urden,' they will say. 'The boy who slew the most honored weapons master in all of Menzoberranzan!' Is this not what you desire?"

"Damn you," Drizzt spat back, but still he made no move to attack.

"Drow warrior?" Zak chided him. "Do not be so quick to claim a title you cannot begin to understand!"

Drizzt came on then, in a fury he had never before known. His purpose was not to kill, but to defeat his teacher, to steal the taunts from Zak's mouth with a fighting display too impressive to be derided.

Drizzt was brilliant. He followed every move with three others and worked Zak low and high, inside and out wide. Zak found his heels under him more often than the balls of his feet, too involved was he in staying away from his student's relentless thrusts to even think of taking the offensive. He allowed Drizzt to continue the initiative for many minutes, dreading its conclusion, the outcome he had already decided to be the most preferable.

Zak then found that he could stand the delay no longer. He sent one sword out in a lazy thrust, and Drizzt promptly slapped the weapon out of his hand.

Even as the young drow came on in anticipation of victory, Zak slipped his empty hand into a pouch and grabbed a magical little ceramic ball—one of those that so often had aided him in battle.

"Not this time, Zaknafein!" Drizzt proclaimed, keeping his attacks under control, remembering well the many occasions that Zak reversed feigned disadvantage into clear advantage.

Zak fingered the ball, unable to come to terms with what he must do.

Drizzt walked him through an attack sequence, then another, measuring the advantage he had gained in stealing a weapon. Confident of his position, Drizzt came in low and hard with a single thrust.

Though Zak was distracted at the time, he still managed to block the attack with his remaining sword. Drizzt's other scimitar slashed down on top of the sword, pinning its tip to the floor. In the same lightning movement, Drizzt slipped his first blade free of Zak's parry and brought it up and around, stopping the thrust barely an inch from Zak's throat.

"I have you!" the young drow cried.

Zak's answer came in an explosion of light beyond anything Drizzt had ever imagined.

Zak had prudently closed his eyes, but Drizzt, surprised, could not accept the sudden change. His head burned in agony, and he reeled backward, trying to get away from the light, away from the weapons master.

Keeping his eyes tightly shut, Zak had already divorced himself from the need of vision. He let his keen ears guide him now, and Drizzt, shuffling and stumbling, was an easy target to discern. In a single motion, the whip came off Zak's belt and he lashed out, catching Drizzt around the ankles and dropping him to the floor.

Methodically, the weapons master came on, dreading every step but knowing his chosen course of action to be correct.

Drizzt realized that he was being stalked, but he could not understand the motive. The light had stunned him, but he was more surprised by Zak's continuation of the battle. Drizzt set himself, unable to escape the trap, and tried to think his way around his loss of sight. He had to feel the flow of battle, to hear the sounds of his attacker and anticipate each coming strike.

He brought his scimitars up just in time to block a sword chop that would have split his skull.

Zak hadn't expected the parry. He recoiled and came in from a different angle. Again he was foiled.

Now more curious than wanting to kill Drizzt, the weapons master went through a series of attacks, sending his sword into motions that would have sliced through the defenses of many who could see him.

Blinded, Drizzt fought him off, putting a scimitar in line with each new thrust.

"Treachery!" Drizzt yelled, painful residual explosions from the bright light still bursting inside his head. He blocked another attack and tried to regain his footing, realizing that he had little chance of continuing to fend off the weapons master from a prone position.

The pain of the stinging light was too great, though, and Drizzt, barely holding the edge of consciousness, stumbled back to the stone, losing one scimitar in the process. He spun over wildly, knowing that Zak was closing in.

The other scimitar was knocked from his hand.

"Treachery," Drizzt growled again. "Do you so hate to lose?"

"Do you not understand?" Zak yelled back at him. "To lose is to die! You may win a thousand fights, but you can only lose one!" He put his sword in line with Drizzt's throat. It would be a single clean blow. He knew that he should do it, mercifully, before the masters of the Academy got hold of his charge.

Zak sent his sword spinning across the room, and he reached out with his empty hands, grabbed Drizzt by the front of his shirt, and hoisted him to his feet.

They stood face-to-face, neither seeing the other very well in the blinding glare, and neither able to break the tense silence. After a long and breathless moment, the dweomer of the enchanted pebble faded and the room became more comfortable. Truly, the two dark elves looked upon each other in a different light.

"A trick of Lolth's clerics," Zak explained. "Always they keep such a spell of light at the ready" A strained smile crossed his face as he tried to ease Drizzt's anger. "Though I daresay that I have turned such light against clerics, even high priestesses, more than a few times."

"Treachery," Drizzt spat a third time.

"It is our way," Zak replied. "You will learn."

"It is your way," snarled Drizzt. "You grin when you speak of murdering clerics of the Spider Queen. Do you so enjoy killing? Killing drow?"

Zak could not find an answer to the accusing question. Drizzt's words hurt him profoundly because they rang of truth, and because Zak had come to view his penchant for killing clerics of Lolth as a cowardly response to his own unanswerable frustrations.

"You would have killed me," Drizzt said bluntly.

"But I did not," Zak retorted. "And now you live to go to the Academy—to take a dagger in the back because you are blind to the realities of our world, because you refuse to acknowledge what your people are.

"Or you will become one of them," Zak growled. "Either way, the Drizzt Do'Urden I have known will surely die."

Drizzt's face twisted, and he couldn't even find the words to dispute the possibilities Zak was spitting at him. He felt the blood drain from his face, though his heart raged. He walked away, letting his glare linger on Zak for many steps.

"Go, then, Drizzt Do'Urden!" Zak cried after him. "Go to the Academy and bask in the glory of your prowess. Remember, though, the consequences of such skills. Always there are consequences!"

Zak retreated to the security of his private chamber. The door to the room closed behind the weapons master with such a sound of finality that it spun Zak back to face its empty stone.

"Go, then, Drizzt Do'Urden," he whispered in quiet lament. "Go to the Academy and learn who you really are."

⚔ ⚔ ⚔ ⚔ ⚔

Dinin came for his brother early the next morning. Drizzt slowly left the training room, looking back over his shoulder every few steps to see if Zak would come out and attack him again or bid him farewell.

He knew in his heart that Zak would not.

Drizzt had thought them friends, had believed that the bond he and Zaknafein had sown went far beyond the simple lessons and swordplay. The young drow had no answers to the many questions spinning in his mind, and the person who had been his teacher for the last five years had nothing left to offer him.

"The heat grows in Narbondel," Dinin remarked when they stepped out onto the balcony. "We must not be late for your first day in the Academy."

Drizzt looked out into the myriad colors and shapes that composed Menzoberranzan. "What is this place?" he whispered, realizing how little he knew of his homeland beyond the walls of his own house. Zak's words—Zak's rage—pressed in on Drizzt as he stood there, reminding him of his ignorance and hinting at a dark path ahead.

"This is the world," Dinin replied, though Drizzt's question had been rhetorical. "Do not worry, Secondboy," he laughed, moving up onto the railing. "You will learn of Menzoberranzan in the Academy. You will learn who you are and who your people are."

The declaration unsettled Drizzt. Perhaps—remembering his last bitter encounter with the drow he had most trusted—that knowledge was exactly what he was afraid of.

He shrugged in resignation and followed Dinin over the balcony in a magical descent to the compound floor: the first steps down that dark path.

✕ ✕ ✕ ✕ ✕

Another set of eyes watched intently as Dinin and Drizzt started out from House Do'Urden.

Alton DeVir sat quietly against the side of a gigantic mushroom, as he had every day for the last tenday, staring at the Do'Urden complex.

Daermon N'a'shezbaernon, Ninth House of Menzoberranzan. The house that had murdered his matron, his sisters and brothers, and all there ever was of House DeVir . . . except for Alton.

Alton thought back to the days of House DeVir, when Matron Ginafae had gathered the family members together so that they might discuss their aspirations. Alton, just a student when House DeVir fell, now had a greater insight to those times. Twenty years had brought a wealth of experience.

Ginafae had been the youngest matron among the ruling families, and her potential had seemed unlimited. Then she had aided a gnomish patrol, had used her Lolth-given powers to hinder the drow elves that ambushed the little people in the caverns outside Menzoberranzan—all because Ginafae desired the death of a single member of that attacking drow party, a wizard son of the city's third house, the house labeled as House DeVir's next victim.

The Spider Queen took exception to Ginafae's choice of weapons; deep gnomes were the dark elves' worst enemy in the whole of the Underdark. With Ginafae fallen out of Lolth's favor, House DeVir had been doomed.

Alton had spent twenty years trying to learn of his enemies, trying to discover which drow family had taken advantage of his mother's mistake and had slaughtered his kin. Twenty long years, and his adopted matron, SiNafay Hun'ett, had ended his quest as abruptly as it had begun.

Now, as Alton sat watching the guilty house, he knew only one thing for certain: twenty years had done nothing to diminish his rage.

PART THREE

THE ACADEMY

The Academy.

It is the propagation of the lies that bind drow society together, the ultimate perpetration of falsehoods repeated so many times that they ring true against any contrary evidence. The lessons young drow are taught of truth and justice are so blatantly refuted by everyday life in wicked Menzoberranzan that it is hard to understand how any could believe them. Still they do.

Even now, decades removed, the thought of the place frightens me, not for any physical pain or the ever-present sense of possible death—I have trod down many roads equally dangerous in that way. The Academy of Menzoberranzan frightens me when I think of the survivors, the graduates, existing—reveling—within the evil fabrications that shape their world.

They live with the belief that anything is

acceptable if you can get away with it, that self-gratification is the most important aspect of existence, and that power comes only to she or he who is strong enough and cunning enough to snatch it from the failing hands of those who no longer deserve it. Compassion has no place in Menzoberranzan, and yet it is compassion, not fear, that brings harmony to most races. It is harmony, working toward shared goals, that precedes greatness.

Lies engulf the drow in fear and mistrust, refute friendship at the tip of a Lolth-blessed sword The hatred and ambition fostered by these amoral tenets are the doom of my people, a weakness that they perceive as strength. The result is a paralyzing, paranoid existence that the drow call the edge of readiness.

I do not know how I survived the Academy, how I discovered the falsehoods early enough to use them in contrast, and thus strengthen, those ideals I most cherish.

It was Zaknafein, I must believe, my teacher. Through the experiences of Zak's long years, which embittered him and cost him so much, I came to hear the screams: the screams of protest against murderous treachery; the screams of rage from the leaders of drow society, the high priestesses of the Spider Queen, echoing down the paths of my mind, ever to hold a place within my mind. The screams of dying children.

—Drizzt Do'Urden

THIS ENEMY, "THEY

Wearing the outfit of a noble son, and with a dagger concealed in one boot—a suggestion from Dinin—Drizzt ascended the wide stone stairway that led to Tier Breche, the Academy of the drow. Drizzt reached the top and moved between the giant pillars, under the impassive gazes of two guards, last-year students of Melee-Magthere.

Two dozen other young drow milled about the Academy compound, but Drizzt hardly noticed them. Three structures dominated his vision and his thoughts. To his left stood the pointed stalagmite tower of Sorcere, the school of wizardry. Drizzt would spend the first sixth months of his tenth and last year of study in there.

Before him, at the back of the level, loomed the most impressive structure, Arach-Tinilith, the school of Lolth, carved from the stone into the likeness of a giant spider. By drow reckoning, this was the Academy's most important building and thus was normally reserved for females. Male students were housed within Arach-Tinilith only during their last six months of study.

While Sorcere and Arach-Tinilith were the more graceful structures, the most important building for Drizzt at that tentative moment lined the wall to his right. The pyramidal structure of Melee-Magthere, the school of fighters. This building would be Drizzt's home for the next nine years. His companions, he now realized, were those other dark elves in the compound—fighters, like himself, about to begin their formal training. The class, at twenty-five, was unusually large for the school of fighters.

Even more unusual, several of the novice students were nobles. Drizzt wondered how his skills would measure up against theirs, how his sessions with Zaknafein compared to the battles these others had no doubt fought with the weapons masters of their respective families.

Those thoughts inevitably led Drizzt back to his last encounter with his mentor. He quickly dismissed the memories of that unpleasant duel, and, more pointedly, the disturbing questions Zak's observations had forced him to consider. There was no place for such doubts on this occasion. Melee-Magthere loomed before him, the greatest test and the greatest lesson of his young life.

"My greetings," came a voice behind him. Drizzt turned to face a fellow novice, who wore a sword and dirk uncomfortably on his belt and who appeared even more nervous than Drizzt—a comforting sight.

"Kelnozz of House Kenafin, fifteenth house," the novice said.

"Drizzt Do'Urden of Daermon N'a'shezbaernon, House Do'Urden, Ninth House of Menzoberranzan," Drizzt replied automatically, exactly as Matron Malice had instructed him.

"A noble," remarked Kelnozz, understanding the significance of Drizzt bearing the same surname as his house. Kelnozz dropped into a low bow. "I am honored by your presence."

Drizzt was starting to like this place already. With the treatment he normally received at home, he hardly thought of himself as a noble. Any self-important notions that might have occurred to him at Kelnozz's gracious greeting were dispelled a moment later, though, when the masters came out.

Drizzt saw his brother, Dinin, among them but pretended—as Dinin had warned him to—not to notice, nor to expect any special treatment. Drizzt rushed inside Melee-Magthere along with the rest of the students when the whips began to snap and the masters started shouting of the dire consequences if they tarried. They were herded down a few side corridors and into an oval room.

"Sit or stand as you will!" one of the masters growled. Noticing two of the students whispering off to the side, the master took his whip out and—crack!—took one of the offenders off his feet.

Drizzt couldn't believe how quickly the room then came to order.

"I am Hatch'net," the master began in a resounding voice, "the master of Lore. This room will be your hall of instruction for fifty cycles of Narbondel." He looked around at the adorned belts on every figure. "You will bring no weapons to this place!"

Hatch'net paced the perimeter of the room, making certain that every eye followed his movements attentively. "You are drow," he snapped suddenly. "Do you understand what that means? Do you know where you come from, and the history of our people? Menzoberranzan was not always our home, nor was any other cavern of the Underdark. Once we walked the surface of the world." He spun suddenly and came up right in Drizzt's face.

"Do you know of the surface?" Master Hatch'net snarled.

Drizzt recoiled and shook his head.

"An awful place," Hatch'net continued, turning back to the whole of the group. "Each day, as the glow begins its rise in Narbondel, a great ball of fire rises into the open sky above, bringing hours of a light greater than the punishing spells of the priestesses of Lolth!" He held his arms outstretched, with his eyes turned upward, and an unbelievable grimace spread across his face.

Students' gasps rose up all about him.

"Even in the night, when the ball of fire has gone below the far rim of the world," Hatch'net continued, weaving his words as if he were telling a horror tale, "one cannot escape the uncounted terrors of the surface. Reminders of what the next day will bring, dots of light—and sometimes a lesser ball of silvery fire—mar the sky's blessed darkness.

"Once our people walked the surface of the world," he repeated, his tone now one of lament, "in ages long past, even longer than the lines of the great houses. In that distant age, we walked beside the pale-skinned elves, the faeries!"

"It cannot be true!" one student cried from the side.

Hatch'net looked at him earnestly, considering whether more would be gained by beating the student for his unasked-for interruption or by allowing the group to participate. "It is!" he replied, choosing the latter course. "We thought the faeries our friends; we called them kin! We could not know, in our innocence, that they were the embodiments of deceit and evil. We could not know that they would turn on us suddenly and drive us from them, slaughtering our children and the eldest of our race!

"Without mercy the evil faeries pursued us across the surface world. Always we asked for peace, and always we were answered by swords and killing arrows!"

He paused, his face twisting into a widening, malicious smile. "Then we found the goddess!"

"Praise Lolth!" came one anonymous cry. Again Hatch'net let the slip of tongue go by unpunished, knowing that every accenting comment only drew his audience deeper into his web of rhetoric.

"Indeed," the master replied. "All praise to the Spider Queen. It was she who took our orphaned race to her side and helped us fight off our enemies. It was she who guided the fore-matrons of our race to the paradise of the Underdark. It is she," he roared, a clenched fist rising into the air, "who now gives us the strength and the magic to pay back our enemies.

"We are the drow!" Hatch'net cried. "You are the drow, never again to be downtrodden, rulers of all you desire, conquerors of lands you choose to inhabit!"

"The surface?" came a question.

"The surface?" echoed Hatch'net with a laugh. "Who would want to return to that vile place? Let the faeries have it! Let them burn under the fires of the open sky! We claim the Underdark, where we can feel the core of the world thrumming under our feet, and where the stones of the walls show the heat of the world's power!"

Drizzt sat silent, absorbing every word of the talented orator's often-rehearsed speech. Drizzt was caught, as were all the new students, in Hatch'net's hypnotic variations of inflection and rallying cries. Hatch'net had been the master of Lore at the Academy for more than two centuries, owning more prestige in Menzoberranzan than nearly any other male drow, and many of the females. The matrons of the ruling families understood well the value of his practiced tongue.

So it went every day, an endless stream of hate rhetoric directed against an enemy that none of the students had ever seen. The surface elves were not the only target of Hatch'net's sniping. Dwarves, gnomes, humans, halflings, and all of the surface races—and even subterranean races such as the duergar dwarves, which the drow often traded with and fought beside—each found an unpleasant spot in the master's ranting.

Drizzt came to understand why no weapons were permitted in the oval chamber. When he left his lesson each day, he found his hands clenched by his sides in rage, unconsciously grasping for a scimitar hilt. It was obvious from the commonplace fights among the students that others felt the same way. Always, though, the overriding factor that kept some measure of control was the master's lie of the horrors of the outside world and the comforting bond of the students' common heritage—a heritage, the students would soon come to believe, that gave them enough enemies to battle beyond each other.

⚔ ⚔ ⚔ ⚔ ⚔

The long, draining hours in the oval chamber left little time for the students to mingle. They shared common barracks, but their extensive duties outside of Hatch'net's lessons—serving the older students and masters, preparing meals, and cleaning the building—gave them barely enough time for rest. By the end of the first tenday, they walked on the edge of exhaustion, a condition, Drizzt realized, that only increased the stirring effect of Master Hatch'net's lessons.

Drizzt accepted the existence stoically, considering it far better than the six years he had served his mother and sisters as page prince. Still, there was one great disappointment to Drizzt in his first tendays at Melee-Magthere. He found himself longing for his practice sessions.

He sat on the edge of his bedroll late one night, holding a scimitar up before his shining eyes, remembering those many hours engaged in battle-play with Zaknafein.

"We go to the lesson in two hours," Kelnozz, in the next bunk, reminded him. "Get some rest."

"I feel the edge leaving my hands," Drizzt replied quietly. "The blade feels heavier, unbalanced."

"The grand melee is barely ten cycles of Narbondel away," Kelnozz said. "You will get all the practice you desire there! Fear not, whatever edge has been dulled by the days with the master of Lore will soon be regained. For the next nine years, that fine blade of yours will rarely leave your hands!"

Drizzt slid the scimitar back into its scabbard and reclined on his bunk. As with so many aspects of his life so far—and, he was beginning to fear, with so many aspects of his future in Menzoberranzan—he had no choice but to accept the circumstances of his existence.

⋊ ⋉ ⋊ ⋉ ⋊

"This segment of your training is at an end," Master Hatch'net announced on the morning of the fiftieth day. Another master, Dinin, entered the room, leading a magically suspended iron box filled with meagerly padded wooden poles of every length and design comparable to drow weapons.

"Choose the sparring pole that most resembles your own weapon of choice," Hatch'net explained as Dinin made his way around the room. He came to his brother, and Drizzt's eyes settled at once on his choice: two slightly curving poles about three-and-a-half feet long. Drizzt lifted them out and put them through a simple cut. Their weight and balance closely resembled the scimitars that had become so familiar to his hands.

"For the pride of Daermon N'a'shezbaernon," Dinin whispered, then moved along.

Drizzt twirled the mock weapons again. It was time to measure the value of his sessions with Zak.

"Your class must have an order," Hatch'net was saying as Drizzt turned his attention beyond the scope of his new weapons. "Thus the grand melee. Remember, there can be only one victor!"

Hatch'net and Dinin herded the students out of the oval chamber and out of Melee-Magthere altogether, down the tunnel between the two guardian spider statues at the back of Tier Breche. For all of the students, this was the first time they had ever been out of Menzoberranzan.

"What are the rules?" Drizzt asked Kelnozz, in line at his side.

"If a master calls you out, then you are out," Kelnozz replied.

"The rules of engagement?" asked Drizzt.

Kelnozz cast him an incredulous glance. "Win," he said simply, as though there could be no other answer.

A short time later they came into a fairly large cavern, the arena for the grand melee. Pointed stalactites leered down at them from the ceiling and stalagmite mounds broke the floor into a twisting maze filled with ambush holes and blind corners.

"Choose your strategies and find your starting point," Master Hatch'net said to them. "The grand melee begins in a count of one hundred!"

The twenty-five students set off into action, some pausing to consider the landscape laid out before them, others sprinting off into the gloom of the maze.

Drizzt decided to find a narrow corridor, to ensure that he would fight off one-against-one, and he just started off in his search when he was grabbed from behind.

"A team?" Kelnozz offered.

Drizzt did not respond, unsure of the other's fighting worth and the accepted practices of this traditional encounter.

"Others are forming into teams," Kelnozz pressed. "Some in threes. Together we might have a chance."

"The master said there could be only one victor," Drizzt reasoned.

"Who better than you, if not me," Kelnozz replied with a sly wink. "Let us defeat the others, then we can decide the issue between ourselves."

The reasoning seemed prudent, and with Hatch'net's count already approaching seventy-five, Drizzt had little time to ponder the possibilities. He clapped Kelnozz on the shoulder and led his new ally into the maze.

Catwalks had been constructed all around the room's perimeter, even crossing through the center of the chamber, to give the judging masters a good view of all the action below. A dozen of them were up there now, all eagerly awaiting the first battles so that they might measure the talent of this young class.

"One hundred!" cried Hatch'net from his high perch.

Kelnozz began to move, but Drizzt stopped him, keeping him back in the narrow corridor between two long stalagmite mounds.

"Let them come to us," Drizzt signaled in the silent hand and facial expression code. He crouched in battle readiness. "Let them fight each other to weariness. Patience is our ally!"

Kelnozz relaxed, thinking he had made a good choice in Drizzt.

Their patience was not tested severely, though, for a moment later, a tall and aggressive student burst into their defensive position, wielding a long spear-shaped pole. He came right in on Drizzt, slapping with the butt of his weapon, then spinning it over full in a brutal thrust designed for a quick kill, a strong move perfectly executed.

To Drizzt, though, it seemed the most basic of attack routines—too basic, almost, for Drizzt hardly believed that a trained student would attack another skilled fighter in such a straightforward manner. Drizzt convinced himself in time that this was indeed the chosen method of attack, and no feint, and he launched the proper parry. His scimitar poles spun counterclockwise in front of him, striking the thrusting spear in succession and driving the weapon's tip harmlessly above the striking line of its wielder's shoulder.

The aggressive attacker, stunned by the advanced parry, found himself open and off balance. Barely a split second later, before the attacker could even begin to recover, Drizzt's counter poked one, then the other scimitar pole into his chest.

A soft blue light appeared on the stunned student's face, and he and Drizzt followed its line up to see a wand-wielding master looking down at them from the catwalk.

"You are defeated," the master said to the tall student. "Fall where you stand!"

The student shot an angry glare at Drizzt and obediently dropped to the stone.

"Come," Drizzt said to Kelnozz, casting a glance up at the master's revealing light. "Any others in the area will know of our position now. We must seek a new defensible area."

Kelnozz paused a moment to watch the graceful hunting strides of his comrade. He had indeed made a good choice in selecting Drizzt, but he knew already, after only a single quick encounter, that if he and this skilled swordsman were the last two standing—a distinct possibility—he would have no chance at all of claiming victory.

Together they rushed around a blind corner, right into two opponents. Kelnozz chased after one, who fled in fright, and Drizzt faced off against the other, who wielded sword and dirk poles.

A wide smile of growing confidence crossed Drizzt's face as his opponent took the offensive, launching routines similarly basic to those of the spear wielder that Drizzt had easily dispatched.

A few deft twists and turns of his scimitars, a few slaps on the inside edges of his opponent's weapons, had the sword and dirk flying wide. Drizzt's attack came right up the middle, where he executed another double-poke into his opponent's chest.

The expected blue light appeared. "You are defeated," came the master's call. "Fall where you stand."

Outraged, the stubborn student chopped viciously at Drizzt. Drizzt blocked with one weapon and snapped the other against his attacker's wrist, sending the sword pole flying to the floor.

The attacker clenched his bruised wrist, but that was the least of his troubles. A blinding flash of lightning exploded from the observing master's wand, catching him full in the chest and hurtling him ten feet backward to crash into a stalagmite mound. He crumpled to the floor, groaning in agony, and a line of glowing heat rose from his scorched body, which lay against the cool gray stone.

"You are defeated!" the master said again.

Drizzt started to the fallen drow's aid, but the master issued an emphatic, "No!"

Then Kelnozz was back at Drizzt's side. "He got away," Kelnozz began, but he broke into a laugh when he saw the downed student. "If a master calls you out, then you are out!" Kelnozz repeated into Drizzt's blank stare.

"Come," Kelnozz continued. "The battle is in full now. Let us find some fun!"

Drizzt thought his companion quite cocky for one who had yet to lift his weapons. He only shrugged and followed.

Their next encounter was not so easy. They came into a double passage turning in and out of several rock formations and found themselves faced off against a group of three—nobles from leading houses, both Drizzt and Kelnozz realized.

Drizzt rushed the two on his left, both of whom wielded single swords, while Kelnozz worked to fend off the third. Drizzt had little experience against multiple opponents, but Zak had taught him the techniques of such a battle quite well. His movements were solely defensive at first, then he settled into a comfortable rhythm and allowed his opponents to tire themselves out, and to make the critical mistakes.

These were cunning foes, though, and familiar with each other's movements. Their attacks complemented each other, slicing in at Drizzt from widely opposing angles.

"Two-hands," Zak had once called Drizzt, and now he lived up to the title. His scimitars worked independently, yet in perfect harmony, foiling every attack.

From a nearby perch on the catwalk, Masters Hatch'net and Dinin looked on, Hatch'net more than a little impressed, and Dinin swelling with pride.

Drizzt saw the frustration mounting on his opponents' faces, and he knew that his opportunity to strike would soon be at hand. Then they crossed up, coming in together with identical thrusts, their sword poles barely inches apart.

Drizzt spun to the side and launched a blinding uppercut slice with his left scimitar, deflecting both attacks. Then he reversed his body's momentum, dropped to one knee, back in line with his opponents, and thrust in low with two snaps of his free right arm. His jabbing scimitar pole caught the first, and the second, squarely in the groin.

They dropped their weapons in unison, clutched their bruised parts, and slumped to their knees. Drizzt leaped up before them, trying to find the words for an apology.

Hatch'net nodded his approval at Dinin as the two masters set their lights on the two losers.

"Help me! " Kelnozz cried from beyond the dividing wall of stalagmites.

Drizzt dived into a roll through a break in the wall, came up quickly, and downed a fourth opponent, who was concealed for a backstab surprise, with a backhand chop to the chest. Drizzt stopped to consider his latest victim. He hadn't even consciously known that the drow was there, but his aim had been perfect!

Hatch'net blew a low whistle as he shifted his light to the most recent loser's face. "He is good!" the master breathed.

Drizzt saw Kelnozz a short distance away, practically forced down to his back by his opponent's skilled maneuvers. Drizzt leaped between the two and deflected an attack that surely would have finished Kelnozz.

This newest opponent, wielding two sword poles, proved Drizzt's toughest challenge yet. He came at Drizzt with complicated feints and twists, forcing him on his heels more than once.

"Berg'inyon of House Baenre," Hatch'net whispered to Dinin. Dinin understood the significance and hoped that his young brother was up to the test.

Berg'inyon was not a disappointment to his distinguished kin. His moves came skilled and measured, and he and Drizzt danced about for many minutes with neither finding any advantage. The daring Berg'inyon then came in with the attack routine perhaps most familiar to Drizzt: the double-thrust low.

Drizzt executed the cross-down to perfection, the appropriate parry as Zaknafein had so pointedly proved to him. Never satisfied, though, Drizzt then reacted on an impulse, agilely snapping a foot up between the hilts of his crossed blades and into his opponent's face. The stunned son of House Baenre fell back against the wall.

"I knew the parry was wrong!" Drizzt cried, already savoring the next time he would get the opportunity to foil the double-thrust low in a session against Zak.

"He is good," Hatch'net gasped again to his glowing companion.

Dazed, Berg'inyon could not fight his way out of the disadvantage. He put a globe of darkness around himself, but Drizzt waded right in, more than willing to fight blindly.

Drizzt put the son of House Baenre through a quick series of attacks, ending with one of Drizzt's scimitar poles against Berg'inyon's exposed neck.

"I am defeated," the young Baenre conceded, feeling the pole. Hearing the call, Master Hatch'net dispelled the darkness. Berg'inyon set both his weapons on the stone and slumped down, and the blue light appeared on his face.

Drizzt couldn't hold back the widening grin. Were there any here that he could not defeat? he wondered.

Drizzt then felt an explosion on the back of his head that dropped him to his knees. He managed to look back in time to see Kelnozz walking away.

"A fool," Hatch'net chuckled, putting his light on Drizzt, then turning his gaze upon Dinin. "A good fool."

Dinin crossed his arms in front of his chest, his face glowing brightly now in a flush of embarrassment and anger.

Drizzt felt the cool stone against his cheek, but his only thoughts at that moment were rooted in the past, locked onto Zaknafein's sarcastic, but painfully accurate, statement: "It is our way!"

13

THE PRICE OF WINNING

"Y ou deceived me," Drizzt said to Kelnozz that night in the barracks. The room was black around them and no other students stirred in their cots, exhausted from the day's fighting and from their endless duties serving the older students.

Kelnozz fully expected this encounter. He had guessed Drizzt's naiveté early on, when Drizzt had actually queried him about the rules of engagement. An experienced drow warrior, particularly a noble, should have known better, should have understood that the only rule of his existence was the pursuit of victory. Now, Kelnozz knew, this foolish young Do'Urden would not strike at him for his earlier actions—vengeance fueled by anger was not one of Drizzt's traits.

"Why?" Drizzt pressed, finding no answer forthcoming from the smug commoner of House Kenafin.

The volume of Drizzt's voice caused Kelnozz to glance around nervously. They were supposed to be sleeping; if a master heard them arguing . . .

"What is the mystery?" Kelnozz signaled back in the hand code, the warmth of his fingers glowing clearly to Drizzt's heat-sensing eyes. "I acted as I had to act, though I now believe I should have held off a bit longer. Perhaps, if you had defeated a few more, I might have finished higher than third in the class."

"If we had worked together, as we had agreed, you might have won, or finished second at the least," Drizzt signaled back, the sharp movements of his hands reflecting his anger.

"Most assuredly second," Kelnozz replied. "I knew from the beginning that I would be no match for you. You are the finest swordsman I have ever seen."

"Not by the masters standing," Drizzt grumbled aloud.

"Eighth is not so low," Kelnozz, whispered back. "Berg'inyon is only ranked tenth, and he is from the ruling house of Menzoberranzan. You should be glad that your standing is not to be envied by your classmates." A shuffle outside the room's door sent Kelnozz back into the silent code. "Holding a higher rank means only that I have more fighters eyeing my back as a convenient place to rest their daggers."

Drizzt let the implications of Kelnozz's statement slip by; he refused to consider such treachery in the Academy. "Berg'inyon was the finest fighter I saw in the grand melee," he signaled. "He had you beaten until I interceded on your behalf."

Kelnozz smiled the thought away. "Let Berg'inyon serve as a cook in some lowly house for all I care," he whispered even more quietly than before—for the son of House Baenre's bunk was only a few yards away. "He is tenth, yet I, Kelnozz of Kenafin, am third!"

"I am eighth," said Drizzt, an uncharacteristic edge on his voice, more anger than jealousy," but I could defeat you with any weapon."

Kelnozz shrugged, a strangely blurring movement to onlookers seeing in the infrared spectrum. "You did not," he signaled. "I won our encounter."

"Encounter?" Drizzt gasped. "You deceived me, that is all!"

"Who was left standing?" Kelnozz pointedly reminded him. "Who wore the blue light of a master's wand?"

"Honor demands that there be rules of engagement," growled Drizzt.

"There is a rule," Kelnozz snapped back at him. "You may do whatever you can get away with. I won our encounter, Drizzt Do'Urden, and I hold the higher rank! That is all that matters!"

In the heat of the argument, their voices had grown too loud. The door to the room swung wide, and a master stepped onto the threshold, his form vividly outlined by the hallway's blue lights. Both students promptly rolled over and closed their eyes—and their mouths.

The finality of Kelnozz's last statement rocked Drizzt to some prudent observations. He realized then that his friendship with Kelnozz had come to an end—and, perhaps, that he and Kelnozz had never been friends at all.

✕ ✕ ✕ ✕ ✕

"You have seen him?" Alton asked, his fingers tapping anxiously on the small table in the highest chamber of his private quarters. Alton had set the younger students of Sorcere to work repairing the blasted place, but the scorch marks on the stone walls remained, a legacy of Alton's fireball.

"I have," replied Masoj. "I have heard of his skill with weapons."

"Eighth in his class after the grand melee," said Alton, "a fine achievement."

"By all accounts, he has the prowess to be first," said Masoj. "One day he will claim that title. I shall be careful around that one."

"He will never live to claim it!" Alton promised. "House Do'Urden puts great pride in this purple-eyed youth, and thus I have decided upon Drizzt as my first target for revenge. His death will bring pain to that treacherous Matron Malice!"

Masoj saw a problem here and decided to put it to rest once and for all. "You will not harm him," he warned Alton. "You will not even go near him."

Alton's tone became no less grim. "I have waited two decades—" he began.

"You can wait a few more," Masoj snapped back. "I remind you that you accepted Matron SiNafay's invitation into House Hun'ett. Such an alliance requires obedience. Matron SiNafay—our matron mother—has placed upon my shoulders the task of handling Drizzt Do'Urden, and I will execute her will."

Alton rested back in his seat across the table and put what was left of his acid-torn chin into a slender palm, carefully weighing the words of his secret partner.

"Matron SiNafay has plans that will bring you all the revenge you could possibly desire," Masoj continued. "I warn you now, Alton DeVir," he snarled, emphasizing the surname that was not Hun'ett, "that if you begin a war with House Do'Urden, or even put them on the defensive with any act of violence unsanctioned by Matron SiNafay, you will incur the wrath of House Hun'ett. Matron SiNafay will expose you as a murderous imposter and will exact every punishment allowable by the ruling council upon your pitiful bones!"

Alton had no way to refute the threat. He was a rogue, without family beyond the adopted Hun'etts. If SiNafay turned against him, he would find no allies. "What plan does SiNafay . . . Matron SiNafay . . . have for House Do'Urden?" he asked calmly. "Tell me of my revenge so that I may survive these torturous years of waiting."

Masoj knew that he had to act carefully at this point. His mother had not forbidden him to tell Alton of the future course of action, but if she had wanted the volatile DeVir to know, Masoj realized, she would have told him herself.

"Let us just say that House Do'Urden's power has grown, and continues to grow, to the point where it has become a very real threat to all the great houses," Masoj purred, loving the intrigue of positioning before a war. "Witness the fall of House DeVir, perfectly executed with no obvious trail. Many of Menzoberranzan's nobles would rest easier if . . ." He let it go at that, deciding that he probably had said too much already.

By the hot glimmer in Alton's eyes, Masoj could tell that the lure had been strong enough to buy Alton's patience.

⚔ ⚔ ⚔ ⚔

The Academy held many disappointments for young Drizzt, particularly in that first year, when so many of the dark realities of drow society, realities that Zaknafein had barely hinted at, remained on the edges of Drizzt's cognizance with stubborn resilience. He weighed the masters' lectures of hatred and mistrust in both hands, one side holding the masters' views in the context of the lectures, the other bending those same words into the very different logic assumed by his old mentor. The truth seemed so ambiguous, so hard to define. Through all of the examination, Drizzt found that he could not escape one pervading fact: In his entire young life, the only treachery he had ever witnessed—and so often!—was at the hands of drow elves.

The physical training of the Academy, hours on end of dueling exercises and stealth techniques, was more to Drizzt's liking. Here, with his weapons so readily in his hands, he freed himself of the disturbing questions of truth and perceived truth.

Here he excelled. If Drizzt had come into the Academy with a higher level of training and expertise than that of his classmates, the gap grew only wider as the grueling months passed. He learned to look beyond the accepted defense and attack routines put forth by the masters and create his own methods, innovations that almost always at least equaled—and usually outdid—the standard techniques.

At first, Dinin listened with increasing pride as his peers exalted in his younger brother's fighting prowess. So glowing came the compliments that the eldest son of Matron Malice soon took on a nervous wariness. Dinin was the elderboy of House Do'Urden, a title he had gained by eliminating Nalfein. Drizzt, showing the potential to become one of the finest swordsmen in all of Menzoberranzan, was now the secondboy of the house, eyeing, perhaps, Dinin's title.

Similarly, Drizzt's fellow students did not miss the growing brilliance of his fighting dance. Often they viewed it too close for their liking! They looked upon Drizzt with seething jealousy, wondering if they could ever measure up against his whirling scimitars. Pragmatism was ever a strong trait in drow elves. These young students had spent the bulk of their years observing the elders of their families twisting every situation into a favorable light. Every one of them recognized the value of Drizzt Do'Urden as an ally, and thus, when the grand melee came around the next year, Drizzt was inundated with offers of partnership.

The most surprising query came from Kelnozz of House Kenafin, who had downed Drizzt through deceit the previous year. "Do we join again, this time to the very top of the class?" the haughty young fighter asked as he moved beside Drizzt down the tunnel to the prepared cavern. He moved around and stood before Drizzt easily, as if they were the best of friends, his forearms resting across the hilts of his belted weapons and an overly friendly smile spread across his face.

Drizzt could not even answer. He turned and walked away, pointedly keeping his eye over one shoulder as he left.

"Why are you so amazed?" Kelnozz pressed, stepping quickly to keep up.

Drizzt spun on him. "How could I join again with one who so deceived me?" he snarled. "I have not forgotten your trick!"

"That is the point," Kelnozz argued. "You are more wary this year; certainly I would be a fool to attempt such a move again!"

"How else could you win?" said Drizzt. "You cannot defeat me in open battle." His words were not a boast, just a fact that Kelnozz accepted as readily as Drizzt.

"Second rank is highly honored," Kelnozz reasoned.

Drizzt glared at him. He knew that Kelnozz would not settle for anything less than ultimate victory. "If we meet in the melee," he said with cold finality, "it will be as opponents." He walked off again, and this time Kelnozz did not follow.

⚔ ⚔ ⚔ ⚔ ⚔

Luck bestowed a measure of justice upon Drizzt that day, for his first opponent, and first victim, in the grand melee was none other than his former partner. Drizzt found Kelnozz in the same corridor they had used as a defensible starting point the previous year and took him down with his very first attack combination. Drizzt somehow managed to hold back on his winning thrust, though he truly wanted to jab his scimitar pole into Kelnozz's ribs with all his strength.

Then Drizzt was off into the shadows, picking his way carefully until the numbers of surviving students began to dwindle. With his reputation, Drizzt had to be extra wary, for his classmates recognized a common advantage in eliminating one of his prowess early in the competition.

Working alone, Drizzt had to fully scope out every battle before he engaged, to ensure that each opponent had no secret companions lurking nearby.

This was Drizzt's arena, the place where he felt most comfortable, and he was up to the challenge. In two hours, only five competitors remained, and after another two hours of cat and mouse, it came down to only two: Drizzt and Berg'inyon Baenre.

Drizzt moved out into an open stretch of the cavern. "Come out, then, student Baenre!" he called. "Let us settle this challenge openly and with honor!"

Watching from the catwalk, Dinin shook his head in disbelief.

"He has relinquished all advantage," said Master Hatch'net, standing beside the elderboy of House Do'Urden. "As the better swordsman, he had Berg'inyon worried and unsure of his moves. Now your brother stands out in the open, showing his position."

"Still a fool," Dinin muttered.

Hatch'net spotted Berg'inyon slipping behind a stalagmite mound a few yards behind Drizzt. "It should be settled soon."

"Are you afraid?" Drizzt yelled into the gloom. "If you truly deserve the top rank, as you freely boast, then come out and face me openly. Prove your words, Berg'inyon Baenre, or never speak them again!"

The expected rush of motion from behind sent Drizzt into a sidelong roll.

"Fighting is more than swordplay!" the son of House Baenre cried as he came on, his eyes gleaming at the advantage he now seemed to hold.

Berg'inyon stumbled then, tripped up by a wire Drizzt had set out, and fell flat to his face. Drizzt was on him in a flash, scimitar pole tip in at Berg'inyon's throat.

"So I have learned," Drizzt replied grimly.

"Thus a Do'Urden becomes the champion," Hatch'net observed, putting his blue light on the face of House Baenre's defeated son. Hatch'net then stole Dinin's widening smile with a prudent reminder: "Elderboys should beware secondboys with such skills."

⚔ ⚔ ⚔ ⚔ ⚔

While Drizzt took little pride in his victory that second year, he took great satisfaction in the continued growth of his fighting skills. He practiced every waking hour when he was not busy in the many serving duties of a young student. Those duties were reduced as the years passed—the youngest students were worked the hardest—and Drizzt found more and more time in private training. He reveled in the dance of his blades and the harmony of his movements. His scimitars became his only friends, the only things he dared to trust.

He won the grand melee again the third year, and the year after that, despite the conspiracies of many others against him. To the masters, it became obvious that none in Drizzt's class would ever defeat him, and the next year they placed him into the grand melee of students three years his senior. He won that one, too.

The Academy, above anything else in Menzoberranzan, was a structured place, and though Drizzt's advanced skill defied that structure in terms of battle prowess, his tenure as a student would not be lessened. As a fighter, he would spend ten years in the Academy, not such a long time considering the thirty years of study a wizard endured in Sorcere, or the fifty years a budding priestess would spend in Arach-Tinilith. While fighters began their training at the young age of twenty, wizards could not start until their twenty-fifth birthday, and clerics had to wait until the age of forty.

The first four years in Melee-Magthere were devoted to singular combat, the handling of weapons. In this, the masters could teach Drizzt little that Zaknafein had not already shown him.

After that, though, the lessons became more involved. The young drow warriors spent two full years learning group fighting tactics with other warriors, and the subsequent three years incorporated those tactics into warfare techniques beside, and against, wizards and clerics.

The final year of the Academy rounded out the fighters' education. The first six months were spent in Sorcere, learning the basics of magic use, and the last six, the prelude to graduation, saw the fighters in tutelage under the priestesses of Arach-Tinilith.

All the while there remained the rhetoric, the hammering in of those precepts that the Spider Queen held so dear, those lies of hatred that held the drow in a state of controllable chaos.

To Drizzt, the Academy became a personal challenge, a private classroom within the impenetrable womb of his whirling scimitars. Inside the adamantine walls he formed with those blades, Drizzt found he could ignore the many injustices he observed all around him, and could somewhat insulate himself against words that would have poisoned his heart. The Academy was a place of constant ambition and deceit, a breeding ground for the ravenous, consuming hunger for power that marked the life of all the drow.

Drizzt would survive it unscathed, he promised himself.

As the years passed, though, as the battles began to take on the edge of brutal reality, Drizzt found himself caught up time and again in the heated throes of situations he could not so easily brush away.

14

PROPER RESPECT

They moved through the winding tunnels as quietly as a whispering breeze, each step measured in stealth and ending in an alert posture. They were ninth-year students working on their last year in Melee-Magthere, and they operated as often outside the cavern of Menzoberranzan as within. No longer did padded poles adorn their belts; adamantine weapons hung there now, finely forged and cruelly edged.

At times, the tunnels closed in around them, barely wide enough for one dark elf to squeeze through. Other times, the students found themselves in huge caverns with walls and ceilings beyond their sight. They were drow warriors, trained to operate in any type of Underdark landscape and learned in the ways of any foe they might encounter.

"Practice patrols," Master Hatch'net had called these drills, though he had warned the students that "practice patrols" often met monsters quite real and unfriendly.

Drizzt, still rated in the top of his class and in the point position, led this group, with Master Hatch'net and ten other students following in formation behind. Only twenty-two of the original twenty-five in Drizzt's class remained. One had been dismissed—and subsequently executed—for a foiled assassination attempt on a high-ranking student, a second had been killed in the practice arena, and a third had died in his bunk of natural causes—for a dagger in the heart quite naturally ends one's life.

In another tunnel a short distance away, Berg'inyon Baenre, holding the class's second rank, led Master Dinin and the other half of the class in a similar exercise.

Day after day, Drizzt and the others had struggled to keep the fine edge of readiness. In three months of these mock patrols, the group had encountered only one monster, a cave fisher, a nasty crablike denizen of the Underdark. Even that conflict had provided only brief excitement, and no practical experience, for the cave fisher had slipped out along the high ledges before the drow patrol could even get a strike at it.

This day, Drizzt sensed something different. Perhaps it was an unusual edge on Master Hatch'net's voice or a tingling in the stones of the cavern, a subtle vibration that hinted to Drizzt's subconscious of other creatures in the maze of tunnels. Whatever the reason, Drizzt knew enough to follow his instincts, and he was not surprised when the telltale glow of a heat source flitted down a side passage on the periphery of his vision. He signaled for the rest of the patrol to halt, then quickly climbed to a perch on a tiny ledge above the side passage's exit.

When the intruder emerged into the main tunnel, he found himself lying back down on the floor with two scimitar blades crossed over his neck. Drizzt backed away immediately when he recognized his victim as another drow student.

"What are you doing down here?" Master Hatch'net demanded of the intruder. "You know that the tunnels outside Menzoberranzan are not to be traveled by any but the patrols!"

"Your pardon, Master," the student pleaded. "I bring news of an alert."

All in the patrol crowded around, but Hatch'net backed them off with a glare and ordered Drizzt to set them out in defensive positions.

"A child is missing," the student went on, "a princess of House Baenre! Monsters have been spotted in the tunnels!"

"What sort of monsters?" Hatch'net asked. A loud clacking noise, like the sound of two stones being chipped together, answered his question.

"Hook horrors!" Hatch'net signaled to Drizzt at his side. Drizzt had never seen such beasts, but he had learned enough about them to understand why Master Hatch'net had suddenly reverted to the silent hand code.

Hook horrors hunted through a sense of hearing more acute than that of any other creature in all the Underdark. Drizzt immediately relayed the signal around to the others, and they held absolutely quiet for instructions from the master. This was the situation they had trained to handle for the last nine years of their lives, and only the sweat on their palms belied the calm readiness of these young drow warriors.

"Spells of darkness will not foil hook horrors," Hatch'net signaled to his troops. "Nor will these." He indicated the pistol crossbow in his hand and the poison-tipped dart it held, a common first-strike weapon of the dark elves. Hatch'net put the crossbow away and drew his slender sword.

"You must find a gap in the creature's bone armor," he reminded the others, "and slip your weapon through to the flesh." He tapped Drizzt on the shoulder, and they started off together, the other students falling into line behind them.

The clacking resounded clearly, but, echoing off the stone walls of the tunnels, it provided a confusing beacon for the hunting drow. Hatch'net let Drizzt steer their course and was impressed by the way the student soon discerned the pattern of the echo riddle. Drizzt's step came in confidence, though many of the others in the patrol glanced about anxiously, unsure of the peril's direction or distance.

Then a singular sound froze them all where they stood, cutting through the din of the clacking monsters and resounding again and again, surrounding the patrol in the echoing madness of a terrifying wail. It was the scream of a child.

"Princess of House Baenre!" Hatch'net signaled to Drizzt. The master started to order his troops into a battle formation, but Drizzt didn't wait to watch the commands. The scream had sent a shudder of revulsion through his spine, and when it sounded again, it lighted angry fires in his lavender eyes.

Drizzt sprinted off down the tunnel, the cold metal of his scimitars leading the way.

Hatch'net organized the patrol into quick pursuit. He hated the thought of losing a student as skilled as Drizzt, but he considered, too, the benefits of Drizzt's rash actions. If the others watched the finest of their class die in an act of stupidity, it would be a lesson they would not soon forget.

Drizzt cut around a sharp corner and down a straight expanse of narrow, broken walls. He heard no echoes now, just the ravenous clacking of the waiting monsters and the muffled cries of the child.

His keen ears caught the slight sounds of his patrol at his back, and he knew that if he was able to hear them, the hook horrors surely could. Drizzt would not relinquish the passion or the immediacy of his quest. He climbed to a ledge ten feet above the floor, hoping it would run the length of the corridor. When he slipped around a final bend, he could barely distinguish the heat of the monsters' forms through the blurring coolness of their bony exoskeletons, shells nearly equal in temperature to the surrounding stone.

He made out five of the giant beasts, two pressed against the stone and guarding the corridor and three others farther back, in a little cul-de-sac, toying with some—crying—object.

Drizzt mustered his nerve and continued along the ledge, using all the stealth he had ever learned to creep by the sentries. Then he saw the child princess, lying in a broken heap at the foot of one of the monstrous bipeds. Her sobs told Drizzt that she was alive. Drizzt had no intention of engaging the monsters if he could help it, hoping that he might perhaps slip in and steal the child away.

Then the patrol came headlong around the bend in the corridor, forcing Drizzt to action.

"Sentries!" he screamed in warning, probably saving the lives of the first four of the group. Drizzt's attention abruptly returned to the wounded child as one of the hook horrors raised its heavy, clawed foot to crush her.

The beast stood nearly twice Drizzt's height and outweighed him more than five times over. It was fully armored in the hard shell of its exoskeleton and adorned with gigantic clawed hands and a long and powerful beak. Three of the monsters stood between Drizzt and the child.

Drizzt couldn't care about any of those details at that horrible, critical moment. His fears for the child outweighed any concern for the danger looming before him. He was a drow warrior, a fighter trained and outfitted for battle, while the child was helpless and defenseless.

Two of the hook horrors rushed at the ledge, just the break Drizzt needed. He rose up to his feet and leaped out over them, coming down in a fighting blur onto the side of the remaining hook horror. The monster lost all thoughts of the child as Drizzt's scimitars snapped in at its beak relentlessly, cracking into its facial armor in a desperate search for an opening.

The hook horror fell back, overwhelmed by its opponent's fury and unable to catch up to the blades' blinding, stinging movements.

Drizzt knew that he had the advantage on this one, but he knew, as well, that two others would soon be at his back. He did not relent. He slid down from his perch on the monster's side and rolled around to block its retreat, dropping between its stalagmite-like legs and tripping it to the stone. Then he was on top of it, poking furiously as it floundered on its belly.

The hook horror desperately tried to respond, but its armored shell was too encumbering for it to twist out from under the assault.

Drizzt knew his own situation was even more desperate. Battle had been joined in the corridor, but Hatch'net and the others couldn't possibly get through the sentries in time to stop the two hook horrors undoubtedly charging his back. Prudence dictated that Drizzt relinquish his position over this one and spin away into a defensive posture.

The child's agonized scream, however, overruled prudence. Rage burned in Drizzt's eyes so blatantly that even the stupid hook horror knew its life was soon to end. Drizzt put the tips of his scimitars together in a V and plunged them down onto the back of the monster's skull with all his might. Seeing a slight crack in the creature's shell, Drizzt crossed the hilts of his weapons, reversed the points, and split a clear opening in the monster's defense. He then snapped the hilts together and plunged the blades straight down, through the soft flesh and into the monster's brain.

A heavy claw sliced a deep line across Drizzt's shoulders, tearing his *piwafwi* and drawing blood. He dived forward into a roll and came up with his wounded back to the far wall. Only one hook horror moved in at him; the other picked up the child.

"No!" Drizzt screamed in protest. He started forward, only to be slapped back by the attacking monster. Then, paralyzed, he watched in horror as the other hook horror put an end to the child's screams.

Rage replaced determination in Drizzt's eyes. The closest hook horror rushed at him, meaning to crush him against the stone. Drizzt recognized its intentions and didn't even try to dodge out of the way. Instead, he reversed his grip on his weapons and locked them against the wall, above his shoulders.

With the momentum of the monster's eight-hundred-pound bulk carrying it on, even the armor of its shell could not protect the hook horror from the adamantine scimitars. It slammed Drizzt up against the wall, but in doing so impaled itself through the belly.

The creature jumped back, trying to wriggle free, but it could not escape the fury of Drizzt Do'Urden. Savagely the young drow twisted the impaled blades. He then shoved off from the wall with the strength of anger, tumbling the giant monster backward.

Two of Drizzt's enemies were dead, and one of the hook horror sentries in the hallway was down, but Drizzt found no relief in those facts. The third hook horror towered over him as he desperately tried to get his blades free from his latest victim. Drizzt had no escape from this one.

The second patrol arrived then, and Dinin and Berg'inyon Baenre rushed into the cul-de-sac, along the same ledge Drizzt had taken. The hook horror turned away from Drizzt just as the two skilled fighters came at it.

Drizzt ignored the painful gash in his back and the cracks he had no doubt suffered in his slender ribs. Breathing came to him in labored gasps, but this, too, was of no consequence. He finally managed to free one of his blades, and he charged at the monster's back. Caught in the middle of the three skilled drow, the hook horror went down in seconds.

The corridor was finally cleared, and the dark elves rushed in all around the cul-de-sac. They had lost only one student in their battle against the monster sentries.

"A princess of House Barrison'del'armgo," remarked one of the students in Dinin's patrol, looking at the child's body.

"House Baenre, we were told," said another student, one from Hatch'net's group. Drizzt did not miss the discrepancy.

Berg'inyon Baenre rushed over to see if the victim was indeed his youngest sister.

"Not of my house," he said with obvious relief after a quick inspection. He then laughed as further examination revealed a few other details about the corpse. "Not even a princess!" he declared.

Drizzt watched it all curiously, noting the impassive, callous attitude of his companions most of all.

Another student confirmed Berg'inyon's observation. "A boy child!" he spouted. "But of what house?"

Master Hatch'net moved over to the tiny body and reached down to take the purse from around the child's neck. He emptied its contents into his hand, revealing the emblem of a lesser house.

"A lost waif," he laughed to his students, tossing the empty purse back to the ground and pocketing its contents," of no consequence."

"A fine fight," Dinin was quick to add, "with only one loss. Go back to Menzoberranzan proud of the work you have accomplished this day."

Drizzt slapped the blades of his scimitars together in a resounding ring of protest.

Master Hatch'net ignored him. "Form up and head back," he told the others. "You all performed well this day." He then glared at Drizzt, stopping the angry student in his tracks.

"Except for you!" Hatch'net snarled. "I cannot ignore the fact that you downed two of the beasts and helped with a third," Hatch'net scolded, "but you endangered the rest of us with your foolish bravado!"

"I warned of the sentries " Drizzt stuttered.

"Damn your warning!" shouted the master. "You went off without command! You ignored the accepted methods of battle! You led us in here blindly! Look at the corpse of your fallen companion!" Hatch'net raged, pointing to the dead student in the corridor. "His blood is on your hands!"

"I meant to save the child," Drizzt argued.

"We all meant to save the child!" retorted Hatch'net.

Drizzt was not so certain. What would a child be doing out in these corridors all alone? How convenient that a group of hook horrors, a rarely seen beast in the region of Menzoberranzan, just happened by to provide training for this "practice patrol." Too convenient, Drizzt knew, considering that the passages farther from the city teemed with the true patrols of seasoned warriors, wizards, and even clerics.

"You knew what was around the bend in the tunnel," Drizzt said evenly, his eyes narrowing at the master.

The slap of a blade across the wound on his back made Drizzt lurch in pain, and he nearly lost his footing. He turned to find Dinin glaring down at him.

"Keep your foolish words unspoken," Dinin warned in a harsh whisper, "or I will cut out your tongue."

⚔ ⚔ ⚔ ⚔ ⚔

"The child was a plant," Drizzt insisted when he was alone with his brother in Dinin's room.

Dinin's response was a stinging smack across the face.

"They sacrificed him for the purpose of the drill," growled the unrelenting younger Do'Urden.

Dinin launched a second punch, but Drizzt caught it in mid-swing. "You know the truth of my words," Drizzt said. "You knew about it all along."

"Learn your place, Secondboy," Dinin replied in open threat, "in the Academy and in the family." He pulled away from his brother.

"To the Nine Hells with the Academy!" Drizzt spat at Dinin's face. "If the family holds similar . . ." He noticed that Dinin's hands now held sword and dirk.

Drizzt jumped back, his own scimitars coming out at the ready. "I have no desire to fight you, my brother," he said. "Know well that if you attack, I will defend. Only one of us will walk out of here."

Dinin considered his next move carefully. If he attacked and won, the threat to his position in the family would be at an end. Certainly no one, not even Matron Malice, would question the punishment he levied against his impertinent younger brother. Dinin had seen Drizzt in battle, though. Two hook horrors! Even Zaknafein would be hard pressed to attain such a victory. Still, Dinin knew that if he did not carry through with his threat, if he let Drizzt face him down, he might give Drizzt confidence in their future struggles, possibly inciting the treachery he had always expected from the secondboy.

"What is this, then?" came a voice from the room's door way. The brothers turned to see their sister Vierna, a mistress of Arach-Tinilith. "Put your weapons away," she scolded. "House Do'Urden cannot afford such infighting now!"

Realizing that he had been let off the hook, Dinin readily complied with the demands, and Drizzt did likewise.

"Consider yourselves fortunate," said Vierna, "for I'll not tell Matron Malice of this stupidity. She would not be merciful, I promise you."

"Why have you come unannounced to Melee-Magthere?" asked the elderboy, perturbed by his sister's attitude. He, too, was a master of the Academy, even if he was only a male, and deserved some respect.

Vierna glanced up and down the hallway, then closed the door behind her. "To warn my brothers," she explained quietly. "There are rumors of vengeance against our house."

"By what family?" Dinin pressed. Drizzt just stood back in confused silence and let the two continue. "For what deed?"

"For the elimination of House DeVir, I would presume," replied Vierna. "Little is known; the rumors are vague. I wanted to warn you both, though, so that you might keep your guard especially high in the coming months."

"House DeVir fell many years ago," said Dinin. "What penalty could still be enacted?"

Vierna shrugged. "They are just rumors," she said. "Rumors to be listened to!"

"We have been accused of a wrongful deed?" Drizzt asked. "Surely our family must call out this false accuser."

Vierna and Dinin exchanged smiles. "Wrongful?" Vierna laughed.

Drizzt's expression revealed his confusion.

"On the very night you were born," Dinin explained, "House DeVir ceased to exist. An excellent attack, thank you."

"House Do'Urden?" gasped Drizzt, unable to come to terms with the startling news. Of course, Drizzt knew of such battles, but he had held out hope that his own family was above that sort of murderous action.

"One of the finest eliminations ever carried out," Vierna boasted. "Not a witness left alive."

"You . . . our family . . . murdered another family?"

"Watch your words, Secondboy," Dinin warned. "The deed was perfectly executed. In the eyes of Menzoberranzan, therefore, it never happened."

"But House DeVir ceased to exist," said Drizzt.

"To a child," said Dinin with a laugh.

A thousand possibilities assaulted Drizzt at that awful moment, a thousand pressing questions that he needed answered. One in particular stood out vividly, welling like a lump of bile in his throat.

"Where was Zaknafein that night?" he asked.

"In the chapel of House DeVir's clerics, of course," replied Vierna "Zaknafein plays his part in such business so very well."

Drizzt rocked back on his heels, hardly able to believe what he was hearing. He knew that Zak had killed drow before, had killed clerics of Lolth before, but Drizzt had always assumed that the weapons master had acted out of necessity, in self-defense.

"You should show more respect to your brother," Vierna scolded him. "To draw weapons against Dinin! You owe him your life!"

"You know?" Dinin chuckled, casting Vierna a curious glance.

"You and I were melded that night," Vierna reminded him. "Of course I know."

"What are you talking about?" asked Drizzt, almost afraid to hear the reply.

"You were to be the third-born male in the family," Vierna explained, "the third living son."

"I have heard of my brother Nal—" The name stuck in Drizzt's throat as he began to understand. All he had ever been able to learn of Nalfein was that he had been killed by another drow.

"You will learn in your studies at Arach-Tinilith that third living sons are customarily sacrificed to Lolth," Vierna continued. "So were you promised.

On the night that you were born, the night that House Do'Urden battled House DeVir, Dinin made his ascent to the position of elderboy." She cast a sly glance at her brother, standing with his arms proudly crossed over his chest.

"I can speak of it now," Vierna smiled at Dinin, who nodded his head in accord. "It happened too long ago for any punishment to be brought against Dinin."

"What are you talking about?" Drizzt demanded. Panic hovered all about him. "What did Dinin do?"

"He put his sword into Nalfein's back," Vierna said calmly.

Drizzt swam on the edge of nausea. Sacrifice? Murder? The annihilation of a family, even the children? What were his siblings talking about?

"Show respect to your brother!" Vierna demanded. "You owe him your life."

"I warn the both of you," she purred, her ominous glare shaking Drizzt and knocking Dinin from his confident pedestal. "House Do'Urden may be on a course of war. If either of you strike out against the other, you will bring the wrath of all your sisters and Matron Malice—four high priestesses—down upon your worthless soul!" Confident that her threat carried sufficient weight, she turned and left the room.

"I will go," Drizzt whispered, wanting only to skulk away to a dark corner.

"You will go when you are dismissed!" Dinin scolded. "Remember your place, Drizzt Do'Urden, in the Academy and in the family."

"As you remembered yours with Nalfein?"

"The battle against DeVir was won," Dinin replied, taking no offense. "The act brought no peril to the family."

Another wave of disgust swept over Drizzt. He felt as if the floor were climbing up to swallow him, and he almost hoped that it would.

"It is a difficult world we inhabit," Dinin said.

"We make it so," Drizzt retorted. He wanted to continue further, to implicate the Spider Queen and the whole amoral religion that would sanction such destructive and treacherous actions. Drizzt wisely held his tongue, though. Dinin wanted him dead; he understood that now. Drizzt understood as well that if he gave his scheming brother the opportunity to turn the females of the family against him, Dinin surely would.

"You must learn," Dinin said, again in a controlled tone, "to accept the realities of your surroundings. You must learn to recognize your enemies and defeat them."

"By whatever means are available," Drizzt concluded.

"The mark of a true warrior!" Dinin replied with a wicked laugh.

"Are our enemies drow elves?"

"We are drow warriors!" Dinin declared sternly. "We do what we must to survive,"

"As you did, on the night of my birth," Drizzt reasoned, though at this point, there was no remaining trace of outrage in his resigned tone. "You were cunning enough to get away cleanly with the deed."

Dinin's reply, though expected, stung the younger drow profoundly.

"It never happened."

ON THE DARK SIDE

I am Drizzt—"

"I know who you are," replied the student mage, Drizzt's appointed tutor in Sorcere. "Your reputation precedes you. Most in all the Academy have heard of you and of your prowess with weapons."

Drizzt bowed low, a bit embarrassed.

"That skill will be of little use to you here," the mage went on. "I am to tutor you in the wizardly arts, the dark side of magic, we call them. This is a test of your mind and your heart; meager metal weapons will play no part. Magic is the true power of our people!"

Drizzt accepted the berating without reply. He knew that the traits this young mage was boasting of were also necessary qualities of a true fighter. Physical attributes played only a minor role in Drizzt's style of battle. Strong will and calculated maneuvers, everything the mage apparently believed only wizards could handle, won the duels that Drizzt fought.

"I will show you many marvels in the next few months," the mage went on, "artifacts beyond your belief and spells of a power beyond your experience!"

"May I know your name?" Drizzt asked, trying to sound somewhat impressed by the student's continued stream of self-glorification. Drizzt had already learned quite a lot about wizardry from Zaknafein, mostly of the weaknesses inherent in the profession. Because of magic's usefulness in situations other than battle, drow wizards were accorded a high position in the society, second to the clerics of Lolth. It was a wizard, after all, who lighted the glowing Narbondel, timeclock of the city, and wizards who lighted faerie fires on the sculptures of the decorated houses.

Zaknafein had little respect for wizards. They could kill quickly and from a distance, he had warned Drizzt, but if one could get in close to them, they had little defense against a sword.

"Masoj," replied the mage. "Masoj Hun'ett of House Hun'ett, beginning my thirtieth and final year of study. Soon I will be recognized as a full wizard of Menzoberranzan, with all of the privileges accorded my station."

"Greetings, then, Masoj Hun'ett," Drizzt replied. "I, too, have but a year remaining in my training at the Academy, for a fighter spends only ten years."

"A lesser talent," Masoj was quick to remark. "Wizards study thirty years before they are even considered practiced enough to go out and perform their craft."

Again Drizzt accepted the insult graciously. He wanted to get this phase of his instruction over with, then finish out the year and be rid of the Academy altogether.

⚔ ⚔ ⚔ ⚔ ⚔

Drizzt found his six months under Masoj's tutelage actually the best of his stay at the Academy. Not that he came to care for Masoj; the budding wizard constantly sought ways to remind Drizzt of fighters' inferiority. Drizzt sensed a competition between himself and Masoj, almost as if the mage were setting him up for some future conflict. The young fighter shrugged his way through it, as he always had, and tried to get as much out of the lessons as he could.

Drizzt found that he was quite proficient in the ways of magic. Every drow, the fighters included, possessed a degree of magical talent and certain innate abilities. Even drow children could conjure a globe of darkness or edge their opponents in a glowing outline of harmless colored flames.

Drizzt handled these tasks easily, and in a few tendays, he could manage several cantrips and a few lesser spells.

With the innate magical talents of the dark elves also came a resistance to magical attacks, and that is where Zaknafein had recognized the wizards' greatest weakness. A wizard could cast his most powerful spell to perfection, but if his intended victim was a drow elf, the wizard may well have found no results for his efforts. The surety of a well-aimed sword thrust always impressed Zaknafein, and Drizzt, after witnessing the drawbacks of drow magic during those first tendays with Masoj, began to appreciate the course of training he had been given.

He still found great enjoyment in many of the things Masoj showed him, particularly the enchanted items housed in the tower of Sorcere. Drizzt held wands and staves of incredible power and went through several attack routines with a sword so heavily enchanted that his hands tingled from its touch.

Masoj, too, watched Drizzt carefully through it all, studying the young warrior's every move, searching for some weakness that he might exploit if House Hun'ett and House Do'Urden ever did fall into the expected conflict. Several times, Masoj saw an opportunity to eliminate Drizzt, and he felt in his heart that it would be a prudent move. Matron SiNafay's instructions to him, though, had been explicit and unbending.

Masoj's mother had secretly arranged for him to be Drizzt's tutor. This was not an unusual situation; instruction for fighters during their six months in Sorcere was always handled one-on-one by higher-level Sorcere students. When she had told Masoj of the setup, SiNafay quickly reminded him that his sessions with the young Do'Urden remained no more than a scouting mission. He was not to do anything that might even hint of the planned conflict between the two houses. Masoj was not fool enough to disobey.

Still, there was one other wizard lurking in the shadows, who was so desperate that even the warnings of the matron mother did little to deter him.

⚔ ⚔ ⚔ ⚔ ⚔

"My student, Masoj, has informed me of your fine progress," Alton DeVir said to Drizzt one day.

"Thank you, Master Faceless One," Drizzt replied hesitantly, more than a little intimidated that a master of Sorcere had invited him to a private audience.

"How do you perceive magic, young warrior?" Alton asked. "Has Masoj impressed you?"

Drizzt didn't know how to respond. Truly, magic had not impressed him as a profession, but he did not want to insult a master of the craft. "I find the art beyond my abilities," he said tactfully. "For others, it seems a powerful course, but I believe my talents are more closely linked to the sword."

"Could your weapons defeat one of magical power?" Alton snarled. He quickly bit back the sneer, trying not to tip off his intent.

Drizzt shrugged. "Each has its place in battle," he replied. "Who could say which is the mightier? As with every combat, it would depend upon the individuals engaged."

"Well, what of yourself?" Alton teased. "First in your class, I have heard, year after year. The masters of Melee-Magthere speak highly of your talents."

Again Drizzt found himself flushed with embarrassment. More than that, though, he was curious as to why a master and student of Sorcere seemed to know so much about him.

"Could you stand against one of magical powers?" asked Alton. "Against a master of Sorcere, perhaps?"

"I do not—" Drizzt began, but Alton was too enmeshed in his own ranting to hear him.

"Let us learn!" the Faceless One cried. He drew out a thin wand and promptly loosed a bolt of lightning at Drizzt.

Drizzt was down into a dive before the wand even discharged. The lightning bolt sundered the door to Alton's highest chamber and bounced about the adjourning room, breaking items and scorching the walls.

Drizzt came rolling back to his feet at the side of the room, his scimitars drawn and ready. He still was unsure of this master's intent.

"How many can you dodge?" Alton teased, waving the wand in a threatening circle. "What of the other spells I have at my disposal—those that attack the mind, not the body?"

Drizzt tried to understand the purpose of this lesson and the part he was meant to play in it. Was he supposed to attack this master?

"These are not practice blades," he warned, holding his weapons out toward Alton.

Another bolt roared in, forcing Drizzt to dodge back to his original position. "Does this seem like practice to you, foolish Do'Urden?" Alton growled. "Do you know who I am?"

Alton's time of revenge had come—damn the orders of Matron SiNafay!

Just as Alton was about to reveal the truth to Drizzt, a dark form slammed into the master's back, knocking him to the floor. He tried to squirm away but found himself helplessly pinned by a huge black panther.

Drizzt lowered the tips of his blades; he was at a loss to understand any of this.

"Enough, Guenhwyvar!" came a call from behind Alton. Looking past the fallen master and the cat, Drizzt saw Masoj enter the room.

The panther sprang away from Alton obediently and moved to rejoin its master. It paused on its way, to consider Drizzt, who stood ready in the middle of the room.

So enchanted was Drizzt with the beast, the graceful flow of its rippling muscles and the intelligence in its saucer eyes, that he paid little attention to the master who had just attacked him, though Alton, unhurt, was back to his feet and obviously upset.

"My pet," Masoj explained. Drizzt watched in amazement as Masoj dismissed the cat back to its own plane of existence by sending its corporeal form back into the magical onyx statuette he held in his hand.

"Where did you get such a companion?" Drizzt asked.

"Never underestimate the powers of magic," Masoj replied, dropping the figurine into a deep pocket. His beaming smile became a scowl as he looked to Alton.

Drizzt, too, glanced at the faceless master. That a student had dared to attack a master seemed impossibly odd to the young fighter. This situation grew more puzzling each minute.

Alton knew that he had overstepped his bounds, and that he would have to pay a high price for his foolishness if he could not find some way out of this predicament.

"Have you learned your lesson this day?" Masoj asked Drizzt, though Alton realized that the question was also directed his way.

Drizzt shook his head. "I am not certain of the point of all this," he answered honestly.

"A display of the weakness of magic," Masoj explained, trying to disguise the truth of the encounter, "to show you the disadvantage caused by the necessary intensity of a casting wizard; to show you the vulnerability of a mage obsessed—" he eyed Alton directly at this point—"with spellcasting. The complete vulnerability when a wizard's intended prey becomes his overriding concern."

Drizzt recognized the lie for what it was, but he could not understand the motives behind this day's events. Why would a master of Sorcere attack him so? Why would Masoj, still just a student, risk so much to come to his defense?

"Let us bother the master no more," Masoj said, hoping to deflect Drizzt's curiosity further. "Come with me now to our practice hall. I will show you more of Guenhwyvar, my magical pet."

Drizzt looked to Alton, wondering what the unpredictable master would do next.

"Do go," Alton said calmly, knowing the facade Masoj had begun would be his only way around the wrath of his adopted matron mother. "I am confident that this day's lesson was learned," he said, his eyes on Masoj.

Drizzt glanced back to Masoj, then back to Alton again. He let it go at that. He wanted to learn more of Guenhwyvar.

⚔ ⚔ ⚔ ⚔ ⚔

When Masoj had Drizzt back in the privacy of the tutor's own room, he took out the polished onyx figurine in the form of a panther and called

Guenhwyvar back to his side. The mage breathed easier after he had introduced Drizzt to the cat, for Drizzt spoke no more about the incident with Alton.

Never before had Drizzt encountered such a wonderful magical item. He sensed a strength in Guenhwyvar, a dignity, that belied the beast's enchanted nature. Truly, the cat's sleek muscles and graceful moves epitomized the hunting qualities drow elves so dearly desired. Just by watching Guenhwyvar's movements, Drizzt believed, he could improve his own techniques.

Masoj let them play together and spar together for hours, grateful that Guenhwyvar could help him smooth over any damage that foolish Alton had done.

Drizzt had already put his meeting with the faceless master far behind him.

⚔ ⚔ ⚔ ⚔ ⚔

"Matron SiNafay would not understand," Masoj warned Alton when they were alone later that day.

"You will tell her," Alton reasoned matter-of-factly. So frustrated was he with his failure to kill Drizzt that he hardly cared.

Masoj shook his head. "She need not know."

A suspicious smile found its way across Alton's disfigured face. "What do you want?" he asked coyly. "Your tenure here is almost at its end. What more might a master do for Masoj?"

"Nothing," Masoj replied. "I want nothing from you."

"Then why?" Alton demanded. "I desire no debts following my paths. This incident is to be done with here and now!"

"It is done," Masoj replied. Alton didn't seem convinced.

"What could I gain from telling Matron SiNafay of your foolish actions?" Masoj reasoned. "Likely, she would kill you, and the coming war with House Do'Urden would have no basis. You are the link we need to justify the attack. I desire this battle; I'll not risk it for the little pleasure I might find in your tortured demise."

"I was foolish," Alton admitted, more somberly. "I had not planned to kill Drizzt when I summoned him here, just to watch him and learn of him, so that I might savor more when the time to kill him finally arrived. Seeing him before me, though, seeing a cursed Do'Urden standing unprotected before me . . . !"

"I understand," said Masoj sincerely. "I have had those same feelings when looking upon that one."

"You have no grudge against House Do'Urden."

"Not the house," Masoj explained, "that one! I have watched him for nearly a decade, studied his movements and his attitudes."

"You like not what you see?" Alton asked, a hopeful tone in his voice.

"He does not belong," Masoj replied grimly. "After six months by his side, I feel I know him less now than I ever did. He displays no ambition, yet has emerged victorious from his class's grand melee nine years in a row. It's unprecedented! His grasp of magic is strong; he could have been a wizard, a very powerful wizard, if he had chosen that course of study."

Masoj clenched his fist, searching for the words to convey his true emotions about Drizzt. "It is all too easy for him," he snarled. "There is no sacrifice in Drizzt's actions, no scars for the great gains he makes in his chosen profession."

"He is gifted," Alton remarked, "but he trains as hard as any I have ever seen, by all accounts."

"That is not the problem," Masoj groaned in frustration. There was something less tangible about Drizzt Do'Urden's character that truly irked the young Hun'ett. He couldn't recognize it now, because he had never witnessed it in any dark elf before, and because it was so very foreign to his own makeup. What bothered Masoj—and many other students and masters—was the fact that Drizzt excelled in all the fighting skills the drow elves most treasured but hadn't given up his passion in return. Drizzt had not paid the price that the rest of the drow children were made to sacrifice long before they had even entered the Academy.

"It is not important," Masoj said after several fruitless minutes of contemplation. "I will learn more of the young Do'Urden in time."

"His tutelage under you was finished, I had thought," said Alton. "He goes to Arach-Tinilith for the final six months of his training—quite inaccessible to you."

"We both graduate after those six months," Masoj explained. "We will share our indenture time in the patrol forces together."

"Many will share that time," Alton reminded him. "Dozens of groups patrol the corridors of the region. You may never even see Drizzt in all the years of your term."

"I already have arranged for us to serve in the same group," replied Masoj. He reached into his pocket and produced the onyx figurine of the magical panther.

"A mutual agreement between yourself and the young Do'Urden," Alton reasoned with a complimentary smile.

"It appears that Drizzt has become quite fond of my pet," Masoj chuckled.

"Too fond?" Alton warned. "You should watch your back for scimitars."

Masoj laughed aloud. "Perhaps our friend, Do'Urden, should watch his back for panther claws!"

SACRILEGE

L ast day," Drizzt breathed in relief as he donned his ceremonial robes. If the first six months of this final year, learning the subtleties of magic in Sorcere, had been the most enjoyable, these last six in the school of Lolth had been the least. Every day, Drizzt and his classmates had been subjected to endless eulogies to the Spider Queen, tales and prophecies of her power and of the rewards she bestowed upon loyal servants.

"Slaves" would have been a better word, Drizzt had come to realize, for nowhere in all this grand school to the drow deity had he heard anything synonymous with, or even hinting at, the word love. His people worshiped Lolth; the females of Menzoberranzan gave over their entire existence in her servitude. Their giving was wholly wrought of selfishness, though; a cleric of the Spider Queen aspired to the position of high priestess solely for the personal power that accompanied the title.

It all seemed so very wrong in Drizzt's heart.

Drizzt had drifted through the six months of Arach-Tinilith with his customary stoicism, keeping his eyes low and his mouth shut. Now, finally, he had come to the last day, the Ceremony of Graduation, an event most holy to the drow, and wherein, Vierna had promised him, he would come to understand the true glory of Lolth.

With tentative steps, Drizzt moved out from the shelter of his tiny, unadorned room. He worried that this ceremony had become his personal trial. Up to now, very little about the society around Drizzt had made any sense to him, and he wondered, despite his sister's assurances, whether the events of this day would allow him to see the world as his kin saw it. Drizzt's fears had taken a spiral twist, one rolling out from the other to surround him in a predicament be could not escape.

Perhaps, he worried, he truly feared that the day's events would fulfill Vierna's promise.

Drizzt shielded his eyes as he entered the circular ceremonial hall of Arach-Tinilith. A fire burned in the center of the room, in an eight-legged brazier that resembled, as everything in this place seemed to resemble, a spider. The headmistress of all the Academy, the matron mistress, and the other twelve high priestesses serving as instructors of Arach-Tinilith, including Drizzt's sister, sat cross-legged in a circle around the brazier. Drizzt and his classmates from the school of fighters stood along the wall behind them.

"*Ma ku!*" the matron mistress commanded, and all was silent save the crackle of the brazier's flames. The door to the room opened again, and a young cleric entered. She was to be the first graduate of Arach-Tinilith this year, Drizzt had been told, the finest student in the school of Lolth. Thus, she had been awarded the highest honors in this ceremony. She shrugged off her robes and walked naked through the ring of sitting priestesses to stand before the flames, her back to the matron mistress.

Drizzt bit his lip, embarrassed and a little excited. He had never seen a female in such a light before, and he suspected that the sweat on his brow was from more than the brazier's heat. A quick glance around the room told him that his classmates entertained similar ideas.

"*Bae-go si'n'ee calamay*," the matron mistress whispered, and red smoke poured from the brazier, coloring the room in a hazy glow. It carried an aroma with it, rich and sickly sweet. As Drizzt breathed the scented air, he felt himself grow lighter and wondered if he soon would be floating off the floor.

The flames in the brazier suddenly roared higher, causing Drizzt to squint against the brightness and turn away. The clerics began a ritual chant, though the words were unfamiliar to Drizzt. He hardly paid them any heed, though, for he was too intent on holding his own thoughts in the overpowering swoon of the inebriating haze.

"*Glabrezu*," the matron mistress moaned, and Drizzt recognized the tone as a summons, the name of a denizen of the lower planes. He looked back to the events at hand and saw the matron mistress holding a single-tongued snake whip.

"Where did she get that?" Drizzt mumbled, then he realized that he had spoken aloud and hoped he hadn't disturbed the ceremony. He was comforted when he glanced around, for many of his classmates were mumbling to themselves, and some seemed hardly able to hold their balance.

"Call to it," the matron mistress instructed the naked student.

Tentatively, the young cleric spread her arms out wide and whispered, "*Glabrezu*."

The flames danced about the rim of the brazier. The smoke wafted into Drizzt's face, compelling him to inhale it. His legs tingled on the edge of numbness, yet they somehow felt more sensitive, more alive, than they ever had before.

"*Glabrezu*," he heard the student say again louder, and Drizzt heard, too, the roar of the flames. Brightness assaulted him, but somehow he didn't seem to care. His gaze roamed about the room, unable to find a focus, unable to place the strange, dancing sights in accord with the ritual's sounds.

He heard the high priestesses gasping and coaxing the student on, knowing the conjuring to be at hand. He heard the snap of the snake whip—another incentive?—and cries of "*Glabrezu!*" from the student. So primal, so powerful, were these screams that they cut through Drizzt and the other males in the room with an intensity they never would have believed possible.

The flames heard the call. They roared higher and higher and began to take shape. One sight caught the vision of all in the room now—caught it and held it fully. A giant head, a goat-horned dog, appeared within the flames, apparently studying this alluring young drow student who had dared to utter its name.

Somewhere beyond the other-planar form, the snake whip cracked again, and the female student repeated her call, her cry beckoning, praying.

The giant denizen of the lower planes stepped through the flames. The sheer unholy power of the creature stunned Drizzt. Glabrezu towered nine feet and seemed much more, with muscled arms ending in giant pincers instead of hands and a second set of smaller arms, normal arms, protruding from the front of its chest.

Drizzt's instincts told him to attack the monster and rescue the female student, but when he looked around for support, he found the matron mistress and the other teachers of the school back in their ritualistic chanting, this time with an excited edge permeating their every word.

Through all the haze and the daze, the tantalizing, dizzying aroma of the smoky red incense continued its assault on reality. Drizzt trembled, teetered on a narrow ledge of control, his gathering rage fighting the scented smoke's confusing allure. Instinctively, his hands went to the hilts of the scimitars on his belt.

Then a hand brushed against his leg.

He looked down to see a mistress, reclined and asking him to join her—a scene that had suddenly become general around the chamber.

The smoke continued its assault on him.

The mistress beckoned to him, her fingernails lightly scraping the skin of his leg.

Drizzt ran his fingers through his thick hair, trying to find some focal point in the dizziness. He did not like this loss of control, this mental numbness that stole the fine edge of his reflexes and alertness.

He liked even less the scene unfolding before him. The sheer wrongness of it assaulted his soul. He pulled away from the mistress's hopeful grasp and stumbled across the room, tripping over numerous entwined forms too engaged to take note of him. He made the exit as quickly as his wobbly legs could carry him, and he rushed out of the room, pointedly closing the door behind him.

Only the screams of the female student followed him. No stone or mental barricade could block them out.

Drizzt leaned heavily against the cool stone wall, grasping at his stomach. He hadn't even paused to consider the implications of his actions; he knew only that he had to get out of that foul room.

Vierna then was beside him, her robe opened casually in the front. Drizzt, his head clearing, began to wonder about the price of his actions. The look on his sister's face, he noted with still more confusion, was not one of scorn.

"You prefer privacy," she said, her hand resting easily on Drizzt's shoulder. Vierna made no move to close her robe. "I understand," she said.

Drizzt grabbed her arm and pulled her away. "What insanity is this?" he demanded.

Vierna's face twisted as she came to understand her brother's true intentions in leaving the ceremony. "You refused a high priestess!" she snarled at him. "By the laws, she could kill you for your insolence."

"I do not even know her," Drizzt shot back. "I am expected to—"

"You are expected to do as you are instructed!"

"I care nothing for her," Drizzt stammered. He found he could not hold his hands steady.

"Do you think Zaknafein cared for Matron Malice?" Vierna replied, knowing that the reference to Drizzt's hero would surely sting him. Seeing that she had indeed wounded her brother, Vierna softened her expression and took his arm. "Come back," she purred, "into the room. There is still time."

Drizzt's cold glare stopped her as surely as the point of a scimitar.

"The Spider Queen is the deity of our people," Vierna sternly reminded him. "I am one of those who speaks her will."

"I would not be so proud of that," Drizzt retorted, clinging to his anger against the wave of very real fear that threatened to defeat his principled stand.

Vierna slapped him hard across the face. "Go back to the ceremony!" she demanded.

"Go kiss a spider," Drizzt replied. "And may its pincers tear your cursed tongue from your mouth."

It was Vierna now who could not hold her hands steady. "You should take care when you speak to a high priestess," she warned.

"Damn your Spider Queen!" Drizzt spat. "Though I am certain Lolth found damnation eons ago!"

"She brings us power!" Vierna shrieked.

"She steals everything that makes us worth more than the stone we walk upon!" Drizzt screamed back.

"Sacrilege!" Vierna sneered, the word rolling off her tongue like the whistle of the matron mistress's snake whip.

A climactic, anguished scream erupted from inside the room.

"Evil union," Drizzt muttered, looking away.

"There is a gain," Vierna replied, quickly back in control of her temper.

Drizzt cast an accusing glance her way. "Have you had a similar experience?"

"I am a high priestess," was her simple reply.

Darkness hovered all about Drizzt, outrage so intense that he nearly swooned. "Did it please you?" he spat.

"It brought me power," Vierna growled back. "You cannot understand the value."

"What did it cost you?"

Vierna's slap nearly knocked Drizzt from his feet. "Come with me," she said, grabbing the front of his robe. "There is a place I want to show to you."

They moved out from Arach-Tinilith and across the Academy's courtyard. Drizzt hesitated when they reached the pillars that marked the entrance to Tier Breche.

"1 cannot pass between these," he reminded his sister. "I am not yet graduated from Melee-Magthere."

"A formality," Vierna replied, not slowing her pace at all. "I am a mistress of Arach-Tinilith; I have the power to graduate you."

Drizzt wasn't certain of the truth of Vierna's claim, but she was indeed a mistress of Arach-Tinilith. As much as Drizzt feared the edicts of the Academy, he didn't want to anger Vierna again.

He followed her down the wide stone stairs and out into the meandering roadways of the city proper.

"Home?" he dared to ask after a short while.

"Not yet," came the curt reply. Drizzt didn't press the point any further.

They veered off to the eastern end of the great cavern, across from the wall that held House Do'Urden, and came to the entrances of three small tunnels, all guarded by glowing statues of giant scorpions. Vierna paused for just a moment to consider which was the correct course, then led on again, down the smallest of the tunnels.

The minutes became an hour, and still they walked. The passage widened and soon led them into a twisting catacomb of crisscrossing corridors. Drizzt quickly lost track of the path behind them as they made their way through, but Vierna followed a predetermined course that she knew well.

Then, beyond a low archway, the floor suddenly dropped away and they found themselves on a narrow ledge overlooking a wide chasm. Drizzt looked at his sister curiously but held his question when he saw that she was deep in the concentration. She uttered a few simple commands, then tapped herself and Drizzt on the forehead.

"Come," she instructed, and she and Drizzt stepped off the ledge and levitated down to the chasm floor.

A thin mist, from some unseen hot pool or tar pit, hugged the stone. Drizzt could sense the danger here, and the evil. A brooding wickedness hung in the air as tangibly as the mist.

"Do not fear," Vierna signaled to him. "I have put a spell of masking upon us. They cannot see us."

"They?" Drizzt's hands asked, but even as he motioned in the code, he heard a scuttling off to the side. He followed Vierna's gaze down to a distant boulder and the wretched thing perched upon it.

At first, Drizzt thought it was a drow elf, and from the waist up, it was indeed, though bloated and pale. Its lower body, though, resembled a spider, with eight arachnid legs to support its frame. The creature held a bow ready in its hands but seemed confused, as though it could not discern what had entered its lair.

Vierna was pleased by the disgust on her brother's face as he viewed the thing. "Look upon it well, younger brother," she signaled. "Behold the fate of those who anger the Spider Queen."

"What is it?" Drizzt signaled back quickly.

"A drider," Vierna whispered in his ear. Then, back in the silent code, she added, "Lolth is not a merciful deity."

Drizzt watched, mesmerized, as the drider shifted its position on the boulder, searching for the intruders. Drizzt couldn't tell if it was a male or female, so bloated was its torso, but he knew that it didn't matter. The creature was not a natural creation and would leave no descendants behind, whatever its gender. It was a tormented body, nothing more, hating itself, in all probability, more than everything else around it.

"I am merciful," Vierna continued silently, though she knew her brother's attention was fully on the drider. She rested back flat against the stone wall.

Drizzt spun on her, suddenly realizing her intent.

Then Vierna sank into the stone. "Goodbye, little brother," came her final call. "This is a better fate than you deserve."

"No!" Drizzt growled, and he clawed at the empty wall until an arrow sliced into his leg. The scimitars flashed out in his hands as he spun back to face the danger. The drider took aim for a second shot.

Drizzt meant to dive to the side, to the protection of another boulder, but his wounded leg immediately fell numb and useless. Poison.

Drizzt just got one blade up in time to deflect the second arrow, and he dropped to one knee to clutch at his wound. He could feel the cold poison making its way through his limb, but he stubbornly snapped off the arrow shaft and turned his attention back to the attacker. He would have to worry about the wound later, would have to hope that he could tend to it in time. Right now, his only concern was to get out of the chasm.

He turned to flee, to seek a sheltered spot where he could levitate back up to the ledge, but he found himself face-to-face with another drider.

An axe sliced by his shoulder, barely missing its mark. Drizzt blocked the return blow and launched his second scimitar into a thrust, which the drider stopped with a second axe.

Drizzt was composed now, and was confident that he could defeat this foe, even with one leg limiting his mobility—until an arrow cracked into his back.

Drizzt lurched forward under the weight of the blow, but managed to parry another attack from the drider before him. Drizzt dropped to his knees and fell face-down.

When the axe-wielding drider, thinking Drizzt dead, started toward him, Drizzt kicked into a roll that put him squarely under the creature's bulbous belly. He plunged his scimitar up with all his strength, then curled back under the deluge of spidery fluids.

The wounded drider tried to scurry away but fell to the side, its insides draining out onto the stone floor. Still, Drizzt had no hope. His arms, too, were numb now, and when the other wretched creature descended upon him, he could not hope to fight it off. He struggled to cling to consciousness, searching for some way out, battling to the bitter end. His eyelids became heavy. . . .

Then Drizzt felt a hand grab his robe, and he was roughly lifted to his feet and slammed against the stone wall.

He opened his eyes to see his sister's face.

"He lives," Drizzt heard her say. "We must get him back quickly and tend to his wounds"

Another figure moved in front of him.

"I thought this the best way," Vierna apologized.

"We cannot afford to lose him," came an unemotional reply. Drizzt recognized the voice from his past. He fought through the blur and forced his eyes to focus.

"Malice," he whispered. "Mother."

Her enraged punch brought him into a clearer mindset.

"Matron Malice!" she growled, her angry scowl only an inch from Drizzt's face. "Do not ever forget that!"

To Drizzt, her coldness rivaled the poison's, and his relief at seeing her faded away as quickly as it had flooded through him.

"You must learn your place!" Malice roared, reiterating the command that had haunted Drizzt all of his young life. "Hear my words," she demanded, and Drizzt heard them keenly. "Vierna brought you to this place to have you killed. She showed you mercy." Malice cast a disappointed glance at her daughter.

"I understand the will of the Spider Queen better than she," the matron continued, her spittle spraying Drizzt with every word. "If ever you speak ill of Lolth, our goddess, again, I will take you back to this place myself! But not to kill you; that would be too easy." She jerked Drizzt's head to the side so that he could look upon the grotesque remains of the drider he had killed.

"You will come back here," Malice assured him, "to become a drider."

PART FOUR

What eyes are these that see
The pain I know in my innermost soul?
What eyes are these that see
The twisted
strides of   GUENHWYVAR
my kindred,
Led on in the wake of toys unbridled:
Arrow, bolt, and sword tip?

Yours . . . aye, yours,
Straight run and muscled spring,
Soft on padded paws, sheathed claws,
Weapons rested for their need,
Stained not by frivolous blood
Or murderous deceit.

Face to face, my mirror;
Reflection in a still pool by light.
Would that I might keep that image
Upon this face mine own.

Would that I might keep that heart
Within my breast untainted.

Hold tight to the proud honor of
your spirit,
Mighty Guenhwyvar,
And hold tight to my side,
My dearest friend.

—Drizzt Do'Urden

17
HOMECOMING

Drizzt was graduated—formally—on schedule and with the highest honors in his class. Perhaps Matron Malice had whispered into the right ears, smoothing over her son's indiscretions, but Drizzt suspected that more likely none of those present at the Ceremony of Graduation even remembered that he had left.

He moved through the decorated gate of House Do'Urden, drawing stares from the common soldiery, and over to the cavern floor below the balcony. "So I am home," he remarked under his breath, "for whatever that means." After what had happened in the drider lair, Drizzt wondered if he would ever view House Do'Urden as his home again. Matron Malice was expecting him. He didn't dare arrive late.

"It is good that you are home," Briza said to him when she saw him rise up over the balcony's railing.

Drizzt stepped tentatively through the entryway beside his oldest sister, trying to get a firm grasp on his surroundings. Home, Briza called it, but to Drizzt, House Do'Urden seemed as unfamiliar as the Academy had on his first day as a student. Ten years was not such a long time in the centuries of life a drow elf might know, but to Drizzt, more than the decade of absence now separated him from this place.

Maya joined them in the great corridor leading to the chapel anteroom. "Greetings, Prince Drizzt," she said, and Drizzt couldn't tell if she was being sarcastic or not. "We have heard of the honors you achieved at Melee-Magthere. Your skill did House Do'Urden proud." In spite of her words, Maya could not hide a derisive chuckle as she finished the thought. "Glad, I am, that you did not become drider food."

Drizzt's glare stole the smile from her face.

Maya and Briza exchanged concerned glances. They knew of the punishment Vierna had put upon their younger brother, and of the vicious scolding he had received at the hands of Matron Malice. They each cautiously rested a hand on their snake whips, not knowing how foolish their dangerous young brother might have become.

It was not Matron Malice or Drizzt's sisters that now had Drizzt measuring every step before he took it. He knew where he stood with his mother and knew what he had to do to keep her appeased. There was another member of the family, though, that evoked both confusion and anger in Drizzt. Of all his kin, only Zaknafein pretended to be what he was not. As Drizzt made his way to the chapel, he glanced anxiously down every side passage, wondering when Zak would make his appearance.

"How long before you leave for patrol?" Maya asked, pulling Drizzt from his contemplations.

"Two days," Drizzt replied absently, his eyes still darting from shadow to shadow. Then he was at the anteroom door, with no sign of Zak. Perhaps the weapons master was within, standing beside Malice.

"We know of your indiscretions," Briza snapped, suddenly cold, as she placed her hand on the latch to the anteroom's door. Drizzt was not surprised by her outburst. He was beginning to expect such explosions from the high priestesses of the Spider Queen.

"Why could you not just enjoy the pleasures of the ceremony?" Maya added. "We are fortunate that the mistresses and the matron of the Academy were too involved in their own excitement to note your movements. You would have brought shame upon our entire house!"

"You might have placed Matron Malice in Lolth's disfavor," Briza was quick to add.

The best thing I could ever do for her, Drizzt thought. He quickly dismissed the notion, remembering Briza's uncanny proficiency at reading minds.

"Let us hope he did not," Maya said grimly to her sister. "The tides of war hang thick in the air."

"I have learned my place," Drizzt assured them. He bowed low. "Forgive me, my sisters, and know that the truth of the drow world is fast opening before my young eyes. Never will I disappoint House Do'Urden in such a way again."

So pleased were his sisters at the proclamation that the ambiguity of Drizzt's words slipped right past them. Then Drizzt, not wanting to push his luck too far, also slipped past them, making his way through the door, noting with relief that Zaknafein was not in attendance.

"All praises to the Spider Queen!" Briza yelled after him.

Drizzt paused and turned to meet her gaze. He bowed low a second time. "As it should be," he muttered.

※ ※ ※ ※ ※

Creeping behind the small group, Zak had studied Drizzt's every move, trying to measure the toll a decade at the Academy had exacted on the young fighter.

Gone now was the customary smile that lit Drizzt's face. Gone, too, Zak supposed, was the innocence that had kept this one apart from the rest of Menzoberranzan.

Zak leaned back heavily against the wall in a side passage. He had caught only portions of the conversation at the anteroom door. Most clearly he had heard Drizzt's heartfelt accord with Briza's honoring of Lolth.

"What have I done?" the weapons master asked himself. He looked back around the bend in the main corridor, but the door to the anteroom had already closed.

"Truly, when I look upon the drow—the drow warrior!—that was my most treasured, I shame for my cowardice," Zak lamented. "What has Drizzt lost that I might have saved?"

He drew his smooth sword from its scabbard, his sensitive fingers running the length of the razor edge. "A finer blade you would be had you tasted the blood of Drizzt Do'Urden, to deny this world, our world, another soul for its taking, to free that one from the unending torments of life!" He lowered the weapon's tip to the floor.

"But I am a coward," he said. "I have failed in the one act that could have brought meaning to my pitiful existence. The secondboy of House Do'Urden lives, it would appear, but Drizzt Do'Urden, my Two-hands, is long dead." Zak looked back to the emptiness where Drizzt had been standing, the weapons master's expression suddenly a grimace. "Yet this pretender lives.

"A drow warrior."

Zak's weapon clanged to the stone floor and his head slumped down to be caught by the embrace of his open palms, the only shield Zaknafein Do'Urden had ever found.

⚔ ⚔ ⚔ ⚔ ⚔

Drizzt spent the next day at rest, mostly in his room, trying to keep out of the way of the other members of his immediate family. Malice had dismissed him without a word in their initial meeting, but Drizzt did not want to confront her again. Likewise, he had little to say to Briza and Maya, fearing that sooner or later they would begin to understand the true connotations of his continuing stream of blasphemous responses. Most of all, though, Drizzt did not want to see Zaknafein, the mentor he had once thought of as his salvation against the realities around him, the one glowing light in the darkness that was Menzoberranzan.

That, too, Drizzt believed, had been only a lie.

On his second day home, when Narbondel, the timeclock of the city, had just begun its cycle of light, the door to Drizzt's small chamber swung open and Briza walked in. "An audience with Matron Malice," she said grimly.

A thousand thoughts rushed through Drizzt's mind as he grabbed his boots and followed his oldest sister down the passageways to the house chapel. Had Malice and the others discovered his true feelings toward their evil deity? What punishments did they now have waiting for him? Unconsciously, Drizzt eyed the spider carvings on the chapel's arched entrance.

"You should be more familiar and more at ease with this place," Briza scolded, noting his discomfort. "It is the place of our people's highest glories."

Drizzt lowered his gaze and did not respond—and was careful not to even think of the many stinging retorts he felt in his heart.

His confusion doubled when they entered the chapel, for Rizzen, Maya, and Zaknafein stood before the matron mother, as expected. Beside them, though, stood Dinin and Vierna.

"We are all present," Briza said, taking her place at her mother's side.

"Kneel," Malice commanded, and the whole family fell to its knees. The matron mother paced slowly around them all, each pointedly dropping his or her eyes in reverence, or just in common sense, as the great lady walked by.

Malice stopped beside Drizzt. "You are confused by the presence of Dinin and Vierna," she said. Drizzt looked up at her. "Do you not yet understand the subtle methods of our survival?"

"I had thought that my brother and sister were to continue on at the Academy," Drizzt explained.

"That would not be to our advantage," Malice replied.

"Does it not bring a house strength to have mistresses and masters seated at the Academy?" Drizzt dared to ask.

"It does," replied Malice, "but it separates the power. You have heard tidings of war?"

"I have heard hinting of trouble," said Drizzt, looking over at Vierna, "though nothing more tangible."

"Hinting?" Malice huffed, angered that her son could not understand the importance. "They are more than most houses ever hear before the blade falls!" She spun away from Drizzt and addressed the whole group. "The rumors hold truth," she declared.

"Who?" asked Briza. "What house conspires against House Do'Urden?"

"None behind us in rank," Dinin replied, though the question had not been asked to him and it was not his place to speak unbidden.

"How do you know this?" Malice asked, letting the oversight pass.

Malice understood Dinin's value and knew that his contributions to this discussion would be important.

"We are the ninth house of the city," Dinin reasoned, "but among our ranks we claim four high priestesses, two of them former mistresses of Arach-Tinilith." He looked at Zak. "We have, as well, two former masters of Melee-Magthere, and Drizzt was awarded the highest laurels from the school of fighters. Our soldiers number nearly four hundred, all skilled and battle-tested. Only a few houses claim more."

"What is your point?" Briza asked sharply.

"We are the ninth house," Dinin laughed, "but few above us could defeat us. . . ."

"And none behind," Matron Malice finished for him. "You show good judgment, Elderboy. I have come to the same conclusions."

"One of the great houses fears House Do'Urden," Vierna concluded. "It needs us gone to protect its own position."

"That is my belief," Malice answered. "An uncommon practice, for family wars usually are initiated by the lower-ranking house, desiring a better position within the city hierarchy."

"Then we must take great care," Briza said.

Drizzt listened carefully to their words, trying to make sense of it all. His eyes never left Zaknafein, though, who knelt impassively at the side. What did the callous weapons master think of all this? Drizzt wondered. Did the thought of such a war thrill him, that he might be able to kill more dark elves?

Whatever his feelings, Zak gave no outward clue. He sat quietly and by all appearances was not even listening to the conversation.

"It would not be Baenre," Briza said, her words sounding like a plea for confirmation. "Certainly we have not yet become a threat to them!"

"We must hope you are correct," Malice replied grimly, remembering vividly her tour of the ruling house. "Likely, it is one of the weaker houses above us, fearing its own unsteady position. I have not yet been able to learn any incriminating information against any in particular, so we must prepare for the worst. Thus, I have called Vierna and Dinin back to my side."

"If we learn of our enemies. . . ." Drizzt began impulsively. All eyes snapped upon him. It was bad enough for the elderboy to speak without being addressed, but for the secondboy, just graduated from the Academy, the act could be considered blasphemous.

Wanting all perspectives, Matron Malice again let the oversight pass. "Continue," she prompted.

"If we discover which house plots against us," Drizzt said quietly, "could we not expose it?"

"To what end?" Briza snarled at him. "Conspiracy without action is no crime."

"Then might we use reason?" Drizzt pressed, continuing against the barrage of incredulous glares that came at him from every face in the room—except from Zak's. "If we are the stronger, then let them submit without battle. Rank House Do'Urden as it should be and let the assumed threat to the weaker house be ended."

Malice grabbed Drizzt by the front of his cloak and heaved him to his feet. "I forgive your foolish thoughts," she growled, "this time!" She dropped him back to the floor, and the silent reprimands of his siblings descended upon him.

Again, though, Zak's expression did not match the others in the room. Indeed, Zak put a hand up over his mouth to hide his amusement. Perhaps there remained a bit of the Drizzt Do'Urden he had known, he dared to hope. Perhaps the Academy had not fully tainted the young fighter's spirit.

Malice whirled on the rest of the family, simmering fury and lust glowing in her eyes. "This is not the time to fear. This," she cried, a slender finger pointing out from in front of her face, "is the time to dream! We are House Do'Urden, Daermon N'a'shezbaernon, of power beyond the understanding of the great houses. We are the unknown entity of this war. We hold every advantage!

"Ninth house?" she laughed. "In short time, only seven houses will remain ahead of us!"

"What of the patrol?" Briza cut in. "Are we to allow the secondboy to go off alone, exposed?"

"The patrol will begin our advantage," the conniving matron explained. "Drizzt will go, and included in his group will be a member of at least four of the houses above us."

"One may strike at him," Briza reasoned.

"No," Malice assured her. "Our enemies in the coming war would not reveal themselves so clearly—not yet. The appointed assassin would have to defeat two Do'Urdens in such a confrontation."

"Two?" asked Vierna.

"Again, Lolth has shown us her favor," explained Malice. "Dinin will lead Drizzt's patrol group."

The elderboy's eyes lit up at the news. "Then Drizzt and I might become the assassins in this conflict," he purred.

The smile disappeared from the matron mother's face. "You will not strike without my consent," she warned in a tone so cold that Dinin fully understood the consequences of disobedience, "as you have done in the past."

Drizzt did not miss the reference to Nalfein, his murdered brother. His mother knew! Malice had done nothing to punish her murderous son. Now Drizzt's hand went up to his face, to hide an expression of horror that only could have brought him trouble in this setting.

"You are there to learn," Matron Malice said to Dinin, "to protect your brother, as Drizzt is there to protect you. Do not destroy our advantage for the gain of a single kill." An evil smile found its way back onto her bone-hued face. "But, if you learn of our enemy, . . ." she said.

"If the proper opportunity presents itself, . . ." Briza finished, guessing her mother's wicked thoughts and throwing an equally vile smile the matron's way.

Malice looked upon her eldest daughter with approval. Briza would prove a fine successor for the house!

Dinin's smile became wide and lascivious. Nothing pleased the elderboy of House Do'Urden more than the opportunity for an assassination.

"Go, then, my family," Malice said. "Remember that unfriendly eyes are upon us, watching our every move, waiting for the time to strike."

Zak was the first out of the chapel, as always, this time with an added spring in his step. It wasn't the prospect of fighting another war that guided his moves, though the thought of killing more clerics of the Spider Queen certainly pleased him. Rather, Drizzt's display of naiveté, his continued misconceptions of the common weal of drow existence, brought Zak hope.

Drizzt watched him go, thinking Zak's strides reflected his desire to kill. Drizzt didn't know whether to follow and confront the weapons master here and now or to let it pass, to shrug it away as readily as he had dismissed most of the cruel world around him. The decision was made for him when Matron Malice stepped in front of him and kept him in the chapel.

"To you, I say this," she began when they were alone. "You have heard the mission I placed upon your shoulders. I will not tolerate failure!"

Drizzt shrank back from the power of her voice.

"Protect your brother," came the grim warning, "or I shall give you to Lolth for judgment."

Drizzt understood the implications, but the matron took the pleasure to spell them out anyway.

"You would not enjoy your life as a drider."

⚔ ⚔ ⚔ ⚔ ⚔

A lightning blast cut across the still black waters of the underground lake, searing the heads of the approaching water trolls. Sounds of battle echoed through the cavern.

Drizzt had one monster—scrags, they were called—cornered on a small peninsula, blocking the wretched thing's path back to the water. Normally, a single drow faced off evenly against a water troll would not have the advantage, but as the others of his patrol group had come to see in the past few tendays, Drizzt was no ordinary young drow.

The scrag came on, oblivious to its peril. A single, blinding movement from Drizzt lopped off the creature's reaching arms. Drizzt moved in quickly for the kill, knowing too well the regenerative powers of trolls.

Then another scrag slipped out of the water at his back.

Drizzt had expected this, but he gave no outward indication that he saw the second scrag coming. He kept his concentration ahead of him, driving deep slashes into the maimed and all but defenseless troll's torso.

Just as the monster behind him was about to latch its claws onto him, Drizzt fell to his knees and cried, "Now!"

The concealed panther, crouched in the shadows at the peninsula's base, did not hesitate. One great stride brought Guenhwyvar into position, and it sprang, crashing heavily onto the unsuspecting scrag, tearing the life from the thing before it could respond to the attack.

Drizzt finished off his troll and turned to admire the panther's work. He extended his hand, and the great cat nuzzled it. How well the two fighters had come to know each other! thought Drizzt.

Another blast of lightning thundered in, this one close enough to steal Drizzt's sight.

"Guenhwyvar!" Masoj Hun'ett, the bolt's caster, cried. "To my side!"

The panther managed to brush against Drizzt's leg as it moved to obey. When his vision returned, Drizzt walked off in the other direction, not wanting to view the scolding that Guenhwyvar always seemed to receive when he and the cat worked together.

Masoj watched Drizzt's back as he went, wanting to put a third bolt right between the young Do'Urden's shoulder blades. The wizard of House Hun'ett did not miss the specter of Dinin Do'Urden, off to the side, watching with more than casual glances.

"Learn your loyalties!" Masoj snarled at Guenhwyvar. Too often, the panther left the wizard's side to join in combat with Drizzt. Masoj knew that the cat was better complemented by the moves of a fighter, but he knew, too, the vulnerability of a wizard involved in spellcasting. Masoj wanted Guenhwyvar at his side, protecting him from enemies—he shot another glance at Dinin—and "friends" alike.

He threw the statuette to the ground at his feet. "Begone!" he commanded.

In the distance, Drizzt had engaged another scrag and made short work of it as well. Masoj shook his head as he watched the display of swordsmanship. Every day, Drizzt grew stronger.

"Give the order to kill him soon, Matron SiNafay," Masoj whispered.

The young wizard did not know how much longer he would be able to carry out the task. Masoj wondered whether he could win the fight even now.

Drizzt shielded his eyes as he struck a torch to seal a dead troll's wounds. Only fire ensured that trolls would not recuperate, even from the grave.

The other battles had died away as well, Drizzt noted, and he saw the flames of torches springing up all across the bank of the lake. He wondered if all of his twelve drow companions had survived, though he also wondered if he truly cared. Others were more than ready to take their places.

Drizzt knew that the only companion who really mattered— Guenhwyvar—was safely back in its home on the Astral Plane.

"Form a guard!" came Dinin's echoing command as the slaves, goblins, and orcs moved in to search for troll treasure, and to salvage whatever they might of the scrags.

When the fires had consumed the scrag he'd set ablaze, Drizzt dipped his torch in the black water, then paused for a moment to let his eyes readjust to the darkness. "Another day," he said softly, "another enemy defeated."

He liked the excitement of patrolling, the thrill of the edge of danger, and the knowledge that he was now putting his weapons to use against vile monsters.

Even here, though, Drizzt could not escape the lethargy that had come to pervade his life, the general resignation that marked his every step. For, though his battles these days were fought against the horrors of the Underdark, monsters killed of necessity, Drizzt had not forgotten the meeting in the chapel of House Do'Urden.

He knew that his scimitars soon would be put to use against the flesh of drow elves.

Zaknafein looked out over Menzoberranzan, as he so often did when Drizzt's patrol group was out of the city. Zak was torn between wanting to sneak out of the house to fight at Drizzt's side, and hoping that the patrol would return with the news that Drizzt had been slain.

Would Zak ever find the answer to the dilemma of the youngest Do'Urden? he wondered. Zak knew that he could not leave the house; Matron Malice was keeping a very close eye on him. She sensed his anguish over Drizzt, Zak knew, and she most definitely did not approve. Zak was often her lover, but they shared little other than that.

Zak thought back to the battles he and Malice had fought over Vierna, another child of common concern, centuries before. Vierna was a female, her fate sealed from the moment of her birth, and Zak could do nothing to halt the assault of the Spider Queen's overwhelming religion.

Did Malice fear that he might have better luck influencing the actions of a male child? Apparently the matron did, but even Zak was not so certain if her fears were justified; even he couldn't measure his influence over Drizzt.

He peered out over the city now, silently watching for the patrol group's return—waiting, as always, for Drizzt's safe return, but secretly hoping, that his dilemma would be ended by the claws and fangs of a lurking monster.

18

THE BACK ROOM

"My greetings, Faceless One," the high priestess said, pushing past Alton into his private chambers in Sorcere.

"And mine to you, Mistress Vierna," Alton replied, trying to keep the fear out of his voice. Vierna Do'Urden coming to see him at this time had to be more than coincidence. "What act has brought me the honor of a visit from a mistress of Arach-Tinilith?"

"No longer a mistress," said Vierna. "I have returned to my home."

Alton paused to consider the news. He knew that Dinin Do'Urden had also resigned his position at the Academy.

"Matron Malice has brought her family back together," Vierna continued. "There are stirrings of war. You have heard them, no doubt?"

"Just rumors," Alton stuttered, now beginning to understand why Vierna had come to call on him. House Do'Urden had used the Faceless One before in its plotting—in its attempt to assassinate Alton! Now, with rumors of war whispered throughout Menzoberranzan, Matron Malice was reestablishing her network of spies and assassins.

"You know of them?" Vierna asked sharply.

"I have heard little," Alton breathed, careful now not to anger the powerful female. "Not enough to report to your house. I did not even suspect that House Do'Urden was involved until now, when you informed me." Alton could only hope that Vierna had no detection spell aimed at his words.

Vierna relaxed, apparently appeased by the explanation. "Listen more carefully to the rumors, Faceless One," she said. "My brother and I have left the Academy; you are to be the eyes and ears of House Do'Urden in this place."

"But . . ." Alton stuttered.

Vierna held up a hand to stop him. "We know of our failure in our last transaction," she said. She bowed low, something a high priestess rarely did to a male. "Matron Malice sends her deepest apologies that the unguent you received for the assassination of Alton DeVir did not restore the features to your face."

Alton nearly choked on the words, now understanding why an unknown messenger had delivered the jar of healing salve some thirty years before. The cloaked figure was an agent of House Do'Urden, come to repay the Faceless One for his assassination of Alton! Of course, Alton had never even tried the unguent. With his luck, it would have worked, and would have restored the features of Alton DeVir.

"This time, your payment cannot fail," Vierna went on, though Alton, too caught up in the irony of it all, hardly listened. "House Do'Urden possesses a wizard's staff but no wizard worthy to wield it. It belonged to Nalfein, my brother, who died in the victory over DeVir."

Alton wanted to strike out at her. Even he wasn't that stupid, though.

"If you can discern which house plots against House Do'Urden," Vierna promised, "the staff will be yours! A treasure indeed for such a small act."

"I will do what I can," Alton replied, having no other response to the incredible offer.

"That is all Matron Malice asks of you," said Vierna, and she left the wizard, quite certain that House Do'Urden had secured a capable agent within the Academy.

⚔ ⚔ ⚔ ⚔ ⚔

"Dinin and Vierna Do'Urden have resigned their positions," said Alton excitedly as the diminutive matron mother came to him later that same evening.

"This is already known to me," replied SiNafay Hun'ett.

She looked around disdainfully at the littered and scorched room, then took a seat at the small table.

"There is more," Alton said quickly, not wanting SiNafay to get upset about being disturbed over old news. "I have had a visitor this day, Mistress Vierna Do'Urden!"

"She suspects?" Matron SiNafay growled.

"No, no!" Alton replied. "Quite the opposite. House Do'Urden wishes to employ me as a spy, as it once employed the Faceless One to assassinate me!"

SiNafay paused for a moment, stunned, then issued a laugh straight from her belly. "Ah, the ironies of our lives!" she roared.

"I had heard that Dinin and Vierna were sent to the Academy only to oversee the education of their younger brother," remarked Alton.

"An excellent cover," SiNafay replied. "Vierna and Dinin were sent as spies for the ambitious Matron Malice. My compliments to her."

"Now they suspect trouble," Alton stated, sitting opposite his matron mother.

"They do," agreed SiNafay. "Masoj patrols with Drizzt, but House Do'Urden has also managed to plant Dinin in the group."

"Then Masoj is in danger," reasoned Alton.

"No," said SiNafay. "House Do'Urden does not know that House Hun'ett perpetrates the threat against it, else it would not have come to you for information. Matron Malice knows your identity."

A look of terror crossed Alton's face.

"Not your true identity," SiNafay laughed at him. "She knows the Faceless One as Gelroos Hun'ett, and she would not have come to a Hun'ett if she suspected our house."

"Then we have an excellent opportunity to throw House Do'Urden into chaos!" Alton cried. "If I implicate another house, even Baenre, perhaps, our position will be strengthened." He chuckled at the possibilities. "Malice will reward me with a staff of great power—a weapon I will turn against her at the proper moment!"

"Matron Malice!" SiNafay corrected sternly. Even though she and

Malice were soon to be open enemies, SiNafay would not permit a male to show such disrespect to a matron mother. "Do you really believe that you could carry out such a deception?"

"When Mistress Vierna returns . . ."

"You will not deal with a lesser priestess with such valued information, foolish DeVir. You will face Matron Malice herself, a formidable foe. If she sees through your lies, do you know what she will do to your body?"

Alton gulped audibly. "I am willing to take the risk," he said, crossing his arms resolutely on the table.

"What of House Hun'ett when the biggest lie is revealed?" SiNafay asked. "What advantage will we enjoy when Matron Malice knows the Faceless One's true identity?"

"I understand," Alton answered, crestfallen but unable to refute SiNafay's logic. "Then what are we to do? What am I to do?"

Matron SiNafay was already considering their next moves. "You will resign your tenure," she said at length. "Return to House Hun'ett, within my protection."

"Such an act might also implicate House Hun'ett to Matron Malice," Alton reasoned.

"It may," replied SiNafay, "but it is the safest route. I will go to Matron Malice in feigned anger, telling her to leave House Hun'ett out of her troubles. If she wishes to make an informant of a member of my family, then she should come to me for permission—though I'll not grant it this time!"

SiNafay smiled at the possibilities of such an encounter. "My anger, my fear, alone could implicate a greater house against House Do'Urden, even a conspiracy between more than one house," she said, obviously enjoying the added benefits. "Matron Malice will certainly have much to think about, and much to worry about!"

Alton hadn't even heard SiNafay's last comments. The words about granting her permission "this time" had brought a disturbing notion into his mind. "And did she?" he dared to ask, though his words were barely audible.

"What do you mean?" asked SiNafay, not following his thoughts.

"Did Matron Malice come to you?" Alton continued, frightened but needing an answer. "Thirty years ago. Did Matron SiNafay grant her permission for Gelroos Hun'ett to become an agent, an assassin to complete House DeVir's elimination?"

A wide smile spread across SiNafay's face, but it vanished in the blink of an eye as she threw the table across the room, grabbed Alton by the front of his robes, and pulled him roughly to within an inch of her scowling visage.

"Never confuse personal feelings with politics!" the tiny but obviously strong matron growled, her tone carrying the unmistakable weight of an open threat. "And never ask me such a question again!"

She threw Alton to the floor but didn't release him from her penetrating glare.

Alton had known all along that he was merely a pawn in the intrigue between House Hun'ett and House Do'Urden, a necessary link for Matron SiNafay to carry out her treacherous plans. Every now and, though, Alton's personal grudge against House Do'Urden caused him to forget his lowly place in this conflict. Looking up now at SiNafay's bared power, he realized that he had overstepped the bounds of his position.

⚔ ⚔ ⚔ ⚔ ⚔

At the back end of the mushroom grove, the southern wall of the cavern that housed Menzoberranzan, was a small, heavily guarded cave. Beyond the ironbound doors stood a single room, used only for gatherings of the city's eight ruling matron mothers.

The smoke of a hundred sweet-smelling candles permeated the air; the matron mothers liked it that way. After almost half a century of studying scrolls in the candlelight of Sorcere, Alton did not mind the light, but he was indeed uncomfortable in the chamber. He sat at the back end of a spider-shaped table, in a small, unadorned chair reserved for guests of the council. Between the table's eight hairy legs were the ruling matron mothers' thrones, all jeweled and dazzling in the candlelight.

The matrons filed in, pompous and wicked, casting belittling glares at the male. SiNafay, at Alton's side, put a hand on his knee and gave him a reassuring wink. She would not have dared to request a gathering of the ruling council if she was not certain of the worthiness of her news. The ruling matron mothers viewed their seats as honorary in nature and did not appreciate being brought together except in times of crisis.

At the head of the spider table sat Matron Baenre, the most powerful figure in all of Menzoberranzan, an ancient and withered female with malicious eyes and a mouth unaccustomed to smiles.

"We are gathered, SiNafay," Baenre said when all eight members had found their appointed chairs. "For what reason have you summoned the council?"

"To discuss a punishment," SiNafay replied.

"Punishment?" Matron Baenre echoed, confused. The recent years had been unusually quiet in the drow city, without an incident since the Teken'duis Freth conflict. To the First Matron's knowledge, no acts had been committed that might require a punishment, certainly none so blatant as to force the ruling council to action. "What individual deserves this?"

"Not an individual," explained Matron SiNafay. She glanced around at her peers, measuring their interest. "A house," she said bluntly. "Daermon N'a'shezbaernon, House Do'Urden." Several gasps of disbelief came in reply, as SiNafay had expected.

"House Do'Urden?" Matron Baenre questioned, surprised that any would implicate Matron Malice. By all of Baenre's knowledge, Malice remained in high regard with the Spider Queen, and House Do'Urden had recently placed two instructors in the Academy.

"For what crime do you dare to charge House Do'Urden?" asked one of the other matrons.

"Are these words of fear, SiNafay?" Matron Baenre had to ask. Several of the ruling matrons had expressed concern about House Do'Urden. It was well known that Matron Malice desired a seat on the ruling council, and, by all measures of the power of her house, she seemed destined to get it.

"I have appropriate cause," SiNafay insisted.

"The others seem to doubt you," replied Matron Baenre. "You should explain your accusation—quickly, if you value your reputation."

SiNafay knew that more than her reputation was at stake; in Menzo-berranzan, a false accusation was a crime on par with murder. "We all remember the fall of House DeVir," SiNafay began. "Seven of us now gathered sat upon the ruling council beside Matron Ginafae DeVir."

"House DeVir is no more," Matron Baenre reminded her.

"Because of House Do'Urden," SiNafay said bluntly.

This time the gasps came out as open anger.

"How dare you speak such words?" came one reply.

"Thirty years!" came another. "The issue has been forgotten!"

Matron Baenre quieted them all before the clamor rose into violent action—a not uncommon occurrence in the council chamber. "SiNafay," she said through the dry sneer on her lips. "One cannot make such an ac-cusation; one cannot discuss such beliefs openly so long after the event! You know our ways. If House Do'Urden did indeed commit this act, as you insist, it deserves our compliments, not our punishment, for it carried it through to perfection. House DeVir is no more, I say. It does not exist!"

Alton shifted uneasily, caught somewhere between rage and despair. SiNafay was far from dismayed, though; this was going exactly as she had envisioned and hoped.

"Oh, but it does!" she responded, rising to her feet. She pulled the hood from Alton's head. "In this person!"

"Gelroos?" asked Matron Baenre, not understanding.

"Not Gelroos," SiNafay replied. "Gelroos Hun'ett died the night House DeVir died. This male, Alton DeVir, assumed Gelroos's identity and posi-tion, hiding from further attacks by House Do'Urden!"

Baenre whispered some instructions to the matron at her right side, then waited as she went through the semantics of a spell. Baenre motioned for SiNafay to return to her seat then faced Alton.

"Speak your name," Baenre commanded.

"I am Alton DeVir," Alton said, gaining strength from the identity he had waited so very long to proclaim, "son of Matron Ginafae and a student of Sorcere on the night House Do'Urden attacked."

Baenre looked to the matron at her side.

"He speaks the truth," the matron assured her. Whispers sprang up all around the spider table, of amusement more than anything else.

"That is why I summoned the ruling council," SiNafay quickly explained.

"Very well, SiNafay," said Matron Baenre. "My compliments to you, Alton DeVir, on your resourcefulness and ability to survive. For a male, you have shown great courage and wisdom. Surely you both know that the council cannot exact punishment upon a house for a deed committed so long ago. Why would we so desire? Matron Malice Do'Urden sits in the favor of the Spider Queen; her house shows great promise. You must reveal to us greater need if you wish any punishment against House Do'Urden."

"I do not wish such a thing," SiNafay quickly replied. "This matter, thirty years removed, is no longer in the realm of the ruling council. House Do'Urden does indeed show promise, my peers, with four high priestesses and a host of other weapons, not the least of which being their secondboy, Drizzt, first graduate of his class." She had purposely mentioned Drizzt, knowing that the name would strike a wound in Matron Baenre. Baenre's own prized son, Berg'inyon, had spent the last nine years ranked behind the wonderful young Do'Urden.

"Then why have you bothered us?" Matron Baenre demanded, an unmistakable edge in her voice.

"To ask you to close your eyes," SiNafay purred. "Alton is a Hun'ett now, under my protection. He demands vengeance for the act committed against his family, and, as a surviving member of the attacked family, he has the right of accusation."

"House Hun'ett will stand beside him?" Matron Baenre asked, turning curious and amused.

"Indeed," replied SiNafay. "Thus is House Hun'ett bound!"

"Vengeance?" another matron quipped, also now more amused than angered. "Or fear? It would seem to my ears that the matron of House Hun'ett uses this pitiful DeVir creature for her own gain. House Do'Urden aspires to higher ranking, and Matron Malice desires to sit upon the ruling council, a threat to House Hun'ett, perhaps?"

"Be it vengeance or prudence, my claim—Alton DeVir's claim—must be deemed as legitimate," replied SiNafay, "to our mutual gain." She smiled wickedly and looked straight to the First Matron. "To the gain of our sons, perhaps, in their quest for recognition."

"Indeed," replied Matron Baenre in a chuckle that sounded more like a cough. A war between Hun'ett and Do'Urden might be to everyone's gain, but not, Baenre suspected, as SiNafay believed. Malice was a powerful matron, and her family truly deserved a ranking higher than ninth. If the fight did come, Malice probably would get her seat on the council, replacing SiNafay.

Matron Baenre looked around at the other matrons, and guessed from their hopeful expressions that they shared her thoughts. Let Hun'ett and Do'Urden fight it out; whatever the outcome, the threat of Matron Malice would be ended. Perhaps, Baenre hoped, a certain young Do'Urden male would fall in battle, propelling her own son into the position he deserved.

Then the First Matron spoke the words SiNafay had come to hear, the silent permission of Menzoberranzan's ruling council.

"This matter is settled, my sisters," Matron Baenre declared, to the accepting nods of all at the table. "It is good that we never met this day."

PROMISES OF GLORY

H ave you found the trail?" Drizzt whispered, moving up beside the great panther. He gave Guenhwyvar a pat on the side and knew from the slackness of the cat's muscles that no danger was nearby.

"Gone, then," Drizzt said, staring off into the emptiness of the corridor in front of them. "'Wicked gnomes,' my brother called them when we found the tracks by the pool. Wicked and stupid." He sheathed his scimitar and knelt beside the panther, his arm comfortable draped across Guenhwyvar's back. "They're smart enough to elude our patrol."

The cat looked up as if it had understood his every word, and Drizzt rubbed a hand roughly over Guenhwyvar's, his finest friend's, head. Drizzt remembered clearly his elation on the day, a tenday before, when Dinin had announced—to Masoj Hun'ett's outrage—that Guenhwyvar would be deployed at the patrol's point position beside Drizzt.

"The cat is mine!" Masoj had reminded Dinin.

"You are mine!" Dinin, the patrol leader, had replied, ending any further debate. Whenever the figurine's magic would permit, Masoj summoned Guenhwyvar from the Astral Plane and bid the cat to run up in front, bringing Drizzt an added degree of safety and a valued companion.

Drizzt knew from the unfamiliar heat patterns on the wall that they had gone the limit of their patrol route. He had purposely put a lot of ground, more than was advised, between himself and the rest of the patrol. Drizzt had confidence that he and Guenhwyvar could take care of themselves, and with the others far behind, he could relax and enjoy the wait. The minutes Drizzt spent in solitude gave him the time he needed in his endless effort to sort through his confused emotions. Guenhwyvar, seemingly non-judgmental and always approving, offered Drizzt a perfect audience for his audible contemplations.

"I begin to wonder the worth of it all," Drizzt whispered to the cat. "I do not doubt the value of these patrols—this tenday alone, we have defeated a dozen monsters that might have brought great harm to the city—but to what end?"

He looked deeply into the panther's saucer eyes and found sympathy there, and Drizzt knew that Guenhwyvar somehow understood his dilemma.

"Perhaps I still do not know who I am," Drizzt mused, "or who my people are. Every time I find a clue to the truth, it leads me down a path that I dare not continue upon, to conclusions I cannot accept."

"You are drow," came a reply behind them. Drizzt turned abruptly to see Dinin a few feet away, a look of grave concern on his face.

"The gnomes have fled beyond our reach," Drizzt said, trying to deflect his brother's concerns.

"Have you not learned what it means to be a drow?" Dinin asked. "Have you not come to understand the course of our history and the promise of our future?"

"I know of our history as it was taught at the Academy," Drizzt replied. "They were the very first lessons we received. Of our future, and more so of the place we now reside, though, I do not understand."

"You know of our enemies," Dinin prompted.

"Countless enemies," replied Drizzt with a heavy sigh. "They fill the holes of the Underdark, always waiting for us to let down our guard. We will not, and our enemies will fall to our power."

"Ah, but our true enemies do not reside in the lightless caverns of our world," said Dinin with a sly smile. "Theirs is a world strange and evil." Drizzt knew who Dinin was referring to, but he suspected that his brother was hiding something.

"The faeries," Drizzt whispered, and the word prompted a jumble of emotions within him. All of his life, he had been told of his evil cousins, of how they had forced the drow into the bowels of the world. Busily engaged in the duties of his everyday life, Drizzt did not think of them often, but whenever they came to mind, he used their name as a litany against everything he hated in his life. If Drizzt could somehow blame the surface elves—as every other drow seemed to blame them—for the injustices of drow society, he could find hope for the future of his people. Rationally, Drizzt had to dismiss the stirring legends of the elven war as another of the endless stream of lies, but in his heart and hopes, Drizzt clung desperately to those words.

He looked back to Dinin. "The faeries," he said again, "whatever they may be."

Dinin chuckled at his brother's relentless sarcasm; it had become so commonplace. "They are as you have learned," he assured Drizzt. "Without worth and vile beyond your imagination, the tormentors of our people, who banished us in eons past; who forced—"

"I know the tales," Drizzt interrupted, alarmed at the increasing volume of his excited brother's voice. Drizzt glanced over his shoulder. "If the patrol is ended, let us meet the others closer to the city. This place is too dangerous for such discussions." He rose to his feet and started back, Guenhwyvar at his side.

"Not as dangerous as the place I soon will lead you," Dinin replied with that same sly smile.

Drizzt stopped and looked at him curiously.

"I suppose you should know," Dinin teased. "We were selected because we are the finest of the patrol groups, and you have certainly played an important role in our attaining that honor."

"Chosen for what?"

"In a fortnight, we will leave Menzoberranzan," explained Dinin. "Our trail will take us many days and many miles from the city."

"How long?" Drizzt asked, suddenly very curious.

"Two tendays, maybe three," replied Dinin, "but well worth the time. We shall be the ones, my young brother, who enact a measure of revenge upon our most hated foes, who strike a glorious blow for the Spider Queen!"

Drizzt thought that he understood, but the notion was too outrageous for him to be certain.

"The elves!" Dinin beamed. "We have been chosen for a surface raid!"

Drizzt was not as openly excited as his brother, unsure of the implications of such a mission. At last he would get to view the surface elves and face the truth of his heart and hopes. Something more real to Drizzt, the disappointment he had known for so many years, tempered his elation, reminded him that while the truth of the elves might bring an excuse to the dark world of his kin, it might instead take away something more important. He was unsure how to feel.

※ ※ ※ ※

"The surface," Alton mused. "My sister went there once—on a raid. A most marvelous experience, so she said!" He looked at Masoj, not knowing how to figure the forlorn expression on the young Hun'ett's face. "Now your patrol makes the journey. I envy you."

"I am not going," Masoj declared.

"Why?" Alton gasped. "This is a rare opportunity indeed. Menzoberranzan—to the anger of Lolth, I am certain—has not staged a surface raid in two decades. It may be twenty more years before the next, and by then you will no longer be among the patrols."

Masoj looked out from the small window of Alton's room in House Hun'ett, surveying the compound.

"Besides," Alton continued quietly, "up there, so far from prying eyes, you might find the chance to dispose of two Do'Urden's. Why would you not go?"

"Have you forgotten a ruling that you played a part in?" Masoj asked, whirling on Alton accusingly. "Two decades ago, the masters of Sorcere decided that no wizards are to travel anywhere near the surface!"

"Of course," Alton replied, remembering the meeting. Sorcere seemed so distant to him now, though he had been within the Hun'ett house for only a few tendays. "We concluded that drow magic may work differently—unexpectedly—under the open sky," he explained. "On that raid twenty years ago—"

"I know the story," Masoj growled, and he finished the sentence for Alton. "A wizard's fireball expanded beyond its normal dimensions, killing several drow. Dangerous side effects, you masters called it, though I've a belief that the wizard conveniently disposed of some enemies under the guise of an accident!"

"Yes," Alton agreed. "So said the rumors. In the absence of evidence . . ." He let the thought go, seeing that he was doing little to comfort Masoj. "That was so long ago," he said, trying to offer some hope. "Have you no recourse?"

"None," Masoj replied. "Things move so very slowly in Menzoberranzan; I doubt that the masters have even begun their investigation into the matter."

"A pity," Alton said. "It would have been the perfect opportunity."

"No more of that!" Masoj scolded. "Matron SiNafay has not given me her command to eliminate Drizzt Do'Urden or his brother. You have already been warned to keep your personal desires to yourself. When the matron bids me to strike, I will not fail her. Opportunities can be created."

"You speak as if you already know how Drizzt Do'Urden will die," Alton said.

An smile spread over Masoj's face as he reached into the pocket of his robe and produced the onyx figurine, his unthinking magical slave, which the foolish Drizzt had come to trust so dearly. "Oh, I do," he replied, giving the statuette of Guenhwyvar an easy toss, then catching it and holding it out on display.

"I do."

⚔ ⚔ ⚔ ⚔ ⚔

The members of the chosen raiding party quickly came to realize that this would be no ordinary mission. They did not go out on patrol from Menzoberranzan at all during the next tenday. Rather, they remained, day and night, sequestered within a barrack of Melee-Magthere. Through nearly every waking hour, the raiders huddled around an oval table in a conference room, hearing the detailed plans of their pending adventure, and, over and over again, Master Hatch'net, the master of Lore, spinning his tales of the vile elves.

Drizzt listened intently to the stories, allowing himself, forcing himself, to fall within Hatch'net's hypnotic web. The tales had to be true; Drizzt did not know what he would hold onto to preserve his principles if they were not.

Dinin presided over the raid's tactical preparations, displaying maps of the long tunnels the group would travel, grilling them over and over until they had memorized the route perfectly.

To this, as well, the eager raiders—except for Drizzt—listened intently, all the while fighting to keep their excitement from bursting out in a wild cheer. As the tenday of preparations neared its end, Drizzt took note that one member of the patrol group had not been attending. At first, Drizzt had reasoned that Masoj was learning his duties in the raid in Sorcere, with his old masters. With the departure time fast approaching and the battle plans clearly taking shape, though, Drizzt began to understand that Masoj would not be joining them.

"Where is our wizard?" Drizzt dared to ask in the late hours of one session.

Dinin, not appreciating the interruption, glared at his brother. "Masoj will not be joining us," he answered, knowing that others might now share Drizzt's concern, a distraction they could not afford at such a critical time.

"Sorcere has decreed that no wizards may travel to the surface," Master Hatch'net explained. "Masoj Hun'ett will await your return in the city. It is a great loss to you indeed, for Masoj has proven his worth many times over. Fear not, though, for a cleric of Arach-Tinilith shall accompany you."

"What of . . ." Drizzt began above the approving whispers of the other raiders.

Dinin cut his brother's thoughts short, easily guessing the question. "The cat belongs to Masoj," he said flatly. "The cat stays behind."

"I could talk to Masoj," Drizzt pleaded.

Dinin's stern glance answered the question without the need for words. "Our tactics will be different on the surface," he said to all the group, silencing their whispers. "The surface is a world of distance, not the blind enclosures of bending tunnels. Once our enemies are spotted, our task will be to surround them, to close off the distances." He looked straight at his young brother. "We will have no need of a point guard, and in such a conflict, a spirited cat could well prove more trouble than aid."

Drizzt had to be satisfied with the answer. Arguing would not help, even if he could get Masoj to let him take the panther—which he knew in his heart he could not. He shook the brooding desires out of his head and forced himself to hear his brother's words. This was to be the greatest challenge of Drizzt's young life, and the greatest danger.

⚔ ⚔ ⚔ ⚔ ⚔

Over the final two days, as the battle plan became ingrained into every thought, Drizzt found himself growing more and more agitated. Nervous energy kept his palms moist with sweat, and his eyes darted about, too alert.

Despite his disappointment over Guenhwyvar, Drizzt could not deny the excitement that bubbled within him. This was the adventure he had always wanted, the answer to his questions of the truth of his people. Up there, in the vast strangeness of that foreign world, lurked the surface elves, the unseen nightmare that had become the common enemy, and thus the common bond, of all the drow. Drizzt would discover the glory of battle, exacting proper revenge upon his people's most hated foes. Always before, Drizzt had fought out of necessity, in training gyms or against the stupid monsters that ventured too near his home.

Drizzt knew that this encounter would be different. This time his thrusts and cuts would be carried by the strength of deeper emotions, guided by the honor of his people and their common courage and resolve to strike back against their oppressors. He had to believe that.

Drizzt lay back in his cot the night before the raiding party's departure and brought his scimitars through some slow-motion maneuvers above him.

"This time," he whispered aloud to the blades while marveling at their intricate dance even at such a slow speed. "This time your ring will sound out in the song of justice!"

He placed the scimitars down at the side of his cot and rolled over to find some needed sleep. "This time," he said again, teeth clenched and eyes shining with determination.

Were his proclamations his belief or his hope? Drizzt had dismissed the disturbing question the very first time it had entered his thoughts, having no more room for doubts than he had for brooding. He no longer considered the possibility of disappointment; it had no place in the heart of a drow warrior.

To Dinin, though, studying Drizzt curiously from the shadows of the doorway, it sounded as if his younger brother was trying to convince himself of the truth of his own words.

THAT FOREIGN WORLD

T he fourteen members of the patrol group made their way through twisting tunnels and giant caverns that suddenly opened wide before them. Silent on magical boots and nearly invisible behind their *piwafwis*, they communicated only in their hand code. For the most part, the ground's slope was barely perceptible, though at times the group climbed straight up rocky chimneys, every step and every handhold drawing them nearer their goal. They crossed through the boundaries of claimed territories, of monsters and the other races, but the hated gnomes and even the duergar dwarves wisely kept their heads hidden. Few in all the Underdark would purposely intercept a drow raiding party.

By the end of a tenday, all the drow could sense the difference in their surroundings. The depth still would have seemed stifling to a surface dweller, but the dark elves were accustomed to the constant oppression of a thousand thousand tons of rock hanging over their heads. They turned every corner expecting the stone ceiling to fly away into the vast openness of the surface world.

Breezes wafted past them—not the sulfur-smelling hot winds rising off the magma of deep earth, but moist air, scented with a hundred aromas unknown to the drow. It was springtime above, though the dark elves, in their seasonless environs, knew nothing of that, and the air was full of the scents of new-blossomed flowers and budding trees. In the seductive allure of those tantalizing aromas, Drizzt had to remind himself again and again that the place they approached was wholly evil and dangerous. Perhaps, he thought, the scents were merely a diabolical lure, a bait to an unsuspecting creature to bring it into the surface world's murderous grip.

The cleric of Arach-Tinilith who was traveling with the raiding party walked near to one wall and pressed her face against every crack she encountered. "This one will suffice," she said a short time later. She cast a spell of seeing and looked into the tiny crack, no more than a finger's width, a second time.

"How are we to get through that?" one of the patrol members signaled to another. Dinin caught the gestures and ended the silent conversation with a scowl.

"It is daylight above," the cleric announced. "We shall have to wait here."

"For how long?" Dinin asked, knowing his patrol to be on the edge of readiness with their long-awaited goal so very near.

"I cannot know," the cleric replied. "No more than half a cycle of Narbondel. Let us remove our packs and rest while we may."

Dinin would have preferred to continue, just to keep his troops busy, but he did not dare speak against the priestess. The break did not prove a long one, though, for a couple of hours later, the cleric checked through the crack once more and announced that the time had come.

"You first," Dinin said to Drizzt. Drizzt looked at his brother incredulously, having no idea of how he could pass through such a tiny crack.

"Come," instructed the cleric, who now held a many-holed orb. "Walk past me and continue through."

As Drizzt passed the cleric, she spoke the orb's command word and held it over Drizzt's head. Black flakes, blacker than Drizzt's ebony skin, drifted over him, and he felt a tremendous shudder ripple across his spine.

The others looked on in amazement as Drizzt's body narrowed to the width of a hair and he became a two-dimensional image, a shadow of his former self.

Drizzt did not understand what was happening, but the crack suddenly widened before him. He slipped into it, found movement in his present form merely an enactment of will, and, drifted through the twists, turns, and bends of the tiny channel like a shadow on the broken face of a rocky cliff. He then was in a long cave, standing across from its single exit.

A moonless night had fallen, but even this seemed bright to the deep-dwelling drow. Drizzt felt himself pulled toward the exit, toward the surface world's openness. The other raiders began slipping through the crack and into the cavern then, one by one with the cleric coming in last. Drizzt was the first to feel the shudder as his body resumed its natural state. In a few moments, they all were eagerly checking their weapons.

"I will remain here," the cleric told Dinin. "Hunt well. The Spider Queen is watching."

Dinin warned his troops once again of the dangers of the surface, then he moved to the front of the cave, a small hole on the side of a rocky spur of a tall mountain. "For the Spider Queen," Dinin proclaimed. He took a steadying breath and led them through the exit, under the open sky.

Under the stars! While the others seemed nervous under those revealing lights, Drizzt found his gaze pulled heavenward to the countless points of mystical twinkling. Bathed in the starlight, he felt his heart lift and didn't even notice the joyful singing that rode on the night wind, so fitting it seemed.

Dinin heard the song, and he was experienced enough to recognize it as the eldritch calling of the surface elves. He crouched and surveyed the horizon, picking out the light of a single fire down in the distant expanse of a wooded valley. He nudged his troops to action—and pointedly nudged the wonderment from his brother's eyes—and started them off.

Drizzt could see the anxiety on his companions' faces, so contrasted by his own inexplicable sense of serenity. He suspected at once that something was very wrong with the whole situation. In his heart Drizzt had known from the minute he had stepped out of the tunnel that this was not the vile world the masters at the Academy had taken such pains to describe. He did feel unusual with no stone ceiling above him, but not uncomfortable. If the stars, calling to his heartstrings, were indeed reminders of what the next day might bring, as Master Hatch'net had said, then surely the next day would not be so terrible.

Only confusion dampened the feeling of freedom that Drizzt felt, for either he had somehow fallen into a trap of perception, or his companions, his brother included, viewed their surroundings through tainted eyes.

It fell on Drizzt as another unanswered burden: were his feelings of comfort here weakness or truth of heart?

"They are akin to the mushroom groves of our home," Dinin assured the others as they tentatively moved under the perimeter boughs of a small forest, "neither sentient nor harmful."

Still, the younger dark elves flinched and brought their weapons to the ready whenever a squirrel skipped across a branch overheard or an unseen bird called out to the night. The dark elves' was a silent world, far different from the chattering life of a springtime forest, and in the Underdark, nearly every living thing could, and most certainly would, try to harm anything invading its lair. Even a cricket's chirp sounded ominous to the alert ears of the drow.

Dinin's course was true, and soon the faerie song drowned out every other sound and the light of a fire became visible through the boughs. Surface elves were the most alert of the races, and a human—or even a sneaky halfling—would have had little chance of catching them unawares.

The raiders this night were drow, more skilled in stealth than the most proficient alley thief. Their footfalls went unheard, even across beds of dry, fallen leaves, and their crafted armor, shaped perfectly to the contours of their slender bodies, bent with their movements without a rustle. Unnoticed, they lined the perimeter of the small glade, where a score of faeries danced and sang.

Transfixed by the sheer joy of the elves' play, Drizzt hardly noticed the commands his brother issued then in the silent code. Several children danced among the gathering, marked only by the size of their bodies, and were no freer in spirit than the adults they accompanied. So innocent they all seemed, so full of life and wistfulness, and obviously bonded to each other by friendship more profound than Drizzt had ever known in Menzoberranzan. So unlike the stories Hatch'net had spun of them, tales of vile, hating wretches.

Drizzt sensed more than saw that his group was on the move, fanning out to gain a greater advantage. Still he did not take his eyes from the spectacle before him. Dinin tapped him on the shoulder and pointed to the small crossbow that hung from his belt, then slipped off into position in the brush off to the side.

Drizzt wanted to stop his brother and the others, wanted to make them wait and observe the surface elves that they were so quick to name enemies. Drizzt found his feet rooted to the earth and his tongue weighted heavily in the sudden dryness that had come into his mouth. He looked to Dinin and could only hope that his brother mistakenly thought his labored breaths the exaltations of battlelust.

Then Drizzt's keen ears heard the soft thrum of a dozen tiny bowstrings. The elven song carried on a moment longer, until several of the group dropped to the earth.

"No!" Drizzt screamed in protest, the words torn from his body by a profound rage even he did not understand. The denial sounded like just another war cry to the drow raiders, and before the surface elves could even begin to react, Dinin and the others were upon them.

Drizzt, too, leaped into the glade's lighted ring, his weapons in hand, though he had given no thought to his next move. He wanted only to stop the battle, to put an end to the scene unfolding before him.

Quite at ease in their woodland home, the surface elves weren't even armed. The drow warriors sliced through their ranks mercilessly, cutting them down and hacking at their bodies long after the light of life had flown from their eyes.

One terrified female, dodging this way and that, came before Drizzt. He dipped the tips of his weapons to the earth, searching for some way to give a measure of comfort.

The female then jerked straight as a sword dived into her back, its tip thrusting right through her slender form. Drizzt watched, mesmerized and horrified, as the drow warrior behind her grasped the weapon hilt in both hands and twisted it savagely. The female elf looked straight at Drizzt in the last fleeting seconds of her life, her eyes crying for mercy. Her voice was no more than the sickening gurgle of blood.

His face the exultation of ecstacy, the drow warrior tore his sword free and sliced it across, taking the head from the elven female's shoulders.

"Vengeance!" he cried at Drizzt, his face contorted in furious glee, his eyes burning with a light that shone demonic to the stunned Drizzt. The warrior hacked at the lifeless body one more time, then spun away in search of another kill.

Only a moment later, another elf, this one a young girl, broke free of the massacre and rushed in Drizzt's direction, screaming a single word over and over. Her cry was in the tongue of the surface elves, a dialect foreign to Drizzt, but when he looked upon her fair face, streaked with tears, he understood what she was saying. Her eyes were on the mutilated corpse at his feet; her anguish outweighed even the terror of her own impending doom. She could only be crying, "Mother!"

Rage, horror, anguish, and a dozen other emotions racked Drizzt at that horrible moment. He wanted to escape his feelings, to lose himself in the blind frenzy of his kin and accept the ugly reality. How easy it would have been to throw away the conscience that pained him so.

The elven child rushed up before Drizzt but hardly saw him, her gaze locked upon her dead mother, the back of the child's neck open to a single, clean blow. Drizzt raised his scimitar, unable to distinguish between mercy and murder.

"Yes, my brother!" Dinin cried out to him, a call that cut through his comrades," screams and whoops and echoed in Drizzt's ears like an accusation. Drizzt looked up to see Dinin, covered from head to foot in blood and standing amid a hacked cluster of dead elves.

"Today you know the glory it is to be a drow!" Dinin cried, and he punched a victorious fist into the air. "Today we appease the Spider Queen!"

Drizzt responded in kind, then snarled and reared back for a killing blow.

He almost did it. In his unfocused outrage, Drizzt Do'Urden almost became as his kin. He almost stole the life from that beautiful child's sparkling eyes.

At the last moment, she looked up at him, her eyes shining as a dark mirror into Drizzt's blackening heart. In that reflection, that reverse image of the rage that guided his hand, Drizzt Do'Urden found himself.

He brought the scimitar down in a mighty sweep, watching Dinin out of the corner of his eye as it whisked harmlessly past the child. In the same motion, Drizzt followed with his other hand, catching the girl by the front of her tunic and pulling her face-down to the ground.

She screamed, unharmed but terrified, and Drizzt saw Dinin thrust his fist into the air again and spin away.

Drizzt had to work quickly; the battle was almost at its gruesome end. He sliced his scimitars expertly above the huddled child's back, cuffing her clothing but not so much as scratching her tender skin. Then he used the blood of the headless corpse to mask the trick, taking grim satisfaction that the elven mother would be pleased to know that, in dying, she had saved the life of her daughter.

"Stay down," he whispered in the child's ear. Drizzt knew that she could not understand his language, but he tried to keep his tone comforting enough for her to guess at the deception. He could only hope he had done an adequate job a moment later, when Dinin and several others came over to him.

"Well done!" Dinin said exuberantly, trembling with sheer excitement. "A score of the orc-bait dead and not a one of us even injured! The matrons of Menzoberranzan will be pleased indeed, though we'll get no plunder from this pitiful lot!" He looked down at the pile at Drizzt's feet, then clapped his brother on the shoulder.

"Did they think they could get away?" Dinin roared.

Drizzt fought hard to sublimate his disgust, but Dinin was so entranced by the blood-bath that he wouldn't have noticed anyway.

"Not with you here!" Dinin continued. "Two kills for Drizzt!"

"One kill!" protested another, stepping beside Dinin. Drizzt set his hands firmly on the hilts of his weapons and gathered up his courage. If this approaching drow had guessed the deception, Drizzt would fight to save the elven child. He would kill his companions, even his brother, to save the little girl with the sparkling eyes—until he himself was slain. At least then Drizzt would not have to witness their slaughter of the child.

Luckily, the problem never came up. "Drizzt got the child," the drow said to Dinin, "but I got the elder female. I put my sword right through her back before your brother ever brought his scimitars to bear!"

It came as a reflex, an unconscious strike against the evil all about him. Drizzt didn't even realize the act as it happened, but a moment later, he saw the boasting drow lying on his back, clutching at his face and groaning in agony. Only then did Drizzt notice the burning pain in his hand, and he looked down to see his knuckles, and the scimitar hilt they clutched, spattered with blood.

"What are you about?" Dinin demanded.

Thinking quickly, Drizzt did not even reply to his brother. He looked past Dinin, to the squirming form on the ground, and transferred all the rage in his heart into a curse that the others would accept and respect. "If ever you steal a kill from me again," he spat, sincerity dripping from his false words, "I will replace the head lost from its shoulders with your own!"

Drizzt knew that the elven child at his feet, though doing her best, had begun a slight shudder of sobbing, and he decided not to press his luck. "Come, then," he growled. "Let us leave this place. The stench of the surface world fills my mouth with bile!"

He stormed away, and the others, laughing, picked up their dazed comrade and followed.

"Finally," Dinin whispered as he watched his brother's tense strides. "Finally you have learned what it is to be a drow warrior!"

Dinin, in his blindness, would never understand the irony of his words.

⚔ ⚔ ⚔ ⚔ ⚔

"We have one more duty before we return home," the cleric explained to the group when it reached the cave's entrance. She alone knew of the raid's second purpose. "The matrons of Menzoberranzan have bid us to witness the ultimate horror of the surface world, that we might warn our kindred."

Our kindred? Drizzt mused, his thoughts black with sarcasm. As far as he could see, the raiders had already witnessed the horror of the surface world: themselves!

"There!" Dinin cried, pointing to the eastern horizon.

The tiniest shading of light limned the dark outline of distant mountains. A surface dweller would not even have noticed it, but the dark elves saw it clearly, and all of them, even Drizzt, recoiled instinctively.

"It is beautiful," Drizzt dared to remark after taking a moment to consider the spectacle.

Dinin's glare came at him icy cold, but no colder than the look the cleric cast Drizzt's way. "Remove your cloaks and equipment, even your armor," she instructed the group. "Quickly. Place them within the shadows of the cave so that they will not be affected by the light."

When the task was completed, the cleric led them out into the growing light. "Watch," was her grim command.

The eastern sky assumed a hue of purplish pink, then pink altogether, its brightening causing the dark elves to squint uncomfortably. Drizzt wanted to deny the event, to put it into the same pile of anger that denied the master of Lore's words concerning the surface elves.

Then it happened; the top rim of the sun crested the eastern horizon. The surface world awakened to its warmth, its life-giving energy. Those same rays assaulted the drow elves' eyes with the fury of fire, tearing into orbs unaccustomed to such sights.

"Watch!" the cleric cried at them. "Witness the depth of the horror!"

One by one, the raiders cried out in pain and fell into the cave's darkness, until Drizzt stood alone beside the cleric in the growing daylight. Truly the light assaulted Drizzt as keenly as it had his kin, but he basked in it, accepting it as his purgatory, exposing him for all to view while its stinging fires cleansed his soul.

"Come," the cleric said to him at length, not understanding his actions. "We have borne witness. We may now return to our homeland."

"Homeland?" Drizzt replied, subdued.

"Menzoberranzan!" the cleric cried, thinking the male confused beyond reason. "Come, before the inferno burns the skin from your bones. Let our surface cousins suffer the flames, a fitting punishment for their evil hearts!"

Drizzt chuckled hopelessly. A fitting punishment? He wished that he could pluck a thousand such suns from the sky and set them in every chapel in Menzoberranzan, to shine eternally.

Then Drizzt could take the light no more. He scrambled dizzily back into the cave and donned his outfit. The cleric had the orb in hand, and Drizzt again was the first through the tiny crack. When all the group rejoined in the tunnel beyond, Drizzt took his position at the point and led them back into the descending path's deepening gloom—back down into the darkness of their existence.

21
MAY IT PLEASE
THE GODDESS

Did you please the goddess?" Matron Malice asked, her question as much a threat as an inquiry. At her side, the other females of House Do'Urden, Briza, Vierna, and Maya, looked on impassively, hiding their jealousy.

"Not a single drow was slain," Dinin replied, his voice thick with the sweetness of drow evil. "We cut them and slashed them!" He drooled as his recounting of the elven slaughter brought back the lust of the moment. "Bit them and ripped them!"

"What of you?" the matron mother interrupted, more concerned with the consequences to her own family's standing than with the raid's general success.

"Five," Dinin answered proudly. "I killed five, all of them females!"

The matron's smile thrilled Dinin. Then Malice scowled as she turned her gaze on Drizzt. "And him?" she inquired, not expecting to be pleased with the answer. Malice did not doubt her youngest son's prowess with weapons, but she had come to suspect that Drizzt had too much of Zaknafein's emotional makeup to ever be an attribute in such situations.

Dinin's smile confused her. He walked over to Drizzt and draped an arm comfortably across his brother's shoulders. "Drizzt got only one kill," Dinin began, "but it was a female child."

"Only one?" Malice growled.

From the shadows off to the side, Zaknafein listened in dismay. He wanted to shut out the elderboy Do'Urden's damning words, but they held Zak in their grip. Of all the evils Zak had ever encountered in Menzoberranzan, this surely had to be the most disappointing. Drizzt had killed a child.

"But the way he did it!" Dinin exclaimed. "He hacked her apart; sent all of Lolth's fury slicing into her twitching body! The Spider Queen must have treasured that kill above all the others."

"Only one," Matron Malice said again, her scowl hardly softening.

"He would have had two," Dinin continued. "Shar Nadal of House Maevret stole one from his blade—another female."

"Then Lolth will look with favor on House Maevret," Briza reasoned.

"No," Dinin replied. "Drizzt punished Shar Nadal for his actions. The son of House Maevret would not respond to the challenge."

The memory stuck in Drizzt's thoughts. He wished that Shar Nadal had come back at him, so he could have vented his rage more fully. Even that wish sent pangs of guilt coursing through Drizzt.

"Well done, my children," Malice beamed, now satisfied that both of them had acted properly in the raid. "The Spider Queen will look upon House Do'Urden with favor for this event. She will guide us to victory over this unknown house that seeks to destroy us."

⚔ ⚔ ⚔ ⚔ ⚔

Zaknafein left the audience hall with his eyes down and one hand nervously rubbing his sword's hilt. Zak remembered the time he had deceived Drizzt with the light bomb, when he had Drizzt defenseless and beaten. He could have spared the young innocent from his horrid fate. He could have killed Drizzt then and there, mercifully, and released him from the inevitable circumstances of life in Menzoberranzan.

Zak paused in the long corridor and turned back to watch the chamber. Drizzt and Dinin came out then, Drizzt casting Zak a single, accusatory look and pointedly turning away down a side passage.

The gaze cut through the weapons master. "So it has come to this,"

Zak murmured to himself. "The youngest warrior of House Do'Urden, so full of the hate that embodies our race, has learned to despise me for what I am."

Zak thought again of that moment in the training gym, that fateful second when Drizzt's life teetered on the edge of a poised sword. It indeed would have been a merciful act to kill Drizzt at that time.

With the sting of the young drow warrior's gaze still cutting so keenly into his heart, Zak couldn't decide whether the deed would have been more merciful to Drizzt or to himself.

✕ ✕ ✕ ✕ ✕

"Leave us," Matron SiNafay commanded as she swept into the small room lighted by a candle's glow. Alton gawked at the request; it was, after all, his personal room! Alton prudently reminded himself that SiNafay was the matron mother of the family, the absolute ruler of House Hun'ett. With a few awkward bows and apologies for his hesitation, he backed out of the room.

Masoj watched his mother cautiously as she waited for Alton to move away. From SiNafay's agitated tone, Masoj understood the significance of her visit. Had he done something to anger his mother? Or, more likely, had Alton? When SiNafay spun back on him, her face twisted in evil glee, Masoj realized that her agitation was really excitement.

"House Do'Urden has erred!" she snarled. "It has lost the Spider Queen's favor!"

"How?" Masoj replied. He knew that Dinin and Drizzt had returned from a successful raid, an assault that all of the city was talking about in tones of high praise.

"I do not know the details," Matron SiNafay replied, finding a measure of calmness in her voice. "One of them, perhaps one of the sons, did something to displease Lolth. This was told to me by a handmaiden of the Spider Queen. It must be true!"

"Matron Malice will work quickly to correct the situation," Masoj reasoned. "How long do we have?"

"Lolth's displeasure will not be revealed to Matron Malice," SiNafay replied. "Not soon. The Spider Queen knows all. She knows that we plan to attack House Do'Urden, and only an unfortunate accident will inform Matron Malice of her desperate situation before her house is crushed!

"We must move quickly," Matron SiNafay went on. "Within ten cycles of Narbondel, the first strike must fall! The full battle will begin soon after, before House Do'Urden can link its loss to our wrongdoing."

"What is to be their sudden loss?" Masoj prompted, thinking, hoping, he had already guessed the answer.

His mother's words were like sweet music to his ears. "Drizzt Do'Urden," she purred, "the favored son. Kill him."

Masoj rested back and clasped his slender fingers behind his head, considering the command.

"You will not fail me," SiNafay warned.

"I will not," Masoj assured her. "Drizzt, though young, is already a powerful foe. His brother, a former master of Melee-Magthere, is never far from his side." He looked up at his matron mother, his eyes gleaming. "May I kill the brother, too?"

"Be cautious, my son," SiNafay replied. "Drizzt Do'Urden is your target. Concentrate your efforts toward his death."

"As you command," Masoj replied, bowing low.

SiNafay liked the way her young son heeded to her desires without question. She started out of the room, confident in Masoj's ability to perform the task.

"If Dinin Do'Urden somehow gets in the way," she said, turning back to throw Masoj a gift for his obedience, "you may kill him, too."

Masoj's expression revealed too much eagerness for the second task.

"You will not fail me!" SiNafay said again, this time in an open threat that stole some of the wind out of Masoj's filling sails. "Drizzt Do'Urden must die within ten days!"

Masoj forced any distracting thoughts of Dinin out of his mind. "Drizzt must die," he whispered over and over, long after his mother had gone. He already knew how he wanted to do it. He only had to hope that the opportunity would come soon.

⚔ ⚔ ⚔ ⚔ ⚔

The awful memory of the surface raid followed Drizzt, haunted him, as he wandered the halls of Daermon N'a'shezbaernon. He had rushed from the audience chamber as soon as Matron Malice had dismissed him, and had slipped away from his brother at the first opportunity, wanting only to be alone.

The images remained: the broken sparkle in the young elven girl's eyes as she knelt over her murdered mother's corpse; the elven woman's horrified expression, twisting in agony as Shar Nadal ripped the life from her body. The surface elves were there in Drizzt's thoughts; he could not dismiss them. They walked beside Drizzt as he wandered, as real as they had been when Drizzt's raiding group had descended upon their joyful song.

Drizzt wondered if he would ever be alone again.

Eyes down, consumed by his empty sense of loss, Drizzt did not mark the path before him. He jumped back, startled, when he turned a corner and bumped into somebody.

He stood facing Zaknafein.

"You are home," the weapons master said absently, his blank face revealing none of the tumultuous emotions swirling through his mind.

Drizzt wondered if he could properly hide his own grimace. "For a day," he replied, equally nonchalant, though his rage with Zaknafein was no less intense. Now that Drizzt had witnessed the wrath of drow elves firsthand, Zak's reputed deeds rang out to Drizzt as even more evil. "My patrol group goes back out at Narbondel's first light."

"So soon?" asked Zak, genuinely surprised.

"We are summoned," Drizzt replied, starting past. Zak caught him by the arm.

"General patrol?" he asked.

"Focused," Drizzt replied. "Activity in the eastern tunnels."

"So the heroes are summoned," chuckled Zak.

Drizzt did not immediately respond. Was there sarcasm in Zak's voice? Jealousy, perhaps, that Drizzt and Dinin were allowed to go out to fight, while Zak had to remain within the House Do'Urden's confines to fulfill his role as the family's fighting instructor? Was Zak's hunger for blood so great that he could not accept the duties thrust upon them all? Zak had trained Drizzt and Dinin, had he not? And hundreds of others; he'd transformed them into living weapons, into murderers.

"How long will you be out?" Zak pressed, more interested in Drizzt's whereabouts.

Drizzt shrugged. "A tenday at the longest."

"And?"

"Home."

"That is good," said Zak. "I will be pleased to see you back within the walls of House Do'Urden." Drizzt didn't believe a word of it.

Zak then slapped him on the shoulder in a sudden, unexpected movement designed to test Drizzt's reflexes. More surprised than threatened, Drizzt accepted the pat without response, not sure of his uncle's intent.

"The gym, perhaps?" asked Zak. "You and I, as it once was."

Impossible! Drizzt wanted to shout. Never again would it be as it once was. Drizzt held those thoughts to himself and nodded his assent. "I would enjoy that," he replied, secretly wondering how much satisfaction he would gain by cutting Zaknafein down. Drizzt knew the truth of his people now, and knew that he was powerless to change anything. Maybe he could make a change in his private life, though. Maybe by destroying Zaknafein, his greatest disappointment, Drizzt could remove himself from the wrongness around him.

"As would I," Zak said, the friendliness of his tone hiding his private thoughts—thoughts identical to Drizzt's.

"In a tenday, then," Drizzt said, and he pulled away, unable to continue the encounter with the drow who once had been his dearest friend, and who, Drizzt had come to learn, was truly as devious and evil as the rest of his kin.

✕ ✕ ✕ ✕ ✕

"Please, my matron," Alton whimpered, "it is my right. I beg of you!"

"Rest easy, foolish DeVir," SiNafay replied, and there was pity in her voice, an emotion seldom felt and almost never revealed.

"I have waited—"

"The time is almost upon you," SiNafay countered, her tone growing more threatening. "You have tried for this one before."

Alton's grotesque gawk brought a smile to SiNafay's face.

"Yes," she said, "I know of your bungled attempt on Drizzt Do'Urden's life. If Masoj had not arrived, the young warrior would probably have slain you."

"I would have destroyed him!" Alton growled.

SiNafay did not argue the point. "Perhaps you would have won," she said, "only to be exposed as a murderous imposter, with the wrath of all of Menzoberranzan hanging over your head!"

"I did not care."

"You would have cared, I promise you!" Matron SiNafay sneered. "You would have forfeited your chance to claim a greater revenge. Trust in me, Alton DeVir. Your—our—victory is at hand."

"Masoj will kill Drizzt, and maybe Dinin," Alton grumbled.

"There are other Do'Urdens awaiting the fell hand of Alton DeVir," Matron SiNafay promised. "High priestesses."

Alton could not dismiss the disappointment he felt at not being allowed to go after Drizzt. He badly wanted to kill that one. Drizzt had brought him embarrassment that day in his chambers at Sorcere; the young drow should have died quickly and quietly. Alton wanted to make up for that mistake.

Alton also could not ignore the promise that Matron SiNafay had just made to him. The thought of killing one or more of the high priestesses of House Do'Urden did not displease him at all.

⚔ ⚔ ⚔ ⚔ ⚔

The pillowy softness of the plush bed, so different from the rest of the hard stone world of Menzoberranzan, offered Drizzt no relief from the pain. Another ghost had reared up to overwhelm even the images of carnage on the surface: the specter of Zaknafein.

Dinin and Vierna had told Drizzt the truth of the weapons master, of

Zak's role in the fall of House DeVir, and of how Zak so enjoyed slaughtering other drow—other drow who had done nothing to wrong him or deserve his wrath.

So Zaknafein, too, took part in this evil game of drow life, the endless quest to please the Spider Queen.

"As I so pleased her on the surface?" Drizzt couldn't help but mumble, the sarcasm of the spoken words bringing him some small measure of comfort.

The comfort Drizzt felt in saving the life of the elven child seemed such a minor act against the overwhelming wrongs his raiding group had exacted on her people. Matron Malice, his mother, had so enjoyed hearing the bloody recounting. Drizzt remembered the elven child's horror at the sight of her dead mother. Would he, or any dark elf, be so devastated if they looked upon such a sight. Unlikely, he thought. Drizzt hardly shared a loving bond with Malice, and most drow would be too engaged in measuring the consequences of their mother's death to their own station to feel any sense of loss.

Would Malice have cared if either Drizzt or Dinin had fallen in the raid? Again Drizzt knew the answer. All that Malice cared about was how the raid affected her own base of power. She had reveled in the notion that her children had pleased her evil goddess.

What favor would Lolth show to House Do'Urden if she knew the truth of Drizzt's actions? Drizzt had no way to measure how much, if any, interest the Spider Queen had taken in the raid. Lolth remained a mystery to him, one he had no desire to explore. Would she be enraged if she knew the truth of the raid? Or if she knew the truth of Drizzt's thoughts at this moment?

Drizzt shuddered to think of the punishments he might be bringing upon himself, but he had already firmly decided upon his course of action, whatever the consequences. He would return to House Do'Urden in a tenday. He would go then to the practice gym for a reunion with his old teacher.

He would kill Zaknafein in a tenday.

⚔ ⚔ ⚔ ⚔ ⚔

Caught up in the emotions of a dangerous and heartfelt decision, Zaknafein hardly heard the biting scrape as he ran the whetstone along his sword's gleaming edge.

The weapon had to be perfect, with no jags or burrs. This deed had to be executed without malice or anger.

A clean blow, and Zak would rid himself of the demons of his own failures, hide himself once again within the sanctuary of his private chambers, his secret world. A clean blow, and he would do what he should have done a decade before.

"If only I had found the strength then," he lamented. "How much grief might I have spared Drizzt? How much pain did his days at the Academy bring to him, that he is so very changed?" The words rang hollow in the empty room. They were just words, useless now, for Zak had already decided that Drizzt was out of reason's reach. Drizzt was a drow warrior, with all of the wicked connotations carried in such a title.

The choice was gone to Zaknafein if he wished to hold any pretense of value to his wretched existence. This time, he could not stay his sword. He had to kill Drizzt.

22

GNOMES, WICKED GNOMES

A mong the twists and turns of the tunnel mazes of the Underdark, slipping about their silent way, went the svirfnebli, the deep gnomes. Neither kind nor evil, and so out of place in this world of pervading wickedness, the deep gnomes survived and thrived. Haughty fighters, skilled in crafting weapons and armor, and more in tune to the songs of the stone than even the evil gray dwarves, the svirfnebli continued their business of plucking gems and precious metals in spite of the perils awaiting them at every turn.

When the news came back to Blingdenstone, the cluster of tunnels and caverns that composed the deep gnomes' city, that a rich vein of gemstones had been discovered twenty miles to the east—as the rockworm, the tho-qquu, burrowed   Burrow warden Belwar Dissengulp had to climb over a dozen others of his rank to be awarded the privilege of leading the mining expedition. Belwar and all of the others knew well that forty miles east—as the rockworm burrowed—would put the expedition dangerously close to Menzoberranzan, and that even getting there would mean a tenday of hiking, probably through the territories of a hundred other enemies. Fear was no measure against the love svirfnebli had for gems, though, and every day in the Underdark was a risk.

When Belwar and his forty miners arrived in the small cavern described by the advance scouts and inscribed with the gnomes' mark of treasure, they found that the claims had not been exaggerated. The burrow-warden took care not to get overly excited, though. He knew that twenty thousand drow elves, the svirfnebli's most hated and feared enemy, lived less than five miles away.

Escape tunnels became the first order of business, winding constructions high enough for a three-foot gnome but not for a taller pursuer. All along the course of these the gnomes placed breaker walls, designed to deflect a lightning bolt or offer some protection from the expanding flames of a fireball.

Then, when the true mining at last began, Belwar kept fully a third of his crew on guard at all times and walked the area of the work with one hand always clutching the magical emerald, the summoning stone, he kept on a chain around his neck.

⚔ ⚔ ⚔ ⚔ ⚔

"Three full patrol groups," Drizzt remarked to Dinin when they arrived at the open "field" on the eastern side of Menzoberranzan. Few stalagmites lined this region of the city, but it did not seem so open now, with dozens of anxious drow milling about.

"Gnomes are not to be taken lightly," Dinin replied. "They are wicked and powerful—"

"As wicked as surface elves?" Drizzt had to interrupt, covering his sarcasm with false exuberance.

"Almost," his brother warned grimly, missing the connotations of Drizzt's question. Dinin pointed off to the side, where a contingent of female drow was coming in to join the group. "Clerics," he said, "and one of them a high priestess. The rumors of activity must have been confirmed."

A shudder coursed through Drizzt, a tingle of prebattle excitement. That excitement was altered and lessened, though, by fear, not of physical harm, or even of the gnomes. Drizzt feared that this encounter might be a repeat of the surface tragedy.

He shook the black thoughts away and reminded himself that this time, unlike the surface expedition, his home was being invaded. The gnomes had crossed the boundaries of the drow realm. If they were as evil as Dinin and all the others claimed, Menzoberranzan had no choice but to respond with force. If.

Drizzt's patrol, the most celebrated group among the males, was selected to lead, and Drizzt, as always, took the point position. Still unsure, he wasn't thrilled with the assignment, and as they started out, Drizzt even contemplated leading the group astray. Or perhaps, Drizzt thought, he could contact the gnomes privately before the others arrived and warn them to flee.

Drizzt realized the absurdity of the notion. He couldn't stop the wheels of Menzoberranzan from turning along their designated course, and he couldn't do anything to hinder the two score drow warriors, excited and impatient, at his back. Again he was trapped and on the edge of despair.

Masoj Hun'ett appeared then and made everything better.

"Guenhwyvar!" the young wizard called, and the great panther came bounding. Masoj left the cat beside Drizzt and headed back toward his place in the line.

Guenhwyvar could no more hide its elation at seeing Drizzt than Drizzt could contain his own smile. With the interruption of the surface raid, and his time back home, he hadn't seen Guenhwyvar in more than a month. Guenhwyvar thumped against Drizzt's side as it passed, nearly knocking the slender drow from his feet. Drizzt responded with a heavy pat, vigorously rubbing a hand over the cat's ear.

They both turned back together, suddenly conscious of the unhappy glare boring into them. There stood Masoj, arms crossed over his chest and a visible scowl heating up his face.

"I shan't use the cat to kill Drizzt," the young wizard muttered to himself. "I want the pleasure for myself!"

Drizzt wondered if jealousy prompted that scowl. Jealousy of Drizzt and the cat, or of everything in general? Masoj had been left behind when Drizzt had gone to the surface. Masoj had been no more than a spectator when the victorious raiding party returned in glory. Drizzt backed away from Guenhwyvar, sensitive to the wizard's pain.

As soon as Masoj had moved away to take his position farther down the line, Drizzt dropped to one knee and threw a headlock on Guenhwyvar.

✕ ✕ ✕ ✕ ✕

Drizzt found himself even gladder for Guenhwyvar's companionship when they passed beyond the familiar tunnels of the normal patrol routes. It was a saying in Menzoberranzan that "no one is as alone as the point of a drow patrol," and Drizzt had come to understand this keenly in the last few months. He stopped at the far end of a wide way and held perfectly still, focusing his ears and eyes to the trails behind him. He knew that more than forty drow were approaching his position, fully arrayed for battle and agitated. Still, not a sound could Drizzt detect, and not a motion was discernible in the eerie shadows of cool stone. Drizzt looked down at Guenhwyvar, waiting patiently by his side, and started off again.

He could sense the hot presence of the war party at his back. That intangible sensation was the only thing that disproved Drizzt's feelings that he and Guenhwyvar were quite alone.

Near the end of that day, Drizzt heard the first signs of trouble. As he neared an intersection in the tunnel, cautiously pressed close to one wall, he felt a subtle vibration in the stone. It came again a second later, and then again, and Drizzt recognized it as the rhythmic tapping of a pick or hammer.

He took a magically heated sheet, a small square that fit into the palm of his hand, out of his pack. One side of the item was shielded in heavy leather, but the other shone brightly to eyes seeing in the infrared spectrum. Drizzt flashed it down the tunnel behind him, and a few seconds later Dinin came up to his side.

"Hammer," Drizzt signaled in the silent code, pointing to the wall. Dinin pressed against the stone and nodded in confirmation.

"Fifty yards?" Dinin's hand motions asked.

"Less than one hundred," Drizzt confirmed.

With his own prepared sheet, Dinin flashed the get-ready signal into the gloom behind him, then moved with Drizzt and Guenhwyvar around the intersection toward the tapping.

Only a moment later, Drizzt looked upon svirfnebli gnomes for the very first time. Two guards stood barely twenty feet away, chest-high to a drow and hairless, with skin strangely akin to the stone in both texture and heat radiations. The gnomes' eyes glowed brightly in the telltale red of infravision. One glance at those eyes reminded Drizzt and Dinin that deep gnomes were as much at home in the darkness as were the drow, and they both prudently ducked behind a rocky outcropping in the tunnel.

Dinin promptly signaled to the next drow in line, and so on, until the entire party was alerted. Then he crouched low and peeked out around the bottom of the outcropping. The tunnel continued another thirty feet beyond the gnome guards and around a slight bend, ending in some larger chamber. Dinin couldn't clearly see this area, but the glow of it, from the heat of the work and a cluster of bodies, spilled out into the corridor.

Again Dinin signaled back to his hidden comrades, and then he turned to Drizzt. "Stay here with the cat," he instructed, and he darted back down around the intersection to formulate plans with the other leaders.

Masoj, a few places back in the line, noted Dinin's movements and wondered if the opportunity to deal with Drizzt had suddenly come upon him. If the patrol was discovered with Drizzt all alone in front, was there some way Masoj could secretly blast the young Do'Urden? The opportunity, if ever it was truly there, passed quickly, though, as other drow soldiers came up beside the plotting wizard. Dinin soon returned from the back of the line and headed back to join his brother.

"The chamber has many exits," Dinin signaled to Drizzt when they were together. "The other patrols are moving into position around the gnomes."

"Might we parley with the gnomes?" Drizzt's hands asked in reply, almost subconsciously. He recognized the expression spreading across Dinin's face, but knew that he had already plunged in. "Send them away without conflict?"

Dinin grabbed Drizzt by the front of his *piwafwi* and pulled him close, too close, to that terrible scowl. "I will forget that you asked that question," he whispered, and he dropped Drizzt back to the stone, considering the issue closed.

"You start the fight," Dinin signaled. "When you see the sign from behind, darken the corridor and rush past the guards. Get to the gnome leader; he is the key to their strength with the stone."

Drizzt didn't fully understand what gnomish power his brother hinted at, but the instructions seemed simple enough, if somewhat suicidal.

"Take the cat if the cat will go," Dinin continued. "The entire patrol will be by your side in moments. The remaining groups will come in from the other passages."

Guenhwyvar nuzzled up to Drizzt, more than ready to follow him into battle. Drizzt took comfort in that when Dinin departed, leaving him alone again at the front. Only a few seconds later came the command to attack. Drizzt shook his head in disbelief when he saw the signal; how fast drow warriors found their positions!

He peeked around at the gnomish guards, still holding their silent vigil, completely unaware. Drizzt drew his blades and patted Guenhwyvar for luck, then called upon the innate magic of his race and dropped a globe of darkness in the corridor.

Squeals of alarm sounded throughout the tunnels, and Drizzt charged in, diving right into the darkness between the unseen guards and rolling back to his feet on the other side of his spell, only two running strides from the small chamber. He saw a dozen gnomes scrambling about, trying to prepare their defenses. Few of them paid Drizzt any attention, though, as the sounds of battle erupted from various side corridors.

One gnome chopped a heavy pick at Drizzt's shoulder. Drizzt got a blade up to block the blow but was amazed at the strength in the diminutive gnome's arms. Still, Drizzt could then have killed his attacker with the other scimitar. Too many doubts, and too many memories, though, haunted his actions. He brought a leg up into the gnome's belly, sending the little creature sprawling.

Belwar Dissengulp, next in line for Drizzt, noted how easily the young drow had dispatched one of his finest fighters and knew that the time had already come to use his most powerful magic. He pulled the emerald summoning stone from his neck and threw it to the ground at Drizzt's feet.

Drizzt jumped back, sensing the emanations of magic. Behind him, Drizzt heard the approach of his companions, overpowering the shocked gnome guards and rushing to join him in the chamber. Then Drizzt's attentions went squarely to the heat patterns of the stone floor in front of him. The grayish lines wavered and swam, as if the stone was somehow coming alive.

The other drow fighters roared in past Drizzt, bearing down on the gnome leader and his charges. Drizzt didn't follow, guessing that the event unfolding at his feet was more critical than the general battle now echoing throughout the complex.

Fifteen feet tall and seven wide, an angry, towering humanoid monster of living stone rose before Drizzt.

"Elemental!" came a scream to the side. Drizzt glanced over to see Masoj, Guenhwyvar at his side, fumbling through a spellbook, apparently in search of some dweomer to battle this unexpected monster. To Drizzt's dismay, the frightened wizard mumbled a couple of words and vanished.

Drizzt set his feet under him, and took a measure of the monster, ready to spring aside in an instant. He could sense the thing's power, the raw strength of the earth embodied in living arms and legs.

A lumbering arm swung out in a wide arc, whooshing above Drizzt's ducking head and slamming into the cavern wall, crushing rocks into dust.

"Do not let it hit me," Drizzt instructed himself in a whisper that came out as a disbelieving gasp. As the elemental recoiled its arm, Drizzt poked a scimitar at it, chipping away a small chunk, barely a scratch. The elemental grimaced in pain—apparently Drizzt could indeed hurt it with his enchanted weapons.

Still standing in the same spot off to the side, the invisible Masoj held his next spell in check, watching the spectacle and waiting for the combatants to weaken each other. Perhaps the elemental would destroy Drizzt altogether. Invisible shoulders gave a resigned shrug. Masoj decided to let the gnomish power do his dirty work for him.

The monster launched another blow, and another, and Drizzt dived forward and scrambled through the thing's stone pillar legs. The elemental reacted quickly and stomped heavily with one foot, barely missing the agile drow, and sending branching cracks in the floor for many feet in either direction.

Drizzt was up in a flash, slicing and thrusting with both his blades into the elemental's backside, then springing back out of reach as the monster swung about, leading with another ferocious blow.

The sounds of battle grew more distant. The gnomes had taken flight—those that were still alive—but the drow warriors were in full pursuit, leaving Drizzt to face the elemental.

The monster stomped again, the thunder of its foot nearly knocking Drizzt from his feet, and it came in hard, falling down at Drizzt, using the tonnage of its body as a weapon. If Drizzt had been even slightly surprised, or if his reflexes had not been honed to such perfection, he surely would have been crushed flat. He managed to get to the side of the monster's bulk, while taking only a glancing blow from a swinging arm.

Dust rushed up from the terrific impact; cavern walls and ceiling cracked and dropped flecks and stones to the floor. As the elemental regained its feet, Drizzt backed away, overwhelmed by such unconquerable strength.

He was all alone against it, or so Drizzt thought. A sudden ball of hot fury enveloped the elemental's head, claws raking deep scratches into its face.

"Guenhwyvar!" Drizzt and Masoj shouted in unison, Drizzt in elation that an ally had been found, and Masoj in rage. The wizard did not want Drizzt to survive this battle, and he dared not launch any magical attacks, at Drizzt or the elemental, with his precious Guenhwyvar in the way.

"Do something, wizard!" Drizzt cried, recognizing the shout and understanding now that Masoj was still around.

The elemental bellowed in pain, its cry sounding as the rumble of huge boulders crashing down a rocky mountain. Even as Drizzt moved back in to help his feline friend, the monster spun, impossibly quick, and dived headfirst to the floor.

"No!" Drizzt cried, realizing that Guenhwyvar would be crushed. Then the cat and the elemental, instead of slamming against the stone, sank down into it!

The purple flames of faerie fire outlined the figures of the gnomes, showing the way for drow arrows and swords. The gnomes countered with magic of their own, illusionists' tricks mostly. "Down here!" one drow soldier cried, only to slam face first into the stone of a wall that had appeared as the entrance to a corridor.

Even though the gnome magic managed to keep the dark elves somewhat confused, Belwar Dissengulp grew frightened. His elemental, his strongest magic and only hope, was taking too long with the single drow warrior far back in the main chamber. The burrow-warden wanted the monster by his side when the main combat began. He ordered his forces into tight defensive formations, hoping that they could hold out.

Then the drow warriors, detained no more by gnomish tricks, were upon them, and fury stole Belwar's fear. He lashed out with his heavy pickaxe, smiling grimly as he felt the mighty weapon bite into drow flesh.

All magic was aside now, all formations and carefully laid battle plans dissolved into the wild frenzy of the brawl. Nothing mattered, except to hit the enemy, to feel the pick head or blade sinking into flesh. Above all others, deep gnomes hated the drow, and in all the Underdark there was nothing a dark elf enjoyed more than slicing a svirfnebli into littler pieces.

✕ ✕ ✕ ✕ ✕

Drizzt rushed to the spot, but only the unbroken section of floor remained. "Masoj?" he gasped, looking for some answers from the one schooled in such strange magic.

Before the wizard could answer, the floor erupted behind Drizzt. He spun, weapons ready, to face the towering elemental.

Then Drizzt watched in helpless agony as the broken mist that was the great panther, his dearest companion, rolled off the elemental's shoulders and broke apart as it neared the floor.

Drizzt ducked another blow, though his eyes never left the dissipating dust-and-mist cloud. Was Guenhwyvar no more? Was his only friend gone from him forever? A new light grew in Drizzt lavender eyes, a primal rage that simmered throughout his body. He looked back to the elemental, unafraid.

"You are dead," he promised, and he walked in.

The elemental seemed confused, though of course it could not understand Drizzt's words. It dropped a heavy arm straight down to squash its foolish opponent. Drizzt did not even raise his blades to parry, knowing that every ounce of his strength could not possibly deflect such a blow. Just as the falling arm was about to reach him, he dashed forward, within its range.

The quickness of his move surprised the elemental, and the ensuing flurry of swordplay took Masoj's breath away. The wizard had never seen such grace in battle, such fluidity of motion. Drizzt climbed up and down the elemental's body, hacking and slashing, digging the points of his weapons home and flicking off pieces of the monster's stone skin.

The elemental howled its avalanche howl and spun in circles, trying to catch up to Drizzt and squash him once and for all. Blind anger brought new levels of expertise to the magnificent young swordsman, though, and the elemental caught nothing but air or its own stony body under its heavy slaps.

"Impossible," Masoj muttered when he found his breath. Could the young Do'Urden actually defeat an elemental? Masoj scanned the rest of the area. Several drow and many gnomes lay dead or grievously wounded, but the main fighting was moving even farther away as the gnomes found their tiny escape tunnels and the drow, enraged beyond good sense, followed them.

Guenhwyvar was gone. In this chamber, only Masoj, the elemental, and Drizzt remained as witnesses. The invisible wizard felt his mouth draw up in a smile. Now was the time to strike.

Drizzt had the elemental lurching to one side, nearly beaten, when the bolt roared in, a blast of lightning that blinded the young drow and sent him flying into the chamber's back wall. Drizzt watched the twitch of his hands, the wild dance of his stark white hair before his unmoving eyes. He felt nothing—no pain, no reviving draw of air into his lungs—and heard nothing, as if his life force had been some how suspended.

The attack dispelled Masoj's dweomer of invisibility, and he came back in view, laughing wickedly. The elemental, down in a broken, crumbled mass, slowly slipped back into the security of the stone floor.

"Are you dead?" the wizard asked Drizzt, the voice breaking the hush of Drizzt's deafness in dramatic booms. Drizzt could not answer, didn't really know the answer anyway. "Too easy," he heard Masoj say, and he suspected that the wizard was referring to him and not the elemental.

Then Drizzt felt a tingling in his fingers and bones and his lungs heaved suddenly, grabbing a volume of air. He gasped in rapid succession, then found control of his body and realized that he would survive.

Masoj glanced around for returning witnesses and saw none. "Good," he muttered as he watched Drizzt regain his senses. The wizard was truly glad that Drizzt's death had not been so very painless. He thought of another spell that would make the moment more fun.

A hand—a gigantic stone hand—reached out of the floor just then and grasped Masoj's leg, pulling his feet right into the stone.

The wizard's face twisted in a silent scream.

Drizzt's enemy saved his life. Drizzt snatched up one of the scimitars from the ground and hacked at the elemental's arm. The weapon sliced in, and the monster, its head reappearing between Drizzt and Masoj, howled in rage and pain and pulled the trapped wizard deeper into the stone.

With both hands on the scimitar's hilt, Drizzt struck as hard as he could, splitting the elemental's head right in half. This time the rubble did not sink back into its earthen plane; this time the elemental was destroyed.

"Get me out of here!" Masoj demanded. Drizzt looked at him, hardly believing that Masoj was still alive, for he was waist deep in solid stone.

"How?" Drizzt gasped. "You . . ." He couldn't even find the words to express his amazement.

"Just get me out!" the wizard cried.

Drizzt fumbled about, not knowing where to begin.

"Elementals travel between planes," Masoj explained, knowing that he had to calm Drizzt down if he ever wanted to get out of the floor. Masoj knew, too, that the conversation could go a long way in deflecting Drizzt's obvious suspicions that the lightning bolt had been aimed at him. "The ground an earth elemental traverses becomes a gate between the Plane of Earth and our plane, the Material Plane. The stone parted around me as the monster pulled me in, but it is quite uncomfortable." He twitched in pain as the stone tightened around one foot. "The gate is closing fast!"

"Then Guenhwyvar might be . . ." Drizzt started to reason.

He plucked the statuette right out of Masoj's front pocket and carefully inspected it for any flaws in its perfect design.

"Give me that!" Masoj demanded, embarrassed and angry.

Reluctantly, Drizzt handed the figurine over. Masoj glanced at it quickly and dropped it back into the pocket.

"Is Guenhwyvar unharmed?" Drizzt had to ask.

"It is not your concern," Masoj snapped back. The wizard, too, was worried about the cat, but at this moment, Guenhwyvar was the least of his troubles. "The gate is closing," he said again. "Go get the clerics!"

Before Drizzt could start off, a slab of stone in the wall behind him slid away, and the rock-hard fist of Belwar Dissengulp slammed into the back of his head.

23

A SINGLE CLEAN BLOW

The gnomes took him," Masoj said to Dinin when the patrol leader returned to the cavern. The wizard lifted his arms over his head to give the high priestess and her assistants a better view of his predicament.

"Where?" Dinin demanded. "Why did they let you live?"

Masoj shrugged. "A secret door," he explained, "somewhere on the wall behind you. I suspect that they would have taken me as well, except . . ." Masoj looked down at the floor, still holding him tightly up to the waist. "The gnomes would have killed me, but for your arrival."

"You are fortunate, wizard," the high priestess said to Masoj. "I have memorized a spell this day that will release the stone's hold on you." She whispered some instructions to her assistants and they took out water skins and pouches of clay and began tracing a ten foot square on the floor around the trapped wizard. The high priestess moved over to the wall of the chamber and prepared for her prayers.

"Some have escaped," Dinin said to her.

The high priestess understood. She whispered a quick detection spell and studied the wall. "Right there," she said. Dinin and another male rushed over to the spot and soon found the almost imperceptible outline to the secret door.

As the high priestess began her incantation, one of her cleric assistants

253

threw the end of a rope to Masoj. "Hold on," the assistant teased, "and hold your breath!"

"Wait—" Masoj began, but the stone floor all around him transformed into mud and the wizard slipped under.

Two clerics, laughing, pulled Masoj out a moment later.

"Nice spell," the wizard remarked, spitting mud.

"It has its purposes," replied the high priestess. "Especially when we fight against the gnomes and their tricks with the stone. I carried it as a safeguard against earth elementals." She looked at a piece of rubble at her feet, unmistakably one eye and the nose of such a creature. "I see that my spell was not needed in that manner."

"I destroyed that one," Masoj lied.

"Indeed," said the high priestess, unconvinced. She could tell by the cut of the rubble that a blade had made the wound. She let the issue drop when the scrape of sliding stone turned them all to the wall.

"A maze," moaned the fighter beside Dinin when he peered into the tunnel. "How will we find them?"

Dinin thought for a moment, then spun on Masoj. "They have my brother," he said, an idea coming to mind. "Where is your cat?"

"About," Masoj stalled, guessing Dinin's plan and not really wanting Drizzt rescued.

"Bring it to me," Dinin ordered. "The cat can smell Drizzt."

"I cannot . . . I mean," Masoj stuttered.

"Now, wizard!" Dinin commanded. "Unless you wish me to tell the ruling council that some of the gnomes escaped because you refused to help!"

Masoj tossed the figurine to the ground and called for Guenhwyvar, not really knowing what would happen next. Had the earth elemental really destroyed Guenhwyvar? The mist appeared, in seconds transforming into the panther's corporeal body.

"Well," Dinin prompted, indicating the tunnel.

"Go find Drizzt!" Masoj commanded the cat. Guenhwyvar sniffed around the area for a moment, then bounded off down the small tunnel, the drow patrol in silent pursuit.

⚔ ⚔ ⚔ ⚔ ⚔

"Where . . ." Drizzt started when he finally began the long climb from the depths of unconsciousness. He understood that he was sitting, and knew, too, that his hands were bound in front of him.

A small but undeniably strong hand caught him by the back of the hair and pulled his head back roughly.

"Quiet!" Belwar whispered harshly, and Drizzt was surprised that the creature could speak his language. Belwar let go of Drizzt and turned to join other svirfnebli.

From the chamber's low height and the gnomes' nervous movements, Drizzt realized that this group had taken flight.

The gnomes began a quiet conversation in their own tongue, which Drizzt could not begin to understand. One of them asked the gnome who had ordered Drizzt to be quiet, apparently the leader, a heated question. Another grunted his accord and spoke some harsh words, turning on Drizzt with a dangerous look in his eyes.

The leader slapped the other gnome hard on the back and sent him off through one of the two low exits in the chamber, then put the others into defensive positions. He walked over to Drizzt. "You come with us to Blingdenstone," he said in hesitant words.

"Then?" Drizzt asked.

Belwar shrugged. "The king'll decide. If you cause me no trouble, I'll tell him to let you go."

Drizzt laughed cynically.

"Well, then," said Belwar, "if the king says to kill you, I'll make sure it comes in a single clean blow."

Again Drizzt laughed. "Do you believe that I believe?" he asked. "Torture me now and have your fun. That is your evil way!"

Belwar started to slap him but held his hand in check. "Svirfnebli don't torture!" he declared, louder than he should have. "Drow elves torture!" He turned away but spun back, reiterating his promise. "A single clean blow."

Drizzt found that he believed the sincerity in the gnome's voice, and he had to accept that promise as a measure of mercy far greater than the gnome would have received if Dinin's patrol had captured him. Belwar turned to walk away, but Drizzt, intrigued, had to learn more of the curious creature.

"How have you learned my language?" he asked.

"Gnomes are not stupid," Belwar retorted, unsure of what Drizzt was leading to.

"Nor are drow," Drizzt replied earnestly, "but I have never heard the language of the svirfnebli spoken in my city."

"There once was a drow in Blingdenstone," Belwar explained, now nearly as curious about Drizzt as Drizzt was about him.

"Slave," Drizzt reasoned.

"Guest!" Belwar snapped. "Svirfnebli keep no slaves!"

Again Drizzt found that he could not refute the sincerity in Belwar's voice. "What is your name?" he asked.

The gnome laughed at him. "Do you think me stupid?" Belwar asked. "You desire my name that you might use its power in some dark magic against me!"

"No," Drizzt protested.

"I should kill you now for thinking me stupid!" Belwar growled, ominously lifting his heavy pick. Drizzt shifted uncomfortably, not knowing what the gnome would do next.

"My offer remains," Belwar said, lowering the pick. "No trouble, and I tell the king to let you go." Belwar didn't believe that would happen any more than did Drizzt, so the svirfneblin, with a helpless shrug, offered Drizzt the next best thing. "Or else, a single clean blow."

A commotion from one of the tunnels turned Belwar away. "Belwar," called one of the other gnomes, rushing back into the small chamber. The gnome leader turned a wary eye on Drizzt to see if the drow had caught the mention of his name.

Drizzt wisely kept his head turned away, pretending not to listen. He had indeed heard the name of the gnome leader who had shown him mercy. Belwar, the other svirfneblin had said. Belwar, a name that Drizzt would never forget.

Fighting from down the passageway caught everyone's attention, then, and several svirfnebli scrambled back into the chamber. Drizzt knew from their excitement that the drow patrol was close behind.

Belwar started barking out commands, mostly organizing the retreat down the chamber's other tunnel. Drizzt wondered where he would fit into the gnome's thinking. Certainly Belwar couldn't hope to outrun the drow patrol dragging along a prisoner.

Then the gnome leader suddenly stopped talking and stopped moving. Too suddenly.

The drow clerics had led the way in with their insidious, paralyzing spells. Belwar and another gnome were held fast by the dweomer, and the rest of the gnomes, realizing this, broke into a wild scramble for the rear exit.

The drow warriors, Guenhwyvar leading the way, charged into the room. Any relief Drizzt might have felt at seeing his feline friend unharmed was buried under the ensuing slaughter. Dinin and his troops cut into the disorganized gnomes with typical drow savagery.

In seconds—horrible seconds that seemed like hours to Drizzt—only Belwar and the other gnome caught in the clerical spell remained alive in the chamber. Several of the svirfnebli had managed to flee down the back corridor, but most of the drow patrol was off in pursuit.

Masoj came into the chamber last, looking thoroughly wretched in his mud-covered clothing. He remained at the tunnel exit and did not even look Drizzt's way, except to note that his panther was standing protectively beside the secondboy of House Do'Urden.

"Again you have found your measure of luck, and more," Dinin said to Drizzt as he cut his brother's bonds.

Looking around at the carnage in the chamber, Drizzt wasn't so sure.

Dinin handed him back his scimitars, then turned to the drow standing watch over the two paralyzed gnomes. "Finish them," Dinin instructed.

A wide smile spread over the other drow's face, and he pulled a jagged knife from his belt. He held it up in front of a gnome's face, teasing the helpless creature. "Can they see it?" he asked the high priestess.

"That is the fun of the spell," the high priestess replied. "The svirfneblin understands what is about to happen. Even now he is struggling to break out of the hold."

"Prisoners!" Drizzt blurted.

Dinin and the others turned to him, the drow with the dagger wearing a scowl both angry and disappointed.

"For House Do'Urden?" Drizzt asked Dinin hopefully. "We could benefit from—"

"Svirfnebli do not make good slaves," Dinin replied.

"No," agreed the high priestess, moving beside the dagger-wielding fighter. She nodded to the warrior and his smile returned tenfold. He struck hard. Only Belwar remained.

The warrior waved his bloodstained dagger ominously and moved in front of the gnome leader.

"Not that one!" Drizzt protested, unable to bear anymore. "Let him live!" Drizzt wanted to say that Belwar could do them no harm, and that killing the defenseless gnome would be a cowardly and vile act. Drizzt knew that appealing to his kin for mercy would be a waste of time.

Dinin's expression was more a look of anger than curiosity this time.

"If you kill him, then no gnomes will remain to return to their city and tell of our strength," Drizzt reasoned, grasping at the one slim hope he could find. "We should send him back to his people, send him back to tell them of their folly in entering the domain of the drow!"

Dinin looked back to the high priestess for advice.

"It seems proper reasoning," she said with a nod.

Dinin was not so certain of his brother's motives. Not taking his eyes off Drizzt, he said to the warrior, "Then cut off the gnome's hands."

Drizzt didn't flinch, realizing that if he did, Dinin would surely slaughter Belwar.

The warrior replaced the dagger on his belt and took out his heavy sword.

"Wait," said Dinin, still eyeing Drizzt. "Release him from the spell first; I want to hear his screams."

Several drow moved over to put the tips of their swords at Belwar's neck as the high priestess released her magical hold. Belwar made no moves.

The appointed drow warrior grasped his sword in both hands, and Belwar, brave Belwar, held his arms straight out and motionless in front of him.

Drizzt averted his gaze, unable to watch and awaiting, fearing, the gnome's cry.

Belwar noted Drizzt's reaction. Was it compassion?

The drow warrior then swung his sword. Belwar never took his stare off Drizzt as the sword cut across his wrists, lighting a million fires of agony in his arms.

Neither did Belwar scream. He wouldn't give Dinin the satisfaction. The gnome leader looked back to Drizzt one final time as two drow fighters ushered him out of the chamber, and he recognized the true anguish, and the apology, behind the young drow's feigned impassive facade.

Even as Belwar was leaving, the dark elves who had chased off after the fleeing gnomes returned from the other tunnel. "We could not catch them in these tiny passage ways," one of them complained.

"Damn!" Dinin growled. Sending a handless gnome victim back to Blingdenstone was one thing, but letting healthy members of the gnome expedition escape was quite an other. "I want them caught!"

"Guenhwyvar can catch them," Masoj proclaimed, then he called the cat to his side and eyed Drizzt all the while.

Drizzt's heart raced as the wizard patted the great cat.

"Come, my pet," Masoj said. "There is hunting left to be done!" The wizard watched Drizzt squirm at the words, knowing that Drizzt did not approve of Guenhwyvar engaging in such tactics.

"They are gone?" Drizzt asked Dinin, his voice on the edge of desperation.

"Running all the way back to Blingdenstone," Dinin replied calmly. "If we let them."

"And will they return?"

Dinin's sour scowl reflected the absurdity of his brother's question. "Would you?"

"Our task is complete, then," Drizzt reasoned, trying vainly to find some way out of Masoj's ignoble designs for the panther.

"We have won the day," Dinin agreed, "though our own losses have been great. We may find still more fun, with the help of the wizard's pet."

"Fun," Masoj echoed pointedly at Drizzt. "Be gone, Guenhwyvar, into the tunnels. Let us learn how fast a frightened gnome may run!"

Only a few minutes later, Guenhwyvar came back into the chamber, dragging a dead gnome in its mouth.

"Return!" Masoj commanded as Guenhwyvar dropped the body at his feet. "Bring me more!"

Drizzt's heart dropped at the sound of the corpse flopping to the stone floor. He looked into Guenhwyvar's eyes and saw a sadness as profound as his own. The panther was a hunter, as honorable in its own way as was Drizzt. To the evil Masoj, though, Guenhwyvar was a toy and nothing more, an instrument for his perverted pleasures, killing for no reason other than his master's joy of killing.

In the hands of the wizard, Guenhwyvar was no more than a murderer.

Guenhwyvar paused at the entrance to the small tunnel and looked to Drizzt almost apologetically.

"Return!" Masoj screamed, and he kicked the cat in the rear. Then Masoj, too, turned an eye back on Drizzt, a vindictive eye. Masoj had missed his chance to kill the young Do'Urden; he would have to be careful how he explained such a mistake to his unforgiving mother. Masoj decided to worry about that unpleasant encounter later. For now, at least, he had the satisfaction of watching Drizzt suffer.

Dinin and the others were oblivious to the unfolding drama between Masoj and Drizzt; too engaged in their wait for Guenhwyvar's return; too engaged in their speculations of the expressions of terror the gnomes would cast back at such a perfect killer; too caught up in the macabre humor of the moment, that perverted drow humor that brought laughter when tears were needed.

PART FIVE

Zaknafein Do'Urden: mentor, teacher, friend. I, in the blind agony of my own frustrations, more than once came to recognize Zaknafein as none of these. Did I ask of him more than he could give? Did I expect perfection of a tormented soul; hold Zaknafein up to standards beyond his experiences, or standards impossible in the face of his experiences?

ZAKNAFEIN

I might have been him. I might have lived, trapped within the helpless rage, buried under the daily assault of the wickedness that is Menzoberranzan and the pervading evil that is my own family, never in life to find escape.

It seems a logical assumption that we learn from the mistakes of our elders. This, I believe, was my salvation. Without the example of Zaknafein, I, too, would have found no escape—not in life.

Is this course I have chosen a better way than

the life Zaknafein knew? I think, yes, though I find despair often enough sometimes to long for that other way. It would have been easier. Truth, though, is nothing in the face of self-falsehood, and principles are of no value if the idealist cannot live up to his own standards.

This, then, is a better way.

I live with many laments, for my people, for myself, but mostly for that weapons master, lost to me now, who showed me how—and why—to use a blade.

There is no pain greater than this; not the cut of a jagged-edged dagger nor the fire of a dragon's breath. Nothing burns in your heart like the emptiness of losing something, some-one, before you truly have learned of its value. Often now I lift my cup in a futile toast, an apology to ears that cannot hear:

To Zak, the one who inspired my courage.

—Drizzt Do'Urden

24
To Know Our Enemies

"Eight drow dead, and one a cleric," Briza said to Matron Malice on the balcony of House Do'Urden. Briza had rushed back to the compound with the first reports of the encounter, leaving her sisters at the central plaza of Menzoberranzan with the gathered throng, awaiting further information. "But nearly two score of the gnomes died, a clear victory."

"What of your brothers?" asked Malice. "How did House Do'Urden fare in this encounter?"

"As with the surface elves, Dinin's hand slew five," replied Briza. "They say that he led the main assault fearlessly, and he killed the most gnomes."

Matron Malice beamed with the news, though she suspected that Briza, standing patiently behind a smug smile, was holding something dramatic back from her. "What of Drizzt?" the matron demanded, having no patience for her daughter's games. "How many svirfnebli fell at his feet?"

"None," Briza replied, but still the smile remained. "Still the day belonged to Drizzt!" she added quickly, seeing an angry scowl spreading across her volatile mother's face. Malice did not seem amused.

"Drizzt defeated an earth elemental," Briza cried, "all alone, almost, with only minor help from a wizard! The high priestess of the patrol named the kill his!"

Matron Malice gasped and turned away. Drizzt had ever been an enigma to her, as fine with the blade as any but lacking the proper attitude and the proper respect. Now this: an earth elemental! Malice herself had seen such a monster ravage an entire drow raiding party, killing a dozen seasoned warriors before wandering off on its way. Yet her son, her confusing son, had defeated one single-handedly!

"Lolth will favor us this day," Briza commented, not quite understanding her mother's reaction.

Briza's words struck an idea in Malice. "Gather your sisters," she commanded. "We shall meet in the chapel. If House Do'Urden so fully won the day out in the tunnels, perhaps the Spider Queen will grace us with some information."

"Vierna and Maya await the forthcoming news in the city plaza," Briza explained, mistakenly believing her mother to be referring to information about the battle. "Surely we will know the entire story within an hour."

"I care nothing for a battle against gnomes!" Malice scolded. "You have told everything that is important to our family; the rest does not matter. We must parlay your brothers' heroics into gain."

"To learn of our enemies!" Briza blurted as she realized what her mother had in mind.

"Exactly," replied Malice. "To learn which house it is that threatens House Do'Urden. If the Spider Queen truly finds favor with us this day, she may grace us with the knowledge we need to defeat our enemies!"

A short while later, the four high priestesses of House Do'Urden gathered around the spider idol in the chapel anteroom. Before them, in a bowl of the deepest onyx, burned the sacred incense—sweet, deathlike, and favored by the yochlol, the handmaidens of Lolth.

The flame moved through a variety of colors, from orange to green to brilliant red. It then took shape, heard the beckons of the four priestesses and the urgency in the voice of Matron Malice. The top of the fire, no longer dancing, smoothed and rounded, assumed the form of a hairless head, then stretched upward, growing. The flame disappeared, consumed by the yochlol's image, a half melted pile of wax with grotesquely elongated eyes and a drooping mouth.

"Who has summoned me?" the small figure demanded telepathically.

The yochlol's thoughts, too powerful for its diminutive stature, boomed within the heads of the gathered drow.

"I have, handmaiden," Malice replied aloud, wanting her daughters to hear. The matron bowed her head. "I am Malice, loyal servant of the Spider Queen."

In a puff of smoke, the yochlol disappeared, leaving only glowing incense embers in the onyx bowl. A moment later, the handmaiden reappeared, full size, standing behind Matron Malice. Briza, Vierna, and Maya held their breath as the being laid two sickly tentacles on their mother's shoulders.

Matron Malice accepted the tentacles without reply, confident in her cause for summoning the yochlol.

"Explain to me why you dare to disturb me," came the yochlol's insidious thoughts.

"To ask a simple question," Malice replied silently, for no words were necessary to communicate with a handmaiden. "One whose answer you know."

"Does this question interest you so greatly?" the yochlol asked. "You risk such dire consequences."

"It is imperative that I learn the answer," replied Matron Malice. Her three daughters watched curiously, hearing the yochlol's thoughts but only guessing at their mother's unspoken replies.

"If the answer is so important, and it is known to the handmaidens, and thus to the Spider Queen, do you not believe that Lolth would have given it to you if she so chose?"

"Perhaps, before this day, the Spider Queen did not deem me worthy to know," Malice responded. "Things have changed."

The handmaiden paused and rolled its elongated eyes back into its head as if communicating with some distant plane.

"Greetings, Matron Malice Do'Urden," the yochlol said aloud after a few tense moments. The creature's spoken voice was calm and overly smooth for the thing's grotesque appearance.

"My greetings to you, and to your mistress, Queen of Spiders," replied Malice. She shot a wry smile at her daughters and still didn't turn to face the creature behind her. Apparently Malice's guess of Lolth's favor had been correct.

"Daermon N'a'shezbaernon has pleased Lolth," the handmaiden said. "The males of your house have won the day, even above the females that journeyed with them. I must accept Matron Malice Do'Urden's summons." The tentacles slid off Malice's shoulders, and the yochlol stood rigid behind her, awaiting her commands.

"Glad I am to please the Spider Queen," Malice began. She sought the proper way to phrase her question. "For the summons, as I have said, I beg only the answer to a simple question."

"Ask it," prompted the yochlol, and the mocking tone told Malice and her daughters that the monster already knew the question.

"My house is threatened, say the rumors," said Malice.

"Rumors?" The yochlol laughed an evil, grating sound.

"I trust in my sources," Malice replied defensively. "I would not have called upon you if I did not believe the threat."

"Continue," said the yochlol, amused by the whole affair. "They are more than rumors, Matron Malice Do'Urden. Another house plans war upon you."

Maya's immature gasp brought scornful eyes upon her from her mother and her sisters.

"Name this house to me," Malice pleaded. "If Daermon N'a'shezbaernon truly has pleased the Spider Queen this day, then I bid Lolth to reveal our enemies, that we might destroy them!"

"And if this other house also has pleased the Spider Queen?" the handmaiden mused. "Would Lolth then betray it to you?"

"Our enemies hold every advantage," Malice protested. "They know of House Do'Urden. No doubt they watch us every day, laying their plans. We ask Lolth only to give us knowledge equal to that of our enemies. Reveal them and let us prove which house is more worthy of victory."

"What if your enemies are greater than you?" asked the handmaiden. "Would Matron Malice Do'Urden then call upon Lolth to intervene and save her pitiful house?"

"No!" cried Malice. "We would call upon those powers that Lolth has given us to fight our foes. Even if our enemies are the more powerful, let Lolth be assured that they will suffer great pain for their attack on House Do'Urden!"

Again the handmaiden sank back within itself, finding the link to its home plane, a place darker than Menzoberranzan. Malice clenched tightly to Briza's hand, to her right, and Vierna's, to her left. They in turn passed along the confirmation of their bond to Maya, at the foot of the circle.

"The Spider Queen is pleased, Matron Malice Do'Urden," the hand-maiden said at length. "Trust that she will favor House Do'Urden more than your enemies when battle rings out—perhaps . . ." Malice flinched at the ambiguity of that final word, grudgingly accepting that Lolth never made any promises, at any time.

"What of my question," Malice dared to protest, "the reason for the summons?"

There came a bright flash that stole the four clerics' vision. When their eyesight returned to them, they saw the yochlol, tiny again, and glaring out at them from the flames of the onyx bowl.

"The Spider Queen does not give an answer that is already known!" The handmaiden proclaimed, the sheer power of its otherworldly voice cutting into the drow ears. The fire erupted in another blinding flash, and the yochlol disappeared, leaving the precious bowl sundered into a dozen pieces.

Matron Malice grabbed a large piece of the shattered onyx and threw it against a wall. "Already known?" she cried in rage. "Known to whom? Who in my family keeps this secret from me?"

"Perhaps the one who knows does not know that she knows," Briza put in, trying to calm her mother. "Or perhaps the information is newly found, and she has not yet had the chance to come to you with it."

"She?" growled Matron Malice. "What 'she' do you speak of, Briza? We are all here. Are any of my daughters stupid enough to miss such an obvious threat to our family?"

"No, Matron!" Vierna and Maya cried together, terrified of Malice's growing wrath, rising beyond control.

"Never have I seen any sign!" said Vierna.

"Nor l! " added Maya. "By your side I have been these many tendays, and I have seen no more than you!"

"Are you implying that I have missed something?" Malice growled, her knuckles white at her sides.

"No, Matron!" Briza shouted above the commotion, loud enough to settle her mother for the moment and turn Malice's attention fully upon her eldest daughter.

"Not she, then," Briza reasoned. "He. One of your sons may have the answer, or Zaknafein or Rizzen, perhaps."

"Yes," agreed Vierna. "They are only males, too stupid to understand the importance of minor details."

"Drizzt and Dinin have been out of the house," added Briza, "out of the city. In their patrol group are children of every powerful house, every house that would dare to threaten us!"

The fires in Malice's eyes glowed, but she relaxed at the reasoning. "Bring them to me when they return to Menzoberranzan," she instructed Vierna and Maya. "You," she said to Briza, "bring Rizzen and Zaknafein. All the family must be present, so that we may learn what we may learn!"

"The cousins, and the soldiers, too?" asked Briza. "Perhaps one beyond the immediate family knows the answer."

"Should we bring them together, as well?" offered Vierna, her voice edged with the rising excitement of the moment. "A gathering of the whole clan, a general war party of House Do'Urden?"

"No," Malice replied, "not the soldiers or the cousins. I do not believe they are involved in this; the handmaiden would have told us the answer if one of my direct family did not know it. It is my embarrassment to ask a question whose answer should be known to me, whose answer someone within the circle of my family knows." She gritted her teeth as she spat out the rest of her thoughts.

"I do not enjoy being embarrassed!"

⚔ ⚔ ⚔ ⚔ ⚔

Drizzt and Dinin came into the house a short while later, exhausted and glad the adventure was over. They had barely passed the entrance and turned down the wide corridor that led to their rooms when they bumped into Zaknafein, coming the other way.

"So the hero has returned," Zak remarked, eyeing Drizzt directly. Drizzt did not miss the sarcasm in his voice.

"We've completed our job—successfully," Dinin shot back, more than a little perturbed at being excluded from Zak's greeting. "I led—"

"I know of the battle," Zak assured him. "It has been endlessly recounted throughout the city. Now leave us, Elderboy. I have unfinished business with your brother."

"I leave when I choose to leave!" Dinin growled.

Zak snapped a glare upon him. "I wish to speak to Drizzt, only to Drizzt, so leave."

Dinin's hand went to his sword hilt, not a smart move. Before he even moved the weapon hilt an inch from the scabbard, Zak had slapped him twice in the face with one hand. The other had somehow produced a dagger and put its tip at Dinin's throat.

Drizzt watched in amazement, certain that Zak would kill Dinin if this continued.

"Leave," Zak said again, "on your life."

Dinin threw his hands up and slowly backed away. "Matron Malice will hear of this!" he warned.

"I will tell her myself," Zak laughed at him. "Do you think she will trouble herself on your behalf, fool? As far as Matron Malice cares, the family males determine their own hierarchy. Go away, Elderboy. Come back when you have found the courage to challenge me."

"Come with me, brother," Dinin said to Drizzt.

"We have business," Zak reminded Drizzt.

Drizzt looked to both of them, once and back again, stunned by their open willingness to kill each other. "I will stay," he decided. "I do indeed have unfinished business with the weapons master."

"As you choose, hero," Dinin spat, and he turned on his heel and stormed away.

"You have made an enemy," Drizzt remarked to Zak.

"I have made many," Zak laughed, "and I will make many more before my day ends! But no mind. Your actions have inspired jealousy in your brother—your older brother. You are the one who should be wary."

"He hates you openly," reasoned Drizzt.

"But would gain nothing from my death," Zak replied. "I am no threat to Dinin, but you . . ." He let the word hang in the air.

"Why would I threaten him?" Drizzt protested. "Dinin has nothing I desire."

"He has power," Zak explained. "He is the elderboy now but was not always."

"He killed Nalfein, the brother I never met."

"You know of this?" said Zak. "Perhaps Dinin suspects that another secondboy will follow the same course he took to become the elderboy of House Do'Urden."

"Enough," Drizzt growled, tired of the whole stupid system of ascension. How well you know it, Zaknafein, he thought. How many did you murder to attain your position?

"An earth elemental," Zak said, blowing a low whistle with the words. "It is a powerful foe that you defeated this day." He bowed low, showing Drizzt mockery beyond any doubt. "What is next for the young hero? A daemon, perhaps? A demigod? Surely there is nothing that can—"

"Never have I heard such senseless words stream from your mouth," Drizzt retorted. Now it was time for some sarcasm of his own. "Is it that I have inspired jealousy in another besides my brother?"

"Jealousy?" Zak cried. "Wipe your nose, sniveling little boy! A dozen earth elementals have fallen to my blade! Daemons, too! Do not overestimate your deeds or your abilities. You are one warrior among a race of warriors. To forget that surely will prove fatal." He ended the line with pointed emphasis, almost in a sneer, and Drizzt began to consider again just how real their appointed "practice" in the gym would become.

"I know my abilities," Drizzt replied, "and my limitations. I have learned to survive."

"As have I," Zak shot back, "for so many centuries!"

"The gym awaits," Drizzt said calmly.

"Your mother awaits," Zak corrected. "She bids us all to the chapel. Fear not, though. There will be time for our meeting."

Drizzt walked past Zak without another word, suspecting that his and Zak's blades would finish the conversation for them. What had become of Zaknafein? Drizzt wondered. Was this the same teacher who had trained him those years before the Academy? Drizzt could not sort through his feelings. Was he seeing Zak differently because of the things he had learned of Zak's exploits, or was there truly something different, something harder, about the weapons master's demeanor since Drizzt had returned from the Academy?

The sound of a whip brought Drizzt from his contemplations.

"I am your patron!" he heard Rizzen say.

"That's of no consequence!" retorted a female voice, the voice of Briza. Drizzt slipped to the corner of the next intersection and peeked around. Briza and Rizzen faced off, Rizzen unarmed, but Briza holding her snake-headed whip.

"Patron," Briza laughed, "a meaningless title. You are a male lending your seed to the matron and of no more importance."

"Four I have sired," Rizzen said indignantly.

"Three!" Briza corrected, snapping the whip to accentuate the point. "Vierna is Zaknafein's, not yours! Nalfein is dead, leaving only two. One of those is female and above you. Only Dinin is truly under your rank!"

Drizzt sank back against the wall and looked behind him to the empty corridor he had just walked. He had always suspected that Rizzen was not his true father. The male had never paid him any mind, had never scolded him or praised him or offered to him any advice or training. To hear Briza say it, though, . . . and Rizzen not deny it!

Rizzen fumbled about for some retort to Briza's stinging words. "Does Matron Malice know of your desires?" he snarled. "Does she know that her eldest daughter seeks her title?"

"Every eldest daughter seeks the title of matron mother," Briza laughed at him. "Matron Malice would be a fool to suspect otherwise. I assure you that she is not, nor am I. I will get the title from her when she is weak with age. She knows and accepts this as fact."

"You admit that you will kill her?"

"If not I, then Vierna. If not Vierna, then Maya. It is our way, stupid male. It is the word of Lolth."

Rage burned in Drizzt as he heard the evil proclamations, but he remained silent at the corner.

"Briza will not wait for age to steal her mother's power," Rizzen snarled, "not when a dagger will expedite the transfer. Briza hungers for the throne of the house!"

Rizzen's next words came out as an indecipherable scream as the six-headed whip went to work again and again.

Drizzt wanted to intervene, to rush out and cut them both down, but, of course, he could not. Briza acted now as she had been taught, followed the words of the Spider Queen in asserting her dominance over Rizzen. She wouldn't kill him, Drizzt knew.

But what if Briza got carried away in the frenzy? What if she did kill Rizzen? In the empty void that was beginning to grow in his heart, Drizzt wondered if he even cared.

⚔ ⚔ ⚔ ⚔ ⚔

"You let him escape!" Matron SiNafay roared at her son. "You will learn not to disappoint me!"

"No, my matron!" Masoj protested. "I hit him squarely with a lightning bolt. He never even suspected the blow to be aimed at him! I could not finish the deed; the monster had me caught in the gate to its own plane!"

SiNafay bit her lip, forced to accept her son's reasoning. She knew that she had given Masoj a difficult mission. Drizzt was a powerful foe, and to kill him without leaving an obvious trail would not be easy.

"I will get him," Masoj promised, determination showing on his face. "I have the weapon readied; Drizzt will be dead before the tenth cycle, as you commanded."

"Why should I grant you another chance?" SiNafay asked him. "Why should I believe that you will fare better the next time you try?"

"Because I want him dead!" Masoj cried. "More than even you, my matron. I want to tear the life from Drizzt Do'Urden! When he is dead, I want to rip out his heart and display it as a trophy!"

SiNafay could not deny her son's obsession. "Granted," she said. "Get him, Masoj Hun'ett. On your life, strike the first blow against House Do'Urden and kill its secondboy."

Masoj bowed, the grimace never leaving his face, and swept out of the room.

"You heard everything," SiNafay signaled when the door had closed behind her son. She knew that Masoj might well have his ear to the door, and she did not want him to know of this conversation.

"I did," Alton replied in the silent code, stepping out from behind a curtain.

"Do you concur with my decision?" SiNafay's hands asked.

Alton was at a loss. He had no choice but to abide by his matron mother's decisions, but he did not think that SiNafay had been wise in sending Masoj back out after Drizzt. His silence grew long.

"You do not approve," Matron SiNafay bluntly motioned.

"Please, Matron Mother," Alton replied quickly. "I would not . . ."

"You are forgiven," SiNafay assured him. "I am not so certain that I should have allowed Masoj a second opportunity. Too much could go wrong."

"Then why?" Alton dared to ask. "You did not grant me a second chance, though I desire Drizzt Do'Urden's death as fiercely as any."

SiNafay cast him a scornful glare, sending him back on his courageous heels. "You doubt my judgment?"

"No!" Alton cried aloud. He slipped a hand over his mouth and dropped to his knees in terror. "Never, my matron," he signaled silently. "I just do not understand the problem as clearly as you. Forgive me my ignorance."

SiNafay's laughter sounded like the hiss of a hundred angry snakes. "We see together in this matter," she assured Alton. "I would no more give Masoj a second chance than I gave you."

"But—" Alton started to protest.

"Masoj will go back after Drizzt, but this time he will not be alone," SiNafay explained. "You will follow him, Alton DeVir. Keep him safe and finish the deed, on your life."

Alton beamed at the news that he would finally find some taste of vengeance. SiNafay's final threat didn't even concern him. "Could it ever be any other way?" his hands asked casually.

⚔ ⚔ ⚔ ⚔

"Think!" Malice growled, her face close, her breath hot on Drizzt's face. "You know something!"

Drizzt slumped back from the overpowering figure and glanced nervously around at his gathered family. Dinin, similarly grilled just a moment ago, kneeled with his chin in hand. He tried vainly to come up with an answer before Matron Malice upped the level of the interrogation techniques. Dinin did not miss Briza's motions toward her snake whip, and the unnerving sight did little to aid his memory.

Malice slapped Drizzt hard across the face and stepped away. "One of you has learned the identity of our enemies," she snapped at her sons. "Out there, on patrol, one of you has seen some hint, some sign."

"Perhaps we saw it but did not know it for what it was," Dinin offered.

"Silence!" Malice screamed, her face bright with rage. "When you know the answer to my question, you may speak! Only then!" She turned to Briza. "Help Dinin find his memory!"

Dinin dropped his head to his arms, folded on the floor in front of him, and arched his back to accept the torture. To do otherwise would only enrage Malice more.

Drizzt closed his eyes and recounted the events of his many patrols. He jerked involuntarily when he heard the snake whip's crack and his brother's soft groan.

"Masoj," Drizzt whispered, almost unconsciously. He looked up at his mother, who held her hand out to halt Briza's attacks—to Briza's dismay.

"Masoj Hun'ett," Drizzt said more loudly. "In the fight against the gnomes, he tried to kill me."

All the family, particularly Malice and Dinin, leaned forward toward Drizzt, hanging on his every word.

"When I battled the elemental," Drizzt explained, spitting out the last word as a curse upon Zaknafein. He cast an angry glare at the weapons master and continued, "Masoj Hun'ett struck me down with a bolt of lightning."

"He may have been shooting for the monster," Vierna insisted. "Masoj insisted that it was he who killed the elemental, but the high priestess of the patrol denied his claim."

"Masoj waited," Drizzt replied. "He did nothing until I began to gain the advantage over the monster. Then he loosed his magic, as much at me as at the elemental. I think he hoped to destroy us both."

"House Hun'ett," Matron Malice whispered.

"Fifth House," Briza remarked, "under Matron SiNafay."

"So that is our enemy," said Malice.

"Perhaps not," said Dinin, wondering even as he spoke the words why he hadn't left well enough alone. To disprove the theory only invited more whipping.

Matron Malice did not like his hesitation as he reconsidered the argument. "Explain!" she commanded.

"Masoj Hun'ett was angry at being excluded from the surface raid," said Dinin. "We left him in the city, only to witness our triumphant return." Dinin fixed his eyes straight on his brother. "Masoj has ever been jealous of Drizzt and all the glories that my brother has found, rightly or wrongly. Many are jealous of Drizzt and would see him dead."

Drizzt shifted uncomfortably in his seat, knowing the last words to be an open threat. He glanced over to Zaknafein and marked the weapons master's smug smile.

"Are you certain of your words?" Malice said to Drizzt, shaking him from his private thoughts.

"There is the cat," Dinin interrupted, "Masoj Hun'ett's magical pet, though it holds closer to Drizzt's side than to the wizard's."

"Guenhwyvar walks the point beside me," Drizzt protested, "a position that you ordered."

"Masoj does not like it," Dinin retorted.

Perhaps that is why you put the cat there, Drizzt thought, but he kept the words to himself. Was he seeing conspiracies in coincidence? Or was his world so truly filled with devious schemes and silent struggles for power?

"Are you certain of your words?" Malice asked Drizzt again, pulling him from his pondering.

"Masoj Hun'ett tried to kill me," he asserted. "I do not know his reasons, but his intent I do not doubt!"

"House Hun'ett, then," Briza remarked, "a mighty foe."

"We must learn of them," Malice said. "Dispatch the scouts! I will know the count of House Hun'ett's soldiers, its wizards, and, particularly, its clerics."

"If we are wrong," Dinin said. "If House Hun'ett is not the conspiring house—"

"We are not wrong!" Malice screamed at him.

"The yochlol said that one of us knows the identity of our enemy," reasoned Vierna. "All we have is Drizzt's tale of Masoj."

"Unless you are hiding something," Matron Malice growled at Dinin, a threat so cold and wicked that it stole the blood from the elderboy's face.

Dinin shook his head emphatically and slumped back, having nothing more to add to the conversation.

"Prepare a communion," Malice said to Briza. "Let us learn of Matron SiNafay's standing with the Spider Queen."

Drizzt watched incredulously as the preparations began at a frantic pace, each command from Matron Malice following a practiced defensive course. It wasn't the precision of Drizzt's family's battle planning that amazed him—he would expect nothing less from this group. It was the eager gleam in every eye.

THE WEAPONS MASTERS

I mpudent!" growled the yochlol. The fire in the brazier puffed, and the creature again stood behind Malice, again draped dangerous tentacles over the matron mother. "You dare to summon me again?"

Malice and her daughters glanced around, on the edge of panic. They knew that the mighty being was not toying with them; the handmaiden truly was enraged this time.

"House Do'Urden pleased the Spider Queen, it is true," the yochlol answered their unspoken thoughts, "but that one act does not dispel the displeasure your family brought upon Lolth in the recent past. Do not think that all is forgiven, Matron Malice Do'Urden!"

How small and vulnerable Matron Malice felt now. Her power paled in the face of the wrath of one of Lolth's personal servants.

"Displeasure?" she dared to whisper. "How has my family brought displeasure to the Spider Queen? By what act?"

The handmaiden's laughter erupted in a spout of flames and flying spiders, but the high priestesses held their positions. They accepted the heat and the crawling things as part of their penance.

"I have told you before, Matron Malice Do'Urden," the yochlol snarled with its droopy mouth, "and I shall tell you one final time. The Spider Queen does not reply to questions whose answers are already known!" In a blast of explosive energy that sent the four females of

House Do'Urden tumbling to the floor, the handmaiden was gone.

Briza was the first to recover. She prudently rushed over to the brazier and smothered the remaining flames, thus closing the gate to the Abyss, the yochlol's home plane.

"Who?" screamed Malice, the powerful matriarch once again. "Who in my family has invoked the wrath of Lolth?" Malice appeared small again then, as the implications of the yochlol's warning became all too clear. House Do'Urden was about to go to war with a powerful family. Without Lolth's favor, House Do'Urden likely would cease to exist.

"We must find the perpetrator," Malice instructed her daughters, certain that none of them was involved. They were high priestesses, one and all. If any of them had done some misdeed in the eyes of the Spider Queen, the summoned yochlol surely would have exacted punishment on the spot. By itself, the handmaiden could have leveled House Do'Urden.

Briza pulled the snake whip from her belt. "I will get the information we require!" she promised.

"No!" said Matron Malice. "We must not reveal our search. Be it a soldier or a member of House Do'Urden, the guilty one is trained and hardened against pain. We cannot hope that torture will pull the confession from his lips; not when he knows the consequences of his actions. We must discover the cause of Lolth's displeasure immediately and properly punish the criminal. The Spider Queen must stand behind us in our struggles!"

"How, then, are we to discern the perpetrator?" the eldest daughter complained, reluctantly replacing the snake whip on her belt.

"Vierna and Maya, leave us," Matron Malice instructed. "Say nothing of these revelations and do nothing to hint at our purpose."

The two younger daughters bowed and scurried away, not happy with their secondary roles but unable to do anything about them.

"First we will look," Malice said to Briza. "We will see if we can learn of the guilty one from afar."

Briza understood. "The scrying bowl," she said. She rushed from the anteroom and into the chapel proper. In the central altar she found the valuable item, a wide golden bowl laced throughout with black pearls.

Hands trembling, Briza placed the bowl atop the altar and reached into the most sacred of the many compartments. This was the holding bin for the prized possession of House Do'Urden, a great onyx chalice.

Malice then joined Briza in the chapel proper and took the chalice from her. Moving to the large font at the entrance to the great room, Malice dipped the chalice into a sticky fluid, the unholy water of her religion. She then chanted, *"Spiderae aught icor ven".* The ritual complete, Malice moved back to the altar and poured the unholy water into the golden bowl.

She and Briza sat down to watch.

⚔ ⚔ ⚔ ⚔ ⚔

Drizzt stepped onto the floor of Zaknafein's training gym for the first time in more than a decade and felt as if he had come home. He'd spent the best years of his young life here—almost wholly here. For all the disappointments he had encountered since—and no doubt would continue to experience throughout his life—Drizzt would never forget that brief sparkle of innocence, that joy, he had known when he was a student in Zaknafein's gym.

Zaknafein entered and walked over to face his former student. Drizzt saw nothing familiar or comforting in the weapons master's face. A perpetual scowl now replaced the once common smile. It was an angry demeanor that hated everything around it, perhaps Drizzt most of all. Or had Zaknafein always worn such a grimace? Drizzt had to wonder. Had nostalgia glossed over Drizzt's memories of those years of early training? Was this mentor, who had so often warmed Drizzt's heart with a lighthearted chuckle, actually the cold, lurking monster that Drizzt now saw before him?

"Which has changed, Zaknafein," Drizzt asked aloud, "you, my memories, or my perceptions?"

Zak seemed not even to hear the whispered question. "Ah, the young hero has returned," he said, "the warrior with exploits beyond his years."

"Why do you mock me?" Drizzt protested.

"He who killed the hook horrors," Zak continued. His swords were out in his hands now, and Drizzt responded by drawing his scimitars. There was no need to ask the rules of engagement in this contest, or the choice of weapons.

Drizzt knew, had known before he had ever come here, that there would be no rules this time. The weapons would be their weapons of preference, the blades that each of them had used to kill so many foes.

"He who killed the earth elemental," Zak snarled derisively. He launched a measured attack, a simple lunge with one blade. Drizzt batted it aside without even thinking of the parry.

Sudden fires erupted in Zak's eyes, as if the first contact had sundered all the emotional bonds that had tempered his thrust. "He who killed the girl child of the surface elves!" he cried, an accusation and no compliment. Now came the second attack, vicious and powerful, an arcing swipe descending at Drizzt's head. "Who cut her apart to appease his own thirst for blood!"

Zak's words knocked Drizzt off his guard emotionally, wrapped his heart in confusion like some devious mental whip. Drizzt was a seasoned warrior, though, and his reflexes did not register the emotional distraction. A scimitar came up to catch the descending sword and deflected it harmlessly aside.

"Murderer! " Zak snarled openly. "Did you enjoy the dying child's screams?" He came at Drizzt in a furious whirl, swords dipping and diving, slicing at every angle.

Drizzt, enraged by the hypocrite's accusations, matched the fury, screaming out for no better reason than to hear the anger of his own voice.

Any watching the battle would have found no breath in the next few blurring moments. Never had the Underdark witnessed such a vicious fight as when these two masters of the blade each attacked the demon possessing the other—and himself.

Adamantine sparked and nicked, droplets of blood spattered both the combatants, though neither felt any pain, and neither knew if he'd injured the other.

Drizzt came with a two blade sidelong swipe that drove Zak's swords out wide. Zak followed the motion quickly, turned a complete circle, and slammed back into Drizzt's thrusting scimitars with enough force to knock the young warrior from his feet. Drizzt fell into a roll and came back up to meet his charging adversary.

A thought came over him.

Drizzt came up high, too high, and Zak drove him back on his heels. Drizzt knew what would soon be coming; he invited it openly. Zak kept Drizzt's weapons high through several combined maneuvers. He then went with the move that had defeated Drizzt in the past, expecting that the best Drizzt could attain would be equal footing: double-thrust low.

Drizzt executed the appropriate cross-down parry, as he had to, and Zak tensed, waiting for his eager opponent to try to improve the move. "Child killer!" he growled, goading on Drizzt.

He didn't know that Drizzt had found the solution.

With all the anger he had ever known, all the disappointments of his young life gathering within his foot, Drizzt focused on Zak. That smug face, feigning smiles and drooling for blood.

Between the hilts, between the eyes, Drizzt kicked, blowing out every ounce of rage in a single blow.

Zak's nose crunched flat. His eyes lolled upward, and blood exploded over his hollow cheeks. Zak knew that he was falling, that the devilish young warrior would be on him in a flash, gaining an advantage that Zak could not hope to overcome.

"What of you, Zaknafein Do'Urden?" he heard Drizzt snarl, distantly, as though he were falling far away. "I have heard of the exploits of House Do'Urden's weapons master! How he so enjoys killing!" The voice was closer now, as Drizzt stalked in, and as the rebounding rage of Zaknafein sent him spiraling back to the battle.

"I have heard how murder comes so very easily to Zaknafein!" Drizzt spat derisively. "The murder of clerics, of other drow! Do you so enjoy it all?" He ended the question with a blow from each scimitar, attacks meant to kill Zak, to kill the demon in them both.

But Zaknafein was now fully back to consciousness, hating himself and Drizzt equally. At the last moment, his swords came up and crossed, lightning fast, throwing Drizzt's arms wide. Then Zak finished with a kick of his own, not so strong from the prone position but accurate in its search for Drizzt's groin.

Drizzt sucked in his breath and twirled away, forcing himself back into composure when he saw Zaknafein, still dazed, rising to his feet. "Do you so enjoy it all?" he managed to ask again.

"Enjoy?" the weapons master echoed.

"Does it bring you pleasure?" Drizzt grimaced.

"Satisfaction!" Zak corrected. "I kill. Yes, I kill."

"You teach others to kill!"

"To kill drow!" Zak roared, and he was back in Drizzt's face, his weapons up but waiting for Drizzt to make the next move.

Zak's words again entwined Drizzt in a mesh of confusion. Who was this drow standing before him?

"Do you think that your mother would let me live if I did not serve her evil designs?" Zak cried.

Drizzt did not understand.

"She hates me," Zak said, more in control as he began to understand Drizzt's confusion, "despises me for what I know." Drizzt cocked his head.

"Are you so blind to the evil around you?" Zak yelled in his face. "Or has it consumed you, as it consumes all of them, in this murderous frenzy that we call life?"

"The frenzy that holds you?" Drizzt retorted, but there was little conviction in his voice now. If he understood Zak's words correctly—if Zak played the killing game simply because of his hatred for the perverted drow—the most Drizzt could blame him for was cowardice.

"No frenzy holds me," Zak replied. "I live as best I can. I survive in a world that is not my own, not my heart." The lament in his words, the droop of his head as he admitted his helplessness, struck a familiar chord in Drizzt. "I kill, kill drow, to serve Matron Malice—to placate the rage, the frustration, that I know in my soul. When I hear the children scream . . ." His gaze snapped up on Drizzt and he rushed in all of a sudden, his fury returned tenfold.

Drizzt tried to get his scimitars up, but Zak knocked one of them across the room and drove the other aside. He rushed in step with Drizzt's awkward retreat until he had Drizzt pinned against a wall. The tip of Zak's sword drew a droplet of blood from Drizzt's throat.

"The child lives!" Drizzt gasped. "I swear, I did not kill the elven child!"

Zak relaxed a bit but still held Drizzt, sword to throat. "Dinin said—"

"Dinin was mistaken," Drizzt replied frantically. "Fooled by me. I knocked the child down—only to spare her—and covered her with the blood of her murdered mother to mask my own cowardice!"

Zak leaped back, overwhelmed.

"I killed no elves that day," Drizzt said to him. "The only ones I desired to kill were my own companions!"

✕ ✕ ✕ ✕ ✕

"So now we know," said Briza, staring into the scrying bowl, watching the conclusion of the battle between Drizzt and Zaknafein and hearing their every word. "It was Drizzt who angered the Spider Queen."

"You suspected him all along, as did I," Matron Malice replied, "though we both hoped differently."

"So much promise!" Briza lamented. "How I wish that one had learned his place, his values. Perhaps . . ."

"Mercy?" Matron Malice snapped at her. "Do you show mercy that would further invoke the Spider Queen's displeasure?"

"No, Matron," Briza replied. "I had only hoped that Drizzt could be used in the future, as you have used Zaknafein all these years. Zaknafein is growing older."

"We are about to fight a war, my daughter," Malice reminded her. "Lolth must be appeased. Your brother has brought his fate upon himself; his actions were his own to decide."

"He decided wrongly."

✕ ✕ ✕ ✕ ✕

The words hit Zaknafein harder than Drizzt's boot had. The weapons master threw his swords to the ends of the room and rushed in on Drizzt. He buried him in a hug so intense that it took the young drow a long moment to even realize what had happened.

"You have survived!" Zak said, his voice broken by muffled tears. "Survived the Academy, where all the others died!"

Drizzt returned the embrace, tentatively, still not guessing the depth of Zak's elation.

"My son!"

Drizzt nearly fainted, overwhelmed by the admission of what he had always suspected, and even more so by the knowledge that he was not the only one in his dark world angered by the ways of the drow. He was not alone.

"Why?" Drizzt asked, pushing Zak out to arm's length. "Why have you stayed?"

Zak looked at him incredulously. "Where would I go? No one, not even a drow weapons master would survive for long out in the caverns of the Underdark. Too many monsters, and other races, hunger for the sweet blood of dark elves."

"Surely you had options."

"The surface?" Zak replied. "To face the painful inferno every day? No, my son, I am trapped, as you are trapped."

Drizzt had feared that statement, had feared that he would find no solution from his newfound father to the dilemma that was his life. Perhaps there were no answers.

"You will do well in Menzoberranzan," Zak said to comfort him. "You are strong, and Matron Malice will find an appropriate place for your talents, whatever your heart may desire."

"To live a life of assassinations, as you have?" Drizzt asked, trying futilely to keep the rage out of his words.

"What choice is before us?" Zak answered, his eyes seeking the unjudging stone of the floor.

"I will not kill drow," Drizzt declared flatly.

Zak's eyes snapped back on him. "You will," he assured his son. "In Menzoberranzan, you will kill or be killed."

Drizzt looked away, but Zak's words pursued him, could not be blocked out.

"There is no other way," the weapons master continued softly. "Such is our world. Such is our life. You have escaped this long, but you will find that your luck soon will change." He grabbed Drizzt's chin firmly and forced his son to look at him directly.

"I wish that it could be different," Zak said honestly, "but it is not such a bad life. I do not lament killing dark elves. I perceive their deaths as their salvation from this wicked existence. If they care so dearly for their Spider Queen, then let them go and visit her!"

Zak's growing smile washed away suddenly. "Except for the children," he whispered. "Often have I heard the cries of dying children, though never, I promise you, have I caused them. I have always wondered if they, too, are evil, born evil. Or if the weight of our dark world bends them to fit our foul ways."

"The ways of the demon Lolth," Drizzt agreed.

They both paused for many heartbeats, each privately weighing the realities of his own personal dilemma. Zak was next to speak, having long ago come to terms with the life that was offered to him.

"Lolth," he chuckled. "She is a vicious queen, that one. I would sacrifice everything for a chance at her ugly face!"

"I almost believe you would," Drizzt whispered, finding his smile.

Zak jumped back from him. "I would indeed," he laughed heartily. "So would you!"

Drizzt flipped his lone scimitar up into the air, letting it spin over twice before catching it again by the hilt. "True enough!" he cried. "But no longer would I be alone!"

26
Angler of The Underdark

Drizzt wandered alone through the maze of Menzoberranzan, drifting past the stalagmite mounds, under the leering points of the great stone spears that hung from the cavern's high ceiling. Matron Malice had specifically ordered all of the family to remain within the house, fearing an assassination attempt by House Hun'ett. Too much had happened to Drizzt this day for him to obey. He had to think, and contemplating such blasphemous thoughts, even silently, in a house full of nervous clerics might get him into serious trouble.

This was the quiet time of the city; the heat-light of Narbondel was only a sliver at the stone's base, and most of the drow comfortably slept within their stone houses. Soon after he slipped through the adamantine gate of the House Do'Urden compound, Drizzt began to understand the wisdom of Matron Malice's command. The city's quiet now seemed to him like the crouched hush of a predator. It was poised to drop upon him from behind every one of the many blind corners he faced on this trek.

He would find no solace here in which he might truly contemplate the day's events, the revelations of Zaknafein, kindred in more than blood. Drizzt decided to break all the rules—that was the way of the drow, after all—and head out of the city, down the tunnels he knew so well from his tendays of patrol.

An hour later, he was still walking, lost in thought and feeling safe enough, for he was well within the boundaries of the patrol region.

He entered a high corridor, ten paces wide and with broken walls lined in loose rubble and crossed by many ledges. It seemed as though the passage once had been much wider. The ceiling was far beyond sight, but Drizzt had been through here a dozen times, up on the many ledges, and he gave the place no thought.

He envisioned the future, the times that he and Zaknafein, his father, would share now that no secrets separated them. Together they would be unbeatable, a team of weapons masters, bonded by steel and emotions. Did House Hun'ett truly understand what it would be facing? The smile on Drizzt's face disappeared as soon as he considered the implications: he and Zak, together, cutting through House Hun'ett's ranks with deadly ease, through the ranks of drow elves—killing their own people.

Drizzt leaned against the wall for support, understanding firsthand the frustration that had racked his father for many centuries. Drizzt did not want to be like Zaknafein, living only to kill, existing in a protective sphere of violence, but what choices lay before him? Leave the city?

Zak had balked when Drizzt asked him why he had not left. "Where would I go?" Drizzt whispered now, echoing Zak's words. His father had proclaimed them trapped, and so it seemed to Drizzt.

"Where would I go?" he asked again. "Travel the Underdark, where our people are so despised and a single drow would become a target for everything he passed? Or to the surface, perhaps, and let that ball of fire in the sky burn out my eyes so that I may not witness my own death when the elven folk descend upon me?"

The logic of the reasoning trapped Drizzt as it had trapped Zak. Where could a drow elf go? Nowhere in all the Realms would an elf of dark skin be accepted.

Was the choice then to kill? To kill drow?

Drizzt rolled over against the wall, his physical movement an unconscious act, for his mind whirled down the maze of his future. It took him a moment to realize that his back was against something other than stone.

He tried to leap away, alert again now that his surroundings were not as they should be. When he pushed out, his feet came up from the ground and he landed back in his original position. Frantically, before he took the time to consider his predicament, Drizzt reached behind his neck with both hands.

They, too, stuck fast to the translucent cord that held him. Drizzt knew his folly then, and all the tugging in the world would not free his hands from the line of the angler of the Underdark, a cave fisher.

"Fool!" he scolded himself as he felt himself lifted from the ground. He should have suspected this, should have been more careful alone in the caverns. But to reach out barehanded! He looked down at the hilts of his scimitars, useless in their sheaths.

The cave fisher reeled him in, pulled him up the long wall toward its waiting maw.

⚔ ⚔ ⚔ ⚔ ⚔

Masoj Hun'ett smiled smugly to himself as he watched Drizzt depart the city. Time was running short for him, and Matron SiNafay would not be pleased if he failed again in his mission to destroy the secondboy of House Do'Urden. Now Masoj's patience had apparently paid off, for Drizzt had come out alone, had left the city! There were no witnesses. It was too easy.

Eagerly the wizard pulled the onyx figurine from his pouch and dropped it to the ground. "Guenhwyvar!" he called as loudly as he dared, glancing around at the nearest stalagmite house for signs of activity.

The dark smoke appeared and transformed a moment later into Masoj's magical panther. Masoj rubbed his hands together, thinking himself marvelous for having concocted such a devious and ironic end to the heroics of Drizzt Do'Urden.

"I have a job for you," he told the cat, "one that you'll not enjoy!"

Guenhwyvar slumped casually and yawned as though the wizard's words were hardly a revelation.

"Your point companion has gone out on patrol," Masoj explained as he pointed down the tunnel, "by himself. It's too dangerous."

Guenhwyvar stood back up, suddenly very interested.

"Drizzt should not be out there alone," Masoj continued. "He could get killed."

The evil inflections of his voice told the panther his intent before he ever spoke the words.

"Go to him, my pet," Masoj purred. "Find him out there in the gloom and kill him!" He studied Guenhwyvar's reaction, measured the horror he had laid on the cat. Guenhwyvar stood rigid, as unmoving as the statue used to summon it.

"Go!" Masoj ordered. "You cannot resist your master's commands! I am your master, unthinking beast! You seem to forget that fact too often!"

Guenhwyvar resisted for a long moment, a heroic act in itself, but the magic's urges, the incessant pull of the master's command, outweighed any instinctive feelings the great panther might have had. Reluctantly at first, but then pulled by the primordial desires of the hunt, Guenhwyvar sped off between the enchanted statues guarding the tunnel and easily found Drizzt's scent.

※ ※ ※ ※ ※

Alton DeVir slumped back behind the largest of the stalagmite mounds, disappointed at Masoj's tactics. Masoj would let the cat do his work for him; Alton would not even witness Drizzt Do'Urden's death!

Alton fingered the powerful wand that Matron SiNafay had given to him when he set out after Masoj that night. It seemed that the item would play no role in Drizzt's demise.

Alton took comfort in the item, knowing that he would have ample opportunity to put it to proper use against the remainder of House Do'Urden.

※ ※ ※ ※ ※

Drizzt fought for the first half of his ascent, kicking and spinning, ducking his shoulders under any outcrop he passed in a futile effort to hold back the pull of the cave fisher. He knew from the outset, though, against those warrior instincts that refused to surrender, that he had no chance to halt the incessant pull.

Halfway up, one shoulder bloodied, the other bruised, and with the floor nearly thirty feet below him, Drizzt resigned himself to his fate. If he would find a chance against the crablike monster that waited at the top of the line, it would be in the last instant of the ascent. For now, he could only watch and wait.

Perhaps death was not so bad an alternative to the life he would find among the drow, trapped within the evil framework of their dark society. Even Zaknafein, so strong and powerful and wise with age, had never been able to come to terms with his existence in Menzoberranzan; what chance did Drizzt have?

When Drizzt had passed through his small bout with self pity, when the angle of his ascent changed, showing him the lip of the final ledge, the fighting spirit within him took over once again. The cave fisher might have him, he decided then, but he'd put a boot or two into the thing's eyes before it got its meal!

He could hear the clacking of the anxious monster's eight crablike legs. Drizzt had seen a cave fisher before, though it had scrambled away before he and his patrol could catch up to it. He had imagined it then, and could imagine it now, in battle. Two of its legs ended in wicked claws, pincers that snipped up prey to fit into the maw.

Drizzt turned himself face-in to the cliff, wanting to view the thing as soon as his head crested the ledge. The anxious clacking grew louder, resounding alongside the thumping of Drizzt's heart. He reached the ledge.

Drizzt peeked over, only a foot or two from the monster's long proboscis, with the maw just inches behind. Pincers reached out to grab him before he could get his footing; he would get no chance to kick out at the thing.

He closed his eyes, hoping again that death would be preferable to his life in Menzoberranzan.

A familiar growl then brought him from his thoughts.

Slipping through the maze of ledges, Guenhwyvar came in sight of the cave fisher and Drizzt just before Drizzt had reached the final ledge. This was a moment of salvation or death for the cat as surely as for Drizzt. Guenhwyvar had traveled here under Masoj's direct command, giving no consideration to its duty and acting only on its own instincts in accord with the compelling magic. Guenhwyvar could not go against that edict, that premise for the cat's very existence . . . until now.

· The scene before the panther, with Drizzt only seconds from death, brought to Guenhwyvar a strength unknown to the cat, and unforeseen to the creator of the magical figurine. That instant of terror gave a life to Guenhwyvar beyond the scope of the magic.

By the time Drizzt had opened his eyes, the battle was in full fury. Guenhwyvar leaped atop the cave fisher but nearly went right over, for the monster's six remaining legs were rooted to the stone by the same goo that held Drizzt fast to the long filament. Undaunted, the cat raked and bit, a ball of frenzy trying to find a break in the fisher's armored shell.

The monster retaliated with his pincers, flipping them over its back with surprising agility and finding one of Guenhwyvar's forelegs.

Drizzt was no longer being pulled in; the monster had other business to attend to.

Pincers cut through Guenhwyvar's soft flesh, but the cat's blood was not the only dark fluid staining the cave fisher's back. Powerful feline claws tore up a section of the shell armor, and great teeth plunged beneath it. As the cave fisher's blood splattered to the stone, its legs began to slip.

Watching the goo under the crablike legs dissolve as the blood of the monster struck it, Drizzt understood what would happen as a line of that same blood made its way down the filament, toward him. He would have to strike fast if the opportunity came; he would have to be ready to help Guenhwyvar.

The fisher stumbled to the side, rolling Guenhwyvar away and spinning Drizzt over in a complete bumping circuit.

Still the blood oozed down the line, and Drizzt felt the filament's hold loosen from his top hand as the liquid came in contact.

Guenhwyvar was up again, facing the fisher, looking for an attack route through the waiting pincers.

Drizzt's hand was free. He snapped up a scimitar and dived straight ahead, sinking the tip into the fisher's side. The monster reeled about, the jolt and the continuing blood flow shaking Drizzt from the filament altogether. The drow was agile enough to find a handhold before he had fallen far, though his drawn scimitar tumbled down to the floor.

Drizzt's diversion opened the fisher's defenses for just a moment, and Guenhwyvar did not hesitate. The cat barreled into its foe, teeth finding the same fleshy hold they had already ripped. They went deeper, under the skin, crushing organs as Guenhwyvar's raking claws kept the pincers at bay.

By the time Drizzt climbed back to the level of the battle, the cave fisher shuddered in the throes of death. Drizzt pulled himself up and rushed to his friend's side.

Guenhwyvar retreated step for step, its ears flattened and teeth bared.

At first, Drizzt thought that the pain of a wound blinded the cat, but a quick survey dispelled that theory. Guenhwyvar had only one injury, and that was not serious. Drizzt had seen the cat with worse.

Guenhwyvar continued to retreat, continued to growl, as the incessant pounding of Masoj's command, back again after the instant of terror, hammered at its heart. The cat fought the urges, tried to see Drizzt as an ally, not as prey, but the urges . . .

"What is wrong, my friend?" Drizzt asked softly, resisting the urge to draw his remaining blade in defense. He dropped to one knee. "Do you not recognize me? How often we have fought together!"

Guenhwyvar crouched low and tamped down its hind legs, preparing, Drizzt knew, to spring. Still Drizzt did not draw his weapon, did nothing to threaten the cat. He had to trust that Guenhwyvar was true to his perceptions, that the panther was everything he believed it to be. What now could be guiding these unfamiliar reactions? What had brought Guenhwyvar out here at this late hour?

Drizzt found his answers when he remembered Matron Malice's warnings about leaving House Do'Urden.

"Masoj sent you to kill me!" he said bluntly. His tone confused the cat, and it relaxed a bit, not yet ready to spring. "You saved me, Guenhwyvar. You resisted the command."

Guenhwyvar's growl sounded in protest.

"You could have let the cave fisher do the deed for you," Drizzt retorted, "but you did not! You charged in and saved my life! Fight the urges, Guenhwyvar! Remember me as your friend, a better companion than Masoj Hun'ett could ever be!"

Guenhwyvar backed away another step, caught in a pull that it could not yet resolve. Drizzt watched the cat's ears come up from its head and knew that he was winning the contest.

"Masoj claims ownership," he went on, confident that the cat, through some intelligence Drizzt could not know, understood the meaning of his words. "I claim friendship. I am your friend, Guenhwyvar, and I'll not fight against you."

He leaped forward, arms unthreateningly wide, face and chest fully exposed. "Even at the cost of my own life!"

Guenhwyvar did not strike. Emotions pulled at the cat stronger than any magical spell, those same emotions that had put Guenhwyvar into action when it first saw Drizzt in the cave fisher's clutches.

Guenhwyvar reared up and leaped out, crashing into Drizzt and knocking him to his back, then burying him in a rush of playful slaps and mock bites.

The two friends had won again; they had defeated two foes this day.

When Drizzt paused from the greeting to consider all that had transpired, though, he realized that one of the victories was not yet complete. Guenhwyvar was his in spirit now but still held by another, one who did not deserve the cat, who enslaved the cat in a life that Drizzt could no longer witness.

None of the confusion that had followed Drizzt Do'Urden out of Menzoberranzan that night remained. For the first time in his life, he saw the road he must follow, the path to his own freedom.

He remembered Zaknafein's warnings, and the same impossible alternatives that he had contemplated, to no resolution.

Where, indeed, could a drow elf go?

"Worse to be trapped within a lie," he whispered absently. The panther cocked its head to the side, sensing again that Drizzt's words carried great importance. Drizzt returned the curious stare with one that came suddenly grim.

"Take me to your master," he demanded, "your false master."

27

UNTROUBLED DREAMS

Zaknafein sank down into his bed in an easy sleep, the most comfortable rest he had ever known. Dreams did come to him this night, a rush of dreams. Far from tumultuous, they only enhanced his comfort. Zak was free now of his secret, of the lie that had dominated every day of his adult life.

Drizzt had survived! Even the dreaded Academy of Menzoberranzan could not daunt the youth's indomitable spirit and sense of morality. Zaknafein Do'Urden was no longer alone. The dreams that played in his mind showed him the same wonderful possibilities that had followed Drizzt out of the city.

Side by side they would stand, unbeatable, two as one against the perverted foundations of Menzoberranzan.

A stinging pain in his foot brought Zak from his slumbers. He saw Briza immediately, at the bottom of his bed, her snake whip in hand. Instinctively, Zak reached over the side to fetch his sword.

The weapon was gone. Vierna stood at the side of the room, holding it. On the opposite side, Maya held Zak's other sword.

How had they come in so stealthily? Zak wondered. Magical silence, no doubt, but Zak was still surprised that he had not sensed their presence in time. Nothing had ever caught him unawares, awake or asleep.

Never before had he slept so soundly, so peacefully. Perhaps, in Menzoberranzan, such pleasant dreams were dangerous.

"Matron Malice will see you," Briza announced.

"I am not properly dressed," Zak replied casually. "My belt and weapons, if you please."

"We do not please!" Briza snapped, more at her sisters than at Zak. "You will not need the weapons."

Zak thought otherwise.

"Come, now," Briza commanded, and she raised the whip.

"I should be certain of Matron Malice's intentions before I acted so boldly, were I you," Zak warned. Briza, reminded of the power of the male she now threatened, lowered her weapon.

Zak rolled out of bed, putting the same intense glare alternately on Maya and Vierna, watching their reactions to better conclude Malice's reasons for summoning him.

They surrounded him as he left his room, keeping a cautious but ready distance from the deadly weapons master. "Must be serious," Zak remarked quietly, so that only Briza, in front of the troupe, could hear. Briza turned and flashed him a wicked smile that did nothing to dispel his suspicions.

Neither did Matron Malice, who leaned forward in her throne in anticipation even before they entered the room.

"Matron," Zak offered, dipping into a bow and pulling the side of his nightshirt out wide to draw attention to his inappropriate dress. He wanted to let Malice know his feelings of being ridiculed at such a late hour.

The matron offered no return greeting. She rested back in her throne. One slender hand rubbed her sharp chin, while her eyes locked upon Zaknafein.

"Perhaps you could tell me why you've summoned me," Zak dared to say, his voice still holding an edge of sarcasm. "I would prefer to return to my slumbers. We should not give House Hun'ett the advantage of a tired weapons master."

"Drizzt has gone," growled Malice.

The news slapped Zak like a wet rag. He straightened, and the teasing smile disappeared from his face.

"He left the house against my commands," Malice went on. Zak relaxed visibly; when Malice announced that Drizzt was gone, Zak had first thought that she and her devious cohorts had driven him out or killed him.

"A spirited boy," Zak remarked. "Surely he will return soon."

"Spirited," Malice echoed, and her tone did not put the description in a positive light.

"He will return," Zak said again. "There's no need for our alarm, for such extreme measures." He glared at Briza, though he knew well that the matron mother had called him to audience to do more than tell him of Drizzt's departure.

"The secondboy disobeyed the matron mother," Briza snarled, a rehearsed interruption.

"Spirited," Zak said again, trying not to chuckle. "A minor indiscretion."

"How often he seems to have those," Malice commented. "Like another spirited male of House Do'Urden."

Zak bowed again, taking her words as a compliment. Malice already had his punishment decided, if she meant to punish him at all, His actions now, at this trial—if that's what it was—would be of little consequence.

"The boy has displeased the Spider Queen!" Malice growled, openly enraged and tired of Zak's sarcasm. "Even you were not foolish enough to do that!"

A dark cloud passed across Zak's face. This meeting was indeed serious; Drizzt's life could be at stake.

"But you know of his crime," Malice continued, easing back again. She liked that she had Zak concerned and on the defensive. She had found his vulnerable spot. It was her turn to tease.

"Leaving the house?" Zak protested. "A minor error in judgment. Lolth would not be concerned with such a trifle issue."

"Do not feign ignorance, Zaknafein. You know that the elven child lives!"

Zak lost his breath in a sharp gasp. Malice knew! Damn it all, Lolth knew!

"We are about to go to war," Malice continued calmly, "we are not in Lolth's favor, and we must correct the situation."

She eyed Zak directly. "You are aware of our ways and know that we must do this."

Zak nodded, trapped. Anything he did now to disagree would only make matters worse for Drizzt—if matters could be worse for Drizzt.

"The secondboy must be punished," Briza said.

Another rehearsed interruption, Zak knew. He wondered how many times Briza and Malice had practiced this encounter.

"Am I to punish him, then?" Zak asked. "I'll not whip the boy; that is not my place."

"His punishment is none of your concern," Malice said.

"Then why disturb my slumber?" Zak asked, trying to detach himself from Drizzt's predicament, more for Drizzt's sake than his own.

"I thought that you would wish to know," Malice replied. "You and Drizzt became so close this day in the gym. Father and son."

She saw! Zak realized. Malice, and probably that wretched Briza, had watched the whole encounter! Zak's head drooped as he came to know that he had unwittingly played a part in Drizzt's predicament.

"An elven child lives," Malice began slowly, rolling out each word in dramatic clarity, "and a young drow must die."

"No!" The word came out of Zak before he realized he was speaking. He tried to find some escape. "Drizzt was young. He did not understand . . ."

"He knew exactly what he was doing!" Malice screamed back at him. "He does not regret his actions! He is so like you, Zaknafein! Too like you."

"Then he can learn," Zak reasoned. "I have not been a burden to you, Mali—Matron Malice. You have profited by my presence. Drizzt is no less skilled than I; he can be valuable to us."

"Dangerous to us," Matron Malice corrected. "You and he standing together? The thought does not please me."

"His death will aid House Hun'ett," Zak warned, grabbing at anything he could find to defeat the matron's intent.

"The Spider Queen demands his death," Malice replied sternly. "She must be appeased if Daermon N'a'shezbaernon is to have any hope in its struggles against House Hun'ett."

"I beg you, do not kill the boy."

"Sympathy?" Malice mused. "It does not become a drow warrior, Zaknafein. Have you lost your fighting will?"

"I am old, Malice."

"Matron Malice!" Briza protested, but Zak put a look on her so cold that she lowered her snake whip before she had even begun to put it to use.

"Older still will I become if Drizzt is put to his death."

"I do not desire this either," Malice agreed, but Zak recognized her lie. She didn't care about Drizzt, or about anything else, beyond gaining the Spider Queen's favor.

"Yet I see no alternative. Drizzt has angered Lolth, and she must be appeased before our war."

Zak began to understand. This meeting wasn't about Drizzt at all. "Take me in the boy's stead," he said.

Malice's narrow grin could not hide her feigned surprise. This was what she had desired from the very beginning.

"You are a proven fighter," the matron argued. "Your value, as you yourself have already admitted, cannot be underestimated. To sacrifice you to the Spider Queen would appease her, but what void will be left in House Do'Urden in the wake of your passing?"

"A void that Drizzt can fill," Zak replied. He secretly hoped that Drizzt, unlike he, would find some escape from it all, some way around Matron Malice's evil plots.

"You are certain of this?"

"He is my equal in battle," Zak assured her. "He will grow stronger, too, beyond what Zaknafein has ever attained."

"You are willing to do this for him?" Malice sneered, eager drool edging her mouth.

"You know that I am," Zak replied.

"Ever the fool," Malice put in.

"To your dismay," Zak continued, undaunted, "you know that Drizzt would do the same for me."

"He is young," Malice purred. "He will be taught better."

"As you taught me?" snapped Zak.

Malice's victorious grin became a grimace. "I warn you, Zaknafein," she growled in all her vile rage. "If you do anything to disrupt the ceremony to appease the Spider Queen, if, in the end of your wasted life, you choose to anger me one final time, I will give Drizzt to Briza. She and her torturous toys will give him to Lolth!"

Unafraid, Zak held his head high. "I have offered myself, Malice," he spat. "Have your fun while you may. In the end, Zaknafein will be at peace; Matron Malice Do'Urden will ever be at war!"

Shaking in anger, the moment of triumph stolen by a few simple words, Malice could only whisper, "Take him!"

Zak offered no resistance as Vierna and Maya tied him to the spider-shaped altar in the chapel. He watched Vierna mostly, seeing an edge of sympathy rimming her quiet eyes. She, too, might have been like him, but whatever hope he had for that possibility had been buried long ago under the relentless preaching of the Spider Queen.

"You are sad," Zak remarked to her.

Vierna straightened and tugged tightly on one of Zak's bonds, causing him to grimace in pain. "A pity," she replied as coldly as she could. "House Do'Urden must give much to repay Drizzt's foolish deed. I would have enjoyed watching the two of you together in battle."

"House Hun'ett would not have enjoyed the sight," Zak replied with a wink. "Cry not . . . my daughter."

Vierna slapped him across the face. "Take your lies to your grave!"

"Deny it as you choose, Vierna," was all that Zak cared to reply.

Vierna and Maya backed away from the altar. Vierna fought to hold her scowl and Maya bit back an amused chuckle, as Matron Malice and Briza entered the room. The matron mother wore her greatest ceremonial robe, black and weblike, clinging and floating about her all at once, and Briza carried a sacred coffer.

Zak paid them no heed as they began their ritual, chanting for the Spider Queen, offering their hopes for appeasement. Zak had his own hopes at that moment.

"Beat them all," he whispered under his breath. "Do more than survive, my son, as I have survived. Live! Be true to the callings in your heart."

Braziers roared to life; the room glowed. Zak felt the heat, knew that contact to that darker plane had been achieved.

"Take this . . ." he heard Matron Malice chant, but he put the words out of his thoughts and continued the final prayers of his life.

The spider-shaped dagger hovered over his chest. Malice clenched the instrument in her bony hands, the sheen of her sweat-soaked skin catching the orange reflection of the fires in a surrealistic glow.

Surreal, like the transition from life to death.

28

RIGHTFUL OWNER

How long had it been? An hour? Two? Masoj paced the length of the gap between the two stalagmite mounds just a few feet from the entrance to the tunnel that Drizzt, and Guenhwyvar, had taken. "The cat should have returned by now," the wizard grumbled, at the end of his patience.

Relief flooded through his face a moment later, when Guenhwyvar's great black head peered around the edge of the tunnel, behind one of the displacer beast statue guardians. The fur around the cat's maw was conspicuously wet with fresh blood.

"It is done?" Masoj asked, barely able to contain a shout of elation. "Drizzt Do'Urden is dead?"

"Hardly," came the reply. Drizzt, for all his idealism, had to admit a tinge of pleasure as a cloud of dread cooled the elated fires in the sinister wizard's cheeks.

"What is this, Guenhwyvar?" Masoj demanded. "Do as I bid you! Kill him now!"

Guenhwyvar stared blankly at Masoj, then lay at Drizzt's feet.

"You admit your attempt on my life?" Drizzt asked.

Masoj measured the distance to his adversary—ten feet. He might be able to get off one spell. Perhaps. Masoj had seen Drizzt move, quick and sure, and had little desire to chance the attack if he could find another way out of this predicament. Drizzt had not yet drawn a weapon, though the young warrior's hands rested easily across the hilts of his deadly blades.

"I understand," Drizzt continued calmly. "House Hun'ett and House Do'Urden are to battle."

"How did you know?" Masoj blurted without thinking, too shocked by the revelation to consider that Drizzt might merely be goading him into a larger admission.

"I know much but care little," Drizzt replied. "House Hun'ett wishes to wage war against my family. For what reason, I cannot guess."

"For the vengeance of House DeVir!" came a reply from a different direction.

Alton, standing on the side of a stalagmite mound, looked down at Drizzt.

A smile spread over Masoj's face. The odds had so quickly changed.

"House Hun'ett cares not at all for House DeVir," Drizzt replied, still composed in the face of this new development. "I have learned enough of the ways of our people to know that the fate of one house is not the concern of another."

"But it is my concern!" Alton cried, and he threw back the cowl of his hood, revealing the hideous face, scarred by acid for the sake of a disguise. "I am Alton DeVir, lone survivor of House DeVir! House Do'Urden will die for its crimes against my family, starting with you."

"I was not even born when the battle took place," Drizzt protested.

"Of little consequence!" Alton snarled. "You are a Do'Urden, a filthy Do'Urden. That is all that matters."

Masoj tossed the onyx figurine to the ground. "Guenhwyvar!" he commanded. "Be gone!"

The cat looked over its shoulder to Drizzt, who nodded his approval.

"Be gone!" Masoj cried again. "I am your master! You cannot disobey me!"

"You do not own the cat," Drizzt said calmly.

"Who does, then?" Masoj snapped. "You?"

"Guenhwyvar," Drizzt replied. "Only Guenhwyvar. I would think that a wizard would have a better understanding of the magic around him."

With a low growl that might have been a mocking laugh, Guenhwyvar loped across the stone to the figurine and dissipated into smoky nothingness.

The cat walked down the length of the planar tunnel, toward its home in the Astral Plane. Ever before had Guenhwyvar been anxious to make this journey, to escape the foul commands of its drow masters. This time, though, the cat hesitated with every stride, looking back over its shoulder to the dot of darkness that was Menzoberranzan.

"Will you deal?" Drizzt offered.

"You are in no position to bargain," Alton laughed, drawing out the slender wand that Matron SiNafay had given him.

Masoj cut him short. "Wait," he said. "Perhaps Drizzt will prove valuable to our struggle against House Do'Urden." He eyed the young warrior directly. "You will betray your family?"

"Hardly," Drizzt snickered. "As I have already said to you, I care little for the coming conflict. Let House Hun'ett and House Do'Urden both be damned, as surely they will! My concerns are personal."

"You must have something to offer us in exchange for your gain," Masoj explained. "Otherwise, what bargain can you hope to make?"

"I do have something to give to you in return," Drizzt replied, his voice calm, "your lives."

Masoj and Alton looked to each other and laughed aloud, but there was a trace of nervousness in their chuckles.

"Give me the figurine, Masoj," Drizzt continued, undaunted. "Guenhwyvar never belonged to you and will serve you no more."

Masoj stopped laughing.

"In return," Drizzt went on before the wizard could reply, "I will leave House Do'Urden and not take part in the battle."

"Corpses do not fight." Alton sneered.

"I will take another Do'Urden with me," Drizzt spat at him. "A weapons master. Surely House Hun'ett will have gained an advantage if both Drizzt and Zaknafein—"

"Silence!" Masoj screamed. "The cat is mine! I do not need any bargains from a pitiful Do'Urden! You are dead, fool, and House Do'Urden's weapons master will follow you to your grave!"

"Guenhwyvar is free!" Drizzt growled.

The scimitars came out in Drizzt's hands. He had never really fought a wizard before, let alone two, but he remembered vividly from past encounters the sting of their spells. Masoj had already begun to cast, but of more concern was Alton, out of quick reach and pointing that slender wand.

Before Drizzt ever decided his course of action, the issue was settled for him. A cloud of smoke engulfed Masoj and he fell back, his spell disrupted with the shock.

Guenhwyvar was back.

Alton was out of Drizzt's reach. Drizzt could not hope to get to the wizard before the wand went off, but to Guenhwyvar's streamlined feline muscles, the distance was not so great. Hind legs tamped a footing and snapped, launching the hunting panther through the air.

Alton brought the wand to bear on this new nemesis in time and released a mighty bolt, scorching Guenhwyvar's chest. Greater strength than a single bolt, though, would be needed to deter the ferocious panther. Stunned but still fighting, Guenhwyvar slammed into the faceless wizard, dropping him off the back side of the stalagmite mound.

The lightning bolt's flash stunned Drizzt as well, but he continued to pursue Masoj and could only hope that Guenhwyvar had survived. He rushed around the base of the other stalagmite mound and came face-to-face with Masoj, once again in the act of spellcasting. Drizzt didn't slow; he ducked his head and barreled into his opponent, his scimitars leading the way.

He slipped right through his opponent—right through the image of his opponent!

Drizzt crashed heavily into the stone and rolled aside, trying to escape the magical attack he knew was coming.

This time, Masoj, standing fully thirty feet behind the projection of his image, was taking no chances with a miss. He launched a volley of magical missiles of energy that veered unerringly to intercept the dodging fighter. They slammed into Drizzt, jolting him, bruising him under his skin.

But Drizzt was able to shake away the numbing pain and regain his footing. He knew where the real Masoj was standing now and had no intention of letting the trickster out of sight again.

A dagger in his hand, Masoj watched Drizzt's stalking approach.

Drizzt didn't understand. Why wasn't the wizard preparing another spell? The fall had reopened the wound in Drizzt's shoulder, and the magical bolts had torn his side and one leg. The wounds were not serious, though, and Masoj had no chance against him in physical combat.

The wizard stood before him, unconcerned, dagger drawn and a wicked smile on his face.

Face down on the hard stone, Alton felt the warmth of his own blood running freely between the melted holes that were his eyes. The cat was higher up the side of the mound, not yet fully recovered from the lightning bolt.

Alton forced himself up and raised his wand for a second strike . . . but the wand had snapped in half.

Frantically Alton recovered the other piece and held it up before his melted, disbelieving eyes. Guenhwyvar was coming again, but Alton didn't notice.

The glowing ends of the wand, a power building within the magical stick, enthralled him. "You cannot do that," Alton whispered in protest.

Guenhwyvar leaped just as the broken wand exploded.

A ball of fire roared up into Menzoberranzan's night, chunks of rubble rocketed off the great cavern's eastern wall and ceiling, and both Drizzt and Masoj were knocked from their feet.

"Now Guenhwyvar belongs to no one," Masoj sneered, tossing the figurine to the ground.

"No DeVir remains to claim vengeance on House Do'Urden," Drizzt growled back, his anger holding off his despair. Masoj became the focus of that anger, and the wizard's mocking laughter led Drizzt toward him in a furious rush. Just as Drizzt got in range, Masoj snapped his fingers and was gone.

"Invisible," Drizzt roared, slicing futilely at the empty air before him. His exertions took the edge from his blind rage and he realized that Masoj was no longer in front of him. How foolish he must seem to the wizard. How vulnerable!

Drizzt crouched to listen. He sensed a distant chanting from up above, on the cavern wall.

Drizzt's instincts told him to dive to the side, but his new understanding of wizards told him that Masoj would anticipate such a move. Drizzt feigned to the left and heard the climactic words of the building spell. As the lightning blast thundered harmlessly to the side, Drizzt sprinted straight ahead, hoping his vision would return in time for him to get to the wizard.

"Damn you!" Masoj cried, understanding the feint as soon as he had errantly fired. Rage became terror in the next instant, as Masoj caught sight of Drizzt, sprinting across the stone, leaping the rubble, and crossing the sides of the mounds with all the grace of a hunting cat.

Masoj fumbled in his pockets for the components to his next spell. He had to be quick. He was fully twenty feet from the cavern floor, perched on a narrow ledge, but Drizzt was moving fast, impossibly fast!

The ground beneath him did not register in Drizzt's conscious thoughts. The cavern wall would have seemed unclimbable to him in a more rational state, but now he gave it not a care. Guenhwyvar was lost to him. Guenhwyvar was gone.

That wicked wizard on the ledge, that embodiment of demonic evil, had caused it. Drizzt sprang to the wall, found one hand free—he must have discarded one scimitar—and caught a tenuous hold. It wasn't enough for a rational drow, but Drizzt's mind ignored the protests of the muscles in his straining fingers. He had only ten feet to go.

Another volley of energy bolts thudded into Drizzt, hammering the top of his head in rapid succession.

"How many spells remain, wizard?" he heard himself defiantly cry as he ignored the pain.

Masoj fell back when Drizzt looked up at him, when the burning light of those lavender orbs fell upon him like a pronouncement of doom. He had seen Drizzt in battle many times, and the sight of the fighting young warrior had haunted him through all the planning of this assassination.

But Masoj had never seen Drizzt enraged before. If he had, he never would have agreed to try to kill Drizzt. If he had, he would have told Matron SiNafay to go sit on a stalagmite.

What spell was next? What spell could slow the monster that was Drizzt Do'Urden?

A hand, glowing with the heat of anger, grabbed the lip of the ledge. Masoj stomped on it with the heel of his boot. The fingers were broken—the wizard knew that the fingers were broken—but Drizzt, impossibly, was up beside him and the blade of a scimitar was through the wizard's ribs.

"The fingers are broken!" the dying mage gasped in protest.

Drizzt looked down at his hand and realized the pain for the first time. "Perhaps," he said absently, "but they will heal."

⋊ ⋉ ⋊ ⋉ ⋊

Drizzt, limping, found his other scimitar and cautiously picked his way over the rubble of one of the mounds. Fighting the fear within his broken heart, he forced himself to peer over the crest at the destruction. The back side of the mound glowed eerily in the residual heat, a beacon for the awakening city.

So much for stealth.

Pieces of Alton DeVir lay scattered at the bottom, around the wizard's smoldering robes. "Have you found peace, Faceless One?" Drizzt whispered, exhaling the last of his anger. He remembered the assault Alton had launched against him those years ago in the Academy. The faceless master and Masoj had explained it away as a test for a budding warrior.

"How long you have carried your hate," Drizzt muttered at the blasted bits of corpse.

But Alton DeVir was not his concern now. He scanned the rest of the rubble, looking for some clue to Guenhwyvar's fate, not certain how a magical creature would fare in such a disaster. Not a sign of the cat remained, nothing that would even hint that Guenhwyvar had ever been there.

Drizzt consciously reminded himself that there was no hope, but the anxious spring in his steps mocked his stern visage. He rushed back down the mound and around the other stalagmite, where Masoj and he had been when the wand exploded. He spotted the onyx figurine immediately.

He lifted it gently in his hands. It was warm, as though it, too, had been caught in the blast, and Drizzt could sense that its magic had diminished. Drizzt wanted to call the cat, then, but he didn't dare, knowing that the travel between the planes heavily taxed Guenhwyvar. If the cat had been injured, Drizzt figured that it would be better to give it some time to recuperate.

"Oh, Guenhwyvar," he moaned, "my friend, my brave friend." He dropped the figurine into his pocket.

He could only hope that Guenhwyvar had survived.

29

ALONE

Drizzt walked back around the stalagmite, back to the body of Masoj
Hun'ett. He had had no choice but to kill his adversary; Masoj had
drawn the battle lines.

That fact did little to dispel the guilt in Drizzt as he looked upon the
corpse. He had killed another drow, had taken the life of one of his own
people. Was he trapped, as Zaknafein had been trapped for so very many
years, in a cycle of violence that would know no end?

"Never again," Drizzt vowed to the corpse. "Never again will I kill a
drow elf."

He turned away, disgusted, and knew as soon as he looked back to the
silent, sinister mounds of the vast drow city that he would not survive long
in Menzoberranzan if he held to that promise.

A thousand possibilities whirled in Drizzt's mind as he made his way
through the winding ways of Menzoberranzan. He pushed the thoughts
aside, stopped them from dulling his alertness. The light was general now
in Narbondel; the drow day was beginning, and activity had started from
every corner of the city. In the world of the surface-dwellers, the day was
the safer time, when light exposed assassins. In Menzoberranzan's eternal
darkness, the daytime of the dark elves was even more dangerous than
the night.

Drizzt picked his way carefully, rolling wide from the mushroom fence of the noblest houses, wherein lay House Hun'ett. He encountered no more adversaries and made the safety of the Do'Urden compound a short time later. He rushed through the gate and by the surprised soldiers without a word of explanation and shoved aside the guards below the balcony.

The house was strangely quiet; Drizzt would have expected them all to be up and about with battle imminent. He gave the eerie stillness no more thought, and he cut a straight line to the training gym and Zaknafein's private quarters.

Drizzt paused outside the gym's stone door, his hand tightly clenched on the handle of the portal. What would he propose to his father? That they leave? He and Zaknafein on the perilous trails of the Underdark, fighting when they must and escaping the burdensome guilt of their existence under drow rule? Drizzt liked the thought, but he wasn't so certain now, standing before the door, that he could convince Zak to follow such a course. Zak could have left before, at any time during the centuries of his life, but when Drizzt had asked him why he had remained, the heat had drained from the weapons master's face. Were they indeed trapped in the life offered to them by Matron Malice and her evil cohorts?

Drizzt grimaced away the worries; no sense in arguing to himself with Zak only a few steps away.

The training gym was as quiet as the rest of the house. Too quiet. Drizzt hadn't expected Zak to be there, but something more than his father was absent. The father's presence, too, was gone.

Drizzt knew that something was wrong, and each step he took toward Zak's private door quickened until he was in full flight. He burst in without a knock, not surprised to find the bed empty.

"Malice must have sent him out in search of me," Drizzt reasoned. "Damn, I have caused him trouble!" He turned to leave, but something caught his eye and held him in the room—Zak's sword belt.

Never would the weapons master have left his room, not even for functions within the safety of House Do'Urden, without his swords. "Your weapon is your most trusted companion," Zak had told Drizzt a thousand times. "Keep it ever at your side!"

"House Hun'ett?" Drizzt whispered, wondering if the rival house had

magically attacked in the night, while he was out battling Alton and
Masoj. The compound, though, was serene; surely the soldiers would have
known if anything like that had occurred.

Drizzt picked up the belt for inspection. No blood, and the clasp neatly
unbuckled. No enemy had torn this from Zak. The weapons master's
pouch lay beside it, also intact.

"What, then?" Drizzt asked aloud. He replaced the sword belt beside
the bed, but slung the pouch across his neck, and turned, not knowing
where he should go next.

He had to see about the rest of the family, he realized before he had
even stepped through the door. Perhaps then this riddle about Zak would
become more clear.

Dread grew out of that thought as Drizzt headed down the long and decorated corridor to the chapel anteroom. Had Malice, or any of them, brought
Zak harm? For what purpose? The notion seemed illogical to Drizzt, but it
nagged him every step, as if some sixth sense were warning him.

There still was no sign of anyone.

The anteroom's ornate doors swung in, magically and silently, even as
Drizzt raised his hand to knock on them. He saw the matron mother first,
sitting smugly on her throne at the rear of the room, her smile inviting.

Drizzt's discomfort did not diminish when he entered. The whole family
was there: Briza, Vierna, and Maya to the sides of their matron, Rizzen
and Dinin unobtrusively standing beside the left wall. The whole family.
Except for Zak.

Matron Malice studied her son carefully, noting his many wounds. "I
instructed you not to leave the house," she said to Drizzt, but she was not
scolding him. "Where did your travels take you?"

"Where is Zaknafein?" Drizzt asked in reply.

"Answer the matron mother!" Briza yelled at him, her snake whip
prominently displayed on her belt.

Drizzt glared at her and she recoiled, feeling the same bitter chill that
Zaknafein had cast over her earlier in the night.

"I instructed you not to leave the house," Malice said again, still holding
calm. "Why did you disobey me?"

"I had matters to attend," Drizzt replied, "urgent matters. I did not wish to bother you with them."

"War is upon us, my son," Matron Malice explained. "You are vulnerable out in the city by yourself. House Do'Urden cannot afford to lose you now."

"My business had to be **hand**led alone," Drizzt answered.

"Is it completed?"

"It is."

"Then I trust that you will not disobey me again." The words came calm and even, but Drizzt understood at once the severity of the threat behind them.

"To other matters, then," Malice went on.

"Where is Zaknafein?" Drizzt dared to ask again.

Briza mumbled some curse under her breath and pulled the whip from her belt. Matron Malice threw an outstretched hand in her direction to stay her. They needed tact, not brutality, to bring Drizzt under control at this critical time. There would be ample opportunities for punishment after House Hun'ett was properly defeated.

"Concern yourself not with the fate of the weapons master," Malice replied. "He works for the good of House Do'Urden even as we speak—on a personal mission."

Drizzt didn't believe a word of it. Zak would never have left without his weapons. The truth hovered about Drizzt's thoughts, but he wouldn't let it in.

"Our concern is House Hun'ett," Malice went on, addressing them all. "The war's first strikes may fall this day."

"The first strikes already have fallen," Drizzt interrupted. All eyes came back to him, to his wounds. He wanted to continue the discussion about Zak but knew that he would only get himself, and Zak, if Zak was still alive, into further trouble. Perhaps the conversation would bring him more clues.

"You have seen battle?" Malice asked.

"You know of the Faceless One?" Drizzt asked.

"Master of the Academy," Dinin answered, "of Sorcere. We have dealt with him often."

"He has been of use to us in the past," said Malice, "but no more, I believe. He is a Hun'ett, Gelroos Hun'ett."

"No," Drizzt replied. "Once he may have been, but Alton DeVir is his name . . . was his name."

"The link!" Dinin growled, suddenly comprehending. "Gelroos was to kill Alton on the night of House DeVir's fall!"

"It would seem that Alton DeVir proved the stronger," mused Malice, and all became clear to her. "Matron SiNafay Hun'ett accepted him, used him to her gain," she explained to her family. She looked back to Drizzt. "You battled with him?"

"He is dead," Drizzt answered.

Matron Malice cackled with delight.

"One less wizard to deal with," Briza remarked, replacing the whip on her belt.

"Two," Drizzt corrected, but there was no boasting in his voice. He was not proud of his actions. "Masoj Hun'ett is no more."

"My son!" Matron Malice cried. "You have brought us a great edge in this war!" She glanced all about her family, infecting them, except Drizzt, with her elation. "House Hun'ett may not even choose to strike us now, knowing its disadvantage. We will not let them get away! We will destroy them this day and become the Eighth House of Menzoberranzan! Woe to the enemies of Daermon N'a'shezbaernon!

"We must move at once, my family," Malice reasoned, her hands rubbing over each other in excitement. "We cannot wait for an attack. We must take the offensive! Alton DeVir is gone now; the link that justifies this war is no more. Surely the ruling council knew of Hun'ett's intentions, and with both her wizards dead and the element of surprise lost, Matron SiNafay will move quickly to stop the battle."

Drizzt's hand unconsciously slipped into Zak's pouch as the others joined Malice in her plotting.

"Where is Zak?" Drizzt demanded again, above the chorus.

Silence dropped as quickly as the tumult had begun.

"He is of no concern to you, my son," Malice said to him, still keeping to her tact despite Drizzt's impudence. "You are the weapons master of House

Do'Urden now. Lolth has forgiven your insolence; you have no crimes weighing against you. Your career may begin anew, to glorious heights!"

Her words cut through Drizzt as surely as his own scimitar might. "You killed him," he whispered aloud, the truth too awful to be contained in silent thought.

The matron's face suddenly gleamed, hot with rage. "You killed him!" she shot back at Drizzt. "Your insolence demanded repayment to the Spider Queen!"

Drizzt's tongue got all tangled up behind his teeth.

"But you live," Malice went on, relaxing again in her chair, "as the elven child lives."

Dinin was not the only one in the room to gasp audibly.

"Yes, we know of your deception," Malice sneered. "The Spider Queen always knew. She demanded restitution."

"You sacrificed Zaknafein?" Drizzt breathed, hardly able to get the words out of his mouth. "You gave him to that damned Spider Queen?"

"I would watch how I spoke of Queen Lolth," Malice warned. "Forget Zaknafein. He is not your concern. Look to your own life, my warrior son. All glories are offered to you, a station of honor."

Drizzt was indeed looking to his own life at that moment; at the proposed path that offered him a life of battle, a life of killing drow.

"You have no options," Malice said to him, seeing his inward struggle. "I offer to you now your life. In exchange, you must do as I bid, as Zaknafein once did."

"You kept your bargain with him," Drizzt spat sarcastically.

"I did!" Matron Malice protested. "Zaknafein went willingly to the altar, for your sake!"

Her words stung Drizzt for only a moment. He would not accept the guilt for Zaknafein's death! He had followed the only course he could, on the surface against the elves and here in the evil city.

"My offer is a good one," Malice said. "I give it here, before all the family. Both of us will benefit from the agreement . . . Weapons Master?"

A smile spread across Drizzt's face when he looked into Matron Malice's cold eyes, a grin that Malice took as acceptance.

"Weapons Master?" Drizzt echoed. "Not likely."

Again Malice misunderstood. "I have seen you in battle," she argued. "Two wizards! You underestimate yourself."

Drizzt nearly laughed aloud at the irony of her words. She thought he would fail where Zaknafein had failed, would fall into her trap as the former weapons master had fallen, never to climb back out. "It is you who underestimate me, Malice," Drizzt said with threatening calm.

"Matron!" Briza demanded, but she held back, seeing that Drizzt and everyone else was ignoring her as the drama played out.

"You ask me to serve your evil designs," Drizzt continued. He knew but didn't care that all of them were nervously fingering weapons or preparing spells, were waiting for the proper moment to strike the blasphemous fool dead. Those childhood memories of the agony of snake whips reminded him of the punishment for his actions. Drizzt's fingers closed around a circular object, adding to his courage, though he would have continued in any case.

"They are a lie, as our—no, your—people are a lie!"

"Your skin is as dark as mine," Malice reminded him. "You are a drow, though you have never learned what that means!"

"Oh, I do know what it means."

"Then act by the rules!" Matron Malice demanded.

"Your rules?" Drizzt growled back. "But your rules are a damned lie as well, as great a lie as that filthy spider you claim as a deity!"

"Insolent slug," Briza cried, raising her snake whip.

Drizzt struck first. He pulled the object, the tiny ceramic globe, from Zaknafein's pouch.

"A true god damn you all!" he cried as he slammed the ball to the stone floor. He snapped his eyes shut as the pebble within the ball, enchanted by a powerful light-emanating dweomer, exploded into the room and erupted into his kin's sensitive eyes. "And damn that Spider Queen as well!"

Malice reeled backward, taking her great throne right over in a heavy crash to the hard stone. Cries of agony and rage came from every corner of the room as the sudden light bored into the stunned drow. Finally

Vierna managed to launch a countering spell and returned the room to its customary gloom.

"Get him!" Malice growled, still trying to shake off the heavy fall. "I want him dead!"

The others had hardly recovered enough to heed to her commands, and Drizzt was already out of the house.

✕ ✕ ✕ ✕

Carried on the silent winds of the Astral Plane, the call came. The entity of the panther stood up, ignoring its pains, and took note of the voice, a familiar, comforting voice.

The cat was off, then, running with all its heart and strength to answer the summons of its new master.

✕ ✕ ✕ ✕

A short while later, Drizzt crept out of a little tunnel, Guenhwyvar at his side, and moved through the courtyard of the Academy to look down upon Menzoberranzan for the last time.

"What place is this," Drizzt asked the cat quietly, "that I call home? These are my people, by skin and by heritage, but I am no kin to them. They are lost and ever will be.

"How many others are like me, I wonder?" Drizzt whispered, taking one final look. "Doomed souls, as was Zaknafein, poor Zak. I do this for him, Guenhwyvar; I leave as he could not. His life has been my lesson, a dark scroll etched by the heavy price exacted by Matron Malice's evil promises.

"Goodbye, Zak!" he cried, his voice rising in final defiance. "My father. Take heart, as do I, that when we meet again, in a life after this, it will surely not be in the hellfire our kin are doomed to endure!"

Drizzt motioned the cat back into the tunnel, the entrance to the untamed Underdark. Watching the cat's easy movements, Drizzt realized again how fortunate he was to have found a companion of like spirit, a true friend. The way would not be easy for him and Guenhwyvar beyond the guarded borders of Menzoberranzan. They would be unprotected and alone—though better off, by Drizzt's estimation—more than they ever could be amid the evilness of the drow.

Drizzt stepped into the tunnel behind Guenhwyvar and left Menzoberranzan behind.

R.A. Salvatore on Homeland

***Homeland* is the first Drizzt novel when they're put in chronological order, but it was actually your fourth FORGOTTEN REALMS® novel featuring Drizzt. What made you want to go back in time and write what amounts to a "prequel"? for The Icewind Dale Trilogy?**

Actually, I didn't make that decision initially. I had planned to end *The Halfling's Gem* right before the retaking of Mithral Hall. However, TSR at that time thought that we had heard enough from this band and requested I wrap it up (hence the epilogue explaining the retaking of the hall).

Not too long after that, I got a call from Mary Kirchoff, then the senior editor, I believe, telling me that there were a lot of people interested in knowing Drizzt's origins. I don't know whether it came from mail or internal discussions among the book group, but the editors decided it would be a good thing for me to go back and tell Drizzt's story and at the same time define the dark elves in the FORGOTTEN REALMS world. I still remember that call, asking me to do three more books—up to that time, I had written each book expecting it to be last. Great relief flooded over me, as I had just quit, or was about to quit, my day job and plunge headlong into full-time writing, and this with three little children at home. I remember walking out of my office for the last time thinking, "Oh great, now I have no health insurance."

But I believed in the gang from Icewind Dale and especially in Drizzt, though I was disappointed that we had to tie up the Mithral Hall story without another book.

That phone call kept it going. It also scared the heck out of me, because I considered the drow to be one of the best creations of those who gave us DUNGEONS & DRAGONS®. When you work with someone else's creation, you don't want to let him down. That's true of working in Ed Greenwood's FORGOTTEN REALMS, and was true again on top of that in working with Gary Gygax's dark elves.

In *Homeland* you really created the drow society of the Underdark and the city of Menzoberranzan. What did you draw on for inspiration for drow civilization?

Mario Puzo's *The Godfather*. Really. I wanted a tough and strong society that survived through personal intelligence and ruthlessness. Of course, we'd have to rename it, "The Godmother," I suppose, when talking about the drow.

The thing that really drives the society of drow is, simply, politics. Nothing is genuine, everything is said for a reason that is buried beneath a web of other possible reasons. When showing the society moving in any direction, I had to constantly step back and look for the layers, the feint within a feint within a feint, and keep taking it deeper and deeper until it got to the point where I wasn't sure why a certain matron mother had really said something or done something. Writing about the drow is actually very exhausting— keeps you thinking in this downward spiral of intrigue until you're ready to leap around, as if expecting that Jarlaxle is standing behind you.

What sort of special research did you do before writing *Homeland* to help bring the Underdark alive. Did you study caves, martial arts, history?

All of the above, which are the same disciplines that I bring to all of my work. I have a great love of caves; I find them fascinating. At more than two hundred pounds, I'm not really built for crawling around in tight tunnels, but I love sitting at the IMAX theatre to see the film work of brave souls who risk the depths.

As for the history element, when I switched my major over to Communications/Journalism in college, all of my electives went to literature courses, and the ones that interested me were those of the middle ages. Shakespeare and Chaucer among others. I tried to take history courses that corresponded with those particular time periods, as well (and no, not so my term papers would work in both classes!).

The martial arts aspect? Well, I play hockey—maybe that's why I chose curved blades. I did a little boxing in high school—club stuff and nothing formal, and I worked as a bouncer for several years at the local nightclubs. I was also a big boxing fan—love those Ali-Frazier fights. What I learned through it all was that, in fighting, where your hands are isn't nearly as important as where your feet are. Balance is everything. It determines the weight of a punch, or slash. It determines your ability to avoid, partially at least, anything thrown your way.

Homeland was the first Dark Elf novel in which you began including excerpts from Drizzt's journal. Why did you decide to do that, and do you feel comfortable writing "as" Drizzt?

The assignment for the Dark Elf Trilogy was to tell Drizzt's story, so I immediately thought of doing the books in first person perspective. Roger Zelazny's amazing Chronicles of Amber came to mind; I think that might be the best example of first-person writing I've ever seen in the genre. I quickly came to realize, though, that first-person would be difficult for me. One of the strengths of my writing, judging from the feedback I was receiving even back then, are those wild battle scenes. I would have a hard time writing those from first person perspective; how would Drizzt know what was happening in a fight behind him if he was involved in his own fight, after all?

So I abandoned the first person idea, but I still wanted to get deeper into the emotions of this character than third person perspective would allow.

Thus, the essays came into being. I've said this before and I'll repeat it now: don't read those essays as if Drizzt is talking (preaching) to you. He's not. Those essays are his diary entries, where he's sitting there emotionally naked, forcing himself to sort through difficult feelings and, yes, faults. I've continued with them—I even went back and put them in the Icewind Dale books for the Collector's Editions—because they've worked.

How much of the complete story of The Dark Elf Trilogy (*Homeland*, *Exile*, and *Sojourn*) did you have in mind when you sat down to write *Homeland*?

Very little. I outline books one at a time, and then, as I'm writing them, usually completely alter that outline. I wouldn't say that I write on the fly, but for the most part, I don't know what's coming. And I don't want to know. This is what makes it fun for me; I'm writing the book in the way that allows me to be surprised. I try to write the book the way the reader reads the book. I didn't know the role Zaknafein would play, for example, although I knew that he would be somewhat of a mentor/inspiration to young Drizzt from the beginning. I had no idea of the progression through *Exile* and *Sojourn* when I started, but I did know that Drizzt would end up in Icewind Dale with Bruenor and Catti-brie at the end of the series.

Is Drizzt based on or inspired by a real person?

Not really. None of my characters are drawn that way, with the exception of Cadderly (who was based on a brilliant young high school flunky I know) and a few choice villains (old bosses) who died horribly. I think Drizzt really is who I wish I had the guts to be. His essays are very personal to me—it's almost like I'm working through my thoughts on particular subjects at some points. I have to constantly pull back from that, however, because these are the thoughts of a character who is carrying around emotional baggage that I never had to deal with, obviously! And there are many times when I don't agree with Drizzt, but I have to spell out his viewpoint anyway.

Creating characters for novels is always an amazing experience, because at some point, those characters take wings and fly away from your control. With Drizzt, that happened very early on, when he was running across the tundra and got jumped by yetis. Characters become very real to the author. After a while, it's almost as if they're sitting next to you in your office, telling you what to write.

Did any or all of the characters from The Legend of Drizzt begin as D&D® game characters?

None of them did. Nor do I play them in my gaming today. The only character I ever tried out in a game was Oliver deBurrows, the high-wayhalfling from *The Sword of Bedwyr*. Oliver is a cross between Inego Montoya from *The Princess Bride* and the little French guy on the wall in *Monty Python and the Holy Grail*. I wanted him in a game because I wanted to see if I could make him annoying enough. We were bouncing along, about six weeks into the campaign when our wizard scried ahead and mistakenly declared that the way was clear. Of course, Oliver then volunteered to take the lead and went dancing up the stairs with his "rahpier-blade" in hand, only to be squished like a bug by a huge ogre who was pressed up against this column. I knew Oliver had to go into the book, because when he died, everyone stood up and cheered.

Do you work from a "character sheet"? to help define what Drizzt can and can't do, or how he might progress in ability as the series continues?

No, not at all. I don't know his level or his ability stats, nor do I care. You really can't think in terms of a game when you're writing a novel. Here's an example, let's say you have a tenth level warrior. He's got perhaps a hundred and twenty hit points. Now, a dagger does a d4 of damage, so if the warrior was leaning against a door jamb, distracted by something, and a young man ran up behind him and plunged the dagger into his back, in game terms, he'd just turn around and swat the impetuous youth. Even granting double/triple/quadruple damage for the strike would do little to disable the warrior. In real life, that guy leaning on the door would go down like a stone.

I'm not interested in CR ratings or anything like that when I'm writing the books. It's that simple.

How do you keep fight scenes so fresh after having written so many? What do you draw on for inspiration for action sequences? Do you have any martial arts or fencing experience?

I don't know, except to say that I actually watch the action taking place in my head, in slow motion, while I'm writing the battles. I go into a frenzy; it's like playing a computer game, almost. I do a thousand to fifteen hundred words a day, typically, but I've had days when writing battle scenes, where I finally look up from the computer to see that the hours have passed and I've put five thousand words down. The scenes remain fresh, I expect, because they're still so much fun to write—sometimes I have to go back through a book and cull some, actually, because they're just so much fun for me that I get carried away.

As for training, see above. I'll add to those experiences the beginning of my DemonWars Saga. I wanted the hero to have a distinctive fighting style, and something different from the rolling and slashing method used by Drizzt, so I enrolled my two boys in fencing classes, and while they went at it on the mat, beating the tar out of each other (kidding!), I grilled their instructor for the details.

What did you do before you became a writer and what would you be doing now if you hadn't started writing fantasy?

I've had many jobs, from bouncing to sustitute teaching to carrying the mail. When I finally got my break, in 1987, I was working as a financial specialist for a computer test equipment company. I was doing well at my job—I've never shied from hard work—and I enjoyed the whole accounting game. At the end of every month, I felt like Sherlock Holmes as I sorted through the numbers, trying to make some sense of them. I expect that I would have stayed in the realm of finance if writing hadn't taken over.

—R. A. Salvatore
November 2003

The Legend of Drizzt

Continues in

EXILE

Featuring an introduction by

Matthew Woodring Stover

and more surprises
June 2004